Also by Nichole Stephens

Someone to Watch Over Me

Zebra Books

Published by Kensington Publishing Corporation

Also by Michelle Stimpson

Falling Into Grace

Last Temptation

Published by Kensington Publishing Corporation

Someone to Watch Over Me

MICHELLE
STIMPSON

Kensington Publishing Corp.
http://www.kensingtonbooks.com

DAFINA BOOKS are published by

Kensington Publishing Corp.
119 West 40th Street
New York, NY 10018

All Kensington Titles, Imprints, and Distributed Lines are available at special quantity discounts for bulk purchases for sales promotions, premiums, fund-raising, and educational or institutional use. Special book excerpts or customized printings can also be created to fit specific needs. For details, write or phone the office of the Kensington special sales manager: Kensington Publishing Corp., 119 West 40th Street, New York, NY 10018, attn: Special Sales Department, Phone: 1-800-221-2647.

Dafina and the Dafina logo Reg. U.S. Pat & TM Off.

ISBN-13: 978-0-7582-4689-9
ISBN-10: 0-7582-4689-7

First trade paperback printing: June 2011
First mass market printing: April 2013

10 9 8 7 6 5 4 3 2 1

Printed in the United States of America

For my hubby.
Thanks for guiding and holding the kite string.
You make me fly high!

Acknowledgments

Thank you, Father, for book number seven. Years ago, I told You I wanted everything I do to have meaning. You have been faithful to my prayer, faithful to arrange my whole life around our relationship, around Your love for me. I look back over what You have done in my life these past two decades and I can only weep in awe of You. Isaiah 55:8, Romans 8:28, and Ephesians 3:20—for real, Father, for real!

Thank you to my family. Mom (Wilma Jean Music), Dad (Michael West Music)—they INSIST that their full names be listed. To aunties, uncles, cousins, and Grandma. Keep the legacy going! When I step back and look at God's faithfulness to our family, I know this is nothing but God.

Steven and Kalen—you've grown up with Mommy's writing. Now the writing has rubbed off—well, kinda. I love seeing this heart for the things of God taking form in you both. You two make me better.

For my longtime friends who encourage me regularly—Kim, Shannon, Jeanne—thanks for the love! To my critique group (i.e., friends, too) who gave me their thoughts on the first few chapters—thanks for your expert eyes—Janice, Lynne, Kellie, Jane, Patricia. Looking forward to many more published manuscripts between us!

Thanks to the people of Mabank ISD who gave me lots of small-town, countrified information; to my sister-in-law, Rebecca, and my mother (again) for medical expertise. Thanks Shewanda and Lynne for helping me through the outline. Shaundale, for sharing your insight about family courts and your child advocate experiences (and just being a great homegirl anyway—miss you much). To my FB friends who share their experience when I'm too lazy to look stuff up, and who cheer me along the way.

Thanks to all the book clubs who continue to discuss/ argue/ debate my previous works. Thank you! Thank you! Thank you! I hope this one will give you much to discuss as well!

Thanks to my agent, Sara Camilli, Selena James, and the good folks at Kensington Publishing. Thanks for believing in me enough to contract these books during such a turbulent time for many. I appreciate the opportunity to write on through!

Thanks to my Anointed Authors on Tour sisters— Vanessa Miller, Kendra Norman-Bellamy, Norma Jarrett, Dr. Vivi Monroe Congress, Tia McCollors, and Shewanda Riley. I am inspired by your daily word counts.

Out of respect for my father, who always made me acutely aware of the fact that air-conditioning is not free, I suppose I should thank all those free Wi-Fi restaurants for letting me use their air-conditioning, Internet connection, and electricity while writing the majority of this book.

God Bless!
Michelle Stimpson

Prologue

1996

"Well, she can't stay here. Not while I'm running for city council," my stepfather, Mr. James, whispered to my mother as though I weren't in the same room. They paced back and forth, his Stacy Adams hitting the ground heel first, toe timbering down seconds later. Mother's pumps shuffled right behind him, like a duckling following a quack.

I sat on the couch, my hands under my chin, wringing my fingers so hard I expected to see blood flowing down my arms. I thought, at that moment, about what the people at church say—that Jesus had prayed so hard that He sweated blood. They also said that Jesus had been through everything I'd been through and paid the price on the cross.

I wondered what Jesus would have done if He were fifteen and pregnant. Fat chance, because in the first place, Jesus wouldn't have given Bootsie Evans His phone number. Secondly, He wouldn't have listened to Dee-Dee Willis, who confirmed that Bootsie couldn't get anybody pregnant because he hurt himself real bad on a ten-speed bike when they were in the fifth grade. And last but not least, He would never have invited Bootsie over to watch the American Music Awards while God was gone to a $200-a-plate fund-raiser. No, I was nothing like Jesus—and Jesus probably didn't understand me seeing as He'd never sinned.

"I guess we could just send her to my aunt Dottie's house," Mr. James considered out loud, tracing his lips with a stiff forefinger.

"James, we're not in the sixties. We don't have to send her away."

He puffed up. "Maybe if people treated pregnant girls like we did in the sixties, more girls would keep their legs closed. We're sending her. There won't be anybody in that little town for her to scr—"

"Ja-aames!" My mother gave his name two syllables, shot her eyes toward me and then back to my stepfather.

"She already knows all about sex now," he said, almost laughing. "No use in trying to protect her anymore. For God's sake, she's pregnant, Margie."

Couldn't they have this conversation without me, like they did everything else? Just go somewhere and deliberate and call me back for sentencing. I was already guilty. I sighed a little too loudly, and my stepfather did a James Brown over to the couch. "You tired of this? Are we borrrring you?" He pushed hot words down onto my face.

"I'm just . . . tired, Mr. James," I said truthfully as I looked away.

In that split second, he could have hugged me. Broken down and cried with me, but he didn't. Instead, he asked, "Did you even think about what this could do to my political career? How can I be elected to run a city when you've got people thinking I can't even run my own house?"

"James, just leave her alone for now. She's tired." I could see my mother's light brown fingers, perfect cylinders, and the shiny red extensions as she pulled him away from me.

Mr. James jerked his arm away and went to their bedroom, leaving my mother and myself to sort things out. "Well, Tori Danielle Henderson"—my punishment name—"you've really done it this time."

It's a funny thing when the bottom drops out, when you've done something horrible and irreversible, something that draws a before-and-after line in your life. No matter how much people try to express their disappointment, nothing can compare to the fact that you let yourself down. After all, it is your own life that you just ruined.

"I'm sorry," was all I could muster up.

She gave a single laugh. "Sorry. Is that all you can say?"

What else *could* I say? Despite the nonchalant attitude, I was scared to death. And ashamed. Not so much for my parents, but for myself. They had their own agenda, which I was sure included a run for the presidency of the United States of America at some point.

Over the lonesome only-child years, I had come to understand my place in the family. To be seen and not heard. And while I played along with their game, I read voraciously and learned the ways of the world. I found out what made people tick, how jealousy and hate and love and passion and insecurity drove people to do things that they wouldn't normally do. It was fascinating, this world of fiction.

That's how I figured out what was going on with my father and our next-door neighbor's wife. The late days at work, the calling and hanging up, the expensive gifts that followed my parents' weeks of counseling. All of that preceding our abrupt move to our new house.

That was their life—politics, scandal, and pretense.

I had wanted better for myself. True love, just like in the romance books, and a family where people came closer in crises rather than falling apart. I wanted to go to college and do something with my life—maybe become a teacher or a doctor. Instead, I'd gone and made myself another statistic: an unwed black teenage mother. How stupid could I be?

I was beginning to feel even more dim-witted for telling my parents about the pregnancy so soon. I should have just waited like Felecia Moore did—wore baggy clothes, wrapped up pads every month and put them in the trash can, and had my momma take me all the way to the emergency room while I complained of severe cramps right up until the very second I pushed the baby out. I heard that Felecia's momma fainted when the nurse came to the waiting room and announced, "It's a boy" instead of, "It's a virus."

There must have been a hundred other girls who'd done it and hadn't gotten pregnant. Why me? I buried my face in my hands, almost wishing I could bury my whole body with this baby inside me, too. Maybe I could just die in my sleep tonight. Then Mr. James could win the election on the sympathy vote and my mother could establish another social coffee group, this one for mothers whose daughters contracted fatal cases of shame.

Momma stood in front of me, warring with her thoughts. She almost came and sat down. I saw it in the way her left foot tapped ever so slightly and I heard it as she whispered my name. But when my stepfather angrily called her to their bedroom, she latched on to his fury and said, "You weren't crying then, so don't start crying now."

I stayed at home until I started to show, around five months. At five foot four and barely a hundred pounds prior to conceiving, my body camouflaged the extra weight well. So far as the people in the community knew, I was simply "filling out." I sang in the choir every Sunday at church, which meant that I had the luxury of putting on a choir robe and blending in right up until the service dismissed, at which point Momma whisked me out the back doors of the church. At school, I had always been the quiet type. Since we'd only lived in Houston for the minimum number of years Mr. James had to be a resident before running for city council, I didn't have any close friends. Nobody believed Bootsie when he said that he "did it" with me—except my unlicensed unplanned parenthood counselor, Dee-Dee, who lied so much that when she tried to go back and tell that I'd sought her advice, nobody believed her either. It helped that I was in a big school where girls popped up pregnant and dropped on and off roll sheets so often, it wasn't a big deal socially.

Everybody had their suspicions, but under penalty of Mr. James, I never confirmed them. Not even to Bootsie. I didn't talk about it at school, at home, at church—I didn't even talk about it to myself when I sat on the toilet. When the baby got big enough where I could feel his kick, I could only blink my eyes.

Right about then they decided it was time for me to go live with Aunt Dottie for the duration of my pregnancy.

Chapter 1

Today

I crossed my fingers in hopes of being named Top Quarterly Producer for my department. I mean, every single one of my clients had experienced Web site traffic and sales above the projected estimates, and I had even received two letters from pleased customers. "Tori's expertise made all the difference in our product launch," one had commented. "We'll be using NetMarketing Results for a long time to come!" Planning and implementing online advertising and marketing campaigns came with its own sense of fulfillment. After all, depending on who you asked, the Web pushes America's economy even more than a good old-fashioned mall.

But even as we stood around the conference room waiting for the announcement, I felt queasy. What if they didn't name me? One look around the room sparked another dose of apprehension.

Lexa Fielder was recently hired, yet she'd already managed to land a pretty impressive list of new customers for the company, though it was rumored she did quite a bit of work on her back.

Brian Wallace was one of the older marketing representatives, but he still had a few tricks up his sleeve. Every once in a while, he pulled off a last-minute record-breaking month for one of his clients and caught management's eyes.

There were only four eyes I wanted to catch, and all of them belonged to Preston Haverty. Okay, he really only had two eyes, but he did wear a set of insistently thick glasses that took on a life of their own at the center of his slight facial features. Every time I saw him, I felt like I was in a scene from *The Emperor's New Clothes*. Like, why won't somebody tell Preston those glasses are ridiculous, that we do have technology to free us from such spectacles? Probably the same reason no one talks to Donald Trump about that comb-over.

Anyway, Preston was good people, glasses and all. I appreciated his "hands off" management style. He didn't really care where or how we worked, so long as we got the job done. I only hoped that I'd done a good enough job to add to my collection of blue and green plaques given to outstanding employees. Lexa and Brian aside, I appreciated being appreciated. And God knows I'd put in enough woman-hours to earn this recognition.

"And the top producer for this quarter is . . ."— Preston announced as everyone in the room beat a drum roll on either the sixteen-foot table or some spot on the surrounding walls that wasn't covered with a motivational poster—"Tori Henderson!"

My cheekbones rose so high I could barely see in front of me. *Is this what it's like to be Miss America?* Everybody applauding, confetti flying, the runners-up on the sideline clapping wildly to distract themselves from their jealousy and impending mental meltdowns following the show?

Okay, maybe it wasn't that serious, but I sure felt like a pageant queen. My fellow coworkers, probably twenty-five people or so, cheered me on as I walked toward the head of the table to receive my plaque. "Good job, Tori!" "You go, girl!" Their affirmations swelled inside me, feeding my self-esteem. *If only my mother could see me now.* Maybe then she'd forget about 1996.

I shook Mr. Haverty's hand and posed for the obligatory picture. In that moment, I wished I'd worn a lighter colored suit. Black always made me look like a beanpole. Gave no testament to all my hours at the gym and the doughnuts I'd turned down to keep the red line on my scale below one hundred and twenty-five.

I wasn't going to pass on the sweets today, though. Jacquelyn, the lead secretary, retrieved a towering pink and white buttercream frosting cake from somewhere and brought it forward now to celebrate my achievement.

Preston offered, "Tori, you get the first piece."

"Get some meat on those bones, girl," from Clara, the Webmaster.

But the mention of meat and the sight of the cake suddenly made me nauseous. To appease the group, I took the first piece. Then Jacquelyn got busy cutting and distributing pieces as everyone stood around milking the moment before having to return to work.

I sat in one of the comfy leather chairs and took a bite of my celebratory sweetness. Almost instantly, my stomach disagreed with my actions. My hand flew to my abdomen, lightly stroking the panel of my suit. People were so busy devouring the cake they didn't notice me catching my breath. *Whew!*

I pushed the plate away from me, as though the pink

mass possessed the power to jump onto my fork and into my mouth. This was clearly not the cake for me. I thought for a moment about how long it had been since I ate something so densely packed with sugar. Maybe this was like red meat—once you stop consuming it, one back-slidden bite tears you up inside.

No, that's not it. I'd eaten a candy bar the previous week, before my monthly visitor arrived. Renegade cramps? I rubbed my palm against the aggravated area again. No. The pain was too high in my torso for female problems. This had to be some kind of bug. Whatever it was, it didn't like strawberry cake, so I quietly tossed my piece in the trash on the way back to my desk.

An hour later, I felt like I could throw up so I sat perfectly still at my desk because . . . well . . . any movement of my torso sparked a pain in my side that might trigger this upchuck. I just didn't *feel* like I wanted to go through the process of throwing up. I would never tell anyone this, but I find vomiting an altogether traumatic experience. Such a nasty feeling in one's throat. And the aftertaste, and the gagging sounds. Not to mention getting a close-up look at the toilet seat. It's just not humanlike and should be avoided at all costs, in my opinion.

Thank God I made it all the way to my apartment before I finally had to look at the inside of a porcelain throne, only this time I hadn't even eaten anything. Bile spewed out of me, splattering in the toilet water. The pain in my side shot up to 7 on a scale of 1 to 10.

Now that I'd done the unthinkable and temporarily lost all self-respect, perhaps my body would relent. I could only hope the worst of whatever this was had passed (albeit out of the wrong end).

I managed to thoroughly brush my teeth and gargle a

great number of times, assuring myself it was safe to swallow my own spit again. The image staring back at me in the mirror was normally me after a good workout— kinky twists dampened slightly at the base by my sweat, light brown face glowing in the accomplishment of burning hundreds of calories. Today, however, my sagging eyelids told the story of a woman who'd . . . vomited. I tried smiling, elevating my cheekbones even higher. No use. Maybe my mother was right when she'd told me, "You're not that pretty, Tori, but you can keep yourself skinny and, when you turn fifteen, I'll let you wear makeup. Fourteen if you're *really* ugly by then."

I closed my eyes and pressed fingers onto my temples, reminding myself that people told me all the time I was cute. One time, I went to this women's empowerment event my client was hosting, and I won a T-shirt that read I'M BEAUTIFUL with some Bible verse on it about being beautifully and wonderfully made. I wore that shirt to Walmart and a total stranger walked up to me and said, "I agree." So why did the only voice ringing now belong to my ever-beautiful mother, the timeless Margie Carolyn James, who bragged of still being carded at age forty?

My side still ached enough for me to call off the evening's kickboxing class. Good thing Kevin was out of town working. He probably would have called me a wimp and dared me to run at least two miles with him. And I probably would have at least attempted to make Kevin eat his words, despite the pain now radiating through my stomach.

After downing a dose of Advil, I trudged to my bedroom, changed into a nightshirt and gently lay across the bed. I didn't have the energy to answer my landline when it rang. I could only listen for the message.

"Hey, I'm gonna lay over tonight. My flight comes in at seven, I leave out again tomorrow morning at eight. See ya."

I was hoping that by the time he got home, I would have awakened from a refreshing nap, totally healed and ready to finish up some of the work I'd had to bring home with me in light of the unproductive afternoon I'd endured. Yet when Kevin returned, he found me hunched over the toilet seat again.

"What are you doing?"

"What does it look like I'm doing? Uuuuck!" The wretching produced another plop of bile into the commode.

"Are you okay?"

"Perfect."

"What's going on?"

"I'm pregnant," I quipped, though the hint of mockery escaped my tone thanks to the reverberating bowl.

"Oh my God, Tori. You're kidding, right? You know how I feel about kids," he yelled. "How could you—"

"Stop freaking out. I'm joking."

He balled up his fist and exhaled into the hole. "Don't give me a heart attack."

"I ate some cake today at work and got sick."

He backed out into the hallway. "Let me know if you need me."

I rested an elbow on the toilet seat and looked up at Kevin. Six foot one looked even taller from my bathroom floor perspective. His deep sandy skin contrasted perfectly with his ivory teeth and hazel eyes that, according to him, had won over many women back in the day. I wasn't one of those eye-color crazy girls, but I was definitely a sucker for track star legs, and Kevin had those for miles and miles. Watching him unveil those limbs when he undressed was definitely the greatest benefit of moving into his condo eighteen months earlier. Well, the legs and the free rent. And the sex, when my mind cooperated.

Kevin was the modern, metrosexual type when it came to clothes, but he had some pretty old-fashioned ideas about finances. Who was I to argue with him? He paid the major bills. I handled groceries, the housekeeper, dry cleaning, and all things communication related since I needed high-speed everything for my job. I often wondered if he was being chivalrous or if he never obligated me to a substantial bill because he still thought of the condo as *his* place.

At first glance, our living quarters still resembled a bachelor pad. Simple furniture, mix-and-match bath towels. Not one picture of us on display, though I had plenty on my computer and stored on my camera waiting to be downloaded someday.

Either way, I'm no fool. Thanks to our financial arrangement, I had a growing stash of rainy-day money I'd earmarked to start my own business after an early retirement.

My stash was chump change compared to Kevin's anyway. I'd seen a few of his pay stubs lying around the condo from his work in telecommunications sales. Made my college degree seem like a huge scam to keep the masses from getting rich.

Thoughts of my master plan to retire well and get rich later compelled me to hoist myself from the floor to a semistanding position and shuffle back to bed. Sick or well, there was work to be done.

Kevin did check on me, but only by default as he changed into his running clothes.

There went those strong, milk chocolate legs again.

"I'm going for a jog at the track. Might head over to Cameron's after to watch the game."

I gave my best big-brown-doe-eyes routine. "But you're leaving again first thing in the morning. Can't we spend time together?"

He held up a cross with his fingers. "I don't want to catch whatever this is you've got. You looked pretty distraught in that bathroom there a minute ago."

"Thanks so much, Kevin."

"Any time, any time," he smirked. "I do feel bad for you, if that helps."

"It doesn't."

"You need me to get you anything while I'm out?"

"A new stomach."

"No can do, babe. How about Pepto-Bismol or Sprite? That's what my mom gave me when I was sick."

I scrunched my face. "Didn't your mom also make you swallow Vicks VapoRub?"

"Yeah," he supported the madness. "Makes you cough the cold up. Worked every time. If you're getting a virus, you might want to give it a shot."

My stomach lurched at the thought. "No. I don't want anything else coming up out of me tonight. Just . . . call and check on me."

He detoured to my side before walking out of the room. A gentle kiss to my forehead was his first affectionate gesture, despite more than a week's passing since we'd seen each other last. I suppose it would have been hard for him to kiss me since I was engulfed in the commode earlier. Still, I wanted him to rub my back or something. What I really wanted was for him to stay home and . . . I don't know, watch me suffer. Hover like they do when women are giving birth in those old movies. Put a damp towel on my forehead and encourage me, "You can do it! You can do it, Tori!"

Who was I kidding? Kevin would hire a birthing coach before he'd subject himself to *my* labor. Not that I'd ever find myself in a position to give birth so long as Kevin stubbornly refused to father a child. I held hope, however, that things would change after a few of his friends settled down. Sometimes guys are the only ones who can convince other guys to grow up. It's a sick reality.

I decided to put the suffering out of my head for a moment. The Advil had taken the edge off the pain, so I carefully reached onto the floor and pulled my laptop bag onto the bed. The sweet challenge of work carried me into a trance that dulled the pain for a while.

I tapped on the mouse to wake my computer and then resumed toggling between the open programs on my computer desktop, making sure my client's newsletter matched the updated blog content precisely. Next to update their social media networks with useful information about the company's new products.

With reviewing several press releases still on my agenda, I really didn't want to stop working. But the pain in my midsection returned with new vigor, biting into my concentration. I powered down my computer for the night and made my way back to the restroom for another bout with bile and a double dose of Advil. If the pain wasn't any better by tomorrow, I'd have to miss work so I could visit the doctor.

Kevin rolled in a little after eleven to assess me again. He slipped a hand beneath the comforter and rubbed my backside. "You all right now?"

"No," I groaned.

He nibbled on my ear, a sure indication of his intentions. "Mind if I make you feel better?"

"That won't help."

"Marvin Gaye says sexual healing is the best thing for you."

"Marvin Gaye never felt this bad. Besides, I might have germs."

Kevin tried again, lapping my neck with his tongue. "I don't care. I miss you."

Now he doesn't care about the germs.

His hand moved around to my stomach, warranting a stern rejection. "Kevin, I cannot do this tonight. Move your hand."

He jumped up from the bed. "Fine. Fine. I understand. I'll be on the couch."

Chapter 2

"Maybe it's because you haven't eaten anything," my secretary speculated when I told her I felt like I'd been kicked by a horse. "You tried crackers?"

"Yes, but they wouldn't stay down," I confessed. Jacquelyn had never seen me so miserable—in fact, no one had ever seen me so miserable because I'd never *been* so miserable in my whole life. I hurt so bad I was close to crying, which is the only reason I decided not to hang around the office another hour before my eleven o'clock semiappointment with Dr. Lightfoot.

His receptionist had assured me, "You may have to wait a bit when you get here, but we'll try to work you in as soon as possible."

I figured if they were going to work me in some way, I might be able to get the ball rolling sooner if I got there earlier. I grabbed my laptop bag and purse, and stopped by Preston's office on my way out the door. By this point, I was nearly doubled over in pain.

"Tori, can I get someone to take you to the doctor?" he asked. "You really don't look well."

Truth be told, I would have preferred a ride. I'd even

considered calling Kevin, but if he came home, he probably wouldn't be able to reschedule his flight and make it
to Chicago in time for his next presentation. Still, the logistics of having a coworker take me—leaving my car in
the parking lot, getting someone else to pick me up when
this was all over—was too much to ask. Plus there was always the possibility I might barf upside someone else's
door panel before they could pull over, like I'd contami-
nated my car only three hours earlier.

"No, I'll make it. I've got my unfinished work here in
my bag, in case I don't get to come back this afternoon." I
raised the black leather satchel for him to see.

To my surprise, he didn't seem impressed. Then again,
who could really tell with those glasses?

"Well, let us know if you need a day off or something."

I frowned and shook my head. "Oh, no. I'll be back at
my desk tomorrow for sure. There's way too much work
to be done."

Now it was Preston's turn to frown. "Take care, Tori."

"Okay. See you tomorrow."

I treaded lightly down the hallway, stabilizing my mid-
section. Movements were the enemy. Movements and
food. Even liquids were suspect.

The beauty-queen wave would have to do as I floated
down the hallway saying good-bye to the few coworkers
who happened to be looking up from their screens as I
passed by. Our gray cubicle partitions definitely prevented outside distractions.

Once down the elevator (which nearly did me in),
through the parking lot, and sitting in my shiny red Cadillac SRX mini-SUV with the lovely lingering aroma of
throw up, I carefully snapped my seat belt and took off for
Dr. Lightfoot's office. My only saving grace was the
weather. February in Houston is still quite cold, thus the

odor from this morning's puke hadn't been baked in yet. The detail shop would have to work me in, too.

Why are there so many lights? I was down to one hand driving now. The other was practically glued to my mid-section, attempting to protect myself from this invading pain. The act itself was impractical because the pain came from inside me, but I couldn't help myself.

I began to doubt whether I could step out of my car if I ever made it to Dr. Lightfoot's office. Agony elicited little animal noises from deep within me. Now, I was thankful for the stoplights. They gave me a chance to catch my breath, refocus myself and gain my wits again. I promise you, the road to this office was turning into that long, ever-extending hallway in *The Shining*.

I think I had maybe two more intersections to go when I decided there was no way I could make it in. I should have taken Preston up on his offer because, at the moment, tears blurred my vision. "Oh my God!" I finally cried out, followed by a long string: "Oh my God, oh my God, oh my God." And I wasn't just saying His name jokingly, either. I felt as though I was, maybe, ten minutes from meeting the Big Man Himself if this pain didn't cease.

Then came this sudden, unquestionable realization that I needed to make a quick right into the hospital's emergency room, which was directly across the street from the physicians' offices. I knew I couldn't sit in Dr. Lightfoot's office and wait to be seen after someone with a mere stuffy nose. I needed someone to see me stat.

A gloriously close spot opened up just as I was pulling into the emergency room parking lot. Couldn't have asked for better without being in an ambulance. I swerved between the white lines and parked, waiting for a moment of diminished pain. No such luck. No reprieve in sight.

I opened the car door and found footing on the nice, steady concrete. Now to push myself up and out of the car. I rolled down the window to get a good grip on the door's frame with my right hand. I'd just grabbed hold of the headrest with my left and was attempting to tilt forward when this band of torture wrapped itself around to my right side and dictated in no uncertain terms: *you ain't goin' nowhere, Tori!*

Yes, Pain has a voice. He sounds like Freddy Krueger and he minces no words. The excruciating fire in my stomach had spread.

"Help!" I whimpered desperately. "Help me!"

The lot was completely void of all human life. Eyeing the building's glass windows, I saw why no one inside the building had noticed me. The shades were pulled down to block out the high sun. Only the patrons' legs were visible.

But wait! A little girl. On the floor. I waved my hand and finally managed to lock gazes with her. She gave me a snaggle-toothed smile that, at that moment, was the sweetest vision I'd ever beheld.

I motioned for her to touch the nearest grown-up and get me some help—or at least I thought that's what I'd motioned. In retrospect, I'm sure I must have looked like I was doing the chicken dance.

The little girl turned away from me and continued playing with some toy on the ground. But a second or two later, she gave me her attention again. This time, I mouthed the word "help" and folded my hands in a pleading gesture.

She laughed, apparently amused. This little girl was not *even* trying to help me. I had to go mean-church-usher on her. I'd never been so glad that 90 percent of communication is body language. Through gritted teeth and flared nostrils, I ordered her with words I'm sure she couldn't hear, "Get your momma! Get your momma!" I wagged my finger angrily toward her. "Get her now!"

The child's face wrinkled with fear and she tapped her mother's leg, then pointed back at me. Seconds later, the bottom of the blinds lifted and a woman's face peeked out at me.

"Help me!"

Nurses came scrambling out with a wheelchair. Thankfully, they had the wherewithal to secure my car and grab my purse. I was transported straight to an examination room. They asked me a ton of questions that I couldn't answer because I was in such agony I couldn't even think straight anymore. Their faces blurred by tears, their words overshadowed by my wailing. I just wanted them to knock me out and do whatever they had to do.

"Who can we notify for you?"

I cried, "Nobody! I came by myself!"

"Have you taken any drugs, Miss Henderson?"

"No!"

"Is there a possibility that you could be pregnant?"

Home-training aside, I managed to say, "No, no, no to everything, all right? Just help me!"

After covering every possible topic—including my insurance—and prolonging my pain to the full extent legally allowable, a doctor finally entered the room. She asked me two questions about my symptoms, had me lie flat on my back, and pressed one area on my stomach that made me want to slap the judge.

I didn't have to tell her she'd hit the spot.

"Looks like it's your appendix. We'll have to operate right away." She glanced at my chart again and ordered the nurses to prepare me for surgery.

"Miss Henderson," the pesky nurse drilled me again,

"we have to notify someone before we can proceed. Don't you have *anyone* we can call? Grandparents? Cousins?"

Surgery? I shook my head violently as, now, a fresh batch of tears spewed from my eyes. These, however, came from a different well. *I don't want to die.*

"How about coworkers or a friend or a boyfriend?"

"He won't answer—he's on a flight."

"It doesn't matter. We can leave a message. We just have to let someone know you're going under sedation. It's the law."

"Kevin Walker." Then I gave her his number and someone whisked me off for surgery. "And call my job for me, okay?"

"We'll do that later."

The last thing I remember was a woman saying, "I'm gonna stick this needle in your arm and you'll be on your way to la-la land."

I remember thinking, "Lady, you can stick a needle in my *eye* if it'll get me out of this misery."

Chapter 3

Unfamiliar surroundings caused a brief panic as I returned to a state of consciousness. An IV in my arm, sterile whiteness all around me.

"Miss Henderson?" a soft voice called.

My voice way obstructed, I instinctively reached for my throat and felt plastic tubing.

"No. Wait just a second—I'll take it out." A red-haired nurse with extremely fair skin stood over me now. Her presence brought everything into focus. The first thing I realized was the absence of excruciating pain that had taken over my entire being earlier in the day, replaced by only a tenderness in the area.

In one sweeping motion, the nurse extracted the cylinder from my mouth. Like ripping tape off someone's skin, there was no use in belaboring the action. A few coughs later, I managed to eke out a request for water.

The nurse obliged me only a sip, saying I shouldn't eat or drink anything until the anesthesia wore off. "Don't want you to lose whatever you put down."

Please. After all I'd been through, I was a professional vomiter.

The next thing I remember with clarity is eating Jell-O, trying to convince myself that it was okay to eat again. The surgery was over, but I still needed to satisfy my psyche. One bite. Wait a minute. Another bite. Wait. Before the next bite, I examined the Jell-O. My taste buds must have been asleep still because I wasn't able to taste much. I had to rely on texture. Gelatin made with real sugar was thicker than Jell-O made with artificial sweetener. My fork sliced through the shiny red goop easily. Splenda.

I'm pretty sure I slept like a baby for most of my two-day hospital stay. There was little to occupy me except an occasional visit from the doctor or a nurse. I could have kicked myself for leaving my laptop in the car. The outside temperature was cool enough to prevent damage to my equipment, but the workload would certainly swell with neglect. If only I'd had someone I knew come by, I could give them my keys and ask them to go get my bag.

Kevin called once, between meetings, to check on me. "How are you feeling?"

"Much better." I powered my bed to an upright position. "How's it going in Chicago?"

"Sweet. I think that pharmaceutical company I told you about is going to award us the account. It's huge. Seriously—huge."

"That's good." I wish I could say I listened to him go on and on about the deal, his residuals from it, and how his team would probably win the contest if they got this one, which meant a trip to Saint Lucia for us both, but as exciting as all that was, something else caught my attention. Actually, it was the *lack* of something that struck me. I didn't have any flowers. Not one balloon, not one card. Nothing.

Voices from the hallway spilled into my room, and I

watched for a moment to see who they belonged to. First appeared a woman about my age with her hair pulled behind a white cloth headband. She wore a full-length halter dress and flip-flops. The child, probably her son, hopped from tile to tile as he traveled alongside her. She told him to stop it; hospitals were no place for leaping. Slowly, a man came into view pushing an IV cart. The patient. They were a family, I figured. The mom and son had come to visit the father. A few more elderly family members trailed the man. Maybe his parents. They talked about whether or not the man would still be able to travel to "D-I-S-N-E-Y land," the grandmother spelled out, presumably so the child wouldn't understand the topic.

As I watched this family's snapshot, the absence of flowers, cards, and balloons seemed minor, to belie my saddest realization. No one had come to see me.

I broke into Kevin's impending-sales-victory train with a question. "Do you think we're ever going to be a family?"

He stuttered, "Wh-what?"

"A family." I spelled it out for him: "Me, you, kids, your parents."

"Tori, we've already talked about this."

I sighed. "I know, I know. It's just that I'm sitting here in this hospital all alone and—"

"You're having a fleeting maternal episode, babe. Don't get down about it, all right? You'll be up on your feet in a few days. This moment will pass," he assured me. "I gotta go. I'll call you when I get a chance." He hung up before I could even say good-bye.

My eyes began to sting and lumps jumbled in my throat. *I'm having a fleeting episode?* A moment of wanting someone to care enough to check on me? This ain't no

Twix commercial, this is life. I didn't want a moment of being cared about—I wanted someone to care about me every day. For a lifetime.

I blinked back the tears because crying, like vomiting, was not my forte. The last time I could remember crying, I mean shoulder-shaking, snot-flying crying, was when my mother told me *not* to cry. I was sixteen and had just delivered a stillborn baby boy.

A nurse brought him to me, swaddled in a white blanket with pink and blue stripes. She said she'd leave me alone with him for a while. To say good-bye.

His little body was perfectly formed, ten fingers and ten toes. He had my lips, his father's nose. If the doctors hadn't told me he was dead, I would have figured he was just sleeping. A guttural wail came from deep inside me as my tears fell onto my deceased son's forehead.

My mother sat beside me on the hospital bed and fingered through my hair. I wasn't expecting her to do that. She'd been so distant—both physically and emotionally—throughout my unexpected pregnancy, I'd forgotten she could actually show affection like most human mothers.

"It's going to be all right, Tori. Everything will work out for the best," she whispered softly. Then she stroked my son's plump cheeks. "He has your lips," she agreed with me.

I laughed slightly. "He kind of looks like Grandpa Henderson, doesn't he, Momma?"

She laughed, too. "Yes, he does look like my father—you're right. He's a handsome little thing."

"You think Grandpa Henderson will recognize him and take care of him in heaven?"

"I'm sure he will, Tori," my mother said as she pulled me and the baby into a hug.

Just then, Mr. James entered the room. My mother stiffened, then jumped up from the bed wiping her eyes with the back of her hands. She walked toward my stepfather and braced him, holding both his arms. Mr. James was short, stocky, and balding on top of his head. His mean black eyes peered from beneath hooded lids. How he'd managed to snag someone as beautiful as my mother was strictly business. She wanted financial stability, he wanted a trophy wife to complement his joke of a political career.

"Give her a minute with the baby, James." My mother attempted to stand her ground with him.

"It's dead, Margie."

I burst into tears again. Why did he always have to be such a jerk?

"No use in crying over spilled milk. What's done is done," he snapped, and pushed past my mother to confront me directly. "I told you and your momma you weren't ready to handle a baby. Even God agreed with me."

I secured the baby in the nook of my left arm, then used my right hand to bop Mr. James upside the head with the hardest thing I could get my hand on—the television remote control.

Mr. James cupped his eye with his hand and stammered, "Are you cr-crazy?"

My mother jumped in between us, as she'd always done. "Tori, stop this! You've lost your mind, hitting your stepfather." No surprise there, either. She almost always took his side. "I'm going to call the nurse. Maybe they can give you a Valium. . . . James, go to the nurses' station and see if you can get an ice pack."

My mother pushed the call button and seconds later, a nurse arrived to assist. I don't know why it didn't occur to me that the nurse would want me to relinquish the baby. But when she rolled that bassinet into the room, reality punched me.

"No! Don't take him!"

"Honey, give me the baby," Mother demanded.

"I'm not ready," I protested. "He's not ready. Aunt Dottie didn't get to see him." I truly wanted my aunt, who had taken me in during the last five months of my pregnancy, to see him. But she was busy working at her store. It was the day before Thanksgiving. There was no way she could close shop on such an important day. She said she'd come and see me as soon as she closed and I knew she would. Aunt Dottie always kept her word.

"Tori, it's all over now," Mother coldly surmised. Somehow, Mr. James always managed to turn my mother into a wicked witch when he was around.

Gently, the nurse and my mother pried my son from me for the last time. "Wait!" I tried to maintain physical contact with him, but they weren't listening. I'd learned no one listened to sixteen-year-old mothers, actually.

When the nurse placed the baby in the clear standard-issue bassinet and rolled him out of the room, I fell apart, sobbing uncontrollably and scrambling to get out of bed.

"Tori, stop this!" my mother ordered. "Stop this. It's over! Stop crying, stop crying this instant! You hear me? What's done is done. Crying won't change anything."

She was right. Crying had never changed one single thing about my miserable life before. I had no reason to think things would change at that point. If anything, things had been worse with my mother and Mr. James since I'd gotten pregnant by one of the neighborhood thugs.

My mother had already decided we weren't having a

funeral. Just a graveside service, which I'd already over-heard my stepfather, Mr. James, tell hospital personnel "cost way too much money for a dead baby. Why can't they just dispose of it?"

He thought I was asleep. I wasn't.

Chapter 4

The doctor ordered me to refrain from driving for at least another three days following the appendectomy. So when the time came for me to check out of the hospital, I was stuck out. Kevin was still in Chicago, so there was absolutely no one on hand to escort me home. My attending nurse asked if I knew how to get in touch with anyone from my job, but since it was Saturday, I had no means of reaching them outside work except e-mail. After all, they were my coworkers, not my friends. I went to an occasional wedding shower or birthday party with those people, but that was about it.

The nurse went down a list of other possibilities: church members, sorority sisters, neighbors. She even went so far as to ask if one of my clients might be willing to transport me. *No, no, no, and are you out of your mind?* The more she asked, the more frustrated I became. She instructed me to go through my cell phone and scan the contacts to see if there might be someone I'd overlooked. "Maybe you're a little foggy, with the drugs and all."

I followed her orders and still turned up nothing. All I had was business contacts, Kevin, my favorite restaurants, and Aunt Dottie, who lived more than three hours away and whom I wouldn't dare bother with my troubles. She was in her seventies. I had no doubt she would hightail it to Houston if she had to, but the last thing I wanted to do was raise Aunt Dottie's blood pressure.

"Can't you just call a taxi for me? Whatever it costs to get me back home, I'll pay," I offered. As if the hospital would have it any other way.

Satisfied that I was indeed a real-life true hermit, the nurse sighed. "I'll call a social worker. He or she will help the checkout and take it from there."

"A social worker?" I attempted to sit up, but the sting in my side reminded me of stitches I still needed to guard. "I'm not a *foster* kid. I'm a grown woman who happens to not have a lot of friends." *Do Facebook friends count?*

When she left the room, I picked up the phone to call a taxi myself. Why were these people acting like everyone has to have a million friends? A zillion contacts? I mean, some of us are busy with work. We've dedicated ourselves to being the best at what we do. Is that so wrong? Isn't that the American dream?

Besides, I did have a boyfriend. He and I had friends. Well, they were mostly his friends, but I knew them. I saw them at Target and McDonald's and said "Hi!" They always said "Hi!" back to me.

The social worker arrived shortly after I'd psyched myself out. *My life isn't so bad, really. I'm perfectly fine.*

"Hello. Tori Henderson?" A chubby Hispanic lady with glasses and a long braid down her back tentatively stuck her head into my room. "I'm Josephine Sanchez with Social Services."

I couldn't be rude to this lady. She was just doing her job. Plus, she was at least twenty years older than me, so I had to be respectful. "Yes, I'm Tori."

"Great." She entered the room and came right over to me, stretching out a hand for shaking purposes.

I returned her gesture and she pulled up a chair. "Well, as I understand it, you're going to need transportation from the hospital to your home. Will you need someone to pick up your prescriptions for you as well?"

"What prescriptions?"

"For pain."

"Well, my boyfriend will be back in a few days. He travels a lot."

She laughed slightly. "I don't think you'll want to be without pain medication in the interim. My son actually had this same surgery a few years ago. Trust me, you'll need it." Her eyes turned to slits when she smiled, but the warmth therein still came across. She had the kind of demeanor I wished I could have when I was in those "What went wrong with your campaign?" meetings with Mr. Haverty.

"Don't hospitals have pharmacies?" I asked.

"Some do," she said, nodding, "but this one doesn't. Don't worry about it though, Miss Henderson. I can help you with that, too." She produced a notepad from her purse and scribbled. "And, by the way, I can also help you to connect with other people in the Houston area so if you're ever in a bind like this again, you'd have people to help you."

I shook my head and smirked. "I don't need help meeting people."

She shrugged. "Well, that's part of what Social Services is all about. If you'd . . . already been meeting people, it might be easier to get along in life. Especially when things like this unexpected surgery happen. Life has lots of surprises. The longer you live, the more you get."

"Ms. Sanchez, I thank you for taking the time to arrange for the taxi and the medications, but I don't *need* any other Social Services. I do have a life, I have a boyfriend, and I'm one of the top producers at my job—"

"Tori." Josephine stopped me, taking off her glasses and peering at me for a moment. She seemed to be deciding something. She looked toward the sky, seemed to nod, and then took a deep breath. "I'm going to tell you something off the record. Something I wish someone had told me a long time ago. Do you want to hear it?"

Do I have a choice? "I guess."

"I think you're ready." She smiled, as though she had been waiting for this moment since she first heard my name. "I used to work for a huge bank. I was well on my way up the corporate ladder, bringing in millions for the company, looking forward to that corner office.

"One day, a colleague in my department died of cancer and we all went to her funeral. We carpooled together that morning. We went to support the family and represent the company, of course.

"When the ceremony was over, about five of us piled into my car. And do you know what was the first thing someone said when we got back into the car?"

It took me a minute to realize her question wasn't rhetorical. "Umm . . . I don't know."

She smiled with a faraway look in her eyes. "The first thing said, I remember it word for word, was, 'Hey, where do y'all want to go for lunch?'"

Call me a little slow still that morning, but I didn't get her right away. "Okay. And?"

"My point is, when you die, the people you work with will move on with their lives just as if you never lived. Your employer will post an opening, there'll be interviews, and your position will be filled as quickly as possible. It'll be just like you never lived. Is that how you want to go?"

My face crinkled in annoyance. "No. No one wants to be forgotten. I'm just . . . very busy living my life."

"And you have no family whatsoever?"

Eyes cast down toward my blank hands, I answered, "None to speak of."

"Who raised you? Are you originally from Houston?" she prodded.

"What's with all the questions?"

Josephine smiled and leveled with me. "I'm also here to make sure you're not in any danger. You'd be surprised how many people use a hospital stay as an opportunity to escape abusive situations."

I took a deep breath, wondering if Josephine worked for the FBI, too. "My mom and stepfather raised me here in Houston until I was fifteen. Then I got pregnant and went to live with my Aunt Dottie in a little country town called Bayford. Ever heard of it?"

Josephine shook her head. "Can't say that I have."

I continued, "I stayed with her until I graduated from high school, then I went to college. After graduation, I got my first entry-level job and worked like crazy. Got another, better paying job I really enjoy. Then I met Kevin. We moved in together. It's just been me, him, and work since then."

Josephine had listened intently, nodding and smiling. She was just listening—not taking any notes. "Why didn't you tell the nurses about your mom or your aunt?"

"I haven't talked to my mom since the day she ripped my son out of my arms and told me to stop crying. And Aunt Dottie . . . I talk to her now and then, but she's elderly. I wouldn't want her to worry about me."

"You love her though, right? I can tell by the way you say her name."

A smile crept up on me. "Yes, I do love my Aunt Dottie very much. If she lived closer to me, there's no way I'd be sitting in this room all alone."

Josephine snapped her notebook shut. "Well, if you ask me—and you didn't—but if you *did,* I'd say you might want to think about getting you some folks. Everybody needs folks, you know?"

I nodded.

"So, I'll get you a taxi and have your prescriptions filled and dropped off at your house. I can also coordinate having meals delivered to you."

I laughed at her offer. "I've got plenty of restaurants in my cell phone." I had those if nothing else.

"Good deal, Tori."

Chapter 5

A normal person probably would have enjoyed lounging around the house for ten days. Relaxing drove me crazy. For one thing, when I finally spoke to Preston about my predicament, I learned that he'd farmed my work out to Lexa and a few other representatives who didn't know diddly-squat about my clients' profiles.

"Tori, you've always kept immaculate, clearly written reports. We should have no problem picking up where you left off. Don't worry. Everything will be fine."

I pleaded, "Can't I at least have proxy to view communication relevant to my accounts?"

Preston let out a condescending laugh. "If it makes you feel better, I'll personally supervise them for you. Take some time off, catch your breath, and come back as soon as you can. All right?"

I did feel a little better knowing Preston would be at the helm. "All right. I'll call back in a few days to see if you all have any questions."

"And I'll put you straight through to voice mail." He stood firm. "I only want you to work on recovery, okay?

I'm serious about this. You're a valuable part of this team, but you're no good to us if you're not well."

He had a point, but I couldn't help thinking I wasn't any good to them sick or well. How could he just divvy up my work—like I didn't even matter?

"Okay, Preston. I'll . . . I'll be in touch later this week."

"Good deal."

The same words Josephine used prior to my hospital checkout. "Good deal," she'd said. Talking to Preston felt like talking to Josephine all over again. Maybe they were both right. Maybe the people at my job really didn't need me. I mean, if what I pride myself on doing can be doled out without so much as a consultation, maybe my work wasn't important. Shoot, a computer could probably do my job, the way Preston acted.

And what if I had died? What if I hadn't made it to the hospital "in the nick of time," as the doctor had phrased it. I think Lexa would have made her lunch plans *before* my funeral. Couldn't blame her, though. All she knew about me was my work record and maybe my birthday because Preston always recognized birthdays. He gave us each gift cards to our favorite venues. Mine had been for Starbucks since I started at NetMarketing Results six years earlier.

This was bad. Really bad. I mean, if my job didn't need me, who did? Kevin certainly didn't. And if no one really cared whether or not I lived, what was the point in me living? Could I possibly be here on earth for eighty-five years or so and then . . . nothing? What would they say at my funeral? "Here lies Tori Danielle Henderson. She lived, she worked, she died. That's it. Y'all can go on to lunch now."

I started thinking about my sixth-grade teacher, Mrs.

Pope. She died of cancer when I was in eighth grade. Her funeral was standing room only. Her family, friends, and former students had so many positive things to say about how she'd touched their lives. At one point, the officiating minister actually curtailed the commentary line because there wasn't enough time to hear all of their testimonies about how thoughtful, selfless Mrs. Pope had helped them. "Please consider expressing your thoughts in writing," the preacher had suggested. But even at the burial grounds, I'd seen people approaching Mrs. Pope's family members to tell them what a wonderful person she had been.

I tried talking to Kevin about my purpose crisis, but he wasn't listening. I think I'd scared him with the mere mention of family the previous week. Not the first time I'd approached the topic, but definitely the first time I'd presented it as more than a rogue thought. Nothing like a hospital room full of nothing to illuminate life's priorities, I suppose.

He left me alone during most of my recovery while he watched basketball at his friends' apartments. He said what I needed most was probably peace and quiet. Since I didn't have work or anything else to fill my time, I fell into a bad combination of reality shows and ramen noodles. With no calorie-burning activity, I had to adjust my intake to less than a thousand calories a day if I wanted to avoid gaining weight. Those college years made for a great experiment in how little one can eat and still survive.

As for the television shows, how could I resist? Real life is way more interesting than anything those screenwriters could imagine. I mean, who would have guessed that someone's mother would suggest her own daughter become a prostitute? And how many dads out there jump for joy when their sons raise fight-winning pit bulls?

The "scientific" channels were my favorite—*Hoarding Life*, *Mites In My Mind*, *Undiagnosed*, and *The Intervention*. I couldn't watch them all, so I started recording them, to Kevin's dismay.

"Is this what you've become?" he asked. "You're turning into a reality-show junkie."

"Better this than chocolate." I shrugged.

He agreed. Kevin had a serious problem with fat people. "They're disgusting," he'd said on more than one occasion. "I don't know how they can live with themselves."

He reminded me of my mother. "You can't control how tall you are or how long your nose gets, but you *can* control how much you eat." She'd said that to me so many times growing up that I almost became anorexic during one of those awkward preteen spells when I packed on eight pounds preceding an upward growth spurt. "Don't sit down—go run around the block!" she'd say when I got home from school.

Aunt Dottie, however, disagreed vehemently with thinness. When I talked to her about losing weight after the baby, she'd said, "Don't nobody want a bone except a dog." The years I lived with her in Bayford warped my sense of the word "healthy," I think. In Bayford, healthy means chubby. In Houston (and apparently the rest of America), healthy meant skinny. I'd tried to explain the height-weight chart to Aunt Dottie, especially when the doctor told her she might want to cut back on fried foods, but she still didn't agree with me. "I ain't studyin' that doctor. I eat everything in moderation with thanksgiving. All this worryin' y'all tryin' to make me do will kill me before the fatback does," she argued.

She carried on as usual and made me eat my words when her doctor died of a heart attack that next year. He was only fifty-six. "Two years younger than me," she'd pointed out as she signed the card for his family. "Tomorrow ain't promised to nobody, fried chicken or not."

The more I thought about Aunt Dottie, the more I missed her. I hadn't talked to her in a couple of months. Truth be told, Aunt Dottie was hard to catch up with. Between running her store and volunteering at the church, she kept pretty busy. I'd call her on birthdays and holidays, of course, and we'd pick right up where we left off. If I caught her at the right time, we'd talk for hours. She'd always ask about my parents and I'd always reply, "I haven't talked to them lately," which translated: I hadn't talked to them at all. There's nothing to say to people who don't want you in their lives anymore.

Aunt Dottie would tell me the latest news in Bayford—who got married, who had a baby, who was going off to college. I'd tell her about my work.

"How's Kevin?" she'd ask, even though I knew she wasn't too crazy about him.

"He's fine," I'd say as I mentioned whatever city he happened to be visiting. Seems like Kevin was always gone somewhere when I had my lengthy talks with Aunt Dottie.

She'd sigh. "Well, I hope he knows what a good woman he's got in you, and I hope you know it, too." Aunt Dottie didn't think Kevin was a good man because he hadn't made an honest woman out of me. I'd heard her talk enough in the corner store about this one or that one shacking up and how men don't buy the cow when they can get the milk for free. "I tell you, it's not so much wrong as it is sad. When are we ever going to figure out that when we do things God's way, it always turns out better, quicker, and easier?"

I knew where Aunt Dottie stood on cohabitation. She didn't have to say anything to me about it. Condemnation and guilt weren't Aunt Dottie's style. She'd sooner smother me in love than beat me over the head with a fire and brimstone sermon. That was the good thing about Aunt Dottie—she granted all this free, unconditional love, and I certainly needed some love right about then.

Aunt Dottie's number was forever seared into my brain. She said she'd had the same phone number for more than fifty years and wasn't planning on changing it. So one can imagine my horror and surprise when a child's voice answered, "Hello."

I double-checked my phone's screen to be sure I'd dialed the correct number. "Hello, is this Dorothy James's residence?"

"No."

"I'm sorry." I ended the call with great peace, but confusion quickly followed. I *had* dialed the right number. Where was Aunt Dottie?

I called again, this time determined to speak to an adult. The child answered again, "Hellllllooooo," with annoyance in his or her voice.

"I'm sorry. I'm trying to reach Dorothy James. This is 5-5-5-7-3-2-1, correct?"

"Yep, but nobody lives here 'cept me and Aunt Dottie," the child informed me between heavy breaths.

I laughed to myself. I forgot—everyone in Bayford called Miss Dorothy James Aunt Dottie whether she was blood kin or not. "May I speak to Aunt Dottie, then?"

"She's not here. She's in the hospital."

"What?!" I tapped the television's mute button and

sat up quickly, thankful that the sting in my side had fully dissipated by then.

"Uh huh. She might be back by tomorrow or maybe not till next week or something 'cause the doctor might make her stay 'cause she got good insurance."

In the background, a woman's shrill tone called, "Who's that on the phone?" Had to be Joenetta. Something must be wrong for Joenetta to be in Aunt Dottie's house unattended. And who was this running-off-at-the-mouth child claiming to live with Aunt Dottie?

"Hello?" Joenetta took over the conversation.

"Hi, Joenetta. This is Tori. How are you?"

"Well, well, well," she cackled, "look what the cat done drug in. How you hear about Aunt Dottie all the way in Houston?"

"I didn't hear anything. I was just calling to check on her. Why is Aunt Dottie in the hospital?" No need in playing these catch-up games with Joenetta. She'd never liked me and the feeling was mutual.

"She had a mild stroke, they say. I think the doctors are just keeping her in there for the insurance," she surmised. "I told your Aunt Dottie she ought to walk out, but I guess it's a bad idea to make your doctor mad at you, especially if he's white. He just might kill you and cover it up." She laughed at her own wacked sense of humor.

"When did she have the stroke?"

"A few days ago. She was workin' at the store and Cassandra said all of a sudden Aunt Dottie was having trouble moving her arm, said she'd had a headache all morning." She paused. "You remember Cassandra Meyers, don't you? Dottie hired her over me. Shame when your own sister won't give you a job. I was one of Dottie's very first customers, you know that?"

I rolled my eyes and jumped in when Joenetta took a breath. "What's the prognosis?"

"The *what*?"

My mind scrambled for a synonymous phrase. "What did the doctor say? Is she going to get better?"

"I know what a pragnesic is, Miss Smartie Pants. I just didn't hear you the first time," Joenetta snapped. "They're going to do a couple more tests. Give it some time. Go to some workout classes.

"You know when Big Daddy had his stroke, they sent him home right away 'cause he didn't have no money. They sure ain't doin' Dottie like that, I tell you."

"What's her room number?" No need in asking what hospital Aunt Dottie was in—there was only one within a fifty-mile radius.

"She's in room one seventeen, but ain't no use in you calling her. I told you she done had a stroke. You can't hardly understand a word she's saying."

The vision of Aunt Dottie barely able to speak broke my heart. Was she in pain? Did she know what had happened to her? Were there flowers in her room? "Is there anything I can do to help?"

Joenetta sighed heavily and took on a gloomy tone. "Well, if you really want to help, you can send some money."

I'd never known Aunt Dottie to be in need of money. She'd always lived beneath her means, a practice she taught me well. Joenetta, on the other hand, was a different story. "Money for what?"

"Money to keep this house going. Electricity, groceries, takin' care of DeAndre."

"Who's DeAndre?"

"The one who answered the phone."

"Okay, but who *is* he?"

"Ray-Ray's boy."

Ray-Ray? Everyone in Bayford had a nickname. Bubba, Pookie, Peaches. I had to ask, "Who's Ray-Ray?"

"My baby son," she practically screamed. "Has the city erased your memory?"

I put two and two together. "So DeAndre is your grandson?"

"That's usually how family trees work."

I had to know. "Why is Aunt Dottie taking care of someone else's child?"

Joenetta gave a nasty laugh. "Hmph, that's the same question I asked when *you* came to Bayford."

I didn't have a comeback for that one. As much as I believed parents should take care of their own children, I didn't have an excuse for why my own mother had quit the job.

Joenetta clicked her teeth. "So, you gonna send some money or what?"

"Is there anything *Aunt Dottie* needs?"

"I already told you all the stuff she needs around here. You don't trust me? Why don't you come see for yourself."

No, I certainly didn't trust Joenetta. I didn't trust her take on Aunt Dottie's medical condition, the financials, or this little DeAndre situation. I needed to lay my own eyes on Aunt Dottie, hug her, look into her face and assess her health for myself so I could sleep in peace at night knowing she was okay.

The only way I could rest was to call Joenetta's bluff. "I'll be there as soon as I can."

Chapter 6

I couldn't believe I was actually calling in to tell Preston I needed to take off a few more days to go visit my ailing aunt. "No worries, Tori. Family first," he assured me. "We've got things under control here."

This was the first time I'd ever heard his "family first" philosophy. Since when did NetMarketing Results become a family-friendly company? Not that I would know, since I'd never called in due to my child's fever or my mother-in-law's surgery. Never had to take off the afternoon for my niece's awards assembly. But when I thought about it, Preston always encouraged people to take off or do whatever they needed to do for family's sake. I was probably due some family-related off days, come to think of it. Maybe this would even give the folk at NetMarketing Results a chance to see what a truly valuable team player I was. Preston had said my clients were asking about me. Always a good sign.

Kevin came home from one of his sports nights with the fellas and found me packing. "Where are you going?"

"I'm going to Bayford. My Aunt Dottie had a stroke.

I need to check on her," I stated coldly while stuffing wrinkle-free fabrics into my largest suitcase.

"Bayford?"

"Yes." I stopped to look at him. His face was contorted, but not with worry. More like annoyance.

"Who's Aunt Dottie?"

"Aunt Dottie Lester. The Lesters? I have family there, remember? People who actually care about me." I couldn't resist. The no-card, no-flower issue still grated me.

He shook his head. "So what are you trying to say?"

"I'm just saying . . . I can't depend on you for everything, obviously."

Shock skittled across his face. "Oh my gosh! I'm like the most dependable person on the face of the planet. I pay almost every bill in this condo, I do everything you ask me to do. What's the problem?"

I sighed. Kevin was right. He was dependable. But high credit score aside, when I needed him to be there for me, he wasn't. "Kevin, you have your life. Your work, your friends, and people in your corner who would drop everything if you had a sudden health scare."

"Babe, I would have come if I could have." He walked around the bed and stood. "It's physically impossible to be in Houston and Chicago at the same time. You know that, right?"

"Yes, I know." He had his point, but he wasn't getting mine and I didn't know how to explain it to him because I think sometimes you have to experience a certain predicament to understand where a person is coming from. "I don't expect you to feel me on this. I just need you to work with me, okay?" I tiptoed to kiss his lips.

He reciprocated, one hand spider-walking down my backside. In the past, I might have fallen for his version of foreplay, but given the circumstances, this felt more like groping than caressing.

"What am I supposed to do with myself while you're gone?"

I pushed him away. "The same things you've been doing since I came home from the hospital, I guess. Go to your friends' places. Watch sports. Carry on with your same bachelor's lifestyle."

"Is this about getting married?" He was so clueless.

Packing resumed. "No. It's about being committed."

"Isn't that the same thing as marriage?"

"Yes and no. I mean, are you committed to me?" I stopped for a moment to read him.

He stumbled through a few expressions—uncertainty and dismay to be exact. "Yeah, I mean, I love you. We've been together all this time."

"That's not what I asked you."

"What's your definition of committed?" Kevin crossed his arms.

"Committed means when I need you, you're there without me asking. You'll drop everything to help me. And when I'm in the hospital, you send flowers." Maybe that last part wasn't quite in Webster's book, but it was definitely in mine.

"Since when have you ever wanted me to send *flowers*?"

"I'm not sure when I decided I liked flowers. Kevin, it's not about the flowers. I just needed to know that somebody cared about me, all right? Is that too much to ask?" Unexpected tears formed in my eyes and fell quickly.

Kevin hugged me again. "Don't freak out, Tori, dang. I'm sorry. You worry too much. I do care about you. I didn't know you wanted flowers. I mean, we're not a touchy-feely couple." He was right. In fact, I rather prided myself on the notion that I wasn't the "needy" type. Where Kevin despised obesity, I could not stand needy, whiny, high-drama people who expected the world to stop because they'd gotten a flat tire or missed a flight.

"We're touchy-feely when we have sex," I suggested, my words muffled by his shirt pressed against my lips.

He leaned down a bit, grabbed my thighs from behind and hoisted me up onto his waist. "You kind of have to touch and feel in order to participate." His hungry gaze met mine now. "I'm sorry for whatever I did or didn't do, okay?"

I wanted to coax more love talk out of him, but there was no use twisting his arm. He simply didn't get it. "Okay," I said, settling for his sincere apology.

Kisses followed, along with our usual sexual routine. My body went through the motions, but no matter how hard I tried to focus (and believe me, I tried) I couldn't make my head get into the game.

Kevin was somewhat distracted by my unresponsive-ness. "Do you want to do this or what?" he asked breath-lessly at one point.

"I'm sorry. My mind is on other things."

I don't suppose any man has ever stopped himself in the act on account of a woman's wandering mind. Kevin was no exception.

The three-and-a-half hour drive to Bayford did little to clarify life for me. I wondered how long I could continue the relationship with Kevin, or if I would even classify what we had as a bona fide romantic relationship. He really did love me in his own low-maintenance way, and I appreciated the space we both allowed each other. I didn't

want a clingy boyfriend who didn't understand my dedication to work or who pressured me to cook and clean
like I imagined most committed women did. Who was I
kidding? I couldn't have my cake and eat it, too. Part of
me wanted a friend who wouldn't place any demands on
me. The other part wanted someone to be so close that our
relationship warranted his presence at all hospital stays,
company parties, and holidays.

I was turning into my own worst needy-chick nightmare.

The closer I got to Bayford, the fewer exits available
on the highway. With my cell phone going in and out of
consciousness, I started to get paranoid. A sense of total
vulnerability settled over me and I began to note every
gas station and Dairy Queen so if I had any type of car
trouble, I'd have an idea of which direction I should walk.
There was an eighteen-wheeler trailing me and a Honda
Accord up ahead. The three of us had been together for at
least fifteen miles, the Honda and I trading the lead a couple of times. I began to imagine that the diesel and the
Honda were a tag team. The Honda would pour out some
nails on the street so my tires would go flat. Then the
diesel man would pull over and kidnap me. Since my cell
phone was dead, I wouldn't be able to call for help. No one
would know I was missing for several days. Why? Because no one cared enough to report me a missing person.

And then I'd be dead for so long before they found
me, my body would have decomposed and they'd have to
wait for forensic dental records to identify me. At my funeral, there'd be hardly anyone present to say good-bye.

I accelerated my cruise control by five more miles
per hour. If anyone was trying to harm me, they'd have to
catch me first.

Snap out of it, Tori! No one is going to kidnap you!

As I got off at the Bayford exit, I breathed easier. I don't know why I let myself get all worked up over the worst-case scenario. Habit, I guess. Maybe habit and watching a few too many crime reality shows.

My drive through town toward the hospital yielded some pleasant surprises. A Sonic drive-in, a Dollar General, even a billboard boasting a new housing development starting in the low hundreds, though I couldn't imagine why anyone would want to move to Bayford. Electricity poles lined the streets and scarcely needed four-way stop signs littered the intersections here and there. Even in the middle of the day, Bayford seemed sleepy compared to Houston, which didn't calm down until well after midnight—and only then for a few hours.

First stop in Bayford: Aunt Dottie's. Since I'd pass her house before nearing the county hospital, I wanted to drop my bag off and change into something other than my riding clothes. The Humble Trail street sign still leaned a little to the right. Every house on the street still looked exactly the same—color, fences, even down to the potted plants on the porches, it seemed. The houses sat on acre lots. Plenty of room for folks to mind their own business, though they rarely did.

The first time I rode down Humble Trail, nearly fifteen years earlier, I was terrified. Being dropped off at a step-relative's house in the middle of nowhere would scare anyone, let alone a pregnant teenager trying to make sense of what to do with her life after thoroughly ruining it.

Aunt Dottie's was the only brick house on Humble Trail. Actually, I think she owned the only brick house for several blocks, which made hers stand out, of course. The brown bricks with green trim amid an immaculate lawn spoke of the home owner's wealth. Back when I was living with Aunt Dottie and helping her run the store, people would always talk about how rich she was.

She'd say, "I'm just blessed."

Sometimes they'd say something smart like, "I'm blessed, too, but not as blessed as you."

And she'd reply, "Well, you might want to talk to the Lord and see what He wants you to do about it 'cause He doesn't play favorites."

Then the person would swagger out of the store as though Aunt Dottie was just blowing hot air, but I know she wasn't. Aunt Dottie was the only person claiming to be a Christian I knew of who actually *did* what Pastor Jacob used to tell us to do on Sundays. Aunt Dottie was so into the Bible and doing what she felt God told her to do, sometimes I wondered why she didn't preach the messages.

I wasn't expecting the front door to be locked. Then again, this wasn't 1996. Bayford was clearly changing just like the rest of the world. Colder, meaner. More dangerous—with the eighteen-wheeler kidnapping schemes and all.

I rang the doorbell a few times, just in case Joenetta was inside. When I got no answer, I walked around to the side of the house and unlatched the six-foot gate. Hopefully, she still kept the back door unlocked. I laughed to myself, thinking of how different Bayford was from Houston, where (by now) someone would have called the police on me.

The expansive backyard where Aunt Dottie planted her own vegetables was still in place. And although it was winter, just the sight of her peach trees made my mouth

water. Nothing like good old country yard-grown produce, even if you do have to pick out a worm every now
and then.

The back door of Aunt Dottie's house was open,
thankfully. I let myself in and, at once, inhaled the smell
of her home, this home that had become mine during the
worst time of my life. The heater's furnace, Pine-Sol, furniture polish, and detergent from the washing machine all
converged. To me, this was the smell of unconditional
love.

She was a skinny old thing, this aunt of mine. "You can
use this room," she said as she hoisted one of my suit-
cases down the main hallway. This place was something
straight out of a magazine—an old folks' magazine.
Hardwood floors, floral print wallpaper, and stark white
baseboards throughout the home screamed "You are now
in the country." At first glance, the kitchen seemed messy.
Counters covered with jars, the refrigerator plastered with
various magnets. Foil paper blocking the sun's rays from
a small area that could probably heat up quickly when the
gas stove activated. A closer look, however, revealed a
kitchen bearing stripes from decades of fellowship—and
good cooking—contained within. No, the kitchen wasn't
messy. It was lived in.

Family portraits lined the main hallway leading to the
bedrooms. I followed her, wobbling slightly with the ad-
ditional weight I carried around my midsection. The door
to what would be my bedroom creaked open, and the
morning's sunshine blasted our faces, temporarily blind-
ing me.

"Ooh! I forgot to pull these shades yesterday." She

rushed over to the window, pushed the lace curtain back, pulled the cord, and the old-fashioned canvas shade flopped down over the pane.

Ever heard of blinds?

She set the largest suitcase on the oblong rug, a coil of thick rope, in the center of the floor. I put the others on the bed, which required a great deal of effort seeing as the bed was a good two or three feet off the floor.

"Don't swing your arms like that!" Aunt Dottie snapped. "You'll choke the baby with the cord—so they say." Then she laughed at herself. "Whew, chile, I don't know nothin' 'bout having babies. All I can tell you is what I've heard other people say."

My eyes bugged out and I lost my breath. Was she actually referring to it? The baby?

This woman (not even my blood relative), whom I knew only from pictures and the occasional family reunion, had in an instant let me know that I wasn't out of my mind. That it really was happening and that I wasn't the only one who could see the basketball sitting at the top of my legs. She stopped for a second, peered down at me above the rim of her glasses and asked, "What's the matter with you, sweetie? You look like you seen a ghost."

"Nothing . . . ma'am."

"Everybody calls me Aunt Dottie, precious."

Aunt Dottie hung up the last of my maternity dresses and dismissed herself. "I'll give you some time to yourself. When you're ready, you can come to the kitchen and eat you some breakfast. I'll be leaving in a little while so I can go open up the store." She shuffled herself out of the room on a pair of worn-out ruby red slippers.

A store? I'd overheard my stepfather talking about the store and how it didn't matter that Aunt Dottie couldn't watch me since I was already pregnant. They just needed me out of town for now.

I unzipped my book bag and searched the room for a suitable home for my best friends, my novels. My mother asked why I'd packed books she knew I'd already read. I shrugged, knowing full well it would have been impossible to leave behind the only people I had left in the world. When I could find no resting place for Carolina, Beatrice, Maxine, and the others, I settled them onto the floor, just to the right of the bed, in eight stacks of five. The last book I pulled from the bag was the Bible. Try as I might, I couldn't get it to line up with the others. It was too thick. Where am I gonna put this? More importantly, I wondered, what exactly am I supposed to do with the Word of God now? I was fifteen and pregnant, had been all but kicked out of my home, and was sent out to the middle of nowhere to live with an old lady who didn't know diddly-squat about being an expectant mother. I was facing an inevitably painful experience, and after all that was over, all I could do was turn the baby over to my Aunt Vivian, whom I knew just about as well as I knew Aunt Dottie at that point.

I put the Bible back into my bag and stuffed the bag to the back corner of the closet. Momma had said there was no use in crying out now—I wasn't crying then. I guess I just figured I was on my own so far as God was concerned.

I finished unpacking my things and placing them throughout the ancient room. The walls were perfect for a baby's nursery: light blue wallpaper with pastel flowers from the midpoint up. The top and bottom were separated by a white, raised wooden bar. Beneath the bar was wood paneling that had obviously been painted white. With some stuffed animals, a bassinet, and a few rugs, it would be the perfect place to nurse a baby. But who was I kidding? If things continued on the way they had been—with arrangements being made on my behalf—I'd be lucky to see the baby's face before my mother and Mr. James shipped him or her off to be adopted by my mother's cousin in Iowa.

Chapter 7

A major reconstruction made the hallways of Saint Frances Hospital a practical maze. PARDON OUR DUST signs posted throughout the corridors excused the unfinished walls and missing tiles on the way to room 117. I couldn't help but think of the last time I'd been inside this facility. That day, I decided I wasn't going home with my parents. I wanted to stay with Aunt Dottie and complete my high school education in Bayford.

My mother did not receive the news well, initially. She felt I should simply return home and carry on with life as usual, as though I'd never gotten pregnant in the first place. "Only this time," she'd warned, "we're going to keep an eye on you." I knew she meant I'd be forced to tag along with Mr. James everywhere, just like my mother did to prevent him from cheating on her again. She wasn't wrong, I don't guess, in her reasoning with regard to me or Mr. James. I mean, it is hard to cheat when you never get a moment away from your wife, and it would be near impossible for me to get pregnant again if I was always with my parents.

What she didn't understand about me, however, was

that having sex with Bootsie was one of the worst experiences in my life. The last thing she needed to worry about was me having sex again for many, many years.

The other thing I don't think she got was how much this whole ordeal had changed our relationship. Before my mother married Mr. James, she always had a boyfriend. Couldn't blame her, though. I imagine it would be hard to stay single when you're breathtakingly beautiful before you even brush your teeth in the morning. My mother was a perfect brick house, 36-24-38. She was honey brown with long wavy hair and light brown eyes. In the seventies, it just didn't get any better than Margie Henderson. Men were always asking my mother out, buying her things, picking up her check in restaurants.

On the other hand, her beauty was a curse. She said she couldn't keep female friends because they feared Margie would steal their man. More than once, a friend's boyfriend came on to my mother, ending the female friendship abruptly. There were also instances when she'd notice a man following her in the grocery store and have to ask security to walk us to the car. The guard, of course, obliged, then promptly asked her for her number when we reached her vehicle.

Marrying Mr. James had been a nice man barrier, at least against men who respected the institution of marriage. The way I see it, my single momma needed stability for herself and her six-year-old daughter, and Mr. James needed a trophy to undergird his political aspirations. With a woman as gorgeous as my mother on his arm, Mr. James got way more publicity than he would have received otherwise since the media tend to gravitate toward beauty.

In the midst of all this, I was simply an addition to Margie Henderson. I knew my mother loved me, but I think what she loved about me most was my "no trouble" persona. According to her, I was the perfect baby—only cried when I was hungry or needed a diaper change. She could take me anywhere and I'd sit and observe without making a fuss. People would comment on what a quiet, well-behaved child I was. If she left me in someone's care, I was content with that person until my mother returned. "I lucked out with you," my mother would say, because even when I did misbehave, as all children do sometimes, a good time-out was all it took to get me back in line.

So I guess the moment I became "trouble" by getting pregnant, my mother didn't really know what to do with me. Maybe she wanted to be my mother, but she wasn't sure how to do this hard thing. And I'd never disappointed her so much in all my fifteen years.

When she told me she was going to watch me like a hawk, I balked, "I'm not a baby anymore. You don't have to treat me like one."

"Tori, you *are* a baby who almost *had* a baby," she argued.

We were both lost, and the easiest thing to do was not figure it out. Walk away and never look back, which is exactly what we both did.

I stayed in Bayford. She and Mr. James stayed in Houston until he realized his big-city political career croaked and got a vision about moving to Africa to live like a king. They sold the house, sold his human resources business, and crossed the seas. The first few years, my mother sent cards and pictures at Christmas. By all appearances, they were indeed living large in Africa, which, according to her, didn't cost much at all. People there thought she and Mr. James were old-money millionaires—right up my mother's alley.

In recent years, I hadn't heard anything from either of them.

The hospital's reconstruction was a welcomed relief because I don't know how I would have handled walking down the corridors again if everything had been exactly the same.

When I reached Aunt Dottie's room, I discovered it was standing room only. Joenetta, her two sons, Uncle Bobby, and a few other Bayford faces I vaguely remembered from the store packed the small space. Whispers abounded as Aunt Dottie slept peacefully. She looked like a little angel. No tubes sticking out of her, no bandages wrapped around her face, her proud, high cheekbones taut against her skin. Still lookin' good. I breathed a tentative sigh of relief, holding final evaluation until she woke.

Visitors were draped across couches and chairs. I should have known Aunt Dottie's hospital room would look nothing like mine in terms of warm bodies present.

Uncle Bobby was the first to greet me. "My, my, my. Dottie's liable to wake up and think she's on her death bed, seeing you here."

Why, thank you, Uncle Bobby, for that warm welcome and your best wishes for Aunt Dottie. "Hi, everybody."

Hugs with varying degrees of sincerity followed, Joenetta's being the coldest. Our bodies barely touched. "I can't believe you actually came."

"I said I would."

Joenetta's deep brown skin matched Aunt Dottie's precisely, but where Aunt Dottie was thin and dainty, Joenetta was large and clumpy. Still wearing those nursing shoes everywhere, like she had a job.

"Hmph." She looked me up and down. "Well, since we

finally got a black president, I reckon anything can happen."

Before I could respond, Aunt Dottie rustled in her bed. Her eyes met mine, and I saw the joy written across her face.

"Hey, Aunt Dottie." I rushed to her bedside and tenderly scooped her into an embrace. She was a little larger than I remembered, but still tiny compared to a lot of women her age in Bayford who'd given up the battle of the bulge after giving birth. Aunt Dottie blamed her lack of girth on the fact that she never had children.

A part of me was waiting for her to say something; then it struck me—she couldn't. I looked at her again and saw her lips moving. Mumbling something unintelligible. Her dentures were on vacation, which wasn't helping. I could only decipher her thoughts with my heart, in the silent language of emotions. She was glad to see me.

"I'm glad to see you, too."

A single tear rolled down her cheek. She tried to wipe it with her right hand, but the muscles wouldn't cooperate. Her arm slapped around for a moment. I jumped in to help, feeling the wetness on my own palm. Aunt Dottie's helplessness was worse than I'd pictured. I guess I figured things weren't really as bad as Joenetta had made them out to be. I was wrong—Aunt Dottie was, as the old folk say, in a bad way. She wasn't knocking on death's door, but she had a long recovery ahead of her.

With her left hand, she motioned for me to come to the other side of her bed. I quickly obeyed and she took my hand in hers, squeezing tightly. I stood there next to her for a good ten minutes, listening to various family members and friends fill me in on Aunt Dottie's condition. Good news, for the most part. Someone said she needed a lot of speech therapy, to which Aunt Dottie flailed her bad arm as if to say "I'm not worried about that."

Dr. Patel, a deeply gray man with a strong Indian accent, came later to give us the results of the most recent test. "The results are virry, virry good so far. You can go home soon, Ms. Lester. Undergo therapy, and you must take better care of yourself. Take your blood pressure pills every day, as we discussed. I tell you, keeping the blood pressure under control may help to prevent future strokes."

Aunt Dottie nodded dutifully.

"No more skipping pills."

She gave him a thumbs-up.

"No more fasting through breakfast—you must take your pills with food."

She gave him a sideways thumb, which sent a slight chuckle throughout the room. Aunt Dottie was the queen of fasting and praying.

The doctor tried one more avenue. "Last thing. Anything that brings stress to you, my friend, try virry hard to let it go."

Another thumbs-up.

"Doctor, when can she go home?" I asked. Aunt Dottie pumped my hand and winked to let me know she'd been wondering the same thing.

"In another day or so. I just want to be sure her blood pressure is regulated and there is no more bleeding at the site where the stroke occurred. Most people who have stroke at her age remain in the hospital for several days."

Joenetta shifted her weight. "Y'all didn't keep Big Daddy in here that long."

Dr. Patel scrunched his face. "Big Daddy?"

Aunt Dottie pointed a warning finger at Joenetta, ending the conversation. Joenetta could only cross her arms and roll her eyes.

Dr. Patel focused his attentions on Aunt Dottie again. "Your therapy will be hard, Ms. Lester. Virry hard. I do not know if you wish to do therapy while staying at your home or if you wish to go to nursing home."

I knew even before Aunt Dottie began vehemently shaking her head that a nursing home was out of the question. She'd sooner live on the streets of Bayford than a nursing home.

"If you go home, you will need much, much help." He looked around at us all. "You have many people here now. This is virry good. But if you go to nursing home, people help you there. The nurse will talk to you more later when I discharge you. Think about it. Talk to your family about it. Right now, we will take you for last X-ray, okay?"

On cue, a nurse came in and wheeled Aunt Dottie away, leaving the rest of us to deal with this huge elephant Dr. Patel had plopped in the middle of the room.

"Well, can we get a calendar going?" I suggested. Seven days a week, six people in the room, not counting myself. "Everybody can sign up for certain days of the week maybe?"

"I work every day but Tuesday, and that's the only day I got off." Uncle Bobby quickly opted out.

Joenetta gave her lame excuse about why she couldn't be depended upon. "I'll help when I can, but my car has been acting up lately." Joenetta's son, Brandon, seconded her excuse and added that he couldn't help because he didn't "do all that good" with helping people.

Sister Meecham, one of Aunt Dottie's fellow church members, said she would have a hard time committing to Aunt Dottie's care because she herself was on dialysis three times a week. She did, however, agree to at least make sure Aunt Dottie had something to eat every night.

Another rap on the door. I recognized the face. "Cassandra?"

"Yes."

"Hey, girl." I pushed past Joenetta to hug Cassandra. "Oh, thanks for getting Aunt Dottie to come to the hospital before things got out of control. How have you been?"

"Good, good." Cassandra had been one of the few girls in Bayford to befriend me while I was pregnant. The rest of the young ladies mostly stayed away from me for fear that pregnancy was contagious or because their parents told them I was a "fast girl." Cassandra's parents might have told her that same thing, but she didn't heed their warnings. She said she'd done "it," too, already, and the only difference between me and her was I got caught but she didn't. I guess that made us bad girls together. Funny how people bond sometimes.

Cassandra and I lingered in an embrace for a moment. "You look great, Tori. Got your hair all kinked up. I see plenty of people on TV with their hair all kee-kee-kee." She created a sound that, apparently, represented the ring of natural hair. "Like what's her name, Whoopi Goldberg?"

"Kinda." I smiled as she took the liberty of tousling my twist-out. "These aren't dreadlocks, though."

"I haven't been able to wrap my mind around the new thinking yet," she said, laughing. "Perms and flatirons are my best friends."

"I heard that," Joenetta added her two cents. "'Specially if you got a bad grade of hair and a way-back hairline, right?"

Always could count on my other aunt to share her unwarranted opinion.

Cassandra waved off Joenetta. "I didn't mean no harm by it. I'm just sayin', it'll take some getting used to. It's cute-rootie though, Tori. Don't worry about it. You go on and do you, girl."

A spark of harmless jealousy peppered Cassandra's tone. She and I were the same age and had gone down such different paths. I'd moved out of Bayford when I got the partial college scholarship. I could only assume she had stayed in this town and was making a living working at Aunt Dottie's store. Couldn't be much of a living, I knew. She had predicted I would go off to college and get rich while she, hopefully, married Baron Williams, the boy she'd been crushing on since middle school. When she and I met, we were entering tenth grade and Baron hadn't noticed her. He still hadn't seen the light by graduation day.

Cassandra and I stood side by side now and exchanged a bit more small talk, then she asked, "So, when are we going to bust Aunt Dottie up out of here?"

"Well, right now we're trying to figure out who's going to care for her when she gets dismissed."

Cassandra raised her hand as though in a classroom. "I can check on her in the evenings, when I'm not watching my nephews."

"That would be great," I sighed, linking arms with Cassandra instinctively. Right about then, I was ready to link up with anyone willing to prove their love for my Aunt Dottie.

I waited a moment for other volunteers to step forward and pledge to Aunt Dottie's care. "So, is there anyone else who can help out?" Everyone present was just as quiet as Kevin when I initiated one of those state-of-the-relationship talks. Dead silence.

My brain scrambled for a solution. "Okay, how about

hiring a nurse? Does anybody know someone we could trust to help Aunt Dottie around the house?"

"I could do it, like, part-time," spurted out of Joenetta. I fired back, "You just said you couldn't help."

"Well, if you gon' pay somebody, might as well pay family."

"How much you thinkin' 'bout payin'?" from Uncle Bobby.

Okay, how is it that the Lesters were interested in money while the church folk and an employee were willing to give of themselves freely? I could have bopped myself on the head for thinking I had missed out on something in Bayford. The Lesters were still triflin'. As I stood there watching their gazes hit the floor, I recalled the few times they'd called out of the blue, shortly after I finished college. They'd ask how I was, if I was still in school; Joenetta even asked once if I had gotten myself pregnant again. They'd eventually gotten around to a sob story ending in an urgent financial request.

Back then, Aunt Dottie had told me that family and money don't mix. "Tori, don't play this game with them. Some folks don't know how to handle money. Don't matter what you give 'em Monday, they'll be broke by Friday. Best thing you can do is pray for God to teach them how to steward what He's already given 'em."

"But Uncle Pete said his lights were going to get cut off tomorrow," I pleaded on his behalf. This man was Aunt Dottie's own brother, for goodness sake.

"So what?" she'd asked.

"And then he won't have lights," I'd reasoned.

She'd prompted, "Okay, and then what?"

"And then he'll be . . . inconvenienced."

She finished the scenario. "And then he'll go stay with his girlfriend until he gets his next check, and then he'll pay to get his lights turned back on, and then he'll think twice about buying all those Lotto tickets next time, or maybe not. Either way, he'll be all right."

Against my sense of compassion, I refused Uncle Pete's request. He had a few choice words for me and hung up in my face.

Aunt Dottie knew her family well. She must have known none of them would step up to the plate to help with her recovery, yet she probably wouldn't say anything to them about their lack of assistance. Somebody had to speak up.

"I think it's a shame that so few people in this room have agreed to help. I remember when she was the only store on our side of the tracks. Aunt Dottie wouldn't let any family in Bayford starve, least of all her own. She's always been there for us."

"She's always been there for *you*," Joenetta piped up. "She took *you* in when you got pregnant and she put *you* through college. She even sent *you* money to get *you* started after *you* finished college. All that for *you,* but she wouldn't even bail her blood nephew out of jail!"

Cassandra tagged into the rink. "So why are you here now, Miss Joenetta?"

"'Cause she's my sister."

I laughed. "Yeah, right. The sister you won't take care of for free."

"Don't talk to *my* sister that way." Uncle Bobby's body struggled to a standing position. "All she sayin' is, if you want to throw some money at the problem, might as well let it land on us."

"Aunt Dottie is not a problem. She's . . . she's Aunt Dottie," I clarified. "Don't y'all care about her? She's raising your grandson anyway, Joenetta."

Joenetta came toward me with her index finger swaying side to side. "Now ain't that the pot calling the kettle black?"

"Shhhh!" Sister Meecham caught our attention, signaling Aunt Dottie's return to the room.

Aunt Dottie must have been fully aware of the tension because she maneuvered her bed to an upright position when the nurse left. She blinked a few times, looking everyone in the eyes as though trying to read the jury before a verdict. She signaled with her left hand that she'd heard us yapping.

My heart sank for her. Again, I stood by her side and grabbed her left hand. "Aunt Dottie, we're just trying to work out the details, that's all. Don't worry. Everything will be all right."

She nodded and sweetly kissed my hand, then drifted off to sleep.

Slowly, the room cleared of visitors. Cassandra was the first to go. She said she had to get back home before her sister dropped off the nephews. Joenetta and Uncle Bobby followed. Sister Meecham lagged behind to comfort me. "What you told Aunt Dottie was right, you know? Everything will indeed work out."

"Yes, ma'am."

"I want you to know, no matter what your family says, Aunt Dottie has always been so proud of you. And don't worry 'bout Joenetta 'nem. They might act ugly, but they love you, too. Every last one of 'em still brags about their cousin who got a degree and moved to Houston. You're the one they hold up as an example for the kids in the family."

I chuckled. "Could have fooled me."

"Don't be fooled. They do love you in their own funny way, hear?" Sister Meecham gave me one last hug and excused herself.

I sat alone, watching Aunt Dottie's chest rise and fall while thinking about Sister Meecham's words. How could they love me and yet be so mean? For that matter, did anyone really love me? My mom's love allowed her to leave me with another caregiver. Kevin loved me enough to live with me, barring commitment. How is it that everyone had this "funny" way of showing love toward me?

Everyone except Aunt Dottie. If I left her to fend for herself in Bayford, she wouldn't get the care she deserved. Between Cassandra, Sister Meecham, and probably a few more church members, they'd do the best they could. Still wouldn't be good enough. Somebody had to return Aunt Dottie's love with the same consistency she'd always doled it out.

Apparently, that someone would have to be me.

Chapter 8

The task of calling Preston to tell him I would be in Bayford longer than I'd planned proved my first major hurdle.
My cell phone wouldn't keep a steady signal while I was
driving through town, forcing me to scramble all over the
city looking for the hot spot. My first thought was to find
a Starbucks and hop on the Internet since my phone was
nearly useless. *Hello! You're in Bayford.* I hadn't seen a
Starbucks sign on the road for miles or leading into town.

I pulled into a gas station to ask for directions to the
nearest . . . tower? Weird question, but I'd learned from
previous Bayford experience that gas stop attendants and
hairdressers knew everything about the town and its in-
habitants.

"Excuse me, do you know where I can go to get a cell
phone signal?"

The frizzy-haired brunette wearing bright red lipstick
squinted her eyes and squawked, "A what, honey?"

I wielded my cell phone and shook my head to
demonstrate the inquiry. "I can't get this phone to work,
and I was wondering—"

"Oh, you want your phone to work," the attendant repeated with a gentle smirk. "You must be new in town."

"Something like that."

"Where are you from? What brings you to Bayford?"

I was at her mercy. "I live in Houston, but I spent some time here in Bayford several years ago. My aunt just had a stroke. I've come to check on her."

"Aunt Dottie, you mean?"

I nodded.

"She's your *real* auntie?"

"Yes."

This, of course, led to a five-minute adulation about how Aunt Dottie had helped this woman and her children get settled again after Hurricane Katrina. "If it hadn't been for Aunt Dottie, I don't know what we would have done. She put in a good word for me and the manager hired me on the spot, paid me in cash until I got copies of all my documents to prove I was legal and everything."

"That's wonderful. Really wonderful. Now, can you tell me—"

"Tell her I'm praying for her."

"Sure will." This woman's testimony warmed my heart, but I still needed to get a line out of Bayford. I read her name tag. "So, Virgie, how about that phone signal?"

Virgie pointed west. "The only place you can get a good signal is up at the church on the hill. You can talk to God or talk to somebody else, either one, but I think talking to God's a whole lot better." She laughed at her own advice. I wondered if she told everyone that, or if a HEATHEN sign was plastered across my forehead.

Not sure how to respond, I grinned and thanked her. I'd almost forgotten how freely people in small towns discuss God and religion, both off-limits for me in the corporate world, which was where I spent most of my waking hours.

You're in Bayford for real now, Tori.

I drove westward, following a steep incline to higher ground. A big yellow house with a white picket fence on a corner lot suddenly jogged my memory. Virgie was sending me straight to Aunt Dottie's house of worship, Mount Pisgah Missionary Baptist Church. The road's sharp turns sparked flashbacks of long-winded preachers and long-skirted saints.

Before moving to Bayford, I'd only attended church sporadically. Mr. James had said it was important to belong to church, so we showed our faces to maintain his political facade. I liked church and wished we could go more often. Mr. James said regular attendance wasn't necessary—just membership.

Aunt Dottie's dedication to her Mount Pisgah congregation, however, placed me in service at least twice a week. I enjoyed being there, except when they talked about sin. The big ball of baby sitting on my lap screamed, "I'm a sinner! I did it!" Even if no one else heard the condemnation, I perceived it.

The hallowed building lay just up ahead, its steeple soaring high above all Bayford. The church campus was somewhat isolated. Only a few cars littered the grass-covered parking lot. Growth overtook the wheels of one vehicle, a testament to the car's prolonged idleness. Another car, a late model Camry, gleamed in the midday sunlight and assured me that someone else was in the vicinity.

I shifted my gear to *P* and held my phone up toward the windshield. Three bars and a well-lit Internet icon. Good enough to make calls, send texts, retrieve voice mail, and check e-mail. Already, I had missed three calls and seven messages populated my in-box.

After responding to less pressing matters—dry cleaner

issues and an unsolicited ad for an MLM—I tackled Net-Marketing. Jacquelyn answered the phone in our department and seemed pleasantly surprised to hear my voice. We exchanged routine chitchat, then I asked, "So tell me, Jacquelyn, how are things *really* going around the office?" Jacquelyn was not one of those blabbermouth administrative assistants, but she had been known to spill the beans when prompted privately.

I'd hoped she would convey a tale of woe, how the office was falling apart at the seams without me—botched publicity campaigns, clients threatening to take their business elsewhere. What she actually said was, "Things are just fine here. No problems, work as usual. How's it going with you?"

How could everything be fine when *I* wasn't there? People had to be complaining about the extra work incurred due to my absence. Surely Preston had been forced to meet with my coworkers and assure them the inconvenience would only be temporary.

"Has Preston called any meetings?" I poked around the issue.

"No. None lately. Why, is something wrong?"

"Oh no, nothing." I had to think of another route. "Have you heard anyone . . . say anything about me being absent? Or maybe . . . complaining about the extra work load?"

"Goodness no, Tori. Everyone's been picking up the slack. No worries." She inadvertently launched the panic button inside me.

I tried once again. "I guess what I'm trying to ask is . . . how can I say it . . . ?"

"Has anyone missed you?" Jacquelyn finally pulled the truth out of me, chuckling.

I admitted, "Yes."

Jacquelyn's voice softened. "Tori, if you ask me, I'd tell you to get back to work as soon as possible, before Preston figures twenty-two people can do the work of twenty-three. Somebody, I'm not saying you necessarily, but *somebody* always loses a job when things like this go on too long."

Oh, great. The entire department was at stake now. "Thanks, Jacquelyn. Could you put me through to Preston?"

"He's not in at the moment."

"Man," I lamented, "I really needed to talk to him."

"I can give him a message," she volunteered.

I sighed. "No thanks. I'll have to call him back later because I may not be in an area with a signal."

"I see. Is there anything you want me to tell him in the meanwhile?"

Movement near the church door snatched my attention from the conversation. A deep chocolate, clean-shaven man wearing jeans and a white T-shirt emerged from the building, cleaning supplies in tow. His muscles bulged just below the cuff of his shirt. He wiped sweat from his forehead, dropped the buckets and mop, and walked toward my car. Looking at this man, I suddenly remembered how much I would miss working out at the gym. I've never been one to go for the popular, hot guys, but bodies can be so beautiful.

The visual examination finally classified his body in the top 20 percent and then scanned the man's face. Boyishly handsome, except for the slight graying at his temples. Definitely premature. The sun beat down on his forehead and, suddenly, I recognized fine-man.

Jacob Carter III. Preacher's kid. Correction, *pastor's* kid. Every girl at Bayford High School had suffered through a crush on Jacob Carter at least one day in her life. I had for weeks, actually, but I gave it up. No need in me pining for the pastor's son, being pregnant and what-not.

Jacob's father was a good pastor, but First Lady Carter had her moments. Aunt Dottie said First Lady's bark was a lot worse than her bite, but she could bark up a storm. First Lady and Aunt Dottie sat on the advisory board of Mount Pisgah, butting heads often about the ushers' uniforms, choir robes, and bake sales. They always seemed to work things out, though, before Sunday.

I'll never forget the night I learned First Lady didn't want Jacob around me, for obvious reasons. I never really knew how or why Aunt Dottie and First Lady were even discussing me, but after an earful of eavesdropping on one of their conversations, I knew better than to call myself liking Jacob. We'd be fellow congregation members, and that was to be the entire scope of our relationship.

Still, Jacob was fine, and by all appearances the fineness had only gotten better with time.

Automatically, my eyes scanned his ring finger. Bare. *Behave! I already have a boyfriend. I am not here for a high school reunion.*

"Tori? Are you there?" Jacquelyn broke the reverie.

"Yes, I'm here. I'll call Preston later. Thanks."

Jacob knocked on my window as I ended the call. I pressed the down arrow on my door's panel. "Hi."

His teeth gleamed more than humanly possible—or maybe it was just my imagination. "Hello. Can I help you with anything?"

"No, thanks. Virgie, at the gas station, told me this was the only place I could get a consistent signal."

He smiled again. "Yeah, she's right about that. Bad thing is, some people wait until Sunday morning service to make long-distance calls."

I hadn't heard the term long-distance in so long, the humor nearly escaped me. "Sorry to hear that."

"I'll be in the church finishing up on some work if you need me. My name is Jacob. I'm the assistant pastor."

I extended one hand and used the other to pull my shades back. "Tori Henderson."

He clapped a hand over his mouth. "You're Aunt Dottie's niece, right?"

He remembered me? "Yes."

Jacob took the liberty of quickly looking me over while I sat in the car. "Good to see you again! How have you been?"

"I'm fine. How about you?"

He pursed his lips and shook his head. "Great. Just working and helping my parents with the church."

"That's good."

"Nice ride," he commented, tapping the hood. "You must be putting that college degree Aunt Dottie's always talking about to good use."

"Can't complain." What happened to my conversational skills?

"Amen and amen," he agreed.

Was I supposed to say something back to him? *Selah? Peace? Right on, my bronze brother?* Church jargon always made me nervous—like there's some secret code language shared only by lifelong members, a code that automatically identifies the reprobate by unorthodox response to insider phraseology.

Jacob ended my uncertainty with a question. "How long will you be in town?"

"Not sure. Depends on what Aunt Dottie needs when she's released from the hospital."

His features slackened with concern. "Aunt Dottie has done so much for my parents and this congregation. So would you please, please let us know what the church can do to help?"

"Sure, certainly."

Jacob reiterated, "I know the hospitality board sent her a card and flowers, but I mean *anything*—money, meals, transportation. I'll see to it personally that her needs are met."

"Thank you, Jacob."

"No problem. And feel free to use our signal waves whenever you need them." He shook his hands in the air.

Talking to Jacob almost made me forget why I'd come up the hill in the first place. "I'm sure I'll be up here again."

He shrugged. "Well, if you see my car in the lot—the blue Camry—you're welcome to come on inside so you won't have to run your AC. Idling is hard on the environment, you know."

"Thanks."

He stepped away. "It really is good to see you again, Tori."

"Same here."

With that, Jacob retreated into the building, allowing me to regain my wits.

Chapter 9

Back at the house, peace covered my decision to stay in Bayford for a while, at least until I could get everything situated for Aunt Dottie. The option of hiring someone still involved research and coordinating, all vying for my time and attention. Bayford might have to become my second home for a while.

I took the liberty of unpacking and organizing my belongings in my old bedroom. The room hadn't changed much—a queen-sized bed with nearly a foot of space beneath, covered by the same blue and white quilt. The cherrywood headboard and coordinating dresser still stood side by side. Across the room sat another bureau. She'd filled the top two drawers with knickknacks. I stuffed my foldables in the bottom two drawers.

In the closet, I discovered some of my old posters—Jodeci, Blackstreet, R. Kelly. "Oh my gosh!" I sat on the bed reminiscing. I used to think I was going to marry K-Ci, for real. *Oooh-yeah.*

A knock on the front door brought me back to the present. I walked to the front entrance, squinting to see if I recognized the silhouette on the porch. Cowboy hat, elderly slump. No one I knew.

"Hello," I asked upon opening the door.

A white man in his late-forties with red, leathery skin tipped his hat toward me. "Hello there. Name's Josiah, from down the road. Saw a new car in the yard and I was just makin' sure everything was okay."

"Yes, sir. Everything's fine."

"Aunt Dottie gettin' better?"

"She's improving. Thanks for asking."

"Alrighty then. Just checking." He studied my face a moment. "Hey, didn't you used to stay with Aunt Dottie long time ago?"

"Yes. I'm Tori. I lived here when I was in high school."

His eyes lit up with remembrance. "That's right, I remember now. That your fancy car?" He pointed toward my Cadillac.

"Yes."

"Mighty fancy, mighty fancy. Looks like you've really made something of yourself. In spite of . . . everything, you know." His eyes traveled to my stomach, rattling my sense of well-being.

The baby.

"Thank you, Josiah."

"Okey-dokey. Believe I'll head on back to my house. Let me know if you need anything, and tell Dottie I'll mow the grass Friday when I do mine. No charge seein' as she's in the hospital and all. See you later."

You'd think I was the first and last unwed mother to walk the streets of Bayford. Give me a scarlet *A* for my dress already. These people didn't forget anything, and they had no problem rudely reiterating the past.

It took me a moment to get past Josiah's playback. I had to remind myself: he came over to make sure things were okay. Lots of good people in Bayford cared about Aunt Dottie. I was there to round them all up and put them to work on her behalf.

A school bus entered my peripheral vision. I remained on the porch, watching the driver slow as the bus approached Humble Trail's halfway point. Back in the day, Bayford bus number 275 transported everyone from kindergartners to seniors to our side of the tracks. Curiosity kept me outside long enough to deduce not much had changed.

Children of various ages poured out of the bus, scrambling north and south.

"What time you coming out to play?" from a robust boy whose shirt didn't fully cover his stomach.

"In a minute," answered another child. This little boy needed a haircut and, judging by the direction he was going, a compass. He ran straight up Aunt Dottie's driveway, past my car, jumped over the steps and landed within an inch of my toe.

He panted, "Where's Aunt Dottie? My grandmomma in there?" The trademark Lester nose, long and low, marked him as a relative. His cheeks held on to the last bit of baby fat. Still pinchable, if he'd hold still long enough.

"Hello. Who are you?"

"DeAndre."

"Hello, DeAndre. How are you?"

He looked beyond me, past the screen door.

I repeated, "How are you?"

"I'm fine. Who are you?"

"Probably your cousin. Tori. And I'm fine, too. Thanks for asking."

Clueless to my home-training lesson, he continued, "Is Aunt Dottie home yet?"

"No. She's still in the hospital."

"Okay." DeAndre breezed past me and opened the door. He threw his lunch box and backpack into the foyer area, pivoted sharply, and took off down the steps again.

"Excuse me." I stopped him. DeAndre faced me, impatience urging him to hop from one foot to the other. "I need you to pick your belongings up off the floor. And are you supposed to be here? Who's watching you?"

He shrugged. "I was gonna get off on my daddy's street, but I saw a car here so I got off now. Can't you watch me while I go play with Chase 'nem?"

"Won't your daddy wonder what happened to you?"

DeAndre shook his head. "No, he don't care where I am, miss."

"Tori," I corrected him, hoping DeAndre had spoken those words regarding his father's nonchalance casually. I reminded myself of the setting. Bayford. People watched each other's children all the time in the country. If people still came over at the sight of an unfamiliar car in someone's driveway, no alarm would sound because a child had decided to get off the bus at a different stop. "You can call me Cousin Tori."

The chubby child appeared at the edge of Aunt Dottie's yard. "Come on, DeAndre! You're *it*!"

DeAndre pressed his hands together in prayer formation. "Ooh, Cousin Tori, please. I gotta go play with Chase. You watchin' me, right?"

What could I do? I mean, DeAndre *was* "it." He had to get out there and redeem himself, the quicker the better if memory served me. I sighed. "Get your stuff off the floor first."

"Here I come!" he answered Chase. DeAndre rushed back into the house, threw the lunch box on the counter, and was off again before I could tell him to tie his shoelaces.

Is he always this rowdy?

The house phone's ring pulled me back inside. Hopefully, one of DeAndre's people had come to claim him. "Hello?"

"Tori?"

"Yes."

"This Joenetta. Did DeAndre get off the bus over there?"

"Yes, he did," I answered, glad to know that someone actually did miss him. "He's outside playing, but I'll go get him and bring him home right now."

"He *is* home."

"Would he be here if I *wasn't*?"

"Maybe not, but you *are* there, so be it. I'll come by later and cook him something to eat."

"Joenetta, I'm not Aunt Dottie. I don't do kids. I'm not *good* with kids, and I'm not going to take care of someone else's child." I mean, really, who did she think she was talking to? I wasn't a teenager anymore. She couldn't treat me like dirt because Aunt Dottie wasn't in earshot.

"What if Dottie had said that to your momma when you got pregnant? 'I'm not going to take care of someone else's child,'" she mocked me. "'Y'all let her get in this mess, y'all figure it out.' Where would you be right now if it wasn't for my sister?"

"I'd be—"

"I tell you where you'd be. You'd be somewhere with probably five or six kids by now and just as many baby daddies, livin' in a government house on food stamps. So if my sister takes it upon herself to save DeAndre like she saved you, you got no right to stop her."

Joenetta's knack for turning tables hadn't diminished

in all these years. And no matter how I (or anyone, for that matter) tried to talk sense into her, she just didn't get it. Aunt Dottie was the only one who could handle Joenetta, but even *she* used to say Joenetta had a "bad understanding," that once she made up her mind about something, she wouldn't change even if Thurgood Marshall proved her wrong.

I'd waste no more breath on Joenetta today. So far DeAndre hadn't been much trouble. This whole situation would have to wait until I could communicate with Aunt Dottie and find out how she wanted me to handle him.

"What time you cooking dinner?" I asked.

"'Round seven." *Click.*

Ooh! She irked me. Aunt Dottie had to hurry up and get better because I couldn't stomach Joenetta too long. What little raising my mother *did* do prevented me from going left on my elders, but this woman was pushing it!

I took a seat in the living room and took a few deep breaths. How could I have forgotten that dealing with Aunt Dottie also meant dealing with Joenetta? Maybe my brain had done me a favor and blocked Joenetta out of my memory.

Calm down, Tori, calm down. Maybe I was getting all worked up for nothing. The drive down had been long, and seeing Aunt Dottie's condition was disconcerting, to say the least. I was hungry and I needed a nap.

Aunt Dottie's refrigerator housed nothing but high-fat, high-sodium, high-carb items galore. This had to be rectified if I planned on helping Aunt Dottie regain her health. Not to mention poor little DeAndre. An early grave awaited him if he absorbed all the preservatives and dyes lining the shelves of this fridge. After searching the pantry, too, I noted several replacements needed, including 2 percent milk, spring water, low-fat mayonnaise, low-cholesterol butter, and no-yolk eggs. How Aunt Dottie had managed to live this long amazed me.

Raisins and half a ham and cheese sandwich sufficed as my lunch. I relaxed in front of the kitchen television for a while. The familiar surroundings lulled me into yet another flashback. This time, I recalled the only time Aunt Dottie and I crossed each other. We'd been standing in this very kitchen when the discussion came to a head. She wanted me to wear stockings with my blue-jean skirt, said it was shameful to go around with my bare legs. "Sweetheart, I'm not telling you what to do. You have a choice. Either put on the stockings or wear a longer skirt."

I told her no one wore stockings anymore. At that moment, the coo-coo clock went off and I remember thinking, *That bird is right! Stockings are coo-coo!*

Aunt Dottie gave her own interpretation. "See, even the clock knows it's crazy to go out of the house with all these legs showing." Though three inches shorter than me, Aunt Dottie always seemed taller. She didn't scream or yell, but she always meant what she said, and she backed her words with a firm love.

I'd seen enough television shows to know the classic teenage line I was supposed to say next: *Well then, maybe I won't live in this house anymore.* Lord knows I was tempted to say it, but I figured Aunt Dottie would call my bluff, still wearing that sweet smile of hers. And where would I go? Really, there's no running away in Bayford. Coyotes and vicious farm animals would probably get me first. My only other option would be moving back to Houston with my mother and Mr. James.

Laughter welled up in my stomach now as I thought about the incident. Those stockings covered my legs quite nicely.

Court TV shows cluttered the local airways, much the same as Houston. I loaded up on other people's drama to make light of my own until heavy eyelids slipped over my eyes one time too many.

My old bedroom faced the front side of the house, so I could keep an ear out for DeAndre while I took a little catnap. I had no idea how long he might be outside playing, but I was pretty sure I'd know the moment he came bounding up the front steps.

The smell of fresh laundry enveloped me as I literally climbed into the bed. Settling into the sheets, aches registered throughout my body, reminding me that I'd undergone a serious surgery only weeks before. Slowing down to take care of Aunt Dottie might actually help me get back to 100 percent, in more ways than one.

Chapter 10

Slam! The screen door jolted me out of a peaceful sleep, hurling me toward the immediate disorientation of waking up in someone else's bed.

"Cousin Tori!" DeAndre ran into the bedroom just as I regained my wits. "Cousin Tori, Chase cut his foot on some glass. He's bleeding real bad. You gotta help him."

I sat up, wiping my eyes. "Where are Chase's parents?"

"They're still at work."

Chase's yowling from beyond the window came into focus now. I surrendered. "Okay. I'll look at him, but I don't do blood."

"You're the one who's watching us, right?"

"I'm watching *you*."

"Come watch me watch Chase." DeAndre took my hand and dragged me to the porch, where Chase's right foot took center stage. Chase sat on the wooden deck rocking himself back and forth, holding his foot between bloodied hands. Tears drenched his cheeks as he attempted to quell another scream.

Poor thing. "Let me see." I kneeled down to get a good look at the injury.

"Don't touch it," he begged while extending his leg toward me.

Had my food not fully digested before I'd lain down, I might have lost it. The deep gash in Chase's small foot spilled over with deep tissue never meant to see daylight. This boy needed stitches.

"You're going to have to call your parents to take you to the hospital," I informed him, hoisting my cell phone from my pocket.

Horror gripped Chase's face. "Wait. Are they gonna put alcohol on it?"

I'd almost forgotten: alcohol on open wounds is every child's worst nightmare. Instinctively, I curbed the alarm in my voice. "Probably not."

"I gotta get stitches?"

"I'm not sure. Maybe they can just put special tape on it."

Chase looked at DeAndre, DeAndre looked at me, then back at Chase again. "Man, this is my cousin Tori. My grandmomma told me all about her. She went to college and everything. She knows stuff."

"I never heard of no tape." Chase shook his head, pulling his foot from my reach.

I couldn't let DeAndre go on record with this tape mumbo-jumbo. "I said *maybe* they can put tape on it. The doctor will have to make the final determination. Just because I went to college doesn't mean I know *everything.*

"What's your mom's work number?"

Chase wailed, "Aaaawwww! I gotta get stitches. No, no, no. I don't wanna get stitches. Please, don't call my momma."

DeAndre intervened. "Chase, we have to. You could get an infection and they'll have to cut off your foot."

"But I'm going to get a whippin' for playing outside without my shoes on," he hollered even louder.

As Judge Judy would say, that falls under the category of *too bad*. "What's your momma's name?"

"Katrina Webb."

"What's her number?"

Through a flood of tears, Chase rattled off the number. After another failed attempt to dial out on my cell phone, I resorted to using Aunt Dottie's land line in the kitchen. Thankfully, her phone was cordless, so I was able to return to the porch with the boys.

I called Chase's mother and calmly explained to her that we weren't facing a life or death situation, but he certainly needed medical attention.

"Shoot, we just had one in the hospital last month with pneumonia," she fussed. "Was he outside playing with his shoes off?"

Chase definitely knew his mother. I looked down at Chase's body quivering through a minor mental meltdown. "Yes, ma'am, I believe so," I replied.

"Uh huh. I told him about keeping his shoes on."

If she could see him now, she might go easy on him later. "Well, an unpleasant trip to the doctor would certainly teach him a good lesson," I offered.

She paused. "I guess so."

I gave a thumbs-up to Chase. He smudged tears and snot across his face with the back of his hand. "What did she say?" he mouthed.

DeAndre begged to know as well. "Is he gonna get a whippin'?"

I silenced them with an index finger over my lips.

"I'll be home in a few minutes," Chase's mother finally acquiesced. "And who is this, again?"

"This is Tori. Aunt Dottie's niece from Houston."

"Oh, yeah," she singsonged. "You're the one who was pregnant and lost the baby and then went to college, right?"

Oh my gosh! The correction came out with attitude. "He was stillborn."

"He was *what*?" from DeAndre.

I whispered, "Not you."

Katrina's voice lowered. "Oh, I'm sorry, sweetie."

Which wrong, exactly, was she apologizing for? And why was she calling me "sweetie" when she was probably only a few years older than me?

She continued, "I tell you what. Your Aunt Dottie sure does brag about you all the time. She's got a copy of your degree on the wall behind the counter. The print is kinda small 'cause I think she wants people to ask her about it so she can tell them all about you." She cackled. "Drives Joenetta crazy."

I joined in Katrina's laughter now. Anyone who read Joenetta the way I read Joenetta was on my side—bad manners notwithstanding.

"How long until you can get here?" I wanted to know.

She blew a breath of concession. "I gotta log out of the system. Fifteen minutes. You think he'll be okay?"

"Yes. I'll keep an eye on him until you get here."

Just before I hung up, I heard her yell, "Thank you, Tori."

"You're welcome."

Chase belted out, "Is she coming?"

"Yes."

"When?"

"Right now."

Chase cried even harder when his mother's classic Cutlass groaned up the driveway. I laughed to myself, knowing his antics were meant to save his hide.

Together, Katrina and I helped situate Chase in the backseat. "Keep the towel pressed against your foot," I instructed him. "The force will stop the blood."

The rims of his eyes had reddened from crying so hard. "Okay," he agreed. "You *are* smart, Miss Tori. Just like DeAndre said."

I winked in response.

DeAndre gave his friend a pat on the back and told him not to worry. Everything would be okay.

After Chase and Katrina left, DeAndre and I were left to await Joenetta's arrival. He followed me from the porch to the kitchen. I made him a sandwich. When he was finished, he plopped himself on the couch right next to me. Obviously, this child hadn't heard the term "personal space."

He scrunched his face. "You like these shows?"

"Yeah, I like court television. What do you like to watch?"

"Cartoons," he replied. "Mostly I watch *Kamen Rider* so I can learn how to fight."

I lowered the television's volume. "Why do you need to know how to fight?"

"'Cause people tease me all the time about my momma since she went to prison for a long time."

Too much information. "Oh. Maybe you should ignore them." TV volume rising again.

He shrugged and hopped up from the couch. "I'm gonna go see if Mike-Mike can play."

"Wait a minute. Don't you have some homework?"

"Ummm . . ."

I didn't know DeAndre well, but I knew a lie-in-the-making when I saw one. "Get your backpack, go to the table, and do your homework."

"But, Cousin Tori, I gotta play before it gets dark outside," he whined.

"Uh uh. Homework first, playing later."

A scowl covered his face as he snatched up his backpack and stomped over to the kitchen table, mumbling under his breath. If this was the kind of flip-flopping attitude Aunt Dottie dealt with day in and day out, no wonder her blood pressure was high. I hadn't witnessed such disrespect except on those nanny shows. My first instinct was to snatch *him* up the way I used to see people at Mount Pisgah rearrange their children's facial expressions, but who was I to jump in? DeAndre was not my problem.

When he finally reached the assigned homework location, he blurted through tears, "You ain't my momma!"

No better words have ever been spoken. *This kid has got to go.*

After his little homework incident, DeAndre and I didn't speak to each other the rest of the day. I just let him vegetate in front of the television and wait for his granny.

Joenetta finally came by at a quarter till six to make dinner. She shuffled through Aunt Dottie's pantry and then declared, "Whew! She ain't hardly got nothin' in here!"

I took her words as my cue to leave. She and that bad DeAndre could starve together, for all I cared. Sonic would be my savior.

I grabbed my purse and headed for the door.

"Where you goin'?" he wanted to know.

Away from you. "To the store."

Joenetta called from the kitchen, "Oh, good. Pick up some flour and hurry back."

I grabbed my purse, my keys, and my laptop. "I'm not going to the grocery store. I'm going someplace else. I'll see you later." The screen door slammed behind me.

Joenetta's fussing followed me to the car. She said something about me not caring, and she was right. How on earth she could claim to care for Aunt Dottie and yet leave her to raise this little boy was beyond me.

Yes, Aunt Dottie had taken me in, but I was a *good* boarder. Okay, yes, I was pregnant, but even in my precarious situation, I never gave her any real trouble. I was respectful, I cleaned up, I helped out around the house and the store. I was good company—Aunt Dottie even said so herself.

This little boy, on the other hand, was a sixty-pound ball of energy with a hair-trigger attitude. He was more than a handful, and no woman past forty-five should be raising him.

Sonic was my first stop, the church my second. After fuming over the situation with DeAndre, I'd mustered up enough gusto to give the out-of-office idea to Preston straight. He often worked late, so I figured I could catch him at the office.

"Preston, it's Tori. My aunt's recovery may take months. I'm proposing a telecommuting arrangement. I can make it back to the office once a week or so for meetings, and the rest I'll handle via the Web, business as usual." There. I got the whole pitch out in one big blurb. Maybe that DeAndre was good for something after all.

Preston cleared his throat. "Sounds like you've given this some thought."

Not really. "Yes, I have."

"How much longer do you expect to be out?"

I took a deep breath and gave my best guestimate. "A month or so."

Preston hesitated. I imagined him sitting there thumbing through his calendar. I hoped he was thinking about my vital role in the team. "We've been talking about offering a telecommuting option at NetMarketing for quite some time. I suppose there's no better person to test the waters than the top producer."

Relief swept over me and my shoulders dropped an inch. "Perfect. I'll contact my colleagues for updates and pick up right where I left off."

I ended the call on an exhilarating high. Maybe there was something to this whole church-mountaintop signal arrangement. I could have my job and take care of Aunt Dottie, too. And if I dug up an Internet connection, I might actually be able to pull this whole thing off.

I left the church parking lot determined to stay away from Aunt Dottie's house as long as possible. Maybe if I rode around long enough, Joenetta and DeAndre would disappear.

I scoured the town for Wi-Fi signs so I could put my files to work. The gas station I'd visited earlier had an ATM light, so Bayford must have some kind of link to the outside world.

Driving through downtown Bayford presented a quaint collection of businesses connected by a cobblestone road. Main Street's charm slowed time. Though most of the businesses had already closed for the day, their window displays spoke of pride in long, hard working hours, not to mention faith. A flower shop, a bakery, a newly remodeled bank on the left. A tea room and an antique mall on the right. The center median flourished with evergreen brush, and I imagined some retired people's horticultural organization would come by in the spring to tend these mini-gardens.

Still no sign of free Web access. I turned a few more corners, desperately hoping, checking every blinking sign for the four magic letters.

The back side of the senior center boasted the best lead yet: COMPUTER CLASSES HELD HERE.

I parked and grabbed my laptop bag from the floorboard. Once inside, I was directed to the adjacent library and thereafter greeted by Mr. Kneebam, the head librarian.

He looked like the type who had been stuck in Stephen King novels all his life. Glasses, scruffy beard, long graying ponytail, fashion rebel. Mr. Kneebam actually favored Stephen King, come to think of it.

"How can I help you?"

"I need to connect to the Internet. Do you have Wi-Fi?"

His face lit up at the mention of this term. "Wi-Fi—music to my ears."

I matched his enthusiasm. "Mine, too."

He rolled his lips inward and shook his head. "Sorry. We don't have it here. The closest Wi-Fi hub is the Starbucks in Henrytown. But you're welcome to utilize our computers." He gestured like a game show hostess, guiding my eyes toward two centers containing a total of eight ancient CPUs with large, boxy monitors.

Is he serious? "How do I get to Starbucks?"

"Hold on a second. I know what you're thinking. I assure you, these computers are actually pretty fast," he bragged in a used-car-salesman tone.

"I work primarily online. I'm not sure—"

"You can get on and off here faster than the twenty minutes it'll take you to get to Starbucks."

He had a point.

I followed him to the main counter to fill out an application for a library card, where I paid a nominal fee for membership since I wasn't a resident of Bayford County.

"You can occupy the computers for an hour at a time, but if there's no one waiting, you can stay on as long as you'd like—or at least until we close," he said with a laugh.

"What time do you close?"

"Eight o'clock on Monday, Wednesday, Friday, six on Tuesday, Thursday, and Saturday. Closed Sunday."

I finished the library's paperwork and logged on to a computer, wondering how on earth I was going to operate within the library's clipped hours. When working away from the office, the internal engine scarcely revved up by eight o'clock. And Sundays were prime production time, in my world.

Mr. Kneebam showed me where to check my time and warned me about inappropriate Web sites. "If you happen to notice a kid on a questionable site, let me know." He winked, as though I had partnered with the Bayford village to raise all these bad kids who don't wear shoes outside and pout when made to do homework.

"I'll be too busy managing my own affairs to monitor anyone else's screen." There. *I am* not *a part of the village.*

Mr. Kneebam tipped his head. "Well, if you happen to observe questionable surfing, please let us know."

The next half hour flashed by quickly. Most of that time was spent carefully wording the e-mail regarding my extended leave to colleagues. I needed to thank them for stepping in while, at the same time, reclaiming my clients and rightful feeding order. I'd leave it to Preston to break news of my telecommuting arrangement because there would surely be backlash to subdue.

I could almost hear them complaining. "First, Tori takes off for weeks and then she gets to telecommute?"

A rush of teenagers—who, I gathered from Mr. Kneebam's impromptu minilecture, had waited until the last minute to do a research project—filled the computer waiting list.

I had to use my last thirty minutes for answering more e-mail messages and posting one press release. I made a mental note to do everything possible off-line and transfer information to my flash drive before coming to the library. Whew!

Mr. Kneebam apologized unnecessarily for kicking me off the machine. "I wish I could let you work longer and teach these kids a lesson. But rules are rules," he sighed.

After logging off, I relinquished my spot to a shaggy-haired frantic kid with an armful of books and two spirals. "Miss, you know anything about *Wuthering Heights*?"

Sympathy laced my response. "It's by Emily Brontë, and I think the main character is a guy named Heathcliff."

"Thanks, miss. That'll help me get started."

Sadly, he was serious.

Stalling in hopes that Aunt Dottie's house might clear out before long, I took the scenic route back to her side of town. Train tracks that used to separate the "black" part of town from mainstream Bayford seemed hardly needed now. From what I could tell, the town had integrated nicely.

Again, the familiar streets greeted me, flagged me through the town. Aunt Dottie's store rested only a few blocks from the tracks, strategically located to serve everyone in Bayford. Aunt Dottie used to claim her store was the melting pot of Bayford. "People need bread and milk no matter what color they are," she'd say. "And all money is green."

As I approached the store, which was actually a frame-house-turned-retail venue, scores of cards and flowers came into view. I threw the car in park and rushed to the porch in awe of the neighborhood's support for my aunt. Even the CLOSED UNTIL FURTHER NOTICE poster board was covered with well wishes. "We're praying for you, Aunt Dottie." "Get well soon!"

Some people had even dropped off teddy bears, and a beautiful ivy with a card from First Baptist Church sat safely under the porch's cover. Even vendors who weren't informed of the store's closing before coming to deliver left personal messages with their nondelivery notices.

I gathered the well-wishers' sentiments and loaded them into the cargo area of my SUV. All I could think about was the numerous times Aunt Dottie had given extra food to people who could barely scrape up enough change to buy a dollar's worth of summer sausage. She'd wink at me and whisper, "It pays to be nice to people."

That sage advice followed me back to the house, where Joenetta griped upon my return, "Took you long enough!" She wiped off the kitchen counters and hung a dish towel on the stove's handle. I had to admit, the smell of whatever she'd scrounged up for dinner teased my taste buds terribly.

DeAndre was nowhere in sight, though I wished he'd appear so he could have helped me unload the gifts from the car.

"What's all that stuff?" she asked.

"Gifts and notes people left at Aunt Dottie's store. Sure was nice of them."

"Would have been *nice* if you'd come home and not been out riding around town. Anything could happen to you out there."

Was this a trace of concern or a threat? *It pays to be nice to people.* "I do have business to handle while I'm here in Bayford."

"Join the club." She stopped straightening and put both hands on her hips. "You should be more considerate. Could have called from a pay phone or something. 'Specially since I couldn't leave DeAndre here by himself."

"I already told you, I am not taking care of DeAndre."

"Since you've taken it upon yourself to step into Aunt Dottie's place, you'll have to," she reasoned.

"But *you're* his grandmother. Why can't *you* step in?"

"You know his mother is—" She stopped abruptly. Her gaze swept over my right shoulder and she cleared her throat as DeAndre's figure materialized in my peripheral vision.

Joenetta raised one eyebrow. "We'll have to finish this conversation some other time."

"You leaving, Granny?"

"Yes, DeAndre. I'll be back tomorrow to cook dinner again and I *hope*"—she darted her eyes toward me—"we have some food around here. Can't eat air, you know."

"Tell my daddy I said good night." DeAndre hugged Joenetta's waist.

She leaned down to reciprocate. "I sure will."

Hated to break up this loving display of affection, but I had to ask, "Can you also tell his daddy to send some money for food? Can't eat air, you know?"

Over DeAndre's head, Joenetta's dark expression mirrored a hostile witness on the stand. "Everybody ain't able to provide like they need to. Some of us didn't have a fairy godmother."

She kissed her grandson good night and walked out the front door. She stopped just shy of the first porch step and picked up the potted ivy. "Somebody left this at the store, too?" she called back toward me.

"Yeah."

Joenetta seized the plant. "Dottie's got enough plants from folk at the hospital. I'll take this one. See y'all tomorrow."

In light of Aunt Dottie's advice about how to treat people, I could only wonder if Joenetta Lester counted as "people."

Chapter 11

DeAndre got off to school the next few days with minimal drama. Toast, eggs, and bacon satisfied the bottomless pit long enough to push him outdoors before the bus arrived.

He came home Wednesday afternoon and begrudgingly started on his homework right away. I fixed him an afternoon snack of sliced apples and graham crackers. "I *hate* math," he mumbled, slamming a fist on the table.

I hate taking care of kids. "Be patient with yourself. You'll get it." I set DeAndre's food down on a napkin and left him alone to continue working while I lay in bed for a little rest. Aside from visiting Aunt Dottie, I'd spent all day on the computer organizing Internet advertising campaigns as much as technically possible without actually being online. And after I'd completed every viable offline task, I transferred the working files to my flash drive so I could utilize every single moment of my one-hour slot at the library. Before the appendix issue, I would have taken a two-mile jog after such a taxing day's work, but now, I still needed naps here and there while my body worked around the missing appendix. Maybe if I mapped out a route in Bayford, I could pick up again with a one-mile walk.

I kicked off my shoes and lay in the bed expecting a light slumber. What I got instead was a soft whimper coming from the kitchen.

"DeAndre," I yelled, "are you okay?"

"No."

Oh, great. "What's the matter?"

"Idon'tknowmynines," he wailed.

"What?"

"I can't multiply by nine!"

My first instinct was to let Joenetta help him when she came to fix dinner, but a wild-blue thought hit me—Joenetta might not know *her* nines, either. Chuckling while scolding myself internally, I joined DeAndre at his work space.

He'd folded his hands and plopped his chin atop them in classic defeat mode. Crocodile tears rolled down his plump cheeks and spilled onto his paper. A snapped pencil signified his white flag.

Hard to believe this was the same kid who'd nearly mouthed off angrily a few days earlier. His deep brown pools of woe told the story of a little boy who cared enough about his academic achievement to cry when he didn't comprehend. I had to give him some kind of credit. Plus, he was awfully cute sitting there looking like Arnold from *Diff'rent Strokes*.

"DeAndre, today is your lucky day." I pulled his chin upward. "I am going to teach you the ancient Chinese secret of multiplying by nines."

He looked up at me, then rolled his eyes. "There's no secret."

"Oh, yes there is."

DeAndre perked up a bit, his head now raised. He waited.

"Well, do you want to know it or not?"

He gave an eager nod.

"Okay, here it goes. The first thing you do is hold both hands out, palms away from you. Like this." I demonstrated, he copied. "Then you think of the number that you want to multiply by nine. Say, nine times three. Starting with your outside pinky finger on your left hand, count to three. When you get to the third finger, which is our middle finger, bend it down so you can't see the top of it anymore."

"Got it," he declared.

"What you have now is two fingers up before the bent finger, and seven fingers up after the bent finger, right?"

I wiggled my digits. He nodded.

"There's your answer. Nine times three is twenty-seven."

His face lit up like a Christmas tree. "Wow! Do it again!"

"Let's do it together. What do you want to try? Nine times six?"

DeAndre tried nine times everything before we finished. His enthusiasm kindled an impression of victory within me that almost rivaled being named Top Producer for a moment there, until I reminded myself this probably wasn't an ancient secret—I'd learned it watching the movie *Stand and Deliver*.

DeAndre picked up the lead end of the broken pencil and quickly finished his homework with the aid of his hands. When he finished the last problem, he hopped out of the chair. "I'm going to play now."

"Get back when you see your granny's car in the driveway." I don't think he heard me.

A second later, his face appeared through the screen door. "Thank you, Cousin Tori."

He skipped away before I could say, "You're welcome."

Truth be told, Joenetta was right about the empty pantry. And there's only so much fast food a health-conscious person can consume. I somewhat happily put grocery shopping on my list of things-to-do, knowing the venture would lead me to Henrytown, Texas, thus Starbucks.

My hips—always the first to speak in a workout drought—warned me of impending thunder thighs if I didn't hop on somebody's treadmill soon. Bayford had no gyms open to the public, so the streets would have to do. I laced up my Nikes and stretched on the porch. My muscles thanked me. Normally, I walked an eleven-minute mile, but given my body's condition (or lack thereof), I might need to shoot for a fifteen-minute mile. Hopefully, I'd land somewhere in between and log three miles within the hour.

Kids off to school, parents off to work, the quiet streets of Bayford lulled me into a peaceful groove. For what it's worth, the air in Bayford was cleaner than the walled-in sweat factories of 24 Hour Fitness. My lungs cycled the fresh air with gratitude.

Seven minutes into my walk, I approached Humble Trail again, marking what I estimated to be the half-mile point. *Back to Aunt Dottie's, then two more laps*. So far, so good. No pain, all gain.

"Woof! Woof!"

Someone's dog (a Rottweiler mix) didn't appreciate me passing his territory. I'm not afraid of dogs, but I don't provoke them, either. I crossed the street to assure him I had no intention of infringing upon his domain. Too late. Next thing I know, this huge dog breaks off his front-yard chain and makes a beeline toward me.

"Aaah!" I screamed, hopping into the bed of an industrial strength pickup truck parked along the street. Wanna-be Cujo tried to follow, but he was too short to make the jump, thank God.

Now that he and I were close, I could see this dog wasn't actually full grown. He was, to put it in human terms, a teenager. Silly, yet volatile. "Go away!" I fussed at him.

He barked louder.

Finally, a little old lady hobbled out with a cane and stood in the yard this dog had been so viciously protecting. "Come back here, Tiny!" she called.

Tiny looked at her, back at me again.

"Tiny!" she bellowed a second time.

I pointed toward his mistress. "Go home, Tiny!"

Tiny barked at me once more and ran back to the lady's side. Call it a Lassie moment, but I understood Tiny perfectly clear. He didn't want any more run-ins with me.

"I'm sorry, sweetheart. He didn't mean no harm," the old lady yelled as I climbed down from the truck. My heart thumped wildly, my right side throbbed painfully from the sudden exertion of energy.

Tiny didn't have to worry about me anymore. Note to self: bring my treadmill.

After I finished my one and only lap, I showered and visited Aunt Dottie in the hospital for the fourth time. I pulled up a chair alongside her bed to catch up. She still couldn't speak, but she was armed with a legal pad and a pen. With her left hand, she scribbled "hi" and "love" on the pad. I hugged her, thankful she and I could finally be alone. The next word was "store."

I told her about the wonderful outpour of support

from her customers. "Oh, Aunt Dottie, you should have seen it. Stuffed animals and cards and notes. Looks almost like this hospital room! And everywhere I go, people ask about you. I think everyone in Bayford is praying for you."

Her eyes glistened with gratitude and she patted my hand. Then she wrote "open."

"No, I don't know how soon you'll be able to open the store. I mean, even after you leave this place, you've still got rehab."

I approached my next concerns cautiously. "I've been meaning to ask you if you had disability insurance or . . . if you were thinking of retiring any time soon. We could sell the store and . . . maybe you could move to Houston with me. I'd bring you back on Sundays for church."

Aunt Dottie shoved her chin into her neck and looked at me like I was the one who'd suffered brain damage. The word "YOU" formed in all caps.

"Me?"

She wrote: "open store," and thrust the pad at me.

"*Me* open the store?"

She nodded.

I rattled off a list of reasons why I couldn't possibly open let alone manage the store in her absence.

She closed her eyes and listened to me, as though my words went in one ear and up to God through her prayers. Only, somehow, she was translating every reason I gave to a prayer request, expecting Him to overturn every obstacle. Not fair!

When I finished explaining myself, I asked, "Do you know what I'm saying, Aunt Dottie? I love you and I'm here to see that you get all the care you need. But I can't run the store. I wish I could, but I can't."

She rubbed my hands, which I hadn't realized were holding on to the bed's railing for dear life.

My breathing returned to normal with her calming gesture. Maybe she did understand the unfeasibility of her proposal.

"Sandra help" appeared on the clipboard.

Okay, so she didn't fully understand me. "Who's Sandra?"

She added "Ca" to the beginning of the name. Cassandra.

"That's a great idea. Cassandra could reopen the store and keep it operating until you get back on your feet."

She wrote: "YOU help Cassandra."

"That I can do. As long as she knows how to manage the books and keep the vendors in line, I can oversee her work."

Aunt Dottie smiled one of those passive-aggressive smiles and I wondered if she'd simply gotten me to agree to what she had in mind to begin with.

A nurse came in with breakfast, and Aunt Dottie ate as best as she could. The right side of her mouth wouldn't stay fully closed, so I had to wipe away the nibblets that dribbled onto her chest. Thankfully, she sucked her juice up through a straw and, with a tilt of her head, managed to slurp with little mess.

We watched the morning news, Aunt Dottie making "Mmmm mmm mmm" sounds whenever the reporters gave bad news, which was every other minute. Somewhere between traffic and weather, Aunt Dottie grew drowsy.

"I'm gonna go now and let you get some rest."

She held up a finger and put pen to paper again. I stood over her and watched as she wrote the name "DeAnd."

Before she could finish writing, I shook my head. "Aunt Dottie, I've been meaning to talk to you about DeAndre."

Her face lit up at the sound of his name. She drew a huge smiley face, covering everything she had written earlier. Then she waited for me to continue.

I wanted to tell her he was driving me crazy, that Joenetta had dumped him on me instead of taking him to Ray-Ray's house, that I suspected he wasn't really stepping into the water when he took a shower.

But I didn't have the heart to ruin her smiley face. "He's fine."

The rapid muted bopping rhythm of my flip-flops marked my gait to the car, giving testament to how much work awaited me that day. On top of all I needed to do for NetMarketing Results, I now had to find Cassandra and talk to her about reopening the store. And I was stuck with DeAndre until I could figure out a way to return him to his rightful owners.

I drove to Sanford Street, a few blocks from Aunt Dottie's house, because I thought I remembered where Cassandra lived. Wrong. The lone resident said he'd been living in that house for thirty-seven years. He said he did know who Cassandra was, thanks to Aunt Dottie's store, and proceeded to tell me where Cassandra's cousin, Benjamin worked, suggesting I go to Benjamin's job so he could then give me directions to Cassandra's deceased grandmother's house, rest her soul, where he believed Cassandra was living. No less than a wild goose chase.

"Thank you, sir." I scrambled off his porch.

A normal person in a normal town might have simply used his/her phone's Internet functions to track her down. But no, no, no. No bars here. Back to the church.

The parking lot was empty. A sense of disappointment registered in my gut. No Jacob. *Stop it!*

I redirected my thoughts to Kevin, calling him in hopes he might be available between presentations. "Hi. This is Kevin Walker . . ."

Again, my heart sank. We hadn't talked since I left Houston. "Hey, babe, let me know when's a good time to call you. Kisses and hugs."

By the time I finished leaving Kevin's message, my phone indicated four voice mails and six e-mails. I tackled e-mail, replying to client inquiries and forwarding a personal request intended for Lexa. Voice mail increased my to-do list significantly.

Rapping on the driver's window startled me, but the shock was quickly replaced by giddiness. Jacob stood outside, waving at me. He signaled for me to roll down the window and I complied. A rush of cool wind filled my vehicle.

"We're going to have to start charging you for cyber access," he teased. "A dollar a minute."

Though his joke wasn't necessarily funny, I found myself tickled pink. "Open a tab for me."

A quick glance at my growing list of tasks yielded a negative response. "Gotta run. Aunt Dottie's put some hefty items on my agenda. . . . By the way, do you know where Sandra lives?"

"Meyers or Jarrett?"

"Meyers."

"Of course I know where my cousin lives. She's in the blue house on Lolita, next street over from Red's Barbecue. You remember where Red's is, right?"

I nodded. "Thanks."

He tapped the hood of my car and shifted the weight of his body. "Let me know if you need anything else."

"Sure will."

Jacob walked away, his image darkening as the tint on my windows glided upward.

I should have gone inside. For what? So I could sit, look into his eyes, and make callow comments like "you're so cute" and "I had a crush on you" all the while feeling guilty on account of Kevin? Why was I even allowing myself to think such silly thoughts?

Driving away from church grounds relieved my internal tension. Maybe if I did a better job of organizing myself before going to the library, I could cut these Mount Pisgah visits to a bare minimum.

Now that I was away from Jacob, the day's plans came back into focus. Cassandra's grandmother's house looked much like the one I'd mistakenly visited earlier. At this point, many of the homes in Bayford were starting to resemble one another in my brain: covered porches, sizable front lawns, chain-link fences, drainage ditches lining the streets.

I reached through the torn screen netting and knocked on the faded wooden door. Cassandra's beaming face greeted me. "Hey, girl. Good to see you again." We hugged and the heavenly aroma of fried chicken emanated from her clothes. "Come on in. You want something to eat?"

My stomach spoke for me. "Love some."

I followed her to the kitchen, noting the worn vinyl floor tiles and vintage seventies wallpaper. Nothing had changed since the last time I entered this house, either. Matter of fact, I think Cassandra was still using that same cast-iron skillet she'd used to cook bacon on Saturday mornings before we'd go to the community pool. By the jar of grease sitting at the back of the stove, Cassandra still ate bacon every morning.

Cassandra herself looked quite the same, too, plus maybe another twenty pounds. Not bad considering how much weight most of my college friends had put on in less than a decade.

"Girl, you ain't changed at all." She laughed while piling our plates with chicken and mashed potatoes.

"What?"

"Always overanalyzing stuff," she teased. "You walk into a room and take stock of everything and everybody."

Her observation made me wonder if I, too, was stuck in some kind of time trap. "I'm sorry."

"Don't apologize. That's just you." She smiled, setting my plate down, joining me at the table. "And this is just me."

She blessed the food and I, for one, dove into the meal head first. Lost all sense of calories and fat grams, and drank sweet tea like it wasn't loaded with sugar.

We caught up on the formals for a while. Neither of us was married. No kids. Since graduating from high school, Cassandra had earned a cosmetology license, but she hated dealing with peoples' unrealistic expectations. "I mean, they come in with a spoonful of hair and want to walk out looking like Beyoncé. I'm not a miracle worker."

I'd forgotten how much Cassandra used to crack me up.

"Plus there's too much gossip in a beauty salon. You know me, I ain't tryin' to be in everybody's business." She shook her head.

"Sandra, please. You were the queen of gossip in high school," I reminded her.

Her mouth fell open. "Me?"

"Yes, you!"

"I am not a gossip . . . anymore," she surrendered, and stuffed her mouth with potatoes.

"Exactly when did the gossip guru relinquish her title?" I examined her.

She laughed slightly, then appeared to give my question thought. "Since God changed me."

Took me off guard. "Really?"

Cassandra squared eyes with mine and she swallowed her food. "Really."

I don't think I'd ever heard anyone under the age of fifty say anything so profound about God. I mean, you get spammy texts about God—"if you love God, forward this" or "send this to five people and you'll be blessed tomorrow by 11:09 A.M." Modern-day equivalent to chain letters, if you asked me.

Cassandra's confession about God, however, rang with authenticity. Made me wonder if we had much in common anymore. I mean, I liked God and I figured He must like me, too, otherwise why would He have taken the time to create me? He was pretty good, from what I could tell, but He hadn't tried to change me. Maybe that's because I was a pretty good person already. *Yeah, that's it.*

The wall clock reminded me I had miles to go before DeAndre returned home from school. "Well, I need to talk to you about something."

"Shoot."

Might as well put it all out there. "Aunt Dottie wanted me to ask you if you'd like to reopen and manage the store until she recovers."

Cassandra almost choked on her drink. "She wants *me* to run the store? Shazooka!"

Her reaction mirrored mine at the news. I, in turn, mimicked Aunt Dottie. "Don't worry, Sandra, I'll help you with the vendors and the paperwork. And you know how Aunt Dottie is—she'll recover in no time."

Cassandra looked at me above the rim of her glasses. "How are you gonna help me run the store from three hundred miles away?"

"I'm not going back to Houston any time soon," I quickly assured her. "I'm here for you."

She sighed pensively and gave me a you-better-be-glad-I-like-you roll of the eyes.

I tried another angle. "Don't you want to . . . get back to work? We all need money, right?"

Couldn't argue that one. She nodded in resignation. "We've got to get in there and clean the store out first. Milk's spoiled, bread's hard by now. When do you wanna get started?"

The concept of cleaning the store hadn't entered my mind, but Cassandra was right. Reopening the store would be a huge undertaking. By the way things looked when I stopped by Dottie's the other day, no one had touched a thing since she suffered the stroke.

"We're gonna need Elgin," she suggested.

"Who's Elgin?"

"Part-timer. He cleans and does all the heavy lifting. He-man for real." She flexed her arms.

Sounded like a good plan. "Call him."

Within a few minutes, my team of three gathered to open the doors of Dottie's. Surprisingly, there was no pungent odor greeting us upon entry. The refrigerators were still plugged in, so nothing had a chance to attract flies. Some dust had settled on the cash register, but aside from that, no trumpet blast.

Upon entrance, the five aisles to the left stocked pantry items—cereal, chips, flour, sugar, bread. To the right, candy and household goods like scissors, paper towels, and toothpaste. Refrigerators cooled dairy products and packaged lunch meat along the back walls. Straight ahead, the counter, my favorite place, secured deli meats and cheeses Aunt Dottie cut to order. And, of course, my college diploma provided the perfect covering for the door leading to the back office.

"Glad to be back," Cassandra declared.

Elgin, a salt-and-pepper-haired man in his midfifties who obviously spent too much time pumping iron, proved a handy addition. He started right away clearing out the lunch meat from the deli area. Cassandra started on the bread aisle, and I holed myself in the back office, contacting vendors to resume deliveries.

After Elgin declared the store ready for business, we gathered at the front counter to figure out a work schedule. Cassandra would open at nine Monday through Friday and work until five. I'd close out the day from five until seven. "I'll be here as long as I need to be here," she said.

Elgin would come in at noon and stay until closing every day. We'd have to play this coming Saturday by ear because, between me and Cassandra, we'd be worked to death by then. We needed to hire someone, quickly. Both Cassandra and Elgin said they knew people who needed part-time work. I told them I'd run those people by Aunt Dottie.

Thank God we were closed Sundays.

I dropped Cassandra off at her house and headed back to the hospital to fill Aunt Dottie in on our progress. Halfway to the hospital, my phone bleeped, marking one of those freak-signal moments. I pulled over to the side of the road, set my blinkers, and made mental note of this hot spot on Opal Street between Dottie's and the hospital. Voice mail flashed: 1 Message.

I dialed quickly, before the cosmos 'rearranged. "Hello, this message is for Tori Henderson. This is Shayna Ash, the principal at Bayford Elementary School. Wanted to let you know that DeAndre has been suspended from school for the next two days for fighting. Please come pick him up as soon as you get this message, since he won't be allowed to ride the bus home this afternoon. Thank you."

My first question: why is she calling me? Secondly, how did she get my number?

I disconnected the call, bristling with annoyance. Had the principal left her number, I would have gladly told her to call Ms. Joenetta or Ray-Ray. Or maybe even DeAndre's mother's family. Where were those people, anyway?

The e-mail icon grabbed my attention before I could process my questions. One from Preston marked urgent caught my eye. I tapped the phone's touch-screen accordingly, my heart thumping even more. The "thinking" emblem circled on the monitor. And it circled, and circled, and circled again.

Cannot retrieve messages at this time. Forced close.

"What?! Open! Open!" I tried to open the application again, but noticed the empty gray bars. "Crazy!" *So, what, a cloud drifts by and my signal disappears?*

My attempted race to the church was thwarted by a school bus ahead of me, stopping at seemingly every possible corner, releasing streams of the slowest-walking kids I'd seen in a while. Obviously, none of DeAndre's friends. *Calm down, Tori.* Another stop, another deep breath.

Glancing down at my console, the time struck me. Three-thirty. By now, DeAndre must have been sitting in the office for fifteen minutes after school dismissed, assuming neither Joenetta nor Ray-Ray had gone to get him. I envisioned his little brown eyes following every passing car as he waited for a ride home. Was he hurt? Did he have a busted lip? What happened to the other kid?

Bayford's elementary, middle, and high schools were so close they all shared a common parking lot. I hopped out of my vehicle and reluctantly trudged toward the office of the smallest building. DeAndre sat just inside the main office, swinging his legs over the edge of a bench.

After an immediate flash of relief, his face settled into a frown. "Hi, Cousin Tori."

"What happened, DeAndre?"

A tall, stout woman emerged from a side door, flipping long blond hair over her shoulder. "Miss Henderson?"

"Yes."

"Hello. Thanks for coming." She clipped her words. Obviously, we shared a mutual distaste for unruly children. She handed me a carbon copy of the document detailing DeAndre's infraction. He and another boy had gotten into an argument in the morning that escalated into a physical confrontation during recess. Pretty cut-and-dry scenario. She closed with, "We'll see DeAndre again Tuesday morning."

"Certainly," I agreed, folding the papers and placing them in my purse for future reference. "Thank you. By the way, Ms. Ash, I don't believe I listed myself as an emergency contact for DeAndre."

"Oh." She softened. "I got your number through Aunt Dottie's nurse. How is she, by the way?"

Should have known. "She's improving, thank you. Let's go, DeAndre."

He sulked all the way back to my car and I wondered why he, suspended-boy, felt perfectly within his rights displaying attitude.

He buckled himself into the passenger's seat and looked straight ahead. Tell me that was not a smirk on his face?

"Why are you smiling?"

He lowered his head, trying to hide the smile.

"DeAndre, you are suspended. In what world is this a happy occasion?" I slammed my hand on the steering wheel with each syllable.

"He was messing with me," DeAndre huffed, "but I bet he won't do it no more."

"*Any* more. And what do you mean messing with you? How?"

DeAndre crossed his arms on his chest. "Calling me names."

"Names like what?"

"DeAndre, DeAndre, got a prison madre." He mimicked the classic playground jump-roping rhyme and rhythm. I had to give it to these kids. They'd come a long way—bilingual teasing.

In this case, however, there was some truth to the mockery. DeAndre's mother actually was incarcerated. If memory served well, usually these taunts could be answered with "Nu uh!" or "Stop lying!" DeAndre couldn't deny facts.

I wasn't crazy about DeAndre, by any means, but there's something about rooting for the underdog. "So what are you going to do the next time someone teases you about your mom?"

He swung a fist in the air. "Pop 'em in the nose, just like I hit Chase today."

"You fought *Chase*?"

He nodded.

"But Chase is your friend."

"He made me mad making fun of my momma." De-Andre's brows furled up again.

I recognized his shut-down tactic and decided not to talk to him again until he calmed down. We rode in silence to the church parking lot so I could finally get a look at the urgent e-mail message.

Panic rushed through my veins. Preston's e-mail "requested" my presence at an impromptu team conference. "It would be best if you could make the meeting Friday." Translation: *be here tomorrow afternoon.*

Knots filled my stomach. Preston Haverty didn't marshal meetings without good reason.

Suddenly, Aunt Dottie's store's appeal and DeAndre's suspension got shoved into the backseat. Maybe even the trunk. I immediately called the office to let Preston know I'd be in attendance.

Chapter 12

Never in a million years would I have imagined I'd be trekking back to Houston with DeAndre by my side. But after a muffled blowup with Joenetta just outside Aunt Dottie's hospital room, I got stuck with him again. This time, I caved in at Aunt Dottie's written request: "Please take him with you. ☺"

Those smiley faces would be the death of me.

We put off the store's reopening until Monday, which also happened to be the projected date for Aunt Dottie's release from the hospital. I had a number of objectives to accomplish before her return, but Houston came first.

DeAndre and I packed our bags for the trip back to civility. For someone who'd just been suspended, he was in awfully high spirits. I heard him up rumbling most of the night before—getting water, going to the restroom, tossing and turning in his bed. All of this while I sat in bed reviewing client campaigns, getting all my ducks in a row before Preston's mysterious last-minute meeting.

DeAndre actually beat me getting up the next morning, like it was Christmas day or something.

"Cousin Tori, is it time?"

"Might as well be," I gave in. We ate a few slices of toast and then rolled onto the highway a little before seven o'clock Friday morning.

He sat up in his seat, looking out the window as we passed cornfields and cow pastures. Nothing foreign until we hit a larger city graced with a shopping center. "Ooh! Look at all those stores!"

Okay. "DeAndre, have you ever been shopping at a mall?"

He looked at me, shook his head.

"Have you been to . . . an amusement park, like Six Flags?"

Another head shake. "No, but I seen one on TV."

"You *saw* one." Let me just break this on down. "Have you ever been outside of Bayford, Texas?"

He sat back and thought for a moment, then proudly conveyed, "I went on a field trip one time. We went to the post office, the police station, and the fire station."

"In Bayford, though, right?"

"Yep." He hoisted himself back up on the edge of the seat and continued to absorb the massive billboards and household icons lining the side roads.

Never been out of Bayford. His obvious excitement plucked a heartstring in my chest. Bayford was a wonderful place full of great people, but the one thing it couldn't boast was exposure to opportunities. I mean, it's one thing to decide to live in a small town, another thing altogether if you never even knew there were other options.

We stopped about an hour into the trip and got another round of breakfast. Though DeAndre was somewhat familiar with the concept of convenience restaurants, he was enamored by the number of options on the food strip. McDonald's, IHOP, Burger King, Jack in the Box, and

Wendy's alone lined one side of the street. "Ummm," he vacillated, "what's Chick-fil-A?"

"It's a chicken place. They have breakfast burritos."

He quizzed me, "They got pancakes?"

"I don't think so."

He turned his attention back to the strip. "Okay, McDonald's. I want pancakes and sausage."

Child-rearing lesson number one: do not let children eat pancakes in a moving car! Maybe if DeAndre had been an infant, I would have known to stay away from sticky foods. Who knew eight-year-olds could still be so messy? DeAndre accidentally drizzled syrup on his shirt, my seats, and the inside door panel. We had to make a second stop for hand sanitizer and wipes to clean his tracks.

DeAndre must have seen the horror written on my face as he put the final dabs on his hands. "I'm sorry, Cousin Tori, for messing up your car."

I wanted to hold a grudge, but I figured the whole thing was as much my fault as his. "It's all right. We'll know better next time."

"No more syrup for me," he chanted.

His willingness to sacrifice this sweet treat seemed a bit drastic. "You can have syrup, just not in this car."

That settled, I popped in an old-school R & B CD and merged with northbound traffic. DeAndre grew restless. He fidgeted with the buttons on his door's panel, which I quickly disabled from the driver's side. He tapped out a tune on the window with his fingertips. He counted the number of people in cars we passed and checked the state-hood of each license plate.

I'm really not sure which of us was more frazzled by his impatience.

"Are we there yet?"

"No."

"Are we getting close?"

"No."

Thirty minutes later. "How about now?"

"Nope."

He exhaled noisily, slumping deeper into the seat. "I've gotta use the restroom."

"Are you serious?"

"Yes. I had a large orange juice, remember?"

At this rate, we'd never make it back to Houston. Another stop, another ten minutes lost. Thank God, he finally fell asleep the last half of the trip. His soft snoring brought about a question that, honestly, hadn't entered my mind a second sooner: what was I going to do with this kid while I was in my meeting at work?

Oh my gosh! How could I have been so silly? This was equivalent to teenage thinking—or, rather, *not* thinking—making dire decisions without considering the ramifications. I didn't have anyone in Houston whom I could ask to watch DeAndre. I mean, some of Kevin's friends might sit with a dog or a kitten, but a child? No way. I know I wouldn't if the shoe were on the other foot.

The stupidest idea ever entered my mind: leave him in the car. Just the very fact that my brain formed this absurd thought was proof I didn't have any business taking care of anyone's kid. This whole scenario was way out of my league.

Kevin wouldn't be back for several days—not that he would have even agreed to keep DeAndre anyway. Maybe there was a recreation center or some kind of children's . . . gated facility I could take him to.

I used my phone's voice-operating system to call a day

care I vaguely remembered passing daily on my way in to NetMarketing.

"Hello," I gasped desperately as I explained my situation to the first person who answered the phone. My speech ended with, "Whatever your fee, I'm willing to pay."

The woman on the other end listened patiently, then bombarded me with questions. Did I have his birth certificate? Shot records? Proof that he was actually enrolled in school? Had his parents given me legal guardianship?

"Ma'am, I just need to bring him in for a few hours," I begged.

"I'm sorry, but we can't accept him without documentation. I mean, we have no way of knowing if he's been kidnapped, if he's allergic to the foods we serve, or if he has some kind of emotional problem that would put the other children in danger."

"But I just need—"

"And we'd have to make some special provisions for him because he's a school-age child. We don't normally keep schoolers during school hours. Do you have documentation showing he's been suspended? I mean, if a state inspector comes and sees we're keeping a child who, by law, should be in school, we have to be able to show them why he's in day care, not school."

Okay, I was getting nowhere with this woman. "Never mind."

I called two more day care centers and the YMCA. I even called a church—they take everyone, right? Same long list of questions I couldn't answer, claims I couldn't prove. What has the world come to when kids can't be ditched, no questions asked? What happened to the whole "village" concept?

I blame the parents. The government. Somebody.

As we approached the city, I fought the urge to wake DeAndre so he could marvel at the lofty buildings and steep highway overpasses. He would have enjoyed the sights, I'm sure, but I enjoyed the sight of his little brown, quiet head propped up against the window even more.

When we finally arrived at my place, I shook DeAndre out of his sleep and announced, "We're here."

He swiped the spittle from his mouth and stretched while taking in the immediate surroundings. My apartment building's garage was pretty uneventful. Gray, dark, nothing but rows of cars.

Nonetheless, DeAndre took one look at the stairwell and gasped, "Ooh! You got a two-story house!"

"Not quite." I laughed under my breath. "This is an apartment."

He crumpled his face. "I thought you was rich?"

"Who told you I was rich?"

"My granny."

Figures. "I'm not rich, but I'm not poor, either."

"Then how come you live in an apartment instead of a house?" he quizzed me sharply. "My momma said rich people live in houses, mostly brick houses with stairs in 'em."

His momma was wrong, of course, but I couldn't call her out like that. "I *choose* to live in an apartment. People have choices, you know? And sometimes an apartment costs more than a house. Just depends on where you live. The city is different from the country."

By the confusion scribbled across his face, I'd given him enough food for thought to last a week.

We had a few hours to kill in the apartment. DeAndre checked out my place and pronounced it officially "cool" on account of the Dyson desktop fan in the living room, which didn't have blades but seemed to blow air from an invisible source. This little wonder wasn't actually a necessity. When Kevin was home, he lowered the thermostat to an un-environmentally-friendly freezing temperature that kept me covered in blankets. This fan he'd purchased was nothing more than a hyperengineered conversation piece.

Once DeAndre had had his fill of the fan, I sat him down in front of the television with a Lean Pocket and apple juice, then hustled onto the Internet to sync my client files in real-time.

I hopped in the shower, changed into business attire, and tore DeAndre from the couch and cartoons. "Where are we going?"

It took nearly all the commuting time from my apartment to the office to explain where we were going and exactly how I expected him to behave. The fact that he was suspended hadn't escaped me, though it didn't seem to phase DeAndre anymore. I wondered how many times he'd been suspended, but the foyer entrance to Net-Marketing didn't seem quite the place to inquire about his previous offenses.

"This office is big," DeAndre commented as the building receptionist, Alma, buzzed us past the front desk.

"Your son?" she wanted to know. I swear, I'd all but walked past this woman tens of thousand times, but never once had she been so interested in my business.

"Cousin," I replied, pulling DeAndre out of her sight. I led him straight to my abandoned cubicle, hoping this home-away-from-home had not been ransacked by fellow employees needing pens, Post-it Notes, or legal pads. Since we arrived during the lunch hour, the office was pretty empty. Bad enough I was telecommuting, now I'd brought a kid into the office. Now, more than ever, I wished I'd had an actual work space with a door so I could hide DeAndre.

I pointed, he parked himself in my seat. "Sit here until I get back from my meeting."

His eyes traversed the countertops in my space, then he questioned, "What am I supposed to *do* while you're in the meeting?"

Do? Who says kids always have to be *doing* something? "You'll sit here and wait."

"You want me to just do nothin'?" DeAndre looked at me like I had lost my marbles.

I opened my desk drawers and pulled out an issue of *Essence* magazine. "Here. Read this."

"Ewww. This is for girls," he whined. He eyed my computer. "You got any video games?"

"Umm . . . maybe there are a few on the Internet. You have a favorite Web site?"

"Web *what*?"

"You know, like w-w-w dot something-something-something dot com," I tried again.

"Oh, you talking about the infernet?"

"In-*ter*-net. Yes."

"No. We don't have the Internet in my class, just at the library."

He was right about that much. We'd have to go "old school" with his entertainment. I grabbed a notepad and pens with various ink colors from another compartment.

"You like to draw?"

"No."

I checked my watch. "Look, I don't have anything else. I don't have any kids, DeAndre. This is all new to me. Give me a break on this one, okay?" Then I resorted to something I'd seen plenty of parents do in grocery stores. "If you sit here and quietly occupy yourself until I come back, we'll go do something fun later. Okay?"

His eyes lit up. "Fun like what?"

"I don't know, but I'll figure it out. Just draw for now. Practice your multiplication tables, too." I drew an imaginary line across the entrance to my cubicle. "Do not move from this area, and don't talk to anyone. If anyone comes by and asks you who you are or what you're doing here, just tell them you're here with Tori Henderson."

"Your last name ain't Lester?"

"No, my last name is *not* Lester."

"So, are we real cousins or play cousins?"

"Real." Why did any of this matter right now?

DeAndre's face brandished a full smile. "Okay. I'm glad, Cousin Tori."

"Yeah. Me, too."

With DeAndre settled, I proceeded to the conference room and took a spot near the head, where I knew Preston would sit. Though I hadn't been away long, already the room possessed a foreign air. The table seemed longer, ceiling higher, lights brighter.

Most of my team (minus Preston) entered at once. Lexa entered first, wearing a power blue suit and black pumps. Brian next, in his signature gray. Two other associates, Kellie and Shane, followed. Obviously, they'd gone to lunch together.

"Hi, Tori!" from Lexa. "Good to see you. How's your grandmother?"

"My aunt," I corrected her fake inquisition. "She's much better. They're releasing her from the hospital Monday."

Brian jumped in. "You'll be back next week, then?"

I tilted my head. "Not exactly. She'll be going to rehab."

They moaned collectively: *oh, I see.*

Lexa took the seat across from me, furtively glanced at the room's door, then blurted out the question I'm sure was on each of my colleagues' minds. "Tori, exactly when *will* you be coming back?"

Something about the sharp tone in her voice didn't sit well with me. Sounded like a teenager home alone, scheming to figure out how much she could get away with in her parents' absence.

Preston saved the day upon entrance. "Hello, Tori! So glad you could make it." He clasped both of my hands in his, a fairly warm gesture for our office.

"Glad to be here."

Preston sat and got straight to business, asking for updates on each person's caseload. I chimed in with the reports, hadn't missed a beat. He shared data supporting everyone's satisfactory productivity and then braced us for his big announcement.

"Looks like we're all on track for another great year, but we'll have to step things up. We're taking on a new client. The biggest one we've ever landed, thanks in great part to Lexa."

Jealousy coursed through my veins. Lexa? She flashed a beauty-queen smile and waved as though gliding down Main Street on a float. My cohorts chuckled at her antics.

Since when did they all find Lexa so humorous? And what on earth could she have done in the few weeks I'd been gone to secure a client worthy of me driving more than three hours to hear this groundbreaking proclamation?

"We just inked a two-year contract with Inner-G drinks. . . ." Preston could barely finish his sentence before the room filled with *oohs* and *aahs*. Inner-G's founder, world-renowned rapper G-Cash, had partnered with a host of basketball players and Hollywood celebrities to launch his version of an energy drink. By all appearances, this line was the urban version of Red Bull.

Why would Preston involve our firm in such a trendy venture? Most of our clients were respectable, mainstream businesses with whom we had proven track records in reaching majority consumers. Researching and accessing a new niche would take us completely out of our market-ing expertise.

Furthermore, I questioned how Lexa had managed to work this deal. I wondered whose behind she'd kissed. Literally.

"In light of this acquisition, we'll be reassigning and hiring. Lexa will, of course, head the Inner-G account. Her enthusiasm and tenacity will lend itself well to their campaigns."

A round of applause for Lexa ensued as a haughty grin snaked across her lips. I forced my hands to clap, but my brain boiled.

"To back Lexa, however, we'll add Tori's experience to the equation." Preston pointed in my direction. Another stupid clapping spell.

Me? This was great. Just great. I don't know what else Preston said in that meeting. He lost me when he ba-sically appointed me assistant to Miss Corporate Bootie-Smacker.

The meeting concluded with my attitude a total wreck. Didn't help to find a group of fellow employees flocked around my desk. *Why are all these people in my work space?*

Before I could say anything, DeAndre hopped down from my seat and stepped toward me. "I'm sorry, Cousin Tori. I didn't know what to do."

"Didn't know what to do about what?"

The small crowd of adults dispersed, their heads hung low, avoiding eye contact. Behind them, one of the custodians emerged toting my trash can with gloved hands at arm's length, as though it might contain nuclear fallout. He walked past me, shaking his head.

"What happened, DeAndre?"

He stood in fig-leaf formation. "I had to pee. But you told me not to go anywhere or talk to anybody. So . . . I peed in the trash can."

Anger and disbelief crawled up my face. "You did what?"

Seth, one of the younger administrative assistants in the office, tapped me on the shoulder and whispered, "I walked by and saw his little rear end sticking out above his pants. You might want to let him know, if he wants to sneak-a-leak, use the opening in his underwear. That's why guys have a flap in the front."

I turned slightly to gauge Seth's facial expression.

"Are you serious?"

He held back laughter. "Trust me, it's a life skill for males." He winked and walked away.

Maybe Seth was used to peeing in trash cans, but this kind of thing was not normal in my world. I returned my attention to DeAndre, still quietly standing in the center of my cubicle.

He rationalized, "Sometimes we pee in the waste-basket at school."

"*Who* is *we*?"

He confessed, "Me and my friends do it, when we're in the restroom. But one time we got caught, and we got suspended."

"So you thought it was a good idea to pee in the wastebasket at my *job*?"

His blank face piled even more fury on top of the

Twilight-Zonish feeling that I was caught in a nightmare. *This boy done peed in my trash can!*

"DeAndre, it's no wonder you're in trouble all the time." I grabbed his elbow. "Let's go."

Suddenly it all made sense. I could understand now why parents always look so stressed and why teachers need two months off in the summer. These kids will drive you crazy.

Chapter 13

All the silent way home, I kept wondering what I should do about this peeing incident. Spank him? Ground him? Make him pee in a wastebasket a hundred times to break him from this nasty habit? Maybe if I Googled "my child peed in a trash can" I might get some ideas, but every kid is different, and this kid wasn't even mine. Was it my fault for telling him to stay isolated in the cubicle? Would I have been more accepting if he'd peed in his pants trying to hold it?

Probably.

Lexa's darn-near promotion (over me) also scraped my nerves. Was there no loyalty at NetMarketing?

Probably not.

I needed to get back to work soon and scrounge up a few good clients, too. Now that we were going hip-hop, taking money from anyone who'd dish it whether we knew their market or not, I was game.

Kevin's bright red Mustang GT always seemed to protrude from its row in our underground parking garage. *What's he doing home?*

I noticed DeAndre pouting as we approached my doorway. How dare he have an attitude. "What's *your* problem?"

"You said we would go do something fun after your meeting if I didn't leave from your desk," he fussed.

He was almost comical at this point. "DeAndre, you don't *get* to have fun when you urinate in trash receptacles at people's jobs."

"I didn't u-ron-ate, I peed."

I gave up. "Whatever."

He muttered, "I knew you were lying."

An image of me backhanding DeAndre flashed through my mind. Scared me, actually, to know I could envision such violent scenarios, and to realize my temper could go from zero to sixty in thirty seconds flat with this little boy.

Breathe. Count to ten.

"I wasn't lying, DeAndre. The deal is off because of you, not me. And don't you ever accuse any adult of lying ever again. You understand?"

Momma mode was in full effect, but I'd have to get this boy back to Bayford quickly before he forced a brief jail stay upon me.

I fumbled through my key ring, searching for the right one. All I wanted was to get inside, fall on my bed face-down, and scream into a pillow. For the past twenty-four hours, I'd been doing nothing except jumping through hoops, thoroughly ashamed at DeAndre's school, upstaged by Lexa, only to be mortified moments later by my cousin's actions. A meltdown would do me just fine.

Alas, I still had DeAndre in custody. And now Kevin, who knew hardly anything about this child. As of this morning, that made two of us.

I leaned down to address DeAndre at eye level. "Listen, my boyfriend, Kevin, is inside. He's probably tired from work, so you need to keep it down," I instructed.

"You got a boyfriend?" DeAndre asked, a twinge of disappointment lining his question.

"Yes."

"How long is he gonna be here?"

"He stays here."

DeAndre covered his lips with both hands. "Ommmm. My granny said a woman ain't supposed to stay with a man she ain't married to." Now he scraped one index finger over the other, giving me the shame-on-you signal. "That's bad, Cousin Tori, super bad."

Give me a break. Yo momma is in the pen.

"Just be quiet, DeAndre."

Kevin's "Hey babe" was cut short at the sight of our little guest. The three of us did a little eye-cutting dance. Kevin confused, me apologetic, DeAndre unimpressed.

I formally introduced them; they shook hands. Kevin promptly called a meeting of the minds in our bedroom. I gave DeAndre orders to stay on the couch, adding, "If you have to use the restroom, it's down the hall."

Once in our bedroom, Kevin closed the door behind me. He barked, "What's he doing here?"

I stepped out of my heels and sunk into the chaise, hoping my routine actions would calm Kevin's impending freak-out. "He got kicked out of school for a few days. I had to bring him with me.

"What are *you* doing home already?" I continued. "I thought you were in St. Louis for the week."

"Plans changed. They needed Romie there instead. Language translation issue. I'm heading out for Milwaukee tomorrow, but don't try to change the subject. Why is there a *kid* in our apartment?"

"You're acting like I brought home a giant squid in a fish tank."

"Might as well. What are you trying to do here—make a little family for us?" He peered into me; I read into him.

"This is not about you, Kevin. Don't flatter yourself."

I brushed past him and took a seat on the toilet to relieve myself, at least physically. Though I was just as upset about having DeAndre in the house, I wasn't in the mood for an argument. Save that for Joenetta.

"Don't worry. I'm taking him back to Bayford tomorrow, and I'll come back to Houston as soon as I possibly can so I can work with Lexa on the new client she single-handedly won over. Preston's really tooting her horn right now."

"What'd you expect? You left your job to take care of family. Now they know where your priorities lie," he fussed from the closet.

"Since when is family so wrong?" I wailed from the bathroom.

He sighed loudly. "Since it slows down production. Everybody knows that's why women don't move up the career ladder as quickly. They're tied to the family rung. Plus they're too loyal. Can't navigate through a dog-eat-dog world when you're tied to people."

"You should know," I pressed.

"Here we go again," Kevin whined. He stepped into the restroom and checked his reflection.

Rather than sporting his workout gear, Kevin had changed into a pair of jeans and a dressier button-down shirt with an angel-wing appliqué on the back side.

I flushed and faced him at the counter. "Where are you going?"

"I was looking forward to a frisky evening with you, but little—what's his name—DeMerrick?"

"DeAndre."

"Yeah, well, he changed those plans." He turned on the faucet and commenced to brushing his teeth. Kevin's brown skin, always a rich reward in itself, brought out the flirt in me.

Crossing my arms, I leaned against the counter. "You plan on kissing someone tonight?"

"Not you."

No he didn't! "What's that supposed to mean?"

He finished brushing, spat out the paste, and rinsed. "Means as long as you've got that kid here, you won't be getting any."

"Kevin—"

"I'm serious, Tori. I don't *do* kids. They make me nervous. Why'd he have to come with you, anyway? Where are his parents?"

"His mom is in prison—"

"Great!" Kevin laughed. "Is he a thief?"

"No, his *mom* is incarcerated—not *him*. Why are you acting so ignorant and rude? What's wrong with you?"

"I should be asking *you* that question. Ever since you came back from the hospital, you've been on this crazy humanitarian kick. Then you go to Bayford and . . . I thought you were supposed to be helping your aunt, not saving the world—or giving me hints."

Okay, he lost me there. I trailed him back to his closet, where he slipped his feet into a pair of loafers.

"What do you think I'm hinting about?"

"That kid! Did you think you'd bring him here, we'd all go to Chuck E. Cheese, and I'd get a warm fuzzy feeling about getting married, having a family?"

"Kevin, I didn't even know you were going to be

here." I prompted his memory. "You're supposed to be in St. Louis right now."

Never defeated, he ignored my observation. "You need to get your priorities back in order. We were good until you got sick."

He stuffed his wallet into his back pocket, grabbed an overnight bag and tossed a few staples inside. I darted in his path and pushed my index finger into his chest. As Aunt Dottie would say, it was time for us to have a come-to-Jesus. "I thought we were good, too, until I saw you couldn't be there for me when I needed you most."

He took a deep breath, rolled his eyes. "Tori, get over your enlightenment. Take the kid back to Bayford, get a nurse for your aunt, come back to Houston, get back to work, and we can pick up where we left off. I don't want all this extra family drama in our relationship. It's not healthy."

He was role-playing either Dr. Phil or a jerk.

"Hypothetically speaking, what if I decide I want a family?"

"Then . . . I guess that's the choice you make."

Kevin grabbed his keys from the dresser and walked past me. "I'm out."

Chapter 14

Sunday morning found me back in Bayford, glad for the solitude of Aunt Dottie's home. I took advantage of the DeAndre-free morning and jogged a whole hour on my treadmill, which I'd transported from Houston. No more run-ins with Tiny.

DeAndre spent most of the day at Ray-Ray's house with Joenetta because Ray-Ray's wife, Fontella, was out of town. I still hadn't figured out all their issues, but none of that mattered at the moment.

I had my own issues to manage: Kevin, my job, Aunt Dottie, the store, which, by the way, still needed another employee to fill in gaps until Aunt Dottie recovered. How was I supposed to deal with all this and keep my sanity, too?

Pride swelled in me as I remembered how proactive I'd been in commissioning Josiah to build a ramp over the porch steps for Aunt Dottie's temporary wheelchair. But a brief visit with a nurse during Aunt Dottie's last day in the hospital burst my bubble. The conversation surfaced a mountain of matters I didn't even know I didn't know. Weakened by the stroke, Aunt Dottie's right side suddenly became my biggest concern. Could I feed her until the physical therapist got her up to speed? How would I lift her? How would I bathe her? That last question freaked me out.

I hadn't seen many people up-close naked. Counting Kevin and myself, the list was up to two. Kevin's body was immaculate, always a pleasure to view. The only other male body I could compare him with belonged in an art gallery.

The first time I had sex (which was the night I got pregnant, incidentally), I only saw parts of Bootsie's body. Kind of impossible to get a good look when he wasn't even fully undressed. Not that I would have looked anyway. I was too embarrassed by the whole situation to scope him out. Our ridiculously clumsy rendezvous was over before it started. He zipped up his pants and left, both of us fearing my parents might come home from work at any moment.

I made him promise not to tell anybody. What a joke.

I'd seen sections of my mother's body when I lived at home. When she sprained her arm roller-skating at my tenth birthday party, I had to help with her front-clasp bra. Her breasts flopped out, to my surprise, when I finally unfastened the hook. I was traumatized by those free-hanging appendages.

I remember turning my head away so I couldn't see them anymore.

My mother had tried to talk some sense into me. "Tori, they're just boobs. You'll have some pretty soon."

I taped my chest down for weeks after, trying to ward off the inevitable.

How was I going to *wash* the tight spots on a seventy-something-year-old woman's body when I couldn't even *look* in the general direction of my mother's bare chest?

We're talking about my beloved Aunt Dottie, here, but . . . the whole idea grossed me out. Maybe I could find some kind of trick. Maybe if I closed my eyes, I could get through it, like holding your nose to eat vegetables blocks the taste.

After leaving the hospital, I stopped at the store to make sure everything was in place before the next day's reopening.

Cassandra's house was next on my list, but I'd have to come back to her later. I forgot—everyone goes to church on Sundays in Bayford.

Of course, the library was closed on Sundays. Actually, almost everything in Bayford was closed on Sunday—at least until twelve. Only the gas station broke ancient Sabbath regulations.

Upon entrance to the gas station store, country gospel music played loudly, probably to shame those of us who were clearly playing church-hookie. Then again, maybe you had to actually be on a church roll sheet to skip.

Virgie waited on me again, asking a ton of questions about Aunt Dottie and the store.

"We'll be open for business tomorrow, bright and early."

"That's wonderful! I'll be sure and tell everybody," she offered. "Let me know if she needs any help. I could use some part-time work."

My ears perked up. "You don't say."

"Yeah, need to pay off those Christmas bills," she said with a laugh.

"Virgie, you've got a deal! Here." I grabbed an old business card from my purse. "Write down your number. I'll call you tonight."

As I filled my gas tank, I thought about how nice Virgie was to inform the town of Dottie's reopening and readily ask for employment. People in Bayford didn't have to worry about competing with the Lexas of the world. Everything was simple. Easy. No conflicts of interest, just people doing what needed to be done.

Aunt Dottie used to tell me, "You do what's right, you won't have to worry about what comes against you. God's real good at fixin' circumstances just right." Then she would recite a verse about things working out for my good. I'd tried to find that verse once in the Bible, but couldn't. The Bible seemed so big to me—how could anyone find quotes they needed with all those different books and verses?

I'd have to wait until church was, presumably, dismissed before using sanctified grounds to check e-mail via cell phone. Hopefully, this wasn't one of those Sundays where everyone ate at the church in anticipation of an afternoon service. Aunt Dottie used to keep me in church from sunup to sundown during Pastor Carter's anniversary month.

Shortly after two, I crept onto the church lot. Jacob's car rested in its usual spot, along with two other vehicles peppering the landscape. The doors leading to the vestibule were still propped open. I could see the diamond-shaped windows in the swinging doors. Visitors would peep through the glass to locate a seat before taking the sanctuary's runway, enduring the scrutiny of hundreds of saints' eyes.

I wondered what would happen if I walked through those doors now. Would the people remember me? Surely they would. I was Aunt Dottie's niece. The pregnant niece. Who had the dead baby. Who went to college, despite the dead baby and all, bless her heart.

My cell phone chimed, noting messages retrieved from cyberspace, now that I had arrived in the twenty-first century zone. Lexa sent me an obligatory state-of-the-Inner-

G account address. Very generic. She obviously didn't want me to know too much at this point. Maybe she feared I'd take over. Or that I wasn't much of a team player. Or maybe she was just a natural-born hater who didn't want to share the spotlight with me.

Do I really care? No. Not about her so much as my job. Not about my job so much as my sense of achievement. Value. Recognition.

Kevin was all but out of the picture. For the time being, our relationship was on hold by default. According to his ultimatum, I had to choose between him and my folks in Bayford. I didn't think he was giving me a fair choice, but I wasn't ready to formally end things because . . . well, I would be back in Houston after a while. Maybe we could work things out then. I had to give him some space—I probably would have freaked out, too, if he'd brought home a child without so much as consulting me.

Kevin and I hadn't talked much before I left for Bayford. He served only the silent treatment. Avoided DeAndre like the plague, turned over the remote to the child, actually, because he wouldn't sit in DeAndre's company watching television. Kevin avoided the house almost entirely while DeAndre was there.

I got the feeling DeAndre was used to feeling like a nuisance around men. I recalled the disturbing tone he'd mustered when I told him Kevin would be inside the apartment. Same tone he'd used that morning when Joenetta told him they were going to Ray-Ray's house.

"Will my daddy be there?"

"For a little while," Joenetta had answered.

"How long?"

Joenetta answered his questions as they got into her car. I eavesdropped on the porch, pretending to have trouble latching the screen.

"He'll be there until Fontella comes home, then they're going out to dinner and to visit Fontella's family."

"Will my baby sister be home?"

"No. You know better than that."

They drove away, DeAndre's sad eyes glued to mine. No love lost on my end. *Go on, Pee-Wee.*

These childless Sunday afternoon hours gave me a moment to remember what it was like to take care of numero uno. I replied to Lexa's superficial e-mail with an equally shallow note. I'd deal with her later.

Jacob's torso entered my peripheral vision, transitioning my thoughts from worry to wonder. Why did he stay in Bayford? What did he see in this little town, other than his father's church? And why wasn't he married by now?

He waved. I waved back. His head dipped into his car while he fumbled around—apparently looking for something. He gave up, then started in my direction.

A million bats beat their wings in my stomach as he approached my car. This time, Jacob walked around to the passenger's side. I unlocked the doors and he took the liberty of setting himself in the front seat, filling my vehicle with an unmistakably manly aroma. Six hours ago, when he'd first entered the sanctuary, he was probably fresh. Now, after he'd probably preached up a storm, as Aunt Dottie would say, he sported an after-service-but-my-deodorant-is-still-hanging-on musk.

My nose reveled in it.

"You doin' all right?"

"Fine." Understatement of the day. My insides liquefied at the sight of Jacob head-on, with nothing but an armrest between us. Was he that hot or was I just a little on edge because Kevin cut me off? Had he really remained this good-looking over time, or was the memory of how cute he was in high school what made him so beautiful now?

"Had a good time at church this morning."

"Good, good, that's really, really good." *Where's my vocabulary?*

"How's Aunt Dottie?"

Finally, something I could talk about. "She's coming home tomorrow."

"Wonderful! I'll share the good news with the prayer team. They've kept her name lifted before the Lord night and day."

Buzz dying. I fidgeted with my air vent. "Mmmm."

"You all right?"

His question startled me into direct eye contact. "Yeah, I'm fine."

"If you say so," he mumbled. "You seem a little upset. Stressed."

I laughed. "How would you know how I seem? We haven't seen each other regularly in years."

Jacob angled himself in front of me. His eyes studied my face, sending a rush to my skin. Thank God for melanin.

"I took a few psychology classes when I was in college. Let's see here—tight brows, tense jawline," he started.

Laughter escaped me before he got any further. Already, I could sense the tension melting away. "You win.

"Where'd you go to school anyway?" I asked.

"U-T-Tyler. You?"

"U of H, business major, marketing minor. You?"

"Double major—counseling and math."

"Odd combination."

He chuckled slightly. "I thought I'd need mad math skills with all the money I'd be making as a big-city psychotherapist."

"Oh, I know. We were all supposed to be millionaires by, what, twenty-five or thirty at the latest, right?

"So what happened to all your suburban money-making dreams?" I asked.

He shrugged. "God had other plans. I use my people skills for pastoring, math skills for managing the church's finances. All things work together for good, you know?"

There it was again! "Okay, where is that verse in the Bible?"

"Romans eight and twenty-eight."

"Romans eight and twenty-eight." I committed the reference to memory. "I was just thinking about this particular verse the other day."

"Well, it's true. All things do work together for the good of those who love the Lord."

"Mmmm." Was I sitting next to warm, dearest Aunt Dottie or hot, beautiful Jacob Carter Jr.? Come to think of it, Jacob was starting to sound a lot like Cassandra—too young to be so . . . churchy and unmotivated to achieve anything outside Bayford. Where was the drive? The ambition? You'd think they'd never heard Dr. King's I Have a Dream speech.

"Looks like things are working out pretty well for you, too." Jacob rubbed a hand across his seat. "Got this nice leather interior. Cold air blowin' through the vents."

I smirked. "Stop. It's not that serious."

"I'm just teasin'. But you're right up there next to God, Jesus, and the Holy Spirit on Aunt Dottie's list. She's really proud of you. You should be proud, too."

What? He's not going to mention the baby? Call me stupid, but for some crazy reason, I felt like I needed to mention the baby *for* him. Like if I put it on the table, he could make his little commentary and get it over with.

Kind of like one of those "now that you mentioned it" things. Save us both some embarrassment.

Casually, I confessed, "Yeah, it's not too often that a girl in my situation ends up doing well for herself."

"What situation?"

"Spare me. I was pregnant, remember?"

"Yeah, but that's not the end of the world." He shook his head. "You weren't the first pregnant teenage girl in Bayford, and you most definitely weren't the last."

"Could have fooled me."

"People are funny, you know? We remember the worst about each other, the bump on someone's nose, the hair sticking out of place. It's human nature to look for what's wrong. We have to be conditioned, trained to look for and remember the best."

"Is that what you do?"

He nodded. "Yeah. That's how I read the stress in your face. I never forgot your smile."

Had to catch myself before all thirty-two showed, front and center. "Thank you."

Jacob grabbed the overhead handle on the passenger's side. "Good talking to you."

"Yeah."

"I'd like to talk again sometime. Some place other than the church parking lot," he suggested.

"O . . . okay." Vocabulary foiled again.

"Would you like to go out later this week?"

"Yes," came out. Then reality hit. "No."

Jacob cast a puzzled glance.

"I mean, yes, I'd like to go out, but I'm too busy. With the store, Aunt Dottie, DeAndre, my work—I can't."

He sat up. "How can I help?"

A puff of air escaped me. "Let me count the ways. You got a day care for bad little boys?"

"You mean DeAndre."

"Who else?"

"He's no trouble. Aunt Dottie brings him to church with her all the time. I've had him in my Sunday school class. Smart as a whip, can't put nothing past him."

"Please! He's suspended from school for fighting, and peed in my trash can at my job, okay?"

Jacob cracked up laughing.

"I'm glad you think it's so funny."

"No"—he calmed himself—"it's not funny, except I did something similar when I was his age."

"Get out," I ordered Jacob, fingering the unlock switch again. "Get out now."

"Wait, wait." He locked the doors. "You remember when those JCPenney and Sears stores used to have those model restrooms set up in the store?"

"You didn't."

"Yes, I did. Number two."

"Jacob, that's nasty!"

"Hey, I didn't know. Maybe I wasn't as old as DeAndre. First grade, I think."

Head shaking, I asked, "Your momma spanked you silly, didn't she?"

He stopped in thought. "Tori, white people get spankings. Black people get whippin's. That's what I got—a whippin'."

"Well, I guess I'm white 'cause I didn't get beat down," I bragged. "My momma didn't hit me often. Her telling me I'd done something wrong was punishment enough for me."

"You're blessed, then, 'cause my hard head needed some hard-core hammering."

The thought of hitting DeAndre had occurred to me, of course, but I didn't think I could actually lay a hand on him. I'd never hit anyone—not even when a mean girl named Roxie Flatsnap slapped me on the playground in fifth grade. Anybody with the name Roxie Flatsnap deserved to get away with something every now and then, for as much as we'd teased her.

With no brothers or sisters to practice my sparring, I was sorely adapted to violence.

"I can't whip DeAndre. He's not mine. And even if he were, I'd try to do time-outs or other punishments first."

"Got an idea. Why don't you let him join our church's Little League baseball team? Brother Reynolds will be coaching, I'll be helping out. I can keep an eye on him, make sure he stays in line. And if he has any more . . . accidents . . . you let me know and I'll make sure he runs laps for it."

"Just make him run for the fun of it, so he'll be dirt tired when he comes home from practice."

"Deal." We shook on it. His hands were soft enough to caress, callous enough to prove he wasn't scared of hard work.

Chapter 15

Cassandra and I met up at eight to open the store. DeAndre's suspended behind tagged alongside me. He was thoroughly miffed at the idea of getting up early this particular Monday morning.

"Why can't I sleep late today since I don't have to go to school?" he'd fussed groggily as I yanked the bedspread off his body.

"Au contraire, mon frère. This is not a free day for you."

Now, as I unlocked the iron bars and padlocks securing the store, DeAndre suddenly came alive. "Wait! Aunt Dottie always prays when she opens the store."

Cassandra nodded. "He's right. She does."

DeAndre scooped my hand and Cassandra's. We all followed DeAndre's lead. "God, please help us to have a great day at the store. Let people find what they need, and help Ms. Cassandra and Mr. Elgin do a good job. Bless the people who come in today. Thank you for this store. Protect us and keep us. In Jesus' name, Amen."

"Amen."

"Oh, wait, God! And bless Cousin Tori, too, Lord. Help her do everything right. Amen."

"Amen."

We hadn't even turned on all the lights before our first customer came rolling in.

"Hey, Miss Mattie!" Cassandra greeted the elderly woman tapping through the entry with her wooden cane.

DeAndre seemed to know his way around the store well enough. He ushered in sunshine through the blinds, clicked on the neon OPEN sign, shouting the news to those traveling westward over the railroad tracks.

With Cassandra and the store set for the first few hours before Elgin came in, DeAndre and I shuttled on over to the hospital to pick up Aunt Dottie.

"Auntie!" DeAndre nearly yelled as we walked into her room.

She held out one arm and braced herself for his zealous hug. Even if she could have talked, she wouldn't have scolded him for nearly knocking her out of the bed.

"I missed you, Aunt Dottie. I'm sorry I got suspended, but I'm going back to school tomorrow," DeAndre rattled off his confession.

Aunt Dottie dipped her chin in disapproval.

"But I'm not going to fight anymore, I promise." DeAndre held up his right hand.

I stood behind him, watching Aunt Dottie's face absorb his enthusiasm. Her crooked smile and twinkling eyes spoke volumes of forgiveness. The same unconditional love she'd shown me when I asked her if God had killed my baby because I'd had sex so young.

"Sweetheart, God is love. He don't kill no babies, but He does welcome when they come back to heaven, just like He'll welcome you at the end of your earthly life."

"But my baby doesn't have anybody in heaven he

knows," I'd cried, wondering where all these wild thoughts were coming from. I'd been taking pain medication to deal with the episiotomy. The haze of drugs and pure sadness blocked out much of my immediate memory following the day I delivered. But I do remember Aunt Dottie's reply. "Time don't pass the same on earth as it does in heaven. To your baby, it'll seem like he's only been there a minute when you get there. You'll see."

I still had questions, of course, but Aunt Dottie's love calmed my inquiry. Love mattered most, in her eyes.

"And Cousin Tori taught me how to multiply by nines, so now I know all my times tables. And guess what else? Cousin Tori said I can play baseball. I'm gonna ask some of my friends to play, too, but Chase got cut and he had to get stitches so I don't know if he can."

Chase must have been forgiven, too.

Aunt Dottie nodded attentively, soaking in DeAndre's overflow of energy. I'd almost forgotten what a great listener she was. Even when she could talk, she preferred to listen.

"So what you think about the baseball team, Aunt Dottie?"

She waggled her head emphatically, agreeing with his plans.

I put a hand on his shoulder. "DeAndre, Aunt Dottie can't talk right now."

"She can't?" As though he didn't believe me.

"Not yet, but don't worry. Once her teacher works with her, she'll be much better."

Worry tramped across his face. He hugged Aunt Dottie again and spoke softly in her ear. "I'll teach you how to talk again, too, Aunt Dottie."

She wrapped him up with her good arm and then kissed him on the cheek twice.

Together, DeAndre and I got Aunt Dottie out of the hospital and propped up in the front seat of my car. The wheelchair collapsed nicely into the back of my SUV.

Upon reentering Bayford, Aunt Dottie spotted friends at every intersection. She'd touch my arm and signal for me to blow, then use her left arm to wave at other drivers. They'd wave back. My first thought: this is *so* country. Then I remembered: this *is* the country.

DeAndre took a special interest in the wheelchair. He quickly reassembled it and rolled it to the passenger's side when we arrived back at the house.

"Lock the wheels first," I told him while showing him how to accomplish this task.

"Got it."

Though she struggled, Aunt Dottie's "working" half was stronger than I'd imagined. She helped us in her own way, holding the screen door open and hoisting herself from the wheelchair as much as possible.

She wrote "THANK YOU!!!" on her tablet after we'd finished arranging the comforter and organizing a tray with the telephone and television remote control at her bedside.

Joenetta showed up unannounced. For once, I was glad to see her. She checked in on Aunt Dottie, then met me in the kitchen as DeAndre and I finished our BLT sandwiches.

I briefed Joenetta on Aunt Dottie's medications and the schedule I'd been able to work out, with the hospital's assistance. Physical therapy Monday, Wednesday, and Friday at one. Speech therapy at three on Mondays and Wednesdays. Checkup with the doctor next week.

Joenetta paid little attention to my words, choosing instead to focus on Aunt Dottie's pill bottles.

"Any of these for pain?"

"I don't think so."

"Hmph. Wonder can you ask the doctor to prescribe some Vicodin?" Her eyes widened with the request. As if.

"I doubt it."

She plunked the bottles back onto the table. "Every household needs some Vicodin around. Never know when you might need it."

"What's Vicodin?" DeAndre interjected.

Stuff people use to get high. "Pain medication."

"Oh."

"Well," Joenetta huffed, "don't come hollerin' to me if she starts hurtin' later on tonight. I tried to tell you."

I promptly changed the subject. "Listen, I've got to run back to the store. Can you stay with Aunt Dottie until this afternoon? Sister Meecham will be over later with food."

Joenetta agreed, but insisted on a trade. "Take DeAndre with you so Dottie can have some peace while she gets settled."

DeAndre stuffed the last bite of his sandwich into his mouth, swished his hands together and announced, "I'm ready."

Great.

Elgin saved the day by putting DeAndre to work. "You're kicked out of school, huh?"

DeAndre nodded.

"Speak up," Elgin commanded.

"Yes, sir."

"What for?"

"Fightin'."

"Fightin' 'bout what?"

"Somebody talkin' 'bout my momma."

The corners of Elgin's lips lowered with understanding. "That'll do it every time. Grab a broom, son."

I joined Cassandra behind the register, filling orders for pressed ham, answering questions about Aunt Dottie's health. Between customers, I talked to Cassandra about hiring Virgie.

"What do you think?"

Cassandra tilted her head to one side. Hesitated. "Everybody already knows her. It might be a good idea."

"Everybody knows everybody in Bayford, Cassandra. What do you *really* think?"

She crossed her arms for a moment. Uncrossed them.

"Spill it, Cassandra."

"Aunt Dottie's never had a white person working here, that's all I'm saying."

Race never even entered my mind. "You think Aunt Dottie would care?"

"No, but the customers might. Black people don't trust white people . . . cleanliness around here. Folks might not want her touching their meat or slicing their cheese. They might be like yowza yowza!" She flopped her head from side to side as though she'd just been slapped by an imaginary hand.

"Cassandra, are you serious?"

"Afraid so."

"Plus," she continued, "this is like the last all-black establishment in Bayford. Except the churches. African Americans are proud we've kept Dottie's open all these years. If you hire Virgie, we might lose some of our older customers. Right now, we can't afford to lose anybody because, I don't know if you heard it or not, but they're building a Walmart in Henrytown."

Walmart? Walmart! This could be the answer to my dreams. If they built it, the people would come. There was tons of research about what happened to mom-and-pop stores once the Walmarts and Targets moved to town.

Aunt Dottie would see the need to close the store and quit while she was ahead, living her golden years in total bliss, except for the slight matter of DeAndre.

"When does the Walmart open?"

"Some time in April, I think."

A month, at best, to help Aunt Dottie arrive at the only sensible solution, save my job, and return to life as usual. Maybe even salvage the thing with Kevin and relinquish DeAndre-duty.

"Let's not worry too much about Virgie. She'll only be part-time anyway." I brought the discussion to a close, hoping this whole thing would be a done deal in a matter of weeks. Liquidation, liquidation, liquidation.

Jacob entered the store a little after five, dressed in business attire. His fresh haircut revealed a wave pattern I remembered quite well from high school. Back then, boys would slap a brush in one palm at a moment's notice. They were worse than the girls sometimes.

"Hey, cuz!" Cassandra called from behind the counter. Several other customers greeted Jacob as well. "You ate up all that pressed ham already?" Cassandra asked him.

"No. Just stopped by to see how things were going." His focus shifted my way—the chip aisle.

"Oh," Cassandra said. "I see. Let me know if you need anything."

He met me at Doritos. "Looks pretty busy."

"Yeah, business is still as good as I remember it."

"Hi, Pastor Jacob." DeAndre gave a hearty handshake. "I've been working with Mr. Elgin. He said he's gonna give me five dollars for helping him, Friday."

"That's right. A man's gotta earn money. Remember when we talked about work ethic at church?"

DeAndre nodded. "I'm gonna get me a good job when I grow up."

"That's what I'm talkin' 'bout." Jacob commended him with dap and DeAndre, enamored by the accolades, skipped back to Elgin.

"I don't want to take up your time," Jacob dismissed himself. "I dropped by to say hi and see if you needed anything."

"Thanks. I think we're good for now." I raised an eyebrow. "You're not going to buy anything?"

"What you got?" he flirted, too.

"Bread, cheese, salami. Classic bachelor food."

"Not for this bachelor. I know my way around a kitchen," he bragged.

"Is that so?"

"Yes, ma'am. Got spaghetti, corn, and salad on the menu tonight. Should I make enough for two?"

His invitation made my stomach growl, but there was no way I could commit to seeing him that night—too much unfinished work.

I reluctantly turned him down. "I'll have to pass this time. Maybe next week?"

His face slackened a bit. "Sure thing." He spoke to the entire store now as he left. "Y'all be blessed."

"All right, Reverend," and "Same to you," from the customers.

Cassandra teased as I finished restocking the Funyuns. "I see my cousin's got his eyes on you."

"Whatever you say, Cassandra."

"I ain't hatin'. Just don't mess over him." She gave a sisterly warning. "He's a good guy."

Wonder if omitting the matter of a live-in boyfriend back in Houston counted as "messing"?

I worked like a woman with purpose that day at the store. Hadn't meant to stay until the end of Cassandra's shift, but the customers kept coming and the cowbell kept ringing. There seemed no opportune moment to leave. When it was time for Cassandra to go, she reciprocated and stayed until seven.

We were both pooped when Elgin flipped the red and white sign to CLOSED.

DeAndre quietly approached me as I wrapped plastic around the ends of lunch meat. "I don't wanna come here anymore. Mr. Elgin makes me work too hard."

"You keep getting in trouble at school, you might as well get used to hard labor," I whispered back, snickering to myself and thinking about Jacob's plan to exhaust De-Andre through baseball practice. These men might be onto something.

Halfway through the day, Cassandra's cousin had come to borrow her car. He still hadn't returned, so I offered her a ride home.

DeAndre hopped in the backseat, snapped into his seat belt, and hummed to himself while Cassandra and I recounted the day. Dottie's was back on track, but the store wouldn't be able to compete with *Great Value* bread at ninety-nine cents a loaf. Might as well prepare Cassandra now.

"So . . . what do you think's gonna happen to Dottie's when Walmart opens?"

She shook her head. "Don't know. I hope we can do a wizzy-wizzy and beat them out. That peanut brittle we purchase from Cleveland Farms don't play. Walmart won't have stuff like that."

"They'll have some kind of pralines there." I was, at least, trying to sound sad about the whole thing. "They've got everything in Walmart. Cheaper, because they order in bulk from the suppliers, you know."

"It's not always about price," Cassandra countered me. "Dottie's belongs to Bayford. You gotta remember, country people don't like to drive more than ten minutes to get anywhere." She laughed at her people. "Plus, you have to go through Oak Mountain to get to Henrytown. The police in Oak Mountain make their living off writing speeding tickets."

I downplayed her reasoning with silence. Then, "We might have to make some changes at Dottie's."

By changes, I meant close, of course, but Cassandra lit up with excitement. "I know! Okay, check, check, check this out." She made an invisible checkmark in the air. "So, we have these special sales. I mean, sales for real, for real. Walmart has *roll* back sales. We'll have *throw*back sales. Get it?"

"Okay . . ."

"Bam—a can of soup for a quarter. Gallon of milk for seventy-five cents, until supplies run out. People come in the store for the cheap milk, but they have to get . . ."

Nothing came to mind, seeing as I don't really *do* milk.

DeAndre hollered from the backseat, "Cereal!"

"Shazam!" Cassandra reached over the seat and slapped hands with my little cousin. "*Gotta* get that cereal, too. The Rice Krispies aren't on sale, but that's all right 'cause the milk was only three quarters. Then you need sugar. Might as well get what you need for dinner while you're at it. Next thing you know, we skiddeefled all this extra money on a gallon of milk!"

"Skiddeefled?"

"Yes!"

"Yes!" From the backseat.

At that moment, I felt completely lucky Cassandra didn't work at NetMarketing because her enthusiasm was highly transmittable.

Almost had me going there. I parked in her driveway and unlocked the doors.

"I can't make those kinds of decisions, Cassandra. It's not my store."

She reached up above my rearview mirror. "Is this the light?"

"Yeah. Pull it back."

A beam filled the car.

Cassandra squared up with me. "Look, Tori, I'm not stupid. I know that Walmart, even if it's twenty minutes away, is a serious threat to Dottie's. But I've been working at the store for years. I know what, when, and why Bayford people buy. I can make this throwback sale blow up all over town—I mean, if you're *really* interested in keeping Aunt Dottie's store alive."

The hairs on my neck bristled. *Busted.* "Fair enough." Silence. "Let me think about it over some Starbucks."

"Love Starbucks."

"What's Starbucks?"

I turned my head slightly. "A coffee shop."

"When you go, take me with you," Cassandra pleaded.

"Me, too," from DeAndre.

"No. Coffee is for grown folks. Too much caffeine for kids." I shot him down flat.

His arms flew across his chest and he had the nerve to kick the back of my seat.

Cassandra reached back and popped his leg before I could even respond. That girl was quick on the draw. "I don't care how mad you get, you don't kick nobody's car! I wouldn't take you nowhere actin' like that. Keep your feet on the floor!"

He mumbled, "Yes, ma'am."

"Apologize!" Cassandra ordered.

"I'm sorry, Cousin Tori."

"Thank you," she ended that episode.

Clearly, I needed to get my poppin' reflexes together.

"Back to Starbucks. When are you going?"

"Umm . . . I was thinking tonight. They don't close until eleven. I have to do some work on the Internet."

"Mind if I tag along?"

"Not at all. Let's go check on Aunt Dottie and put DeAndre to bed first."

"You are my kind of homegirl, Tori. Ooh, I keep tryin' to tell my sister about Starbucks, but she's all heebie-jeebie about it. It's so good to have somebody in Bayford who understands the power of a Caramel Macchiato! Girl, that stuff will make you slap your grandmomma!"

"Ommm," DeAndre sang out, "that's bad. Super bad."

Cassandra and I cracked up laughing.

At Starbucks, she lapped up her special treat and I reveled in mine. "This is sooooo good. Mmmmmm," I hummed.

"Amen," Cassandra seconded.

"One of these days, I'm going to have to bring Aunt Dottie to Starbucks."

"I'm coming with you," Cassandra insisted.

"Guess that means I'll have to bring DeAndre, too. I don't know why his father doesn't spend more time with him."

Cassandra swallowed quickly. "Really?"

"You know something I don't?"

"Uh, yeah." She took another swig. "Zoletha—that's DeAndre's mom, everybody calls her Z—she and Ray-Ray had a little fling-a-ring not too long after he married Fontella. Fontella can't stand the sight of DeAndre, so Ray-

Ray and Joenetta try to put distance between DeAndre and his stepmother so she won't be reminded of the affair."

"That's crazy. None of this is DeAndre's fault."

"Normal people understand these things. Fontella? Not normal. She's just like Joenetta. Ray-Ray married his mother, basically."

Great. Just great.

Chapter 16

Running Dottie's with Cassandra, Elgin, and (later in the week) Virgie proved a full-time job. Even when I wasn't at the store, there was paperwork to shuffle.

At a little after three, I'd rush home to check on Aunt Dottie and make sure DeAndre was settled after school. Sometimes he came with me to the shop, other times he wanted to hang with Chase and the other neighborhood boys. I actually preferred him to stay at home so he could look in on Aunt Dottie every so often.

Joenetta's visits dwindled since Sister Meecham brought enough food for both DeAndre and Aunt Dottie, and I began to notice something: DeAndre wasn't so bad when he knew exactly what he was supposed to be doing. So long as I was specific—"take your bath at seven-thirty" instead of "take your bath some time before you go to bed"—we got along just fine. I also discovered that if I made a big fuss about how great he smelled, he'd actually wash himself in the shower.

"How do I smell, Cousin Tori?" He'd bound toward me when I got home from the library.

I'd sniff his neck. "Wonderful! I can tell you're really scrubbing yourself clean!"

The first time I played this game with him, he surprised me with a bear hug and a smack on the cheek. Took me off guard, but his ability to forget the problems we'd had and enjoy that good moment helped me to remember he was just a kid. A kid who didn't have a mom and had found a way to ensure a squeeze each night after his bath.

Speaking of baths and such, my biggest nightmare had come and gone. I got over myself when I realized this had to be ten times more embarrassing for Aunt Dottie than for me.

We established a routine. I ran a deep tub of water and helped her inside, where she sat for about fifteen minutes just soaking. The physical therapist said a good hot bath could soothe her muscles after all the exertion she'd spent trying to rebuild them. I watched television in Aunt Dottie's bed so I could keep an eye on her while she relaxed.

After a while, I'd turn on some gospel music and she'd hum along while I bathed her. As the week wore on, her pitch matched almost perfectly.

By Saturday night, I was a pro at this whole bath thing. Get in, get out, keep it moving. Almost silly how much I'd worried about what turned out to be nothing.

Aunt Dottie's favorite part of our evenings together, by far, was Bible time.

"Could you please read me a few chapters every night?" she wrote to me.

Simple enough request. We tackled Job, Proverbs, and most of Psalms that first week.

"'I will instruct you and teach you in the way you should go, I will counsel you and watch over you. Do not be like the horse or the mule, which have no understanding but must be controlled by bit and bridle or they will not come to you. Many are the woes of the wicked, but the Lord's unfailing love surrounds the man who trusts in him.' That's from Psalm thirty-two."

Aunt Dottie closed her eyes and listened, taking a second bath in comforting words. As I read the scriptures one after another, in full context, I began to see patterns I'd never noticed before. God came through for these people in the Bible. Though I still wasn't too sure about why God allowed Job to experience horrendous loss, everything worked out fine in the end.

And David, in Psalms, was an undiagnosed mess. One week fighting victoriously, the next week crying out to God in despair. Up, down, up, down. David had some serious mood swings, but he always knew where to turn for help.

One night, I found myself so engrossed in the wisdom of Proverbs, I lost track of time. I looked up and Aunt Dottie had fallen asleep somewhere along the way. I kept reading until I'd had my fill.

Store-wise, I'd managed to resolve all management issues—including paying Dottie's employees.

No more problems at DeAndre's school. Kevin on hold, NetMarketing work progressing nicely. I wasn't getting much sleep at night, but I was surviving and looking forward to the only day of rest I could reasonably expect—Sunday.

"Nooooo!"
What's that sound? Am I dreaming?
"Nooooo!"
DeAndre's wailing startled me, conjuring up a worst-

case scenario with Aunt Dottie. *Oh, God, no.* I threw back the covers and rushed to her bedroom first. She, too, was scrambling to get out of bed—with little success.

"I'll check on him," I assured her.

I rushed down the hallway to his room and busted through the door. "What's wrong?"

He sat up in bed crying. "She didn't come."

"Who didn't come?"

"The tooth fairy."

"You didn't tell me you lost a tooth."

His brows pinched together. "Why I gotta tell you? You ain't the tooth fairy."

I blinked. "Right, right. Well . . . did you put it under the *correct* pillow? She might have been looking in the wrong place."

"Yes, I did," he whimpered. He reached under his pillow and produced the sacrificial exchange offering, centering it in his palm. "Here it is right here. She skipped me, I *know* she did."

"No, she didn't. Maybe she just got really busy last night," I explained. "Tooth fairies are people, too. Kinda."

"She's just stupid."

"No, she's not. You better hope she didn't hear you or you won't be getting any more money ever again. And she *might* tell Santa Claus what you said," I played along, giggling like crazy inside.

DeAndre's eyes widened. "No! I didn't mean it—she's not stupid. She's smart."

"Very smart. Put your tooth back under the pillow. I'm sure she'll pay up tonight."

"Sure?"

"Yes, I'm sure."

He sighed. "Okay, if you say so, Cousin Tori."

Later, Aunt Dottie had to slap my hand to stop me from laughing. "He's soooo serious about that tooth fairy!"

She wrote: "You probably were too."

I conceded. "You're right, Aunt Dottie. I just have to remember to put money under his pillow tonight. But he scared me half to death, screaming like that!"

Aunt Dottie held a hand to her chest.

"I'm going back to bed," I told her.

She looked at me like I'd told her I was joining the circus.

"What?"

"CHURCH!" she scribbled.

"Oh, Aunt Dottie, this is the only day I have to rest. Plus you just got out of the hospital—are you sure you're up to this?"

"Missed two Sun. and Wed. already. Going today. Let's get go."

So much for relaxation.

The last time I set foot inside Mount Pisgah, I didn't actually know it would be my final visit. I was already out of college, working, and living with Kevin when Aunt Dottie had asked me to attend an appreciation ceremony for Pastor Carter.

"I'm not sure if I can make it back to Bayford this weekend. I've got a lot of work to finish," I'd told her.

In her signature no-pressure style, Aunt Dottie said she understood. "Well, if anything changes, we'd love to see you."

Of course, the only "thing" I really had to change was my mind. I took another look at my calendar and realized that upcoming Saturday marked what would have been my son's eighth birthday.

Eight years already.

I fell into a funk and decided the best thing to do would be go to Bayford, eat some of Aunt Dottie's good cooking, and sit with her for a while. Ask her to pull out the pictures we requested the hospital staff to take right after he was born. Morbid, I know, but he was so perfectly formed. Looked like he was sleeping, all curled up in a little ball. Aunt Dottie had agreed to keep the two snapshots tucked away. Said I didn't need to look at them too often. "What's done is done, sweetie."

When I arrived in Bayford and went inside Aunt Dottie's house to freshen up for church, I asked her if I could see the pictures. Briefly.

"Why don't you wait until we come back from church, all right?" she'd said, pulling me toward the front door.

The whole time I sat in service, I thought about those pictures. I began to weep. Aunt Dottie put an arm around me, rocked me gently while some man went way over an appropriate time frame for preaching, even by Southern Baptist standards.

After the appreciation, we'd gone back to Aunt Dottie's and sat at the kitchen table eating fried chicken, macaroni and cheese, and greens. True to her word, Aunt Dottie produced an old box of pictures from her bedroom. She showed me the pictures of my baby again. Just for a moment.

She commented, "He sure was a handsome little rascal, wasn't he?"

"Yeah," I laughed through tears. My body collapsed onto her chest. "He would have been a great son."

"Don't you worry, Tori. One day, you'll be a great mom to another child who's just as good lookin'." She rubbed my back, then gently slipped his pictures from my hand. "I'm gonna put these away for now. But any time you need to see 'em, you let me know. You are his mother. Always will be."

Driving back to Houston later that evening, relief swept over me. Leaving Bayford behind meant no crazy memories, no pictures of a dead baby. I vowed then to stay away as long as possible. Keep in touch with Aunt Dottie, slap a Band-Aid on everything else Bayford represented.

With the adjustments for dressing Aunt Dottie and maneuvering her wheelchair, we were late for church. Yet, Aunt Dottie's entrance to Mount Pisgah seemed perfectly timed. The choir was singing a song about thankfulness as DeAndre held the sanctuary's swinging door open. I pushed her wheelchair past the threshold and suddenly, the entire congregation erupted in high praise.

The choir kept singing, "Thank You, Lord, for all you've done for me."

Aunt Dottie lifted her left hand and, I promise you, those people came undone. Several of them rushed the aisles. "Praise the Lord!" "Bless your name!" Bending down to hug and kiss her.

But Aunt Dottie kept on waving that good arm, flashing that diagonal smile, while I kept on pushing the wheelchair forward because I knew if I stopped before I sat down, I'd be overwhelmed by this sudden sense of belonging within me.

This wasn't just Aunt Dottie's church, God's house. The people in the building welcomed Aunt Dottie, but the church itself enveloped me. I swiped at my eyes, wondering why on earth—or heaven—I was crying. These tears spilled over from a long-abandoned well of emotions within me.

Aunt Dottie motioned for me to stop at the second pew. An usher quickly moved the offering bucket from the floor, just beneath the bench's siding. I parked her wheelchair, locked her wheels, and sat right next to her at the end of the row. I was sitting in Aunt Dottie's usual spot, actually—don't think I'd ever seen anyone sit there except her in all those years of coming to Mount Pisgah.

DeAndre positioned himself next to me, but his behind didn't actually hit the cushioning for another ten minutes while the church rejoiced over Aunt Dottie's return.

Somewhere in all this, I locked eyes with Jacob. I wanted to return his clandestine smile, but my quivering bottom lip wouldn't cooperate. I bit down to stop the shaking and quickly turned my head in a different direction.

Senior Pastor Carter took the pulpit and tried to move on in the service, but even he got "happy" when he started talking about how the doctors said Aunt Dottie might have suffered irreparable damage if Cassandra hadn't convinced her to go to the hospital when she did.

"Saints, you know that wasn't nothin' but God!"

The congregation roared, "Amen," myself included.

"Aunt Dottie's so full of love, always opening her doors, always feeding the needy. Helping folks find jobs, raise their kids, keeping an eye out for the community through her store. She's blessed!"

"Hallelujah!"

"Stroke can't stop her!"

The organist hit a chord.

"Hospital can't hold her!"

Another chord, higher octave.

"Doctors underestimate her."

Higher still.

"Yeah!" from the church.

" 'Cause many are the afflictions of the righteous—but the Lord delivers him out of them all!"

They shouted another round before someone started singing a congregational hymn to get everyone back on track.

"Now, Sister Dottie," Pastor Carter said, "when the Lord *does* call you home, He gonna call you home in one, good piece. We all know these earthly bodies won't last forever. But while we're still here doing the Lord's work, He'll make what we've got work for as long as He needs it in service."

The worshippers agreed. Aunt Dottie seconded His presage with another gesture, and the ceremony continued.

My chest beat so hard I could see my blouse thumping when Pastor Carter gave the invitation to accept Christ. *Why am I so nervous?* I'd already walked down a church's center aisle once before. When I was ten. Mr. James was about to embark on another campaign, and we'd joined a huge church with a pastor who used to play for the Dallas Cowboys.

"Everybody who's anybody in Houston goes to his church," I remember Mr. James saying. "White people, too. Wonderful networking opportunity."

The three of us had walked down and repeated the minister's prayer of faith. Then we shook hands forever with a lingering line of people.

Back then, my mother had told me to confess to Jesus, so I did. Maybe I'd done this whole "accept Christ" thing under the wrong pretenses, but I did do it. I *did* say the words, and I hoped they were true.

Now was different. My mother wasn't forcing me to walk down the aisle. Something in me caused my legs to straighten and propel me toward the front of Mount Pisgah. Was it my grieving heart? Rebellion against my mother now that I could do things on my own terms?

Either way, if Jesus could rid me of all the worries constantly running through my head, I needed Him. I needed Him for *real* for real.

Aunt Dottie had me read Romans chapters five through eight that evening. Paul's account of life with Christ was more real than ever to me now. The all-encompassing truth of verses 38 and 39 of chapter eight jumped straight off the page and into my heart. "For I am convinced that neither death nor life, neither angels nor demons, neither the present nor the future, nor any powers, neither height nor depth, nor anything else in all creation, will be able to separate us from the love of God that is in Christ Jesus our Lord."

Nothing could ever cut me off from His love for me. Unlike my mother, He wouldn't abandon me when I needed Him most. Wouldn't run off to Africa and never look back. I had to laugh at myself—He's already *in* Africa.

I put Aunt Dottie to bed and set myself up for a long night in front of the computer screen, doing as much work as possible off-line. Midnight came and went. Half an hour later, my forehead bonked the top of my laptop and I knew it was time to call it a night. The open word-processing file on the monitor was filled with the letter S for pages. I'd been pressing the button when I fell asleep at the helm. No telling what I might mess up if I made unconscious keyboard strokes again.

My head had scarcely hit the pillow when I remembered DeAndre. The tooth fairy. I pleaded with myself internally: *do I really have to get up?* Maybe I could tell him the tooth fairy was like every other venue in Bayford—she was closed on Sundays. *Isn't he a little too old to still believe in the tooth fairy anyway?*

Try as I might, I couldn't rest well again until I'd settled the matter of the fairy money. DeAndre had been heartbroken when he thought she'd skipped him. Between Z and Ray-Ray, he'd been skipped more than enough.

I got up, found a few dollars in my purse, and tiptoed into DeAndre's room. Moonlight outlined a path to his bedside. The soft, deep, raspy sound of DeAndre's breathing assured me that he was conked out. *Wish I could say the same for myself.*

I reached beneath his pillow, keeping one eye on his face. *Got it!* Tooth in hand, I slipped the money in place. When I pulled my hand back, a small piece of paper cascaded to the floor. Instinctively, I grabbed the paper and crept out of the room.

Just beyond his door, I switched on the hallway lamp and read.

> *Dear Tooth Fairy,*
>   *I am sorry I have been bad lately, but I lost my tooth and I hope you will forgive me so I can get some money. I am really sorry, so if you can leave me some money I will know you still like me no matter about my mother.*
>   *The End,*
>   *DeAndre Lester in Bayford—I live with Aunt Dottie and Cousin Tori*
>
> *P.S. If you see my mother, please tell her I said hello. Her name is Zoletha Simpson, but she is also Z. Amen.*

Chapter 17

Of course, Aunt Dottie's church routine placed me at Mount Pisgah on Wednesday nights for Bible study. Jacob Jr. led the meeting, adding even more insight to my nightly readings with Aunt Dottie.

After service, DeAndre and I had plenty of help carting our aunt back to the Caddy. Several members volunteered to hold her bag, open the doors, etc. For the first time, I noticed women flocked around Jacob at the church entrance.

Hmmm.

Once we'd put her in the car, I set my mind on the next shift. I needed to get to Starbucks for some online time. Lexa had finally come up against a snag in Inner-G's marketing plan. None of the keywords she'd researched for targeted Web site impressions had enough search demand to warrant a massive campaign. *Can you say "didn't do your homework"?*

Her e-mail had asked for "my input," but she really needed my help. Not that she would ever admit this, mind you. Part of me wanted to see her crash and burn. Really, if the buzz about her sleeping around to get accounts was true, she'd set women back fifty years. She deserved whatever she lost.

But I couldn't let Inner-G go out like that. Not with my name and a portion of my paycheck tied to it, anyway. I had a long night ahead of me.

Before I could get one of my own legs in the car, Jacob dashed toward my car. "Hold up."

"Yeah?"

He leaned into my car to acknowledge my family members, then continued, "You got a minute?"

He seemed to have a knack for approaching me at the worst possible moments. "Not really. I've got to get to Starbucks for an Internet connection, fast."

"You're going all the way to Henrytown by yourself at this time of night?"

Aunt Dottie beeped my horn, nearly startling me out of my skin. She wagged her index finger at me. I'd gotten pretty good at reading her body language—she agreed wholeheartedly with Jacob.

"I'll go with you," he insisted with heartfelt sincerity.

Aunt Dottie gave us a thumbs-up.

I couldn't resist. "Let me take them home first."

Jacob followed me back to the house and helped get both Aunt Dottie and DeAndre settled for the night.

"What time are you coming back?" my pesky little overseer queried.

"Too late for you to be up when I return."

He squinted at Jacob, who was standing in the bedroom doorway, then whispered, "Is this a date?"

Not sure how to answer—or if I should answer—I sidestepped him. "Good night, DeAndre."

He roused to his knees in bed and gave me a hug. "Night, Cousin Tori. Ooh! Did you hear what I said?"

"What?"

"When I say your name real fast, it sounds like 'cussin' Tori,' you get it? Cousin Tori, cussin' Tori?" He fell over laughing at himself. DeAndre could be downright delirious when he was sleepy. "Your name is superbad!"

His giggling touched a silly nerve within me. In a moment's time, we were both laughing. Jacob, shaking his head, walked toward the front door. "Cussin' Tori," I repeated. Each time, another wave of delirium swept over him, his eyes blinking slowly, barely able to stay above board. He'd be a goner in no time.

"Don't forget—if you need anything, phone numbers are on the refrigerator."

Jacob met me in the living room. With my laptop bag on one shoulder and purse on the other, I looked more like I was on my way to a conference room with Preston than Starbucks with Jacob. I wished we were going on the romantic date DeAndre suspected, but this would have to be clinical.

"You want me to drive?" Jacob pulled his keys from his pocket before I could answer.

"Sure. Thanks."

He opened the passenger's door for me, waited until I'd settled my belongings on the floorboard, and then closed my side.

The interior of his car boasted top-of-the-line gadgets. More bells and whistles than I'd ever seen or than anyone in Bayford would ever need. The sound system enhancing the gospel lyrics spewing from speakers I could understand. But a built-in GPS device?

Curiosity got the best of me before we even made it to the highway. "Okay, Jacob. I have to know why you have a navigation system in this car."

He raised an eyebrow. "I do get out of Bayford sometimes, you know?"

"Really?"

"Yes. Other churches invite me to preach. I go into town to meet friends. Pick people up from the airport, plus I dabble in real estate throughout the county."

I gasped. "I didn't know you were a realtor." This bit of information might come in handy when we got ready to sell Dottie's.

He nodded. "Keeps me in touch with people's everyday lives. Pastoring has a tendency to distance men and women of God from their flocks. Makes for unrealistic sermons and theology with no practicality."

"You did a great job of breaking down the scriptures tonight, by the way," I complimented him. "When you teach, I understand His message to us."

"Thanks for the encouragement; it's all God."

We crossed the official city limits, reminding me of the last time I'd left town. "I took DeAndre to Houston with me and he nearly hyperventilated at the sight of a shopping center."

"Wow."

"I know, right? I wonder what he'll do when I take him to a mall."

"Hmmm." Jacob rubbed his temple slightly.

"Hmmm what?"

"You've really taken to DeAndre, huh?"

"No." I creased my brow. "He's . . . eight. He's . . . always into things, always asking questions. Seriously, he can't walk past a rock without picking it up and throwing it."

"And he's crazy about you," Jacob observed.

I sang, "Come again?"

"He asked if we were going on a date—he's trying to

protect you. And when he hugged you, I wish you could have seen his face. Contentment. He's really going to take it hard when you move back to Houston."

What?! "DeAndre has . . . Joenetta."

Jacob pursed his lips. "Wrong answer."

"So, you know Joenetta, I gather?"

"Know her well. Been praying for her for years now. Aunt Dottie keeps her sister high on the prayer team's list." Jacob smiled to himself.

"I recommend you all keep Joenetta a priority 'cause she sure needs all the prayer she can get."

He laughed slightly. "We all do, my sister, we all do."

"So, what are you praying for yourself?" My spiritual way of getting nosy.

He responded quickly, "Guidance."

Too generic for me. "Guidance in what area of your life?"

"Pastoring. Work. My parents. What about you?"

"I *should* be praying about work, Aunt Dottie, and the store."

"What about DeAndre?"

"I'll pray that his mother gets out of prison soon, I guess."

"Don't hold your breath. She's in for armed robbery and aggravated assault. She already had a record before this. It's gonna be a while before she sees the other side of the barbed wire."

My heart sank. DeAndre would probably be a man by the time Z was released. She wouldn't even recognize him.

"What's his mother like?"

"I don't know. She's a lot younger than us. Twenty-four, maybe. Some of the Simpsons attend New Jerusalem Temple, about ten miles north of here. From my understanding, she's always been in trouble. In and out of jail, fighting, running with a bad crowd, short temper."

That would explain DeAndre's sharp attitude and penchant toward violence. Couple his mother's model with Joenetta's influence, it's a wonder the child had any sense at all.

We listened to music the rest of the trip. Jacob sang along softly with whoever was bellowing praise to Christ. There's just something comforting about a man who can sing.

One of my earliest memories is of my maternal grandfather, who used to walk around their grand old house crooning the blues. When PaPa wasn't singing, he whistled marvelously. He tried to teach me how to whistle once, to no avail. Soon thereafter, my grandmother and my mother had a falling out and I never saw my grandparents again. I asked my mother if I could go see PaPa once.

"No. He and Granny are no longer a part of our lives. He's not your *real* grandfather anyway."

"Oh." Her statement led me to one that I'd been asking since the first time I saw *Good Times* on television. "Momma, who's my real daddy?"

She grabbed the section of hair she was combing and yanked my head to the side. "Your don't have a daddy. You've got me, and I'm good enough."

Despite the pain coursing through my scalp, I pressed, "Doesn't everybody have a daddy?"

She sighed and (thankfully) eased up on my do. "No, Tori, not everyone has a daddy. I didn't have a real one, and neither do you. You're a momma's girl right now. But I'll find you another daddy soon."

Years later, she told me Mr. James would be my daddy.

He was more like a custodian than a father figure. My mother never did tell me who my biological father was. I tried an Internet search in later years, but without her help, I couldn't proceed. By that time, my grandmother was dead, so the buck stopped there.

I finally figured whoever he was, if he didn't care enough about me to find me, I didn't want to know him. He'd only add to the stack of disappointments in my life.

Starbucks came into view much sooner with Jacob behind the wheel. He nabbed the front parking spot, helped me out of the car, and even opened the door for me. It was almost too much chivalry, but I had to remember: Jacob was probably born, and definitely raised, in Bayford.

The distinct aroma of coffee beans wafted through the air, a barista whipped up a Caffè Latte. *Ahh, the sounds and smells of civilization.* The house was nearly packed, so I quickly claimed one of the few empty tables with my laptop case. Jacob and I got in line to order food.

"What do you like?" I asked.

He waved me off. "Nothing. I don't drink coffee."

"Hmm." I studied the menu. "Why don't you try a Strawberries and Crème Frappuccino? My . . . friend drinks those." *Good Lord, I almost mentioned Kevin.*

"What's the taste?"

"Kinda reminds you of a milkshake."

"Cool."

Jacob paid for both drinks and led the way back to the seat I'd staked.

Time to get to business. "I hope you don't mind, I really do have a lot of work to do."

"No problem." Jacob held his palms toward me. "I'm only here to accompany you. But I am gonna run back to the car and get some things I need to cover, too."

When our drinks became available, Jacob thanked me profusely for recommending the frappuccino. "This drink is anointed," he remarked in a most holy tone.

I giggled like DeAndre.

For the next hour, we worked in isolation. Me with my laptop, Jacob with the Bible, a pen, and a spiral.

I couldn't make heads or tails of Lexa's keyword search information. Hadn't she factored in global competition? This girl was way off track. I checked my phone for the time. 10:42. If she was half the workaholic she projected herself to be, she should still be in front of her screen, too.

"Hello?"

"Hi, Lexa, it's Tori. Did I wake you?"

"No, I'm up. Glad you called. Have you had a chance to review the data?"

"Yeah, there's no way we're to hit the numbers we need with these terms unless we bid much higher, and that would take us over the budget." I went on to explain exactly how she should refine the keywords, get with Alex in research and have him run another report with different parameters, and go from there.

"Do I have to go to Alex?"

Duh? "Yes. He knows back-end research. It's going to take a little while for him to pull it all together, but we don't need to go any further without the numbers to back us."

"Ugh. Time is money. And Alex talks too much," she balked. "I don't want the office thinking I don't know what I'm doing."

You don't. "You gotta do what you've gotta do, Lexa."

"Thanks, Tori. You're a godsend."

Of course, she'd never say those words to me within hearing distance of our team. "Good night."

"Hey, when are you coming back into the office?"

"I don't know. Why?"

She clicked her teeth. "Just asking."

"You need me for something? Has Preston said anything?"

"No, no. Just . . . stay put. No worries."

I was tired of playing games with Lexa. "Look, if there's something going on that I need to know about, I'd really appreciate a heads-up."

Jacob glanced up at me for a moment.

Lexa gushed, "It's not rocket science, Tori, and Preston might not realize it yet, but you need to be *at* your job in this industry. I mean, I've had to wait a whole day for a response from you about this account. I think you know how big this is for me, for everyone at NetMarketing. We're trying to take this company to another level, and you're not here. You don't even reply to e-mails in a timely manner."

"I already told *Preston,* who was my boss the last time I checked, that I'm in a small town where there's no signal except—"

"*Not* my problem."

My lips curled with disgust. "This entire Inner-G account fiasco is your problem, Lexa. You should have done your homework and planned this whole movement better. Doesn't make sense to take on a huge client if you don't have the resources to make the campaign work."

"Are you trying to sabotage me?" she accused.

"No. I'm trying to get you to slow down and go to the drawing board with this client. You can't use the same tactics with Inner-G that you use with, say, P-T-C Books. It's a totally different market, a totally different consumer you're trying to reach. You're going to need help—"

"I *have* help. I have *you,* if you'd ever come to work."

She cut me off one time too many. "Listen, I am here to assist you, *not* lead this account. If you want to do your job right, you're going to have to start from scratch. I don't know what you've promised the people at Inner-G already, but you cannot proceed without backing up first. That's all there is to it. Good night, Lexa."

She disconnected without another word. I slapped my phone onto the table and ran my fingers through the nape of my fro.

"Sounded like a heated conversation," Jacob commented.

I released a prolonged exhale. "Just work as usual. I don't know how much longer I can keep up with everything."

Jacob's probing gaze made me uneasy. "What?" I asked.

"Your entire facial expression morphed during your business chat," he said.

Suddenly, the muscles in my face screamed from overuse. I intentionally relaxed them. "Is that better?"

"Much better. Does your job always make you so uptight?"

"Not usually. Just lately, since I've been telecommuting, there's added stress from my coworkers. I thought working away from the office would be heaven—and maybe it would be if I weren't in Bayford. But here I am at Starbucks, hoping I can haul my share of the load before the baristas start blinking the lights."

He nodded.

"Doesn't everyone feel pressure from their job now and then?"

"I suppose so," he acquiesced. "But there's a difference between pressure and stress. I see stress written all over your face, your eyes, your neck." He scooted my laptop aside, creating an open space between us. "Here. You need a hand massage."

"A *hand* massage?"

He winked. "Ancient Egyptian practice."

Without question, I complied. Jacob Carter Jr. asked for my hands. If only the girls from Bayford High could see me now.

"You right-handed?"

I affirmed using my head, afraid my voice had taken flight.

He rubbed the back of my dominant hand, then turned it over and began kneading my palm with his thumbs. Starting at the base of each finger, pressing warm lines as he worked his way up to my wrist. Then he started his movements higher on each finger, working from the nails downward. He finished the massage with an upward rubbing motion, which sent heat racing from my hands straight up my arms. *Am I sweating?*

"You want me to do the other hand?"

I swear, a drop of spit was almost about to fall from my lips. Quickly, I drew in my breath. "Yeah. Sure."

He repeated the heavenly process, giving the left hand its fair share of attention. "Feel better?"

My pulse slammed in my ears now. "Mmm hmmm." Not quite sure if his massage had the intended effect on me. Sure, I was relaxed, but I was also . . . shall we say . . . happy to be touched.

He's a preacher, Tori. Stop it!

Flickering lights brought my therapy session to an official end.

"Guess we'd better get out of here." Jacob slammed his spiral shut as I collected my belongings—and myself.

His gentlemanly acts still punctuated our transition. I couldn't help but ruin the moment by thinking of Kevin.

Were we still together? Was I cheating on him? *I haven't done anything.*

I'm sure my body was tired, but being in Jacob's presence energized me. Smelling him, hearing him, listening to him talk about his involvement with the interdenominational pastors' alliance. "The body of Christ has been segregated too long. It's time we came together."

His comment had me reflecting on Cassandra's viewpoint on hiring Virgie, which had proven somewhat true. I'd seen a couple of customers wait just shy of the counter until they saw Cassandra approach, then they'd rush forward to order sliced meats before Virgie had an opportunity to take the request.

"I agree with you, Jacob. People need to stop with all these stereotypes."

We floated on back to Bayford with few words between us. Gospel music, songs of eternal love and peace, encased the mood.

"Whose album is this?" I asked upon return.

"The new Myron Williams. Want mine? I'll get myself another one next time I'm online."

I suggested, "I can just burn a copy and give you back the original."

He winced slightly. "No, I'll get another one. You keep this." He ejected the disc and carefully handed it to me.

I paused, wondering what had just transpired. "You don't duplicate CDs?"

"Naa."

Awww, man. Just when I thought we might have some common ground. "Jacob, *everybody* copies music."

"I don't."

"It's the American way," I argued. *Does he have to do everything by the Good Book?*

He made his case. "I know if I produced a CD, I wouldn't want anyone making unauthorized copies of my work."

"So, this is a Karma thing to you?"

"Some people call it Karma, I call it sowing and reaping." He paused. "I treat people right, and I expect them to treat me right, too."

Guilt crept up my spine. I wondered if Jacob would have even given me the time of day if he'd known I was living with Kevin.

Jacob walked me to Aunt Dottie's porch. The sounds of crickets chirping and dogs barking in the distance surrounded us now. Back to the country.

"Thanks," he said as we ascended the ramp.

"For what? Shouldn't this be the other way around?"

"For letting me be me," he testified.

"Who else would you be?"

"Assistant Pastor Carter. Little Jacob Junior. Who or whatever people here have pegged me to be. It's nice to spend time with someone who just thinks of me as Jacob."

"That makes two of us. I'm glad to be around someone who doesn't remember me as the pregnant girl," I admitted.

He made a clicking sound with his cheek. "I have a confession to make."

Worst-case scenarios flitted through my mind: he's engaged, he's dying, he's gay. Hey—stranger things have happened in the movies.

"When you first moved to Bayford, I had a huge crush on you." A coy grin replaced his confident air. "You were quiet, pretty—without a bunch of makeup. Obviously smart, because every time I checked out the honor roll, your name was there."

I stood in amazement.

"When I told my parents that I was going to ask you to the junior prom, they told me I was crazy. Said it wouldn't look good for the pastor's son to take a fast girl to the dance. They told me I should go with someone raised in the church who knew right from wrong."

He motioned for me to move over to the swing so we could sit. Jacob pushed us off and the rickety hinges hummed a smooth, unhurried tune.

He continued, "So I went to the prom with Shonda Rhymes, and we actually did everything it takes to make a baby. Out of rebellion, you know."

"T-M-I, Jacob."

"I'm sorry. I just remember thinking to myself, how is Shonda different from Tori, except Shonda's loud and mean and happened to be a deacon's daughter? The hypocrisy of the situation bothered me for a long time."

"Hmmm." How was I supposed to respond?

"Anyway, life goes on. And sometimes we're blessed with a second chance."

"Jacob, I'm sure you've had *lots* of chances with *lots* of women." He was not about to convince me he'd been pining for me all these years, not with all that fineness dripping off his body.

"Not really," he denied. "I've been busy. Working, keeping my father's church above water, juggling life's responsibilities."

I slapped his back. "Sounds like we're both on the same treadmill."

"I like my treadmill, but I wouldn't mind slowing it down a notch, you know?"

Slowing down wasn't in my personal encyclopedia. "Why would anyone want to slow down? I mean, life's too short to spend it"—*in Bayford*—"on turtle speed."

"I think the reverse is true," he countered me. "You can speed through life so quickly until it becomes nothing more than a big blur. And at the end, maybe on your deathbed, you look back and realize you blew past everything that mattered."

The swing's rhythm, slow and steady, seemed to undergird Jacob's illustration, reminding me of why I'd returned to Bayford in the first place. Aunt Dottie was here. Love was here, even if this town moved on the lowest setting. Most importantly, this was where I first believed.

"You remember when we used to have youth night?" I pondered.

"Every fourth Friday night," he recalled. "How could I forget?"

"When I started coming to the group, Mother Ash made the girls and boys sit on separate rows. You remember that, too?"

"Yeah. I'm sorry. I should have said something," he apologized.

"Oh, no. I was glad she split us up. I would have been too nervous to sit next to you."

His eyes, barely visible now, still bore a twinkle from the moon's light. "A little confession of your own?"

"Yes, I liked you, too, but I knew you were off limits. The only boys who expressed any interest in me were the ones who figured I'd be easy, given my background."

"I didn't think you'd be easy. I don't think you're easy *now*." He counted off on his fingers. "I have to hang out at the church hoping you'll need the tower signal. Gotta come up to your job and buy some lunch meat I don't even need. Had to practically invite myself to Starbucks so I could spend time with you. I mean, come on! I've been trying to make up for lost time here."

"You've been doing all that for me?"

He smirked. "Kind of. I don't want to miss a second chance at getting to know you. Especially not now that I know we're both moving in the same direction, spiritually."

A heavy puff of air escaped my lungs. Once again, the male/female roles seemed flip-flopped. "I'm terribly flattered, Jacob, but don't think I'm ready for anything . . . serious right now."

He gave the baseball signal for "safe" with his hands. "No worries, no pressure. If nothing else, I'd like to stay in touch with you about Aunt Dottie and DeAndre. I could be your ears and eyes in Bayford."

"That would be a great relief." I let my hand rest on his shoulder.

He stood, jolting the swing's rhythm. "I'd better be going."

Once again, he grabbed my hand. This time to pull me up from the swing.

"Thanks for everything, Jacob."

His embrace was polite, yet tentative. "Good night, Tori."

"Night."

Chapter 18

Another week passed before Aunt Dottie was able to speak her first post-stroke words. She gave a written testimony at church the following Sunday. I stood next to her and read her script aloud. Halfway through the letter, my voice wavered. Though I spoke on Aunt Dottie's behalf, the truth of her message hit me.

"No matter what you think or how things look, God's plan is *always* the best way and His love is *always* true. *Always* there for you."

I passed the microphone back to Senior Pastor Carter and let the church carry on with worship while I took my seat, shaking with emotion. DeAndre draped an arm across my back and whispered into my ear, between sniffles, "It's all right, Cousin Tori. People cry in church all the time."

Despite the past week's after-school detention for throwing a ketchup packet across the lunchroom, DeAndre won the prize for compassion.

My Bayford weekdays now consisted of two miles on the treadmill, getting DeAndre out of the house, then running to the church to hear/view voice/e-mail messages. I was usually at Dottie's for opening, then back to the house to get the real Dottie ready for either physical or speech therapy. Library by noon, working until time to meet DeAndre after school. Help him with homework, get him settled. Back to Dottie's to work until close. Starbucks if the library was closed or if I had more than an hour's worth of online duties to tackle. The final item on my agenda, if fatigue hadn't completely won out, was to dab oil on my hair and braid it into five cornrows for a softer texture the next morning.

I'd actually gotten quite good at streamlining and prioritizing, thanks to this hectic schedule. No more junk e-mail lists, and every phone conversation cut straight to the point.

Joenetta might help out. Or not. Just depended on what Sister Meecham brought for dinner.

The only opportunity to sit down and catch my breath came when I read the Bible aloud to Aunt Dottie. She liked to revisit Proverbs eight almost every other night. Several of the verses found their way into my memory bank and resurfaced throughout the day.

Kevin called once that week to ask me if we should keep the housekeeper, since neither of us was really home much.

"Guess not," I conceded. The housekeeper had been my idea.

"Tori, when are you coming back to Houston? We really need to sit down and sort things out."

"You mean as in work things out or, like, figure out who's taking what from the apartment?"

"However you want it."

Why was the ball always in my court? "So, you're fine with whatever I decide?"

"Don't have a choice."

I muttered, "Do you even care?"

"Of course I care. What kind of question is that? You're the one who's putting us through all these changes, remember?"

He had a point. "I'll try to come home in the next few weeks. What's your schedule like?"

Kevin rambled through an impossibly full agenda that crisscrossed the country. New York, Arizona, Indiana.

"How are we supposed to spend any time together with you traveling so much?"

He chortled. "The same way we've always done it, babe."

I wondered if this was how we'd do it if we ever got married. Had kids. "Just give me a few solid dates when you're home for at least forty-eight hours."

We decided on the following week, which meant I'd have to find someone to take Aunt Dottie and DeAndre to church Wednesday night. Going back to Houston wasn't so easy anymore.

I texted Lexa to let her know I'd be in the office as early as Tuesday afternoon so we could have two glorious days of sit-down meetings to help her get Inner-G afloat. The more I looked at the account, the more I realized we'd need to involve Preston in some serious renegotiation if we planned to satisfy this client. The budget Lexa projected, and Inner-G had agreed to in their package, simply wasn't enough to produce the outcome she'd all but guaranteed.

As far as I was concerned, the only thing we needed to discuss the following week was how *she* was going to tell Preston that he needed to go to bat for us.

*   *   *

Cassandra and Virgie were all too willing to work more hours at Dottie's while I was out of town. For Cassandra, this meant time and a half.

"Hey, sooky-sooky now. Just in time for E-, E-, E-aster Sunday." She scratched on an imaginary turntable. "Gonna get some extra P-, P-, Peeps!"

"No, no, no," I bellowed while wiping down the countertops nearest the deli case. "You are not going to kill me with all these sound effects!"

"I put up with her all day long, Miss Tori." Elgin teased as he switched off the neon sign, silencing the electric buzzing sound, which never registered until he disconnected power.

"Hey—I keep it exciting in here," Cassandra boasted.

"That's for sure," Virgie agreed. "But Joenetta—she blows the top off."

Cassandra threw a visual dagger at Virgie, who immediately put a hand over her own mouth.

"What's going on with Joenetta?"

Virgie mouthed "sorry" to Cassandra.

"It's okay. Might as well clear the air."

"What?" I bugged.

Cassandra smacked her lips. "We cut her off."

"Okay . . . ?"

"You remember I told you I know how, when, and what people in Bayford buy?"

"Yeah."

"Well, Joenetta buys everything—never."

I closed my eyes. "You're not making sense."

"She doesn't pay for things. She comes in, she gets what she wants, she leaves without paying. 'Course she only does it when you're not here."

"How long has she been using her five-finger discount?"

Elgin piped up. "She's *always* thought her sister owed her something."

"Did Aunt Dottie let her take things from the store before now?"

Cassandra rolled her eyes. "You know, every once in a while Joenetta'll come in and say she forgot her purse at home, or she'll pay next week when she gets her SSI. She never pays. So, in a way, Aunt Dottie puts up with it, but not like *this*. She's taking twenty-five or thirty dollars worth of groceries out of the store every other day. We're about to be in competition with Walmart. We can't be tiffy-tiffyin' no more with Joenetta."

From the context, "tiffy-tiffyin'" meant providing hookups.

"Miss Tori, I've seen Aunt Dottie help plenty people who couldn't afford to buy food. You know how big her heart is." Elgin got no objections. "But everybody who's able, family included, ought to pay for what they get. Even Aunt Dottie's mother, when she was alive, paid for what she got here. I saw that with my own eyes. Joenetta's downright taking advantage of Aunt Dottie's sickness."

I shouldn't have been surprised by any of this. Nothing could be put past Joenetta. Must be why she was avoiding me, hoping I wouldn't confront her about pilfering inventory.

"The other day, I saw her taking items for her friends, too," Virgie contributed, shifting her weight nervously. "She came with a carload of people. They all walked around the store with her, putting things in her basket. Then she led them to the door without even looking at the cash register. When I tried to stop them, Joenetta cussed me like a drunken sailor, called me everything but a child of God. Told me I had no business working in here anyway on accounta I'm white."

"I'm so sorry, Virgie." I apologized on behalf of the Lester family, I supposed.

Cassandra wiped her forehead. "So that's why we cut Joenetta off, Tori. Something had to be done."

No arguments from me. Aunt Dottie, on the other hand, might feel differently. I zipped the dolphin pendant across my necklace a few times. "Well, she *is* Aunt Dottie's sister, and Aunt Dottie *did* know that Joenetta wasn't paying for some things. I need to tell her what's going on. I mean, the name of the store *is* Dottie's."

"Uh," Cassandra grunted, "the new name of the store will be Brokie's if Joenetta has her way while Aunt Dottie's recovering."

Couldn't help but giggle, which actually eased the tension mounting in this small, frame-house store. "Good job, Cassandra. That was a profitable executive decision."

She saluted. "Thank you."

Elgin and Virgie finished their routines and said their good-byes while Cassandra and I stayed behind to run tape and balance the drawer.

"Do you think Aunt Dottie would be angry if she knew what Joenetta was doing?" I asked Cassandra.

She finished counting the stack of fives first. "I don't think she'd be angry. Hurt maybe a teench, but she's known her sister all their lives. No biggie."

"Yeah, you're right."

"Hey!" Cassandra nearly scared me out of my skin.

"What?"

"Your cell phone working now?"

"Yeah, when I'm at the church."

"Nuh uh. Now. Here." She stomped the floor. "That Walmart put up a snooty-pooty power tower. There's a man up at the Dairy Queen selling cellular phones now. I'm gonna get me one next week, if it doesn't cost an arm and leg, which it obviously doesn't since Rokeshia got one and—"

"Cassandra, stop. Are you kidding me?"

"I'm serious as a preacher trying to hide from the cameras in Las Vegas."

Never mind her analogy. I reached beneath the counter and extracted my mobile device from the front pocket of my purse. Pressed the power icon, bouncing on the balls of my feet. Could this be true?

A moment later, three—*three!*—lighted bars. Quickly, I sent a call through to the first contact on my list. "It's ringing! It's ringing!"

Still no guarantees unless someone answered.

"Applebee's. Would you like to place a to-go order?"

"Oh my gosh! Yes!"

"Okay, what would you like?"

"No. I'm sorry, no. Bye." I ended the call. "Yes! This is awesome, Cassandra. Thank you so much for telling me."

I waltzed around the store with my cell phone for a partner, singing "The hills are alive with the sound of cell phones." Neither Cassandra nor I knew all the words to the song. We improvised with more gobbledygook.

"Thank God I won't have to go to the church anymore to make phone calls," I declared.

Cassandra lowered her forehead and feigned a European accent. "I rather thought you enjoyed a bit of dilly-dallying at the temple with Sir Jacob."

"How'd you know?"

"My dear, this is a very small town."

Stunned, I could only rub my tongue across my teeth. "For the record, I went to the church on business."

"I see, my love, I see." She dragged the apron over her head, ruffling the back of her hair. Cassandra didn't bother to fix it. "Well, taa-taa."

I put a hand on her arm. "Wait! You can't just leave. When . . . I mean, what did you hear?"

Foreign accent intact, she demurred, "A true lady never repeats gossip."

"Cassandra, you are not British. This is Bayford. I wanna know the Bayford juice."

She gushed, "He got a thang for you, girl."

Chapter 19

Now that I had a signal and could be reached at a moment's notice, I felt more comfortable leaving Aunt Dottie alone for longer periods. Her left arm could pick up a phone and dial out. Even though she probably couldn't tell me what she needed, I would know to come home.

I instructed DeAndre to call me when he got off the bus every day. He read the therapists' notes to me (if they weren't written in cursive) and made sure Aunt Dottie was comfortable. He found it thoroughly fascinating to know I was communicating with him wirelessly.

"Where are you, Cousin Tori?"

"I'm at the library."

"*Then* where are you going?"

"Back to the store, probably."

"Oh, can you bring me some Sprees?" As though this wasn't the main point of our conversation.

"Only if you finish your homework and your chores before I get home."

"Yes, ma'am. And get the sour Sprees, all right?"

I nearly broke my neck trying to get to the box of sour

Sprees in the back storage room. When I got home later, the beam across DeAndre's face compensated for near-death teetering.

"Thank you, Cousin Tori."

I gave Jacob my number under the premise of him being my eyes and ears. He called me later that week, too, on his own superficial grounds. "Baseball practice starts Tuesday. We'd love to see DeAndre there."

Just when I'd gotten one area of my life simplified, I was adding Little League sports? "What time?"

Jacob must have heard the distress in my voice. "Six—but I can pick him up, along with several other boys, in the church van. Bring him home, too, if need be."

"That would be really great, Jacob. I'm going back to Houston."

"Um"—panic seeped through his voice—"how long will you be gone?"

"Just a few days."

"Oh, okay. I thought you were out of here, homegirl," he chided.

"Not quite."

"Will you be back in time for Wednesday service?"

What's with all these questions? "Maybe. You got something special going on?"

"No. I was hoping we could do another Starbucks run. You got me fiending for a grande frappuccino."

Truth be told, the Starbucks concoctions didn't have anything on the memory of that hand massage. I'd drive to L.A. and back for a second appointment. "I can't promise I'll be here when church starts—just depends on traffic coming out of Houston. But I should definitely be back before you dismiss."

"Hey"—he lowered his tone—"don't worry about

DeAndre and Aunt Dottie while you're gone. I'll look out for 'em."

"Thanks, Jacob."

The last time I drove into Houston, I'd felt like I was coming home. Now, the landmarks leading back to the city struck me differently. Kind of like when you return from a weeklong vacation. Feels like you're rediscovering your own house.

Anxiety followed me into the building, but one of the scriptures I'd been reading to Aunt Dottie sprang up in defense. "God's peace guards my heart and mind." Philippians 4:7. I don't think it had ever occurred to me before then how helpful it was to have God's word handy in my heart.

"Hey, babe." Kevin met me at the door and relieved me of my overnight bag.

"Hey."

He leaned in for a kiss. I pulled back, surprised. "What's that for?"

"Because I'm glad to see you," he explained, half annoyed. He tried again.

I blocked him with an index finger. "Wait. I thought we were supposed to be talking."

"May I speak first?" he asked.

"Give me a second to . . . unwind, okay?"

"Fair enough."

Our place wasn't quite as fresh as when the housekeeper came regularly. Quite stale, actually, since there'd been no life inside. I set my purse on the nightstand, my work case on the bed.

I slipped my knees onto the floor, arranging myself in classic prayer position. Maybe God would know what to do about all this. All through Proverbs, He harped on asking Him for help. No time like the present.

God, thank You for a safe trip back, but that's not really what I want to talk about. You already knew, though, so here it goes: what do I do about Kevin?

"Oh my God. Are you praying?" Kevin nearly shouted at the doorway.

Glancing up, I nodded.

"Wow." He exited the room in shock.

Sorry about that, God. Anyway, Kevin and I have been together for a while, but I don't know where things are supposed to go from here. Please show me exactly what to do.

I'm also not sure about the next step at NetMarketing. I guess I just don't know what to do with my life in general, so I'm asking for Your wisdom and help because You said You'd guide me if I asked. Aunt Dottie's always telling me about Your faithfulness, and I see what You've done in her life. I believe You can bless my life, too.

Amen.

I waited, perfectly still, for a while, hoping all the answers would miraculously pop into my head. Nothing.

What *did* appear was a string of doubt: *What makes you think He's going to answer you? He's not concerned about you. You just started going to church again a few Sundays ago. Who do you think you are, anyway—Aunt Dottie?*

Fear relentlessly kicked me about the room as I fiddled around for a while, delaying the inevitable. Rebuttal came in the form of music. One of Mount Pisgah's most frequent congregational songs landed squarely on my lips. "Call on Jesus. He will answer prayer."

A text from Lexa gave another reprieve. When will u be in?

I replied: an hour

I flipped outfits and stuffed my feet into a pair of pumps. Kevin, slumped on the couch watching ESPN, straightened his posture when I entered the living area. I sat next to him. Maybe *he* had a proper resolution. "I'm listening."

"Babe, I miss you. I love you, I need you. I love the way things were. Why do we have to change everything? You had your health scare, but it's over now. Your aunt's getting better . . . right?" His eyes pleaded for the best of both worlds—comfort without allegiance.

An internal news flash scrolled across my spirit: *this is the first time Kevin has asked about Aunt Dottie.* Quickly, I scrambled through my memory bank to verify. Negative. Now I could throw this tidbit of information on the table. "You've never asked about her before now."

"Who?"

"My aunt."

He shrugged. "I . . . I just assumed her health was improving."

"Does it matter to you that I love her? That she's the closest thing to family I have left on earth?"

Blankness covered his face. "I mean, we're not into each other's families. Or politics or religion—although I'm not so sure about you right now. No matter, that's what makes us so great. We don't argue, there's no drama. There's no pressure here. Don't rock the boat, Tori."

No words came to mind. Thumbs twiddled. Ankles crossed twice. Waiting for the right answer certainly made me look stupid.

"So, what do you have to say?" Kevin pressed.

"Nothing right now."

"You have to say *something.*"

Maybe if I'd been trying really hard to have my own

way, I could have met his demand by either agreeing with him or issuing his walking papers. Neither of those options seemed appropriate. "I can't respond yet."

The muscles in his jaw twitched as wrinkles puckered his brow. "I made a pit stop in Houston so we could have this discussion face-to-face, remember?"

"I'm sorry, Kevin. I'm not trying to be contrary. I *really* don't know what to say yet. What do you want me to do—pull the answer out of a hat?"

Anger settled over his features. "I should have caught the flight to Arizona."

I swear, Kevin looked like he wanted to spit on me, so I left.

During the drive to work my mind streamed a constant replay of our conversation. Or was that an argument? In all the time we'd been dating, this was as close to a real clash as Kevin and I had ever come. I knew Kevin thrived on competition—had to in his line of work. But he wasn't confrontational. He'd make five phone calls to maneuver people's actions before he'd tackle a person head-on. "My approach is far more diplomatic," he'd say.

Though I still wasn't sure where to go with the relationship, Kevin made a serious point. We were drama-free. I'd seen people fight like cats and dogs on *Divorce Court* over how to fry okra. I'd even witnessed Mr. James throwing soft objects—wadded paper or clothes—at my mother in the midst of heated disputes. They used to scare me, actually. I never could figure out how they patched up their quarrels in time for city hall meetings.

Nevertheless, I wasn't my mother and Kevin wasn't Mr. James . . . *or is he?* His little temper tantrum sure linked him with Mr. James, throwing fits when the world (or my mother) refused to follow his master plan.

So, what's Kevin's agenda? As far as I could tell, he

didn't have one, other than work. Neither did I, until after the surgery. I couldn't put all the blame on Kevin.

Our solution would have to wait until after today's business with NetMarketing. I shook my head clear of Kevin, put on my game face, and hoisted my good-to-see-you-again grin in place for the office. Several new faces peppered the department, as Preston had promised.

My cubicle, if that's what they still called it, had apparently been converted to mini-storage. *Okay?* Six boxes of copy paper, a broken chair, a small file cabinet, and a pile of unreturned U.S. Postal Service bins occupied what used to be called Tori Henderson's work space.

"Oh, Tori, I had no idea you'd be back today. Sorry about your office," Jacquelyn acknowledged. "With all the new hires, we had to move things around. I haven't had time to send in the request to have these things stored off site, but don't you worry. I'll get this out of your way soon. Um, are you back for good?"

Sometimes a bad attitude is just an inch away. Back or not, my office wasn't Storage Depot. *Then again, a certain someone did use it as a restroom. . . .*

Laughing to myself, I answered Jacquelyn's question. "No worries. I'm only here for a few days. I'll try to call you a day or two before I need the area cleared."

Save all the hostility for Lexa.

Relief flattened Jacquelyn's features. "Okay. Thanks, Tori. And by the way"—she took a step toward me, closing the gap between us—"Preston's just about figured out we bit off more than we could chew with Inner-G, and Lexa's looking to blame somebody."

"Would that somebody be me?"

"Bingo."

"Great. Thanks for the heads-up."

"Any time."

Preston and Lexa were waiting for me in the conference room. She certainly looked the part of a competent marketer. Reading glasses, hair pulled back into a working, messy ponytail. Reminded me of how political consultants ramped up Sarah Palin to gain acceptance with the GOP.

Stacks of charts and reports covered the oblong cherry-wood table, making the room look more like Santa's workshop the night before Christmas.

"Hello." I tried a cheerful approach.

Preston's mouth tightened. He checked his watch. "We were expecting you hours ago."

"I sent Lexa a text saying I'd be in this afternoon."

Lexa lifted her phone from the table and scarcely glanced at the screen. "I didn't get that message."

"I certainly sent it. I can show you—"

She stammered, "Well, you're here now. All we can do is move forward."

I gave her the old I-know-you-know-I-know-you're-lying glower.

"Did you bring the numbers I asked you to research?" she prodded on.

"Yes. I have them." I dealt the manila files like cards, one for each of us.

Preston opened his and took a deep, calming breath. "This is good information," he complimented. After a battery of questions, he and I talked strategy based on data for the next half hour. Lexa tried to interject with her feelings, but Preston shot her down every time.

"What market research do you have to support your opinion?" he'd ask.

She didn't.

"Has our competition tried this strategy already, and if so, what was their success rate?" he wanted to know.

She had no clue. Just shooting from the hip.

"I know you're incredibly talented and creative, Lexa, but if Tori's numbers don't back your proposals, I won't approve them. This isn't one of those if-you-build-it-they-will-come accounts. Don't build it unless you *know* they will come."

She blasted, "I don't have a crystal ball, Preston."

"But you do have data from Tori and even Alex. Why do you think I put you on a team with Tori in the first place?"

She passed the buck. "If Tori would come to work, maybe we'd have the opportunity to consult with each other."

Preston turned the tables. "Tori, would you say your performance has suffered since you began telecommuting?"

I nodded slightly. "Yes, I'd say so, but only because there's an adjustment period for every virtual employee." No need to bring up the whole no phone signal thing. Moot point, currently.

"I'd be glad to produce research proving my line of reasoning." This addendum, of course, directed at Lexa.

Her bratty "ha-ha" must have gotten under Preston's skin. He grabbed his folder and dismissed himself. "I'll leave you two to work out the rest. Tori, can you give me an update next week?"

"Glad to."

"Looks like I'm going to have to meet with Inner-G's executives again soon," he said.

"No problem," I assured him. "We'll make sure you have empirical backup."

I resisted the urge to bury my thumbs in my ears, wiggle my fingers, and stick out my tongue, taunting "I'm better than you are from hundreds of miles away!" Instead, I attempted to steer our remaining time back to the facts.

"So, I'll get busy working on our Facebook—"

Lexa railed, slamming a well-manicured hand on the table, "You are *not* going to take this account from me." She stormed out, leaving me in total confusion. *Father, what is wrong with this girl?*

Then Lexa number two entered. Hair dangling free of its clasp, reading glasses tucked in her pocket. "Let's get started."

"Whatever. And for the record, let me tell you something: I don't want your job. I have well-established clients of my own whose campaigns aren't running at optimum success because I spend half my day trying to return calls and e-mail messages from you."

Red splotches crawled up her neck as she attempted to lead our discussion. Her hands shook so badly, she couldn't hold up a sheet of paper between us, had to lay it on the table so we could see the numbers clearly. Part of me felt sorry for her. I know what it's like to be second-guessed. The difference between Lexa and me, however, was her denial of facts. She'd been second-guessed because her first guess was wrong. She would have been better off throwing up the white flag so Preston and the rest of the team could intervene.

Alas, I was in no position to tell her all this. She was the boss of me on this account, remember?

We worked well past five o'clock. I got into my zone and forgot all about Lexa's attitude. The problem-solving groove felt good. Familiar. In this world, I knew all the answers.

Too bad the wisdom train fizzled out when I got back to the apartment with Kevin. "Babe," he immediately started upon my arrival home, "I want you to know how much I love you." My eyes scanned the dining room. He'd prepared a hot, healthy dinner for us both—turkey spaghetti with steamed broccoli. Kevin's idea of a sugar splurge, fruit pizza, would top off our meal.

"Looks nice," I had to admit.

He pulled out my chair and waited until I was comfortably seated before presenting me with a plateful of his masterpiece. He filled both our wineglasses, then he announced a toast. "To us."

Couldn't leave a brother hanging, so I clinked his glass and added to the toast. "To the life fate has planned for us."

I didn't believe in fate, but I knew Kevin wasn't too big on God. Or Jesus, for that matter. Bringing up the Holy Spirit was out of the question. "The universe" was as close as Kevin ventured toward any kind of spiritual talk.

He drank, peering at me above the rim of his flute. His withering stare didn't phase me, however. I saw clear through him, as though his daddy made Saran Wrap. This wasn't about me, him, or us. It was about sex. *Watch*.

"So, what are your plans tonight?" I asked.

"Spending time with you."

My cell phone's all-encompassing genius button came in quite handy. "Find AMC theater, Houston, Texas."

"What are you doing?"

"Finding a movie for us."

He rubbed a foot against my leg. "Let's produce our own movie tonight."

As if. "No can do."

"Why not?"

"Mother nature's in the house."

The flicker in his eyes flatlined. He sucked turkey from between his teeth. "So much for makeup sex."

We both climbed into bed a little before ten, early by our standards. He monopolized the remote control, setting the television on a sports channel to play through the night.

I turned my back to him and studied the knickknacks resting on my nightstand. Among them, a quaint nativity scene that I failed to store every year. Joseph, Mary, and baby Jesus.

I wondered if Kevin would be the kind of husband who'd put up Christmas lights around the house every year. What kind of wife or mom would I be? I couldn't see myself making angel-shaped chocolate chip cookies, leaving them out for Santa. Shoot, I could barely hold the tooth fairy gig together at this point.

"Tori." I nearly jumped at his voice.

"Yeah."

He lowered the television's volume. "I do care about you."

"I know." In his own special, give-me-my-space kind of way, I'm sure he did.

"So what do you want from me?" he asked.

"I want everything."

"Define everything."

"Everything a woman wants from a man."

Moments later, a sports announcer's voice blared through the speakers again.

Chapter 20

By Wednesday afternoon, I still didn't know what to tell Kevin. He moped around the apartment, dishing out the noisiest silent treatment on record. He slammed doors and cabinets, cursed under his breath when he ripped the last paper towel from the holder. Reminded me of DeAndre, really, and prompted me to give my little cousin a call.

"Lester residence," he answered, as I'd trained him.

"Hello, DeAndre. How are you?"

"Cousin Tori!" he squealed. "When are you coming home?"

I laughed to myself. He thought Bayford was home for me. "Tonight."

"Yes!" he hissed.

"How was school today?"

"I got a hundred on my spelling test."

"That's wonderful, DeAndre. I can tell you've been studying." An elective class I got shoved into at the last minute had come in handy. The instructor told us not to praise kids for being inherently "smart" or "pretty," but rather for effort exerted toward accomplishments. Suppose I knew a little something after all.

"And how was baseball practice with Pastor Jacob?"

His tone declined sharply. "It was all right."

"Why just all right?"

DeAndre blew air before answering. "I had to run extra laps because my teacher called the house yesterday."

Hand against my forehead, I prompted, "Keep going."

"'Cause she thinks maybe I'm the one who wrote a bad word on the wall in the bathroom, but it wasn't me," he explained. "I told her, I don't even write like that, all messy and scribble-scrabble."

"So why does she think you did it?"

He reluctantly admitted, "'Cause I was in the restroom without permission."

With the phone held tightly to my ear, I pushed past Kevin to grab a bottle of Gatorade from the refrigerator. He lurched in the opposite direction, dodging elbow-to-elbow contact.

A puff of air escaped my lungs, signaling my disgust.

Back to more serious matters. "Well, DeAndre, I hope you learned a lesson from this. If you had been in the right place, you couldn't have been accused."

"That's the same thing Pastor Jacob said."

"He's right."

DeAndre lamented, "I know."

"So from now on, you stick with your class. Got it?"

"Yes, ma'am."

"How's Aunt Dottie?"

"She's fine, except she makes me read the Bible to her at night and there's a lotta old words I can't read."

I nearly choked on my drink. "Just keep reading to her. What else is up?"

DeAndre gave a detailed account of Aunt Dottie's ins and outs. He said Joenetta had taken Aunt Dottie to the doctor yesterday, as arranged. Then they had come home with a "whole buncha food." Not part of the deal, but I imagine Cassandra let those groceries roll out the door since Joenetta probably paraded Aunt Dottie around the store, wheelchair and all.

"I'm gonna get off the phone now, DeAndre."

"Cousin Tori," he blurted out, "I was thinking about something."

"Yes?"

"My momma's birthday is coming up. I was thinking maybe I could go visit her."

That's not what I was thinking. "We'll see."

"Okay. Bye."

I pressed the red disconnect icon, wondering how on earth I'd gone from a peaceful, ho-hum life to possibly planning a trip to the state penitentiary.

Kevin's shenanigans continued until time came for me to leave. His flight out of Bush Intercontinental Airport would depart only a few hours later, so we found ourselves in the bedroom packing simultaneously.

He grabbed the largest suitcase in the closet first, which left me stuffing every square inch of the intermediate-sized piece and the carry-on. There were several other bags to choose from, mind you, but I guess we both coveted the *good* luggage with intact handles.

Nosiness finally got the best of Kevin. "You're packing almost everything. Are you moving out or what?"

"No. I'm just tired of wearing the same two pairs of jeans."

"So why'd you take the treadmill? Don't they have sidewalks in Breyton?"

"Bayford," I enunciated, "is filled with animals. Loose animals."

"You should call animal control," he suggested.

I answered his question while zipping the front pocket

of the smallest bag. "People in Bayford don't call the city on each other's pets. It's rude. If they have a problem, they talk to their neighbors or they figure out a way around it. Live and let live."

He stopped and faced me, peering down his nose contemptuously. "You owe me an answer. Are you calling it quits?"

"I'm not calling anything until I have an answer."

"From who?"

"From God, Kevin, all right? I'm waiting to hear from God." Can of worms now open.

"Are you some kind of super-Christian now?" He circled index fingers around his ears. "Have they *brainwashed* you? Can't you think for yourself?"

Have to let that one slide this time. "I don't expect you to understand, but that's the way it is."

"So, God is in control of your life now?"

Everything in me stood erect for this lightbulb moment. "Yes. He is."

He looked toward the sky, then down at me. "Let me know when the real Tori Henderson comes back, okay?"

I didn't justify his response.

"And don't drink the red Kool-Aid!" he yelled, slamming the front door behind himself.

Rain slowed my exit from the city, placing me in the parking lot of Mount Pisgah shortly before church dismissed. In the past, I might have considered my arrival perfect timing. The well-explained Word, however, had become a pleasant addition to my Bayford stint. Maybe I could get a personal review later.

As I waited for the congregation's dismissal, my phone's chiming called for attention. I clicked on an ur-

gent e-mail from Lexa—cc'd to Preston—asking about
another report that I failed to produce prior to leaving. I
quickly replied: Lexa, I never received your request for
this report. However, I anticipated the need and I have already asked Alex to configure the statistics for you. Have
a great evening.

I, too, copied Preston. Two can play that game. *Lord,
she's gonna get enough of trying to throw me under the
bus one day.*

The first few churchgoers descended the steps, my cue
to locate my people. DeAndre's little head bobbed diago-
nally as he struggled with Aunt Dottie's bag. Another
church member wheeled her down the ramp. I waved toward DeAndre, but he didn't see me. *Hey, I'm in the country.* "DeAndre!" *I can do this here.*

He scampered toward me, doing his best to keep the
oversized bag in check. I braced myself for his hug. "Hey,
you."

"I'm glad you're here," he said, slinging the purse off
his back and handing it to me. "I don't like carrying no
purse."

"You don't like carrying *a* purse?"

"Nu uh."

I accepted the bag and placed it in the backseat.
Jacob sauntered toward us and took over the task of rout-
ing Aunt Dottie safely in her seat.

"We still on for tonight?" he asked once we'd gotten
my two passengers situated.

"Yep."

DeAndre's ultrainquisitive ears must have caught the
private exchange between Jacob and me. He kept turning
around in the backseat, checking to see if Pastor Jacob
was still following us. "Where are you going with Pastor
Jacob tonight?"

Aunt Dottie looked at me out of the corner of her eye, obviously stifling a grin.

"None of your beeswax."

"Are you going to that place with the coffee?"

"Why?"

Aunt Dottie reached across the center console and gently squeezed my arm. Studying her face didn't quite reveal what she wanted to say. "You all right?" I asked.

She nodded. She stealthily pointed at DeAndre, touched her chest, then directed her finger toward me. *He loves you.*

Reverence for Aunt Dottie's wordless commentary quieted me the rest of the way home. Jacob had perceived this same fondness. What exactly was I supposed to do with the information, though? I was only a temporary character in DeAndre's life. Pretty soon, he'd get back to life with Joenetta. I wished him well.

After I tucked both Aunt Dottie and DeAndre in bed, Jacob escorted me to java heaven again. We ordered the same drinks, occupied the same table. Only this time, I wasn't consumed with work. I'd have the opportunity to swim in Jacob's eyes and soak up his hearty brown skin.

"How was your trip?"

"Productive." I reveled in the soft coolness of my beverage. "How was church?"

"Church is always good. We looked at first Corinthians thirteen tonight—the famous love chapter."

Maybe it was famous to him, but I'd never heard of it. "What's it all about?"

He paraphrased the scripture. "Love is patient, kind, it does not envy, is not proud. Love is not rude, self-seeking, or easily angered, keeps no record of wrongs. The scripture goes on to say love always protects, always trusts, always hopes, always perseveres. Love never fails."

An ache in my chest belied the fact that I spent most of my childhood without love. "Wow. Those are beautiful verses." My lashes couldn't blink fast enough to stave the tears.

"What's wrong?"

I tilted my head backward, forcing my sockets to re-absorb, reabsorb quickly.

He asked again. Woman 101 advised me to deny distress despite obvious signals. Jacob's probing glance, however, would settle for nothing less than the truth.

"I came to Bayford looking for that kind of love, hoping to get it from Aunt Dottie again because I never got it from my mother. But Aunt Dottie . . . she can't even express herself." The reality of her stroke hit me full blast right there in Starbucks, perhaps because I hadn't stopped long enough to let myself feel anything before.

Jacob's eyes brimmed with joy. "Tori, you already *have* the love you're looking for. That kind of love, in chapter thirteen, is the kind of love God has for you. He *is* love. You don't have to travel to Bayford or any place else to know His love."

Truth slowly trickled into my heart, negated by my experiences, my past. Other people's problems, too.

"I pray for a revelation—a Rhema word—on the love of Christ," he professed.

"What's a Rhema word?"

"A word from God through His Holy Spirit within you, just when you need it." Jacob's voice began to take on a pulpit quality. "A Rhema word will put you in re-membrance of a deeper understanding of God's view-point about a specific matter. The Rhema word can always be supported by scripture."

The incident at the apartment with Kevin—when I

recalled the scriptures about guidance—came to mind. "I think I'm already getting those, just not quickly enough."

He opened his palms. "I'm not God, but if you've got something on your mind, I'm a pretty good sounding board."

Not totally likely, since my biggest problem was Kevin. I half accepted his offer, asking him what he thought of DeAndre's suggested field trip to prison.

"Going to visit someone in prison isn't a simple exploit," he explained. "The prisoner has to put you on their visitor's list, then you have to pass a background check—and those were the rules, what fifteen, almost twenty years ago. I can only imagine how much tighter security is now."

Eyes widened, I asked, "And how do you know so much about prison protocol?"

"My uncle got incarcerated for embezzlement when I was in high school, but he wouldn't have gotten so many years if he'd had more money."

"How about he wouldn't have gone to prison in the first place if he hadn't committed the crime?" I countered.

Jacob nodded. "True, true. But our justice system is so skewed by money, it's ridiculous."

How dare he try to make this whole thing about money. One thing Kevin and I always agreed on was the sanctity of people's choices and resulting consequences. "Right is right, wrong is wrong. Right?"

"Yes. But the legal obligation of the justice system is to fairly try each case—not play legal games exhausting the defendant's resources until they have no choice except to plea.

"I mean, one time they were all set for trial. My uncle's lawyers had made arrangements for and flown in all these experts to testify on my uncle's behalf—all on my uncle's tab, of course. When the prosecuting attorney saw my uncle's team was ready to put up a fight, the attorney asked the judge for a stay due to some frivolous technicality. The judge granted the delay for a week. Wasted thousands and thousands of dollars.

"The prosecutors kept playing games until my uncle ran out of money. When he was finally broke and could no longer afford to fly in experts and witnesses, the prosecutors were suddenly ready for trial. He was tried, convicted, and heavily sentenced. That's the way it goes in our courts."

Flabbergasted, I coughed. "Did the judge know how much trouble your uncle's team had gone through to assemble a defense?"

Jacob's nostrils contracted. "Yeah, he knew. He didn't care. Lawyers find loopholes, judges interpret laws however they see fit any given day."

Since O. J., I hadn't really thought much about court cases. I always felt he'd gotten away with murdering his ex-wife and her friend, and his "not guilty" verdict came as a result of shoddy police work rather than financial influence.

Jacob's account of his uncle's incident, however, caused me to reexamine the accused's options, or lack thereof, depending on wealth. I wondered if DeAndre's mother would have landed so much time in prison if she'd been rich. I imagined a lot of things in her life would have been different if she had money. Really, whose wouldn't?

With this change of heart, I asked Jacob if he'd help me get in touch with the Simpsons so we could get the ball rolling toward this prison visit. "I just don't want DeAndre to be distracted, you know? He's more focused in school, now that I'm trying to get him into a routine. Maybe I should wait until school's out to throw in this visit to his mother."

"No worries." He nodded. "I'll get in touch with DeAndre's peeps. And trust that God will work things out so DeAndre will see his mother again at the right time. People talk about how He's never late, but sometimes we have to realize, He's also never early. His timing is exact."

"Thanks. I'll remember that."

Jacob glanced toward the ordering counter. "How are their sandwiches? I'm hungry, actually."

"I hear they're pretty good."

He excused himself and later returned with turkey on wheat, cut down the middle. Watching him unwrap the entrée suddenly reminded me I hadn't eaten for several hours. My eyes must have given me away.

"You want one?" Jacob offered between bites.

Might be too much bread for me to eat the whole thing. "No. But . . . can I have just a little taste of yours?"

He scooted the untouched half across the table. "Here."

"Oh, I can't ask you for *half,*" is what came out of my mouth, though my taste buds said otherwise.

"You know you want to eat this sandwich, Tori," Jacob teased. "It's printed all up in your cheekbones."

Humor and hunger overtook me. I grabbed the sandwich, laughing unashamedly. "How do you always know what's going on in my head?"

"I don't," he refuted. "But I know hungry when I see it."

I asked him if he'd ever watched the television show *Lie to Me.* "It's all about reading people's body language to solve mysteries."

"Hmmm . . ." Jacob slanted his eyes, scrutinizing my face. "So what's the mystery behind you?"

I looked left, then right. "No mystery here. I should be asking you that question. They say preachers' kids have the darkest secrets."

"You just made that up," he sneered.

"Yes, but it's probably true. What gives? What deep, dark secret are you hiding?"

"I already told you."

My nose wrinkled. "What?"

"Shonda. And the likes," he uttered.

Gulping couldn't occur fast enough. "*Sex* is the worst thing you've ever done?" *I did that just the other week.*

"Doesn't get much worse than dishonoring your own temple."

He seemed almost annoyed at me for making light of his most sordid sin. I had to explain myself. "I mean, there's extortion, armed robbery, mass murder—you know, stuff that affects other people negatively."

"There's also hypocrisy," he stated. He leaned in toward me, his eyes glinting with sincerity. "Do you know how difficult it is to stand in the pulpit and preach holiness to God's people when you just crept out of someone's bed—and that *someone* is sitting in the audience?"

I had to give it to him. "Can't say that I do."

He lowered his lashes. "I couldn't even look at myself in the mirror after church. On top of my sin, I damaged her faith in Christ. I couldn't witness to her to save her life."

Jacob's regret over what I considered everyday (or at least every week) action hit me hard. *He's really serious about God.* Bayford must have something in the water because both he and Cassandra, who were both in my age bracket, seemed to have this holy thing all worked out.

"So, to clarify, you're celibate?"

"Yes."

"And you have no desire to . . . you know?"

"I didn't say all *that*," he corrected me. "But this isn't about sex. Everyone has their own struggles. Some people struggle with gambling, drinking, overeating, lying. The list of human vices goes on and on."

I clamped and unclamped my teeth. "I thought we were supposed to be free from our wicked selves when we accepted Jesus. What's the song the choir sang last week? 'You will never be the same again.'"

Jacob raised one brow. "We are new creatures in Christ. Most of us just don't believe it."

Chapter 21

Just when we'd gotten our weekly schedule down pat, DeAndre's school dismissed for spring break. Back in the day, the second week of March meant much-needed relaxation. Now, from the guardian's angle on the school calendar, this five-day recess signaled double duty.

The first few days passed uneventfully. DeAndre stayed at home with Aunt Dottie while I kept all my plates spinning, popping in between stops to make sure they ate and Aunt Dottie got to use the restroom. When I really thought about it, I don't know what I would have done without DeAndre's help. Most of the time, he played outside with Chase and the other boys. But he checked on Aunt Dottie regularly (at least through the screen door) and called me when he wasn't sure about something.

"Can me and Chase make a cake?"

"No, you *may* not."

Next day. "Mike-Mike's pit bull big brother dog had puppies. Can I have one?"

"What?"

"Mike-Mike big brother Phillip dog."

I slowed him down. "Mike-Mike has an older brother named Phillip?"

"Yes."

"And Phillip's pit bull has given birth to puppies."

"Yes." DeAndre begged impatiently. "So *may* I please have one?" He probably thought using proper English would strengthen his case.

"No."

I guess by Wednesday, DeAndre decided he wasn't going to ask me if he could do anything else because the answer was always negative. Rain limited his entertainment options. I asked him if he wanted to hang with me at the store and at the library, but he declined on the grounds that Elgin might make him work too hard and the library bored him when there was no puppet show. Deep down inside, I knew I should have made him come anyway. The only reason I didn't was because I didn't feel like hearing him whine the whole day. "Are you ready to go yet?" and "How much longer?"

The blabbering howls on the other end of the phone line later cut my extended library time short. "Ooooow, Cousin Tori! It hurts! It hurts!"

"DeAndre, what's going on?"

"My leg."

"What happened to your leg?"

"Waaaaaw!"

I asked again. He screamed again. We weren't getting anywhere. "Where's Aunt Dottie?"

He hollered, "She's right here."

"Put the phone up to her ear."

I waited a moment, then directed her. "Aunt Dottie, if I really need to come home, press a button one time."

Beep.

"I'm on my way," I said, hanging up. A million terrifying images scrambled through my mental camera. Was his leg cut? Broken? Burned? Bitten? Should I have called 9-1-1?

In the interim, I placed a call to Joenetta. "Can you get over to Aunt Dottie's? DeAndre hurt himself."

"Who's watching him?" she barked.

"He's with Aunt Dottie."

She hmphed me. "Like I said, who's watching *him*?"

"You know, either you or his father is more than welcome to come get DeAndre any day of the week—especially this week since school is out."

"I'm just sayin' little boys have a tendency to get in trouble when left to their own imaginations. You should have asked someone to come sit with Dottie while you ran your errands," she accused, as though she were incapable of pitching in with her own grandson.

I wondered whom she thought that someone should be. Nevertheless, her words teamed up with the guilt already simmering inside me. I had no rebuttal. "Just meet me there. Bye."

"Mmmm hmmm. That's what I thought."

She beat me to the house and rallied at the door with dramatics worthy of an Oscar nomination. "Good Lord, this boy's leg is almost clear gone in the front."

Never having heard such an inept description, I threw my purse on the couch next to Aunt Dottie and braced myself for the worst. Joenetta led me to my own bedroom, an odd triage for someone who had no business in my room in the first place.

DeAndre lay still on his backside with a scantly reddened hand towel covering the lower portion of his right leg. The lack of major blood loss lowered my anxiety level significantly.

His crying picked up again the moment our eyes met.

"You're all right, DeAndre," I assured him, rubbing his head. He covered his face with a forearm, his body jerking with each fresh whimper.

"He wouldn't let me touch it. Said he only wanted you." She murmured, "I don't know why, since you're the one who let him get into this mess."

No mood for an argument. Time for the great reveal. With Joenetta literally looking over my shoulder, I gently lifted the towel. She gasped, I breathed a sigh of relief. About six inches of skin covering DeAndre's shin had somehow been . . . rubbed off? Scraped off, maybe, but he'd survive. How on earth had he managed to engineer this freak accident? "What happened?"

He squealed between huffs. "I was . . . on your . . . treadmill . . . and then it . . . started going real fast . . . and I fell . . . and my leg got caught on the machine."

"He's lucky he didn't break his neck," Joenetta pointed out.

"Why were you on my treadmill?"

Joenetta answered for him. "Because he's eight years old and unsupervised, that's why."

Guess even a broken clock is right twice a day.

She added, "Both of y'all need a whippin'."

"Don't get carried away," I warned.

Save DeAndre's lecture for later. Joenetta and I coaxed him into allowing us to douse the wound with water. We agreed that he could test the water temperature before we positioned his leg under the bathtub faucet. No one would touch the wound itself.

"Okay," he finally consented.

Next came the big peroxide scene.

"We have to kill any possible bacteria, DeAndre," I tried to reason with him.

"How do you know there's bacteria on a treadmill?" he retorted tearfully, keeping his eyes on my hands.

I set the brown peroxide bottle on the rim of the tub so he could focus on the words that were coming out of my mouth. "The belt on that treadmill is covered with germs from the bottoms of my shoes. You don't want spit and smashed up bugs and dog poop getting inside your body, do you?"

He needed a moment to deliberate.

All of a sudden, Joenetta seized him, grabbed the peroxide and upturned the bottle, sending a river of liquid down his leg.

It all happened so fast, DeAndre barely had time to shriek, "Noooo!"

I yelled, "Joenetta!" and tried to jerk DeAndre from her clutch, but it was too late. White bubbles fizzed under the clamor of DeAndre's heart-wrenching protest.

After the initial oxidizing sting had visibly and audibly subsided, Joenetta loosed her grip on the child. He immediately wrapped himself around my waist and buried his face in my neck. The tone of his weeping altered now to include the pain of betrayal.

I stammered with rage, "How could you be so evil, Joenetta?"

She tsked. "I ain't got time to sit up here and talk through all this nonsense."

"What else do you have to do, Joenetta? I mean, you don't work, you're not helping with Aunt Dottie, and you've been relinquished of your store . . . pilfering duties." I'd wanted to pick a synonym for robbery so DeAndre wouldn't realize I'd accused his grandmother of being a thief. Turns out Joenetta didn't know the word, either.

"What you mean by store piftering?"

Conscious of DeAndre's attentive ears, I asked him to go in the other room with Aunt Dottie because his granny and I needed to talk privately.

"I ain't got nothin' to say to you," Joenetta declared, stomping out of the bathroom ahead of DeAndre.

I remained on the tub's edge for a moment, collecting myself. *Ten. Nine. Eight.* Was this my fault? *Seven. Six. Five. Four.* Did we need to put DeAndre in day care? *Three. Two. One.* Why was I even raising him to begin with?

Joenetta had already hopped her broom and flown away by the time I joined DeAndre and Aunt Dottie in the living room. Peace abounded. DeAndre had propped his leg across Aunt Dottie's lap, and she'd used her left arm to blot wetness from the abrasion. She motioned for me to stand near her. She grabbed DeAndre's hand. He took mine, and I stooped down to take hold of her weaker hand. She tipped her head toward me.

"Father, we thank You for watching over DeAndre. This injury could have been worse, but we thank You that he'll recover nicely. God, help us all continue to work through Aunt Dottie's recovery and with the store." There was too much on my plate to even start listing my needs. "Just help us with everything, God. Amen."

"Amen," from DeAndre, nodding from Aunt Dottie.

DeAndre and I had our after-the-fact discussion with Aunt Dottie sitting between us, participating via hand and head motions. My treadmill was off limits. DeAndre was not to stick a toe in my room. He apologized profusely. "I hear ya, Cousin Tori. I'm not goin' in your room ever again without permission."

That settled, he and I made a trip to the nearest pharmacy, ten minutes away, to purchase gauze, tape, and a huge tube of ointment. We came back to the house and plotted an elaborate scrape-care plan.

"Do I have to use peroxide again?"

"Probably so, but it won't be as bad as the first time," I explained. "You've toughed through the worst part already."

Pride bloated his chest as he dabbed Neosporin with latex-gloved hands. The gloves were his addition—he'd found them in Aunt Dottie's bathroom next to the hair dye.

Soon after his leg was properly medicated and covered, Wendy, the physical therapist, arrived for Aunt Dottie's session. I needed to get back to the store but, truth be told, I was too afraid to leave DeAndre home again. He'd have to stick with me during the last two days of this ridiculously unnecessary spring break.

A flash of horrifying magnitude barged through my head. *What's going to happen over* summer *break?* Really, I couldn't even allow my mind to go there. Aunt Dottie's right side grew stronger daily. She'd even begun muttering vowel sounds lately, weeks ahead of the speech therapist's prediction. Her brain had already begun to reroute some of her verbal functions. Hopefully, prayerfully, Aunt Dottie would be in much better shape by the time DeAndre finished third grade.

DeAndre and I returned to the store after Wendy left. The bandage, his new source of honor, sparked several sympathetic conversations with customers. "It hurt *real* bad," he recounted.

Virgie pumped him up, reminding him to give each customer the whole story. "Tell 'em about the blood," she'd yell from across the store. "You forgot about the peroxide part."

By the store's closing hour, DeAndre's humble narrative about the accident had turned into a full-blown, harrowing tall tale worthy of a war hero.

Cassandra laughed, saying I should take a picture of the wound and put it in his baby book.

"I don't know if he has one." I tidied the cashier area.

"Have you tried to get in touch with the Simpsons?"

"Not yet, but I will soon. DeAndre wants to visit his mother in prison."

Cassandra's lips compressed. She glanced around the store, obviously checking for DeAndre's location. "If you knew Z like I knew Z, you'd think twice about taking him to see her—unless the power of God z-zapped her prison cell and changed her permanently."

"Changed how?"

"She came in here a few times with DeAndre before Aunt Dottie took over his care. I never liked how Z treated him. She'd cuss and yell at him, tell him he was stupid. Pop him way too hard, in my opinion."

This news coming from the speedy poppin' queen herself.

"I see."

"All I'm saying is if you decide to go, be prepared to snatch him out of the booth at a moment's notice. Aunt Dottie's is the best place for DeAndre. She's the best thing to happen to him. Well, her and you."

"Thanks."

Cassandra switched gears. "Hey, check this out." She reached into the side pocket of her jeans. "Behold. My new cell phone." She showcased a simple flip-style phone in the palm of her hand. "What do you think?"

"Nice, nice." I surveyed the phone for her sake. I probably had one just like it . . . three years ago. Alas, things were 'a changing in Bayford. "What kind of calling plan did you get?"

"I got a thousand minutes a month, though I doubt I'll use 'em all."

I disagreed, "You say that now, but once you get used to calling for the least little conversation, a thousand minutes won't be nearly enough. What about texting?"

"Unlimited," she replied. "Came with the plan, but I really don't get how you type words with all these numbers."

"Let me see your phone." I changed her text settings to T9 and showed her how to use the phone's intuitive features advantageously.

"Wacka wacka wacka!"

Eighties children's television. "Come on now, Sandra, the Muppets?"

"I loved Miss Piggy. She made chubbiness acceptable."

"She was a *pig*."

"Still, she was the *prettiest* muppet. Everyone wanted a piece of Miss Piggie."

"For breakfast, maybe."

She held the time-out sign. "Zinch! Flink! Stop and think. Okay, back to my phone. I was thinking. Remember the throwback sale I mentioned? Okay, everybody and their momma has gone to the barbershop and gotten a phone. And I do mean *everybody* from all sides of the track. So, if we send out Dottie's throwback deal in a text every day at the same time—say ten o'clock, before people have a chance to get up and drive to Henrytown—we could get their money first, before they sprinkle and prinkle on over to Walmart."

With a hopeful look at me, she prodded, "What you think?"

Truth was, I hadn't given her proposal much thought at all. I was so busy running daily operations, there was no occasion to analyze an entire marketing strategy. I barely had enough time to cover my NetMarketing plans without adding this to my spinning plate routine.

Plus, the store was constantly full of talk about the new Walmart. People wanted to know if we intended to stay open. Rumors circulated that some of Bayford's oldest family-owned businesses had already planned their exit strategies. From Red's Tire Shop to Macie's Craft Closet, owners who feared the worst were closing on their own terms rather than facing uncertainty.

With those circumstances in mind, I couldn't possibly impart false hope. "I have to think about it some more, Cassandra."

She returned to the quarters, counting all the way to six seventy-five before she addressed me again. "You need to make some decisions soon. I know you have to get back to your real world in Houston, but the rest of us will still be here in Bayford doing life as usual." She motioned for Elgin to join our conversation.

"Elgin, tell Tori what you said earlier about our customers." She put one hand on my shoulder.

He withdrew a small piece of paper from a hidden compartment in his apron. "Well, I've been keeping track of our traffic. Seems like we get a lot of folks in here from three till five, getting stuff for dinner and such. Plus the kids are getting out of school. But that's only for now. When it gets hot outside, people get out early in the morning or they'll wait until closer to sundown."

Cassandra grabbed my hand and Elgin's, and led us to the back office, where she literally unrolled an elaborate chart detailing store trends, best-selling items, and other factors to consider with the throwback plan.

"You've really thought this through, huh?"

"Had to. I've been watching you and"—finger quotes—"overhearing. When you talk to the people at your job in Houston, y'all talk numbers. I do numbers, too."

"Clearly."

Elgin remarked, "Looks like a real professional put this chart together."

"Shazaam! I *am* a real professional!"

We laughed at her antics. That Cassandra was something else.

Chapter 22

DeAndre's baseball practices consumed Tuesday and Thursday evenings. True to his word, Jacob taxied a van-load of little boys to and from the middle school diamond. The brisk spring air, still clutching remnants of cooler days gone by, beckoned Bayford occupants outside to enjoy the last round of tolerable outdoor activity. It was simply too pleasant to spend time indoors.

I packed up Aunt Dottie and her wheelchair, and we trailed the van across town to watch DeAndre and his poorly coordinated teammates practice. They were supposed to be the Yellow Jackets, but they looked more like the Bad News Bears out there on the field. Dropping fly balls, running bases at a snail's pace. Jacob and the father of one of the boys, assumably an assistant coach, could barely keep straight faces watching the team train.

Our first game against the Longhorns forecasted a miserable season. Of course, the boys didn't really care so much whether they won or lost so long as they got their after-game snacks. Sometimes I wondered if they even realized how badly we'd been pounded by almost every team we faced. Jacob always praised them for their effort no matter the score. The boys were oblivious.

Joenetta and Ray-Ray came to a few of DeAndre's games. DeAndre was absolutely beside himself when his father sat in the stands. However, I think I scared them off when I asked Ray-Ray if he could contribute to the cost of DeAndre playing baseball. My exact words were, "Is there any way you can put twenty dollars toward his registration fee? Not right away, just whenever you get the chance." I give him some credit. He didn't lie and say he would when he knew he wouldn't.

With the advent of a nonstop communication signal anywhere in town—courtesy of the future Walmart—I invested in a mobile wireless connection. Now I could get on the Internet anywhere, even outdoors, which made my life considerably easier. My only excuse for going to the library now was to get books for DeAndre. Since he'd been forced to spend more time with me, I begged the librarian to work with DeAndre and find books he would enjoy. After a few hit-or-miss authors, he fell in love with a faith-based series about the adventures of a young boy with ADHD. I even had to stop him from reading one Sunday in church.

After that particular service, Senior Pastor Carter invited us to their home for dinner. Now that Aunt Dottie had improved visibly, she might be able to accept such invitations. "You sure you up to this, Aunt Dottie?" I asked as we followed behind the Carters in my vehicle. Sarah, Aunt Dottie's speech therapist, had cautioned me against putting Aunt Dottie in situations where several different dialogues occurred simultaneously. Aunt Dottie might get overwhelmed by the words whizzing past.

Aunt Dottie patted my arm, assuring me she could handle this.

I almost didn't want to take DeAndre to dinner with us, though, because he was so impatient when it came to boring, grown-up talk. And his table manners needed some serious upgrading. Unfortunately, Joenetta sharply declined when I told her why I needed her to babysit DeAndre.

"Why you tryin' to get all goody-goody with the pastor?" she contested.

"We're just breaking bread together." Not that I owed her an explanation anyway.

She insisted, "I know what you're up to. Trying to seduce the pastor's son to swim in your hot tub of sin."

"What are you talking about?"

"People been talking about you two runnin' off to some place in Henrytown, supposed to be some kind of coffee place. Don't no black people I know hang out at no coffee house long as you two been there." She added, "Ain't that many coffee beans in the world."

I didn't even answer her. I made up my mind right then and there—Joenetta was officially on my I-choose-not-to-deal-with-you-anymore list, right up there with my mother, my biological father, and Mr. James.

Back when I was in college and on-campus counseling was free, I'd talked to a psychotherapy intern about the gulf between my mother and I. He'd asked me if I *wanted* to fill it. That was the first time I'd ever been given the option to let my mother go if she didn't want to be tethered to me. Let Margie be Margie. We talked a little about personality disorders—when people, for a plethora of reasons, have a hard time sustaining lifelong relationships outside of what's required of them. For as much as she'd fussed and complained about me, she made sure I had food, clothing, shelter, and even insurance. She didn't abuse me physically, and she generally did what she thought was best for me.

"That's more than I can say for half the parents of people who come through this door. I mean, I think it's sad that your mother has chosen to cut ties with you, but you can live a full and complete life without her," he'd cheerfully informed me. "She believes she fulfilled her motherly duties to you. She has a right to move to Africa and live life within her definition of peace. You have to make up in your mind. She doesn't owe you anything."

Well, it was past time to stop trying to make sense of Joenetta. She was what she was, and I wasn't going to let her bother me anymore. She didn't owe me anything. She didn't have to act right, do right, be right. All she had to do was pay taxes and die. No, make that die, because she didn't have a job or property.

Jacob Junior, his sister, Priscilla, and Priscilla's family—husband and three teenage children—joined us as well. We crossed the unhealthy threshold only three minutes into dinner, when First Lady Carter produced a basket of hot, buttery rolls drizzled with honey. No doubt, I'd be forgetting carbs today.

"Certainly enjoyed your sermon this morning, Pastor Carter," I complimented him. Though father and son had two different preaching styles, they both packed potent messages.

"Thank you, Sister Tori. Ain't nobody but the Lord." He smiled at me with the same warm eyes his son possessed. Even at probably twice our age, Senior Pastor Carter's handsome features hadn't faded. I wondered if Jacob Junior would age as gracefully. Looking at both his parents, his gene pool was definitely well maintained.

We passed oversized platters around the table, each

person spooning or forking generous helpings of turkey, dressing, yams, and green beans. DeAndre smacked heartily, rudely, at the table. I whispered to him, "Slow down. The food's not going anywhere." You'd have thought we didn't feed the boy.

When he stuffed another humongous spoonful of yams into his mouth, I gave him the evil eye. Jacob did even better. He asked sternly, "Didn't you hear Miss Tori ask you not to eat so fast?"

Casting an anxious glance at his coach, DeAndre placed the spoon beside the plate and deliberately prolonged the swallowing process, one portion at a time until he'd downed the entire mouth full of disobedience. "I'm sorry."

Having watched Jacob and DeAndre's interactions on the field, I was always amazed at how quickly DeAndre responded to Jacob's discipline. Aunt Dottie helped me understand, in writing, that their interaction was a man thing. Whatever it was, I was thankful for Jacob's influence. Using Jacob's name was right up there with invoking Santa Claus. If DeAndre got testy about practicing his spelling words, I'd threaten, "Uh, don't make me call your coach." Problem solved.

"Is it Thanksgiving?" DeAndre wanted to know.

Pastor laughed. "Well, it's not the Thanksgiving holiday, but every day is a day of thanksgiving."

"Aaaama."

Time froze. Every eye zoomed in on Aunt Dottie. She slurred again, "Aaaama."

Joy flooded through every inch of my frame. "Aunt Dottie, you can speak!"

"She said 'amen,'" DeAndre translated.

"Praise God!" I exclaimed, hugging my aunt. Tears spilled from my eyes as I cried into her shoulder. "Thank

You, Lord." My Aunt Dottie was back. I'd heard grunts and sounds from her since the stroke, but this was the first intelligible word I'd heard from her lips since arriving in Bayford.

The table rejoiced with me, and laughter soon accompanied our elation. "We won't be able to keep her quiet now," Pastor teased.

Aunt Dottie pointed her index finger at him. "Waa ou."

Again, DeAndre interpreted. "She said 'watch out.'"

I'm sure the meal First Lady Carter prepared was scrumptious, but I couldn't savor it. My taste buds took a backseat to concealed emotions coursing through me. When Aunt Dottie spoke, my whole world changed. There was light at the end of my tunnel. Sooner than later, she'd be able to comfort me with words, advise me, convey her needs.

Tell me she loved me.

On the way back from Pastor's house, DeAndre asked if he could spend the rest of the day outside with several friends. They had big plans to build a fort in Chase's backyard. "I finished all my homework already," he added to clinch the deal. Given Chase's foot incident and DeAndre's treadmill episode, I really wasn't sure this whole fort thing was such a great idea. This proclivity toward accidents wore my nerves thin.

"I don't know, DeAndre."

"Why not?" he protested. "Chase's mom will be home."

"Yeah, but she probably won't be outside to make sure you guys don't burn down the neighborhood."

Aunt Dottie tapped my shoulder. "Bah."

I couldn't make out her words. "Say that again."

DeAndre piped up, "She said 'boy.'"

She nodded. Boy. I drew a deep breath, filling in the gaps with my own reasoning. I would have to accept the fact that this was the way of boys. Trying things, getting hurt, learning lessons. But why did their lessons have to involve stitches and gauze?

"DeAndre, how do you know what she's saying anyway?"

"She talks to me all the time," he revealed. "I seen what Miss Sarah did to help Aunt Dottie talk, and I practice with Aunt Dottie every day even after Miss Sarah leaves. At first I couldn't understand Aunt Dottie, but now I do."

Giggling from Aunt Dottie.

Cassandra got in the habit of texting encouraging words to her phone contacts throughout the day. Like clockwork, my phone chimed each morning at ten and every evening at six. Sometimes her message was no more than a scripture, but somehow it was always the right scripture for the moment.

"How many numbers do you have in your phone now?" I asked her at the end of another hard day's work.

"One hundred sixty-seven," she proudly announced.

I surmised, "That's like every single person in Bayford with a cell phone."

"You tight-right on that *one,* sugar*plum,*" she forced the rhyme. "And more people keep signing up every day. This contact list will come in very handy when we start the throwbacks." She winked at me as though I'd already endorsed her plan. "I'm going to keep a pen and paper at the register so people can sign up for the throwback texts."

"Cassandra, I haven't really talked to Aunt Dottie about this—"

She blurted, "I know, I know. I also know that Aunt Dottie will support anything that keeps the store open.

So, what do you say? We'll start with sugar next week. Five-pound bag for a quarter, while supplies last." She jerked her eyebrows up and down.

What did we have to lose? "Okay."

"Yowza!" She held up both hands for a high-five. "Hit me, my sister."

I obeyed.

"Don't worry, Tori. God's going to see this through. I can feel it in my spirit already."

Then she and Elgin holy danced around the store singing, "I've got a feeling everything's gonna be all right."

Chapter 23

"Are you absolutely, positively sure?" Lexa's line of questioning vexed me to no end.

"Yes. I'm sure about this data. I've considered every demographic—ethnicity, age group, geographic location, income, etcetera." I lowered my speed on the treadmill so I could hear her better. Maybe I shouldn't have informed Lexa I had a phone signal.

She sighed heavily. "If you say so, I guess I'll have to just . . . trust you on this one, Tori."

I was sick of her asking for my expertise and then second-guessing my proficiency. "Do what you want to do, Lexa. Adios."

I really didn't have time to fool with her anyway. We were only a day away from launching Dottie's Throwbacks as a proactive attack against the Walmart scheduled to open the following week. In preparation, I'd made copies of flyers and worked in the back office, constructing an obnoxious floor display for the bargain of the day. The town's newspaper had been kind enough to run a story about the upcoming daily special sales, so people were chomping at the bit for the announcement of the first deal.

I wanted to be excited, for Cassandra's sake, but in actuality, I held onto hope that when Aunt Dottie fully recovered and realized she needed to slow down, she would liquidate. Maybe even move back to Houston with me.

I hadn't talked to Kevin directly in weeks. We texted regarding logistics only. He asked me twice when I would be home again. Not sure, I replied.

Need 2 know. Lost without you. How could he be lost without me when he was hardly ever home? I have to admit, however, part of me wished that he would come running to Bayford, knock on Aunt Dottie's door, beg me to forgive him for taking our relationship for granted, then bend down on one knee and pop the question. Not that I would say yes, just that it would be nice to be treasured. Or at least be somebody's one-that-got-away. Selfish, I know. Fact was, I assumed, at some level, we had already broken up minus the formal announcement. It's kind of hard to break up something that obviously never really meant anything to one party in the relationship. Still, it hurt to say good-bye in my heart.

Two years down the drain.

Jacob stopped by the store during his early lunch break. Since this would, hopefully, be one of our last slow mornings, I figured it best to take him up on his offer for brunch. "I've missed seeing you on church grounds now that the tower is in place."

One of our regular customers, Miss McDermott, passed an all-knowing glance over Jacob and me. She sang under her breath, "Looks like love is in the air."

Jacob and I transported our conversation to the next aisle. "Can you get away for an hour or so?" he pressed.

Cassandra and Elgin said they could handle things at the store. Cassandra mocked, "Don't ever let it be said I blocked Cupid's route."

Were it not for the very technological innovation that relieved me from the church parking lot, I wouldn't have had the luxury of a few free hours in the middle of the day. But as the Walmart windfall would have it, Net-Marketing had become a virtual breeze. I still had a full load. However, learning to prioritize under fire had paid off greatly. What used to take me an entire eight or nine hours a day only took me five now. I amazed myself, quite honestly.

As Jacob and I rode several miles outside city limits to this mystery location, I wondered how far this rumor about the two of us had traveled. Joenetta knew. Cassandra knew, though I could easily trace her information's path. She was, after all, Jacob's first cousin. Aw, who was I kidding? Everybody in Bayford was kin. This might have given me reason to investigate Jacob's lineage further if I had been related to the Lesters by blood.

Jacob's undisclosed location turned out to be a TGIF establishment. He laughed as we walked through the door. "I know it's not an exclusive steak house, but have you tried their sizzling chicken and cheese?"

I shook my head, knowing I couldn't stomach a heavy meal this early in the morning. "Sounds good, but I'm gonna have to pass."

We were seated in a booth almost immediately.

"All right," Jacob joked, "have your bunny rabbit salad, but don't ask me for half my food later."

I rolled my eyes. "I won't."

We talked some about DeAndre's wretched baseball team and their 1–5 record.

"I tell them over and over," Jacob dramatically lamented,

"when you hit the ball, don't sit there and watch—run to first base, man!"

Jacob's frustration gave us both cause for laughter. "Seems like some of these kids haven't seen one baseball game in action their entire lives. Not even on television. I don't know how to teach them things they've never observed."

I took the opportunity to encourage Jacob. "Don't be too hard on yourself, Coach. You're doing a great job with the boys."

"I could say the same about you with DeAndre. Which brings me to one of the reasons I wanted to talk to you. I heard back from his other grandmother."

"She called you?"

"Yes, and I tried to give her your number, but she wouldn't accept it."

Okaaay? "What did she say?"

"She said wherever DeAndre is now, he needs to stay put. Said her daughter needed a child like she needed a hole in her head."

"Wow. That's pretty harsh, coming from her own mother."

"I told you, Z's family is different. This woman talked about her own daughter like the girl was a dog. I can only imagine the kind of verbal abuse Z must have suffered."

"Did you get to ask her about visitation?"

He shook his head. "We didn't make it that far. She must have thought I was calling to ask for financial help with DeAndre. She spent five minutes talking about how broke she was and what a hard time she had raising her other daughter's children. Matter of fact, she asked *me* for money by the end of our talk. When I told her I couldn't help her, she promptly called me a hypocrite and hung up the phone."

"Are you serious?"

Blank gaze. "As a heart attack."

"That is so wild, Jacob."

"You tellin' me?"

Our waiter, an older Asian woman with a high-pitched voice, laid our plates before us. "Here you go, folks."

Jacob blessed the food and prayed a special prayer for the Simpsons.

After amen, I resumed. "So, I guess that's a no for visiting DeAndre's mom?"

"As far as I know."

There had to be another way. "I wonder if we can write Z a letter and ask her to add us to her visitors' list."

He shrugged. "I guess that's an option, if her mother will give you the prison address and her inmate ID number."

"Prison records are public information. Has to be somewhere on the state's Department of Corrections Web site."

Jacob shook his head. "I'll bet you look up everything on the Internet, don't you?"

"Mmmm . . . not necessarily."

"Have you Googled me?" he flirted.

"No. Should I?"

"Maybe. I Googled you."

Both my eyebrows shot up. "Why?"

"I wanted to know more about you. You're everywhere. LinkedIn, Myspace, Facebook—although you really do need to update your status notifications. You haven't been on in months."

"Haven't had time. Plus my employer has advised us to stay off those social media sites for personal use. I've already blocked information that might be remotely personal. Back up, though." I gave him the stop-sign hand. "What's up with all the private investigation?"

"Wanted to make sure you didn't have a criminal record." He couldn't hold a straight face for long. "I don't know. I was just playing around on the Internet one day and thought it would be fun to see what old Tori Henderson's been up to. Nice profile pictures, by the way."

I wriggled under his gaze. "Thank you." Suddenly, my salad needed eating. Jacob followed my lead and took a bite of his onion-layered chicken dish. Cheese didn't rank high on my list of desires, but there was something enticing about the food on Jacob's plate. I must have looked at his cuisine too long.

"Tori, take a bite."

We'd been through this before, might as well. "Just a little piece."

"Go for it."

I stuck my fork and knife into his entrée, mentally calculating how many minutes this tidbit would cost me in workout currency.

Worth every minute. "I can't dine with you or your family too often—I'd have to live on my treadmill."

"Naaa," he disagreed. "Every woman ought to have a little meat on her bones."

"What are you trying to say?"

He shifted nervously. "Nothing, nothing. You're fine the way you are."

"You think I've got meat on my bones?"

"No. Um, yes. You do have *some* meat."

"Clean it up," I admonished him.

"Oh, you crack me up," he said with a laugh. "I like you, Tori."

"I like you, too, Jacob. You're cool with me."

His smile morphed into a serious flatline. "I don't mean in a 'cool' way."

Maybe it was time we put it all on the table. For real,

Jacob had to be one of the most coveted bachelors in Bayford. No way was he eyeing me, and no way was I in the running for a preacher, no matter how attractive, fun, and caring he was.

"Jacob, I can't like you as . . . more than a friend. To be honest, I *do* like you as more than a friend, but I'm soooo . . . not . . . preacher's girlfriend material."

He kept his mouth shut, too busy chewing to respond.

"I mean, you're all . . . holy. Your father is a preacher. Your grandfather was a preacher, too. I saw his picture in the church foyer."

"And?" Jacob interrogated.

"And you come from this long heritage of preachers, men and women of God. When I'm around you, I have to totally forget you're a preacher in order to be comfortable. I have to think of you as Jacob Carter—football player. Jacob Carter—boy who sat beside me in Spanish two class."

"I sat *behind* you in Spanish two," he interrupted.

"Behind me?"

"Yeah. You wore your hair in one of those diagonal, architecture styles." He made a triangle with his hands. "And you had this one long section in the back. What was that style?"

"We called it an asymmetrical mushroom, and it was the bomb, thank you very much," I declared for the record.

"For real, you kept your do in check every day. Never a hair out of place."

"Is it safe to assume you were watching me?"

He winked at me. Giddy heat swooshed through my circulatory system.

"So anyway, like I was explaining . . ." I cleared my

throat. "I can't *date* you date you, if that's what you're asking."

"Depends on your definition of dating," Jacob chided. "According to the Bayford grapevine, we're already a couple."

"I'll bet your mom is having a cow."

Jacob nearly choked.

See there, what kind of mess is this? Who in their right mind accuses the church's first lady of having a cow? "I'm sorry."

He took a swig of water. "No, no need to apologize. I can assure you, she has given birth to many cows on many occasions."

Eased by his joke, shame subsided.

"My mom knows I respect her opinion, but I'm a grown man with a mind of my own. Plus, she's changed."

"How so?"

"She's not as judgmental as she used to be."

"What changed her?"

"The Word. Study, meditate, and apply it long enough, it'll change anybody for good."

"You're doing it again," I stopped him.

"Doing what?"

"Going into preacher mode. This is when I have a hard time seeing you as . . . someone who's regular."

"You think I sit up at night reading the Bible and praying?" he asked.

"Yeah."

"You're right. I do," he confirmed.

"Thanks, Jacob. That really helps," I kidded.

He held up a finger. "But, eventually, I go to the restroom, brush my teeth, get ready for bed. Might watch me a little *Sanford and Son* before I hit the sack."

"So you read the Bible every single night?"

"I try to," he testified.

I buried my eyes in the salad again. "Aunt Dottie reads the Bible every night, too. Actually, I've been reading it to her."

"Have you noticed the Word changing you already—entering your train of thought throughout the day?"

"Well, yes, but my train jumps right back to the old tracks in a hot minute. Not everything I think about is right. I'm a long way from the kind of life God has in mind," I testified.

"Don't worry about it—God will keep perfecting us all until the day of Christ. Takes a while." He'd paraphrased a verse I recognized but couldn't quite place.

His comment brought me to a grave rebuttal. "All right, so here's my question. I don't want to sound bad or evil. I mean, I really felt good about rededicating my life to Christ. But what if I don't *want* to be this other person God's trying to turn me into?"

I waited for accusation to cross Jacob's expression, but there was none. He simply asked, "What's wrong with her—this other person you think God wants you to be?"

I looked around the restaurant, trying to find an unwitting example. An older Aunt-Dottieish-looking woman with a Bible in hand, or maybe even a younger, domestic-hearted lady with no career aspirations wearing a long, Amish-looking skirt.

"Bring it on," he prodded. "What would the new, triple-holy, sanctified Tori Henderson be like? Worst-case scenario."

"Okay," I sighed. "She's super-submissive. A wimp. A pushover. Old-acting. She's always reading the Bible. I mean, she loves God and everything, but she's boring and she can't relate to the real world because all she thinks about is Jesus all day."

He tugged, "What else?"

"She also sews."

"Anything else?" He took the last bite of his chicken.

"That's bad enough," I smarted-off.

"And you think that's the kind of woman I should be dating?" he asked.

"Well, yeah. You *are* a man of God, except for *Sanford and Son,* maybe. Depends on the episode."

"I love your wit," he remarked, wiping his mouth with a napkin. His skin, thick with masculinity, beckoned to be touched. *How long has it been?* Again, my heart took a detour. How could he be this holy and sexy simultaneously? *I can't be a virtuous woman, not with these unrighteous thoughts running through my mind.*

He steered us back on track. "It's like this. The more you study the Word and spend time in prayer, in God's presence, the person you want to be and the person God wants you to be become one and the same. But He's smooth about it—He changes your desires first, and your actions follow. Inside out. One day you'll look up and realize you've changed. And you'll like the new you."

Jacob plucked a phone from his pocket. "Let me show you something."

One look at the fancy contraption, and I exclaimed, "Et tu, Jacob?"

"Of course. I've needed a cell phone for years." He wielded the phone left to right. "Signed up for a data plan and everything. I am now officially in the twenty-first century."

"You go!"

Quickly, I added his phone number and e-mail to my contacts. "Got it."

"Check this out." We pushed our plates aside and leaned toward each other, but the table's width prevented an adequate view.

"I'll come on your side." *Good Lord!* Jacob's solid frame scooted in toward me. His cologne drifted up my nostrils and down my spine, distracting me from the task at hand. *Focus, Tori. Focus.*

Jacob positioned the phone's display so we could both scrutinize the scripture he'd called into play. "Colossians three and three. For you died, and your life is now hidden with Christ in God. So, the old you died with Christ. You can't be anyone *but* a child of God, according to the Word."

"What about all the bad things I still think and do?"

"That's the old you, your natural self who doesn't realize she's dead."

I played along. "Who's keeping her alive? I mean, in order to have the ability to *think* you're alive, you have to be alive at some level, right?"

He pinched his lips together, let his eyes drift to the left. Thinking. "You know any amputees?"

"Not personally."

"My uncle lost one of his legs to diabetes. For a while after he lost the leg, he still felt like the leg was there. Said it was the weirdest thing to have the sensation of that leg, but look down and see it missing. They call it phantom leg.

"So long as you have an earthly body, sin dwells in this body. All our bodies are programmed for death. But that's just your body. Your inner man was renewed with Christ. When you find yourself doing things that don't line up with who you are, that's the phantom. You can feel and act and think like something you're not. What matters is when God looks at you, He doesn't see that old you. He views you in Christ. He's trying to get us all to behold what He sees."

Part of me wanted to believe Jacob. Maybe that was the Christian part of me. But I still knew me. I was Tori Henderson. No, I hadn't killed anybody, but I could have a short temper. I was impatient, yet sometimes a pushover. *Hate when I don't speak up for myself.* I'd embarrassed my mother so badly she sent me away and never really looked back. Honestly, how many people can say they caused their own mother to abandon them? That's gotta be a record.

"Just read it for yourself." He slid the qwerty keypad behind the screen. "Romans eight, Colossians three, First Corinthians two."

After noting the references in my phone, I snapped mine shut, too.

"All this knowledge because you want to date me?" I snarled.

He shot thumbs-up. "First and foremost, as your out-of-town assistant pastor, I'm concerned about your spiritual growth."

I acknowledged, "As you should be. Aren't you, like, my shepherd?"

"Right. But I do have my own selfish reasons for explaining all this to you and showing you how to rightly divide the scriptures. I want you to know I'm a regular person who's been changed by the Lamb. I don't want you to be nervous around me because I wear the fragrance of Christ. I really *am* regular."

"You know you sound like a Metamucil commercial, right?" I teased.

He smirked. I zoomed in on his lips again. *Behave, Phantom Tori!*

"How's *normal*?"

"Normal is good," I agreed.

"You know what I like about you?" he asked.

Time stood still. I closed my mouth, shook my head *no*.

"You're honest. True. You challenge me. And you don't treat me like I'm the last available African American male on earth, which is what most females have done my whole life."

Unsure of how to respond, I didn't.

"And beautiful. Not too much meat on your bones."

"Whatever!" I shoved his arm. *Oh snap!* Brother had some serious biceps hiding under all those starched sanctified shirts.

He smiled for a moment, then our eyes locked. Firecrackers couldn't have been louder than the sparks flying across the five inches between us.

"You still don't think I'm a regular—sorry—*normal* person?"

Honesty prevailed. Slight left and right motion with my head. I didn't have the wherewithal to speak.

With his eyes still set on mine, Jacob cupped my chin. He leaned in, tilted his head. My lids shut, anticipating the kiss. He planted a soft one on my lips.

"Normal enough for you?"

"I think I can work with that."

Chapter 24

That night, I told Aunt Dottie I had a few scriptures of my own in mind.

She agreed. "Aaaa."

Romans, Colossians, Corinthians. According to the table of contents, all these were in the New Testament.

"Aunt Dottie, what's the difference between the Old Testament and the New Testament?"

"Jeeeees," she slurred.

Jesus. Surely, there was more to it. I'd have to ask Jacob later. But I guess, for now, Jesus was the simple explanation.

I read the chapters Jacob suggested as Aunt Dottie listened. She bobbed her head up and down, concurring with the main points. There were so many, in fact too many to keep straight in my head.

"Ooh, Aunt Dottie, I wish you could help me understand all this."

She pointed toward the ceiling, then poked my chest.

"God and me?"

She smiled. She grabbed her ever-present pen and paper. "Holy Spirit reveal."

"How?"

"Just read. He will," she wrote.

Sounded like something super-spiritual Jacob would say. I kissed my aunt on her forehead. "Good night, Aunt Dottie."

On the way to my room, I noticed a thin stream of light emanating from under DeAndre's door. I checked my watch. 9:48. He should have been asleep a long time ago.

Pushing the door open, I confronted him. "DeAndre, why is your lamp still on?"

His body rustled under the covers. "Please, Cousin Tori, can I finish reading this chapter of my book? It's really good."

I chuckled. "Looks like we both found good books to keep us up all night."

He leaned up against his pillows. "Whatchu readin'?"

"The Bible."

"Oh. I like the Bible, too. 'Specially when there's lions."

"Yeah, the lions are fun." I laughed.

"I been prayin', too."

"Really?"

"Yeah." His face knit with sentiment.

"About what?"

"My momma. Her birthday is almost here."

I motioned for him to scoot over in bed, then joined him under the covers. He giggled with excitement.

"Kiddo, I'm going to see what I can do about getting in touch with your mother. But I can't make any promises. It may be a long time before you hear from her or see her again."

His warm face rested against my shoulder. "I know. The judge said thirty years."

Instinctively, I rubbed the top of his head. His tears trickled down my arm.

"I'm so sorry about your mom, DeAndre."

He bucked with emotion. "Why did the police have to catch her? And that stupid judge! I wish I could punch him in the face!"

"You're not going to punch anyone in the face, DeAndre." I calmed him with a soft tone, wondering if he'd ever considered maybe his mother had a hand in her own demise.

"I want her to come back. Why won't they let her come home?"

Tread lightly. "Well, sometimes people don't always make good choices. They have to pay a price for doing the wrong thing. Just like you have rules at school, grown-ups have rules outside school."

"I thought grown-ups could do anything they want."

"Not if their actions cause problems for other people. Everybody has rules, DeAndre. Everybody."

He wiped his tears. I moved to leave. He grabbed my arm. "No. Don't go yet."

I sank into his grip, wrapped him in my arms. We lay there in perfect stillness. Me and DeAndre. He stalled. "What were you and Aunt Dottie talking about?"

"We were reading the Bible."

He altered his position, peering into my face. "Is Aunt Dottie your real momma?"

"No. My real momma lives far, far away from here."

He settled back into me again. "Oh. So who watched over you?"

"My Momma watched over me for a while. Then I came to live with Aunt Dottie, like you. Now I watch over Aunt Dottie."

"Oh." He waited for a moment. "So who's gonna watch over you when you get old like Aunt Dottie if your momma don't come back?"

His timing was off, but I'd wondered that same thing. "I don't know, DeAndre."

He squeezed. "I'll watch over you, Cousin Tori. Don't worry."

I kissed his forehead. "Thanks, DeAndre."

Not ten minutes later, he was out cold. I gently eased from his hold, letting his head fall on the pillow. I marked his place in the book with a scrap of paper.

Putting the Bible research aside for a while, I detoured to the Internet. Took me a while, but I finally found the only Zoletha Simpson in the state database of prisoners past and present. Big brown eyes and chubby cheeks confirmed her relation to DeAndre. I jotted down her inmate number and the unit address, presumably the information I'd need to send a letter. Out of curiosity, I scrolled down to survey the rest of her page, reading her charges and sentences. Drug trafficking. Prior convictions: grand theft auto, assault, theft, drug trafficking. Probation, probation violation, two years of incarceration, parole, revoked parole.

What surprised me most about Z's record was how long it took for them to finally throw the book at her. DeAndre was lucky to have had her present in his life for as long as he did. Matter of fact, given DeAndre's age, I really don't know how she had time to form a relationship with Ray-Ray (assuming there was one) and *create* DeAndre. *Whew! She works fast!*

I shut down the computer and, while my nerves were still in motion and the residue from DeAndre's tears still stained my arms, I penned a letter to DeAndre's mother.

Dear Zoletha,
    Hello. My name is Tori Henderson. I'm Aunt Dottie's niece. DeAndre has been in her care since

your incarceration began. I don't know if you know this or not, but Aunt Dottie had a stroke. I am staying with her for now, so I have had the opportunity to play a part in DeAndre's life. I'm sure you already know this, but he is a wonderful young man. He keeps us all very busy with baseball, homework, and reading.

That said, DeAndre would love to be able to come see you for your birthday. If you can add us to your visitors' list, we will make arrangements to come see you soon.

Again, DeAndre is a great kid. You should be very proud.
Sincerely,
Tori

DeAndre and I both were at the mercy of the justice system and his mother, it seemed. How long would it take for the letter to reach her? What if she didn't reply? What would I tell DeAndre?

I treaded back to Aunt Dottie's room, hoping to find her still up. I rapped on the door. "You still up?"

"Aaaah."

She sat in her bed, still reading through the scriptures.

"I need to talk to you about something."

She closed the book, patted the space beside her.

"I'm writing a letter to DeAndre's mom. Her birthday is around the corner. He wanted to get in touch with her."

Aunt Dottie scribbled. "Call grandmother."

"Jacob and I already tried. She's wasn't very . . . reasonable."

Aunt Dottie threw her head back, then wrote, "I see. Pray."

"Pray for what?"

She looked at me quizzically, like she didn't know the answer any more than I did.

"Pray for God to do something?"

"Aaah."

"Something like what?"

She jotted. "Leave it to Him."

Dumbfounded, I returned to my room to pray. I asked God to intervene and do whatever He does to comfort little boys with incarcerated mothers.

It was almost eleven. Definitely too late to call Jacob. *Unless.*

I scrambled to the living room and turned on the television. Searching the guide, I found the show time for *Sanford and Son*. Eleven-thirty. Jacob should be winding down. I envisioned him brushing his teeth, running a towel over his face. Taking a shower.

The thought of Jacob showering, as enticing as it was, reminded me not so much of his sexiness but his claim of normalcy.

The day I saw my first-grade teacher in the grocery store, she toppled from grace. "Miss Johnson, you're *here*?"

"Yes, Tori. Teachers shop."

"But I thought you lived at the school."

She and my mother shared one of those confusing what's-so-funny grown-up laughs.

"No, I live at a house with my husband and our children. Teachers are people, too."

She really shook me up. Before then, I didn't even think teachers used the restroom.

I laughed at myself now. If Miss Johnson could be normal, maybe Jacob could be normal, too.

I grabbed my phone, opened a text box and sent him a message. U up?

No immediate response. No reply after five minutes. No *Sanford and Son* tonight, I guessed. Then came a ring.

"Hello?"

"Hey. I didn't want to call this late, that's why I texted you."

He hesitated. "I don't know how to text yet."

"I'm sorry." Amusement escaped my manners.

"Go ahead, laugh now. Give me one month with this phone, we'll see who's laughing then."

I teased him for a while longer before getting to the business of scriptures. Jacob's insight generated even more questions. After going back and forth about this new life in Christ, which I already possessed but, apparently, wasn't experiencing, Jacob finally said, "Tori, stop trying to understand this with your head. Ask God to give you a revelation of His Word."

Did I not get the memo stating "revelation" was the word of the day?

A heavy sigh spewed from my lips. "I'm going to sleep, Jacob." The mention of snoozing triggered a yawn. "Thanks for trying."

"Wait. What do you mean 'thanks for trying'?"

"I just don't get all this spiritual . . . stuff. Plus I'm tired."

"Okay. Get your rest. But don't give up on God. He's faithful. I'll be praying for you."

"Thanks."

"Good night, Tori."

"Night."

God, thank You for DeAndre. Thank You for his soft heart, despite all the hardness he's been around. God, go with this letter to his mother. Let it accomplish Your purposes.

Ummm . . . the other thing I want to know about is Your Word. Not just the words printed on the page, but I want to have this wonderful revelation everyone keeps talking about.

Thank you. In Jesus' name, Amen.

Chapter 25

After only a week into the Dottie's Throwbacks movement, we had more business than we could have imagined. The new cell phones had been the clincher. So many things converged at just the right time to propel Cassandra's marketing plan toward success—Aunt Dottie's absence, the tower, the cell phones. Totaling each day's sales with Cassandra was fast becoming a drum roll experience.

"Girl, fazooshi!" she exclaimed when I showed her the final numbers Friday night. "You sure this ain't somebody's social security number?"

Bayford residents, along with people from surrounding towns, appeared and reappeared throughout the week, snapping up the bargains at record speed. No sooner than Cassandra sent out the mass texts, people came pouring in.

Cassandra, of course, was practically dripping with pride. Her passion for Dottie's spanned the long hours she worked to make sure every customer had the throwback deal as well as any complementary items they might need to make the purchase complete. I was almost ashamed that I'd suppressed her efforts for weeks. We could have been raking it in sooner.

"Oompa Loompa doopity doo!" she sang one Saturday evening after closing.

"No!" I screamed. "Not *Charlie and the Chocolate Factory*!"

Elgin dropped his broom and exploded with laughter, clapping both hands on his knees.

"That's a good one, Sandra!" Virgie added.

We must have all been delirious from working so much at the store because it took us half an hour to regain our composure. "Oooh, I am so glad we're closed tomorrow, I don't know what to do," I exclaimed.

"Gotta get ready for *next* week's throwbacks," Cassandra advised. "Monday is flour for a dime."

"Save me a few," Elgin requested.

"Oh, no, my brother. You've got to buy your own."

Elgin and Virgie doubled over in laughter again. Cassandra laughed at her own joke. Must have been a country joke. "What's so funny?" I asked.

Cassandra squinted her eyes. "Oh, Tori, you remember that commercial for the *Hey Love* soul music compilation? The one where the guy asks to borrow a record so he can seduce his woman?"

"Never."

"Never?" Elgin asked. I repeated.

Virgie angled her head down. "Even I know that one, Tori."

"You poor deprived black child." Cassandra tsked. "Didn't you watch black shows growing up in the city?"

"Sure, I did."

"What did you watch?"

I listed on my fingers, "*Get Christie Love!, Good Times,*

That's My Mama, What's Happening!, A Different World,
after I moved to Bayford."

"What about black *movies*?" Elgin started in on me.

This was a little harder. "Ummm . . . *Stir Crazy*?"

"Nope. Gene Wilder." Cassandra discounted my attempt. "I mean an all black cast."

Virgie threw me a line. "Did you see *Mahogany*?"

"No."

"*Sparkle*?" from Elgin.

"Nope."

"Okay." Cassandra called our attention. "Now, if you didn't see this next movie, you're going to have to leave."

I braced myself. "What?"

"*The Wiz.*"

"*The Wizard of Oz?*" I asked.

"No," Cassandra yelled, slapping her hands together. "*The Wiz.* Diana Ross played Dorothy. The late, great Michael Jackson was the scarecrow?"

"Sounds like a good movie," I tried to redeem myself.

"Oh my gosh." Cassandra reeled. "You cannot carry on like this! I'm going to have to help you, my sister. Like Reeeer! Reeeer! Reeeer! Here comes the ambulance. What you doin' tonight?"

Virgie chimed in, "Probably seeing that handsome Jacob Junior."

"No," I quickly refuted. Our relationship had, by all appearances, become almost as popular as Dottie's Throwbacks. "Jacob's at a revival, thank you."

"You didn't want to go?" Virgie inquired.

I balked at her suggestion. Sunday morning and Wednesday night services gave me enough spiritual homework to last all week.

"You'd better get used to traveling if you plan on marryin' a preacher man," Elgin piped up.

"Who says I'm getting married. Ever?"

Elgin lowered his gaze, sweeping the floor again. "All I'm sayin' is, a halfway-decent-looking guest preacher runnin' a revival brings all kinds of Jezebels and Delilahs out of the woodwork. I seen that with my own eyes back when I was a deacon in my hometown."

"Hey, I'm keeping my nephews tonight," Cassandra said. "If you want to bring DeAndre and Aunt Dottie over to the house, we can watch at least one good black movie. Catch you up to speed. Can't be up too late, though. Church tomorrow."

After a long day already—up at seven to review Net-Marketing matters, DeAndre's baseball game at ten, then working at the store all afternoon—I should have been pooped. But Cassandra had infused me with her Oompa Loompa energy. "Sounds like a plan to me."

"You're invited, too, Virgie. Elgin, I would invite you, but I know you've probably got two dates lined up for the evening."

He smiled so widely, the space where his back teeth should have been showed. "You know me well, Sandra."

"Don't break too many hearts, Elgin," I ragged.

"Oh no, oh no. I don't break hearts. I just bend 'em."

We all had to crack up then.

Quickly, we finished our closing routine. I called DeAndre to let him know he'd have a little excitement in his life tonight. "We goin' to see Fred and Vernell?"

With one hand over the phone, I asked Cassandra her nephews' names. She confirmed and I passed the news on to DeAndre.

"Yes! Ooh, they got Legos and everything."

I didn't even know kids still played with Legos. From the news reports, seemed like all the boys were stuck on video games.

When I dropped by the house to pick up my two house-mates, I found Aunt Dottie fast asleep in bed with the Bible laid flat against her chest.

"Aunt Dottie," I whispered, shaking her gently. Her lids parted slightly. "DeAndre and I are going to Sandra's. Will you be all right by yourself?"

"Mmmm hmmm."

"You need to go to the restroom?"

She frowned "no."

"There's something else I wanted to tell you."

Her eyes widened slightly. She was awake now.

"The store almost doubled business this week."

"Yeeh!" She raised her left hand for a high five.

"Cassandra's marketing plan worked beautifully. If things continue this way, you should have no problem remaining viable after the Walmart comes."

She aimed a pen at my lips, then heaven, signaling a phrase I'd heard many times before. "I know. From my lips to God's ears," I said.

She winked at me.

DeAndre scrambled into Aunt Dottie's room with a backpack full of toys. "You ready, Cousin Tori?"

"Give me a second to change clothes."

"What's wrong with the clothes you got on right now?"

"The clothes I *have* on right now need to be washed. I've been around meat and packages all day. I really need to take a shower—"

"Awww," he groaned. "We won't have a lot of time to play."

I relented. "So just let me change clothes, capiche?"

"Ommm! You said a super-bad word."

"Capiche means 'you understand.'"

"Oh. Okay."

The car's gear barely hit park in Cassandra's driveway before DeAndre hopped out of the backseat. Rather than fuss at him, I took a moment to set the child safety lock. There were so many things to remember with kids, I had a new appreciation for parents. Single parents, especially.

As I sat there kid-proofing my car, the reality of DeAndre's plight hit me. Aunt Dottie would be back on her feet—or at least her wheelchair—soon. Once she regained the ability to speak, she'd be able to take care of herself reasonably well.

Cassandra could, obviously, handle the store. With God's help, Dottie's would take care of itself.

But DeAndre would be at the mercy of Joenetta and Ray-Ray again. They wouldn't take him to the library or check his homework. They rarely came to any of his baseball games. Bottom line, they didn't care about him.

Watching *Sparkle* wasn't the best therapy. The story line actually depressed me even more, made me remember how my mother and I drifted apart. I excused myself a few times to "check on the boys," stopping off at the restroom to dab my eyes.

DeAndre, Fred, and Vernell busied themselves with a three-foot Lego castle. "Nice!"

"Thanks, Cousin Tori," from all three.

Since Cassandra cried at the end of the movie, too, my tears flowed unchecked.

"*Sparkle* is, like, one of the best movies ever made," Cassandra commented, removing the DVD from the tray. "They tried to remake this movie a while back, but the attempt flopped sorely. Caput!"

"Remakes never live up to the hype."

Cassandra made no bones about her bedtime. "Girl,

you and DeAndre gotta scattle. I'm ushering tomorrow morning. Have to be at church by eight o'clock in my white."

I pushed myself off the couch. "I hear you. Getting Aunt Dottie together adds another hour to my morning."

"How is Aunt Dottie doing? I stopped by the house the other day. DeAndre said you were gone with Jacob, which—zippy news—is *always* where you seem to be when I drop by the house these days."

In Bayford, Jacob and Tori sightings equated with paparazzi reports. "Sometimes I am with Jacob, other times I think DeAndre just assumes I'm with Jacob."

Cassandra grabbed a comb from an end table and proceeded to wrap her long, black hair as we spoke. "I ain't mad at you. Like I said, my cousin deserves a good woman like Miss Tori Henderson. Woot! Woot!"

"You think I'm good?" *As in good enough for him?*

She looked me up and down. "Sure you are. Why *wouldn't* you be good enough?"

"I don't know," I struggled. Maybe Cassandra could give me a better perspective. "He's a minister."

"He's also a man," she countered. "Don't be scared of Jacob. He doesn't bite, and he's not wearing an invisible halo."

"I feel like a spiritual baby around him. You, too, for that matter."

"When did you say you accepted Christ? Last month?"

"Yeah."

"You are a spiritual baby. Don't get mad at yourself because you can't drive yet. Thing is, you don't want to be a Christian for twenty years, slurping up strained carrots because you still haven't cut teeth yet. Sloop! Sloop!"

This girl had missed her calling. "Cassandra, have

you ever thought about moving to Houston or any other big city?"

"Why—so I can pay a house note? No, thank you. I like visiting places, but I love to come home to a paid-for residence even more."

She had a point. "Well, if you ever decide to move my way, give me a call. Your creativity could really be put to great use."

She tied the knot on her hair rag. "I am putting my ingenuity to work. At Dottie's."

"I mean, like, for a bigger company."

"Nothing wrong with Dottie's. Nothing wrong with Bayford. No offense, Tori, but when you first came to Bayford, you were uptight. Worried about everything and everybody, wondering how you were going to make your life work. But once you got in and started hooking up with people—like moi, of course—you calmed down. This is the most relaxed I've seen you since you arrived in town.

"I wouldn't trade my life here for the world." She placed both hands on her hips. "Now, how many people working at those big fancy corporations in Houston can agree?"

"Touché, my friend. Touché."

DeAndre was so weary from his travels through Legoland, he fell asleep during the short drive home. In the absence of a decent radio station, watching DeAndre's head bobble with every lump in the road provided minimal entertainment.

He trudged up the porch ramp at Aunt Dottie's house, and on into his room. I heard him shuffling around only for a minute or two, then nothing.

I planned to follow suit, but a text from Kevin sent a

SOMEONE TO WATCH OVER ME

new ball in motion. In Houston 2nite. Will be in Phx 2morrow. Love you.

Maybe if I'd lived in Phoenix, this might be a good thing. But I was in Bayford. Even more of a problem were the last two words. Kevin never told me he loved me unless I asked him.

Chapter 26

Sleep eluded me all night. Most of the week, actually. I was so restless, I did something different with my hair every night. Twists, blow-out, deep conditioning.

"Tooor," Aunt Dottie asked Wednesday night after service, "uukaaaay?"

"No, I'm not really okay, Aunt Dottie. There's a lot I need to figure out when I get back to Houston."

I'd saved Kevin's text, reviewed it repeatedly. *Maybe I shouldn't jump to conclusions. Or maybe I shouldn't be this stupid.* I had a mind to hop the next plane to Phoenix and see what this "Love you" was all about.

Praise God for Sunday service, but first thing Monday morning, I called Lexa and told her I'd be in to work later that afternoon through Wednesday. This, of course, set me up for a mandatory return to Houston. No turning back now.

"'Tis about time," she tried an Irish accent.

I made arrangements with Jacob and Joenetta to help with DeAndre. Maybe it would do DeAndre good to get back in the habit of being with his grandmother again.

Now that he'd become a bookworm, he could escape her madness through literature.

Driving back home gave me the chance to solidify thoughts. Nothing like three hours alone with yourself to build up nerve, talk yourself into an air-tight case.

When I finally arrived in the building, I had my confrontation speech ironed out like a button-down cotton blouse. "Kevin," I'd say, "I need to talk to you."

He'd say, "What's up, babe?"

I'd ask him twice—no, three times—if he was seeing someone else. He'd deny it, of course, then ask me where I got such a silly idea.

Then I'd say, "I have my sources."

I'd let him panic for a few days, then I'd drop his text blunder on him before heading back to Bayford. He'd deny it, but I'd have proof and he'd eventually have to confess. Then I'd promptly break up. For the record, the official reason for our demise would be his cheating. His guilt would give me a while to figure out the logistics of this breakup. I needed a place to stay. Needed a moving date.

Kevin could live the rest of his life feeling like an idiot. The end. Well, unless he found Jesus or something, which I wouldn't bet on considering his distaste for all things religious.

My heart pounding with adrenaline, I flung the door open. Then my heart came to an abrupt halt. There was Kevin. Naked Kevin. Naked woman. They both jumped from the couch, reaching for blankets, pillows. She screamed, "Oh my God! Kevin, who is this?"

I wanted to ask the same question, but I couldn't speak. Couldn't move. She ran back to *my* bedroom, her plastic breasts barely bobbing. She was short, blond, and thin, from what I could gather of the flickering image blurring past me.

Kevin, too, fell speechless. Eyes fixed on each other, we both knew this was the end.

The end. For some reason, the realization of finality unleashed a fury of tears. All the good times we'd had together flashed before my eyes. The cruise. His brother's graduation. Logging hundreds of miles around our block. Maybe we weren't the most romantic, sentimental couple, but we were a couple. Or so I thought. *The end.*

"I'm sorry, Tori," he apologized. "I've wanted to tell you, but the opportunity never presented itself."

"Well, you sure couldn't have planned a better unveiling than this one here." Sarcasm to the rescue.

He lowered his head. "You're right. I'm—I'm a dog. I'm a dog, okay? You deserve better."

Miss Stiff-Breasts appeared again wrapped in *my* terry-cloth bathrobe. "What's going on here, Kevin? Why does this woman have a key to your apartment?"

"It's *our* apartment," I corrected her. "And that's *my* robe you're wearing."

She flashed a smug grin. "Oh no. See this *T* on the pocket?" She pointed at the embroidery. "This stands for *Taylor.*"

"Well, my name is *Tori,* which also starts with a *T.* Kevin gave me that robe last year for Christmas."

She flipped her hair back and landed her gaze directly on Kevin. He secured the blanket under his elbows and buried his face in his hands. I'd never seen anyone look so stupid.

Pity took a backseat to anger, however, as I continued the interrogation. "So where do you live, Taylor?"

She answered me but continued staring at Kevin. "N'Orleans."

Even better. "So, who's in Phoenix, Kevin?"

"Everybody out," he muttered.

"Are you crazy? I'm not leaving. I live here."

"I'm not leaving, either," Taylor huffed. "Not until I get to the bottom of why my son's father has a woman living with him in Texas."

My mouth gaped open. "You two have a child?"

She smacked her lips. "Yep. Five months old." Now it was her turn to cry. "How could you do this to us, Kevin? You know how much I love you!" She snatched up the lamp from the end table and threw it at his head.

Lucky for him, he ducked just in time. He lost the blanket, though. The lamp crashed against the bar, showering glass on the bar stools and floor.

"Hey! Get a hold of yourself!" he yelled. Standing there in the buff, his command seemed almost comical.

"Don't tell me to get hold of myself! I hate you! I hate both of you!" Taylor grabbed one of Kevin's dress shoes from the floor and pitched it at me this time.

Her force was sapped by sadness, and I easily dodged the shoe. "Kevin, you betta get your baby's momma."

"I'm not his baby's momma. I'm his fiancée!" She lunged toward me, but Kevin stepped between us. His bare backside blocked my view of Taylor.

"You're engaged, Kevin?"

"Yes, we're engaged!" Taylor screeched.

Suddenly, her knee appeared between Kevin's legs. He went down with a strident moan and a few choice cuss words for Taylor.

She and I were face to face now. I hadn't fought anyone since second grade (when Amy Crawford dunked my shoe in a toilet) so I was rusty. This Taylor girl was obviously well-practiced in hostility.

Calm words turn away wrath. "Look, I'm not going to

fight you." I pointed toward Kevin's body, curled up in the fetal position. "He's not worth it."

Taylor kicked him square in the behind.

"Yowwww!" And another string of expletives.

She spit on him. "You're right. He's trash."

She stomped off to our bedroom again. Kevin had barely struggled to his feet when the deafening sound of a single gunshot rang in my ears and I watched him tumble over again.

Taylor stood at my bedroom door's entryway looking like a straight-up Charlie's angel.

"Are you crazy?" he bellowed, grasping his arm as blood spilled onto our hardwood floor.

"Taylor, think!" I reasoned with her from behind the bar. Don't even ask me how I got there because I can't tell you.

"He doesn't deserve to live." She cocked the gun again. "I could kill you and claim postpartum depression on top of temporary insanity."

Wait until I leave, Taylor. "Think about your son, Taylor. He needs a mom. I know. I have . . . a son, too." Anything to make her give up the gun.

Kevin cried out in sheer terror, "Listen to her, for the love of God. Don't shoot me again!"

God, please don't let her pull the trigger.

The faint resonance of police sirens caused Taylor's arms to shake. She dropped the gun, grabbed her purse from the love seat and left the scene of this crime she'd committed.

I sank to the floor, catching my breath as the sirens drew nearer.

"Tori," Kevin called to me. "Help me."

"The police are coming."

"I know," he winced. "I'm freakin' naked." His warped

sense of priority eased any doubt that he'd survive the injury.

"You're also bleeding, Kevin. Stay where you are." For real, I wasn't blowing my cover until officers secured the premises.

"Will you . . . will you go with me to the hospital?"

Every ounce of common sense within me said this was the perfect opportunity to give Kevin a taste of his own medicine. I could leave him high and dry. And hurt.

When I didn't answer immediately, he begged, "Please. I don't have anyone else I can call."

Stay.

Once the police were sure I wasn't the trigger woman, they wrapped up their investigation quickly. I followed the ambulance closely, wondering why on earth I'd agreed to help Kevin through this ordeal. Maybe he could get his Arizona woman to fly out and tend to his needs. Or maybe he had one in New Mexico. Might have had one down the street, for all I didn't know about him. This was a hot mess.

Tears poured again, though I wasn't quite sure why. Hadn't I been planning to break up with him in a few days anyway? Confusion, utter confusion.

I called Lexa and told her I might not make it in today after all.

"What the heck?!" she practically shouted at me.

In my most professional tone, I requested that she lower her voice before we proceeded any further with our conversation.

"I . . . I can't believe you're not coming in today."

"You act as though we'd been planning this meeting for weeks. We spoke *this morning,*" I reminded her.

"Ugh. How soon can you get here?"

"I'm caravanning with an *ambulance* right now, Lexa—I have no idea how long I'll be at the hospital. My guess is late afternoon."

"Oh my gosh, an ambulance?"

Finally, she'd shown a sense of humanity.

"Yes, I'm behind the ambulance."

"Well, if the sick person's already in an ambulance, *they* don't need you. *I* need you!"

Wrong on so many levels. "Good-bye, Lexa."

"No. Fine. I'll wait here all night if I have to."

"Have it your way."

X-rays showed the low-caliber bullet missed all major blood vessels and bones. The doctor simply sewed up both sides of Kevin's arm and sent him away with a prescription for antibiotics, an anti-inflammatory drug, and pain medication.

Kevin whined for his pain medication all the way home. I had to stop at CVS and fill the prescription before we even left downtown. He swallowed the pills with the warm water—my water—stationed in the console.

After the day's events, him taking my water without permission was the straw that broke the camel's back. "Did you ever love me, Kevin?"

"Of course."

"When?"

"I still do."

"Your drugs haven't kicked in yet, but you're talking crazy."

He reached up and fingered my afro.

I shirked away from him. "Don't touch me."

"I seriously do love you, Tori. These other women . . .

they just happened. I'm always on the road working. Talking to people, wheeling and dealing. Sometimes I want someone to listen to my heart, not my sales pitch."

"*I* don't listen to you?"

"You listen, but you don't *adore* me. You don't drink every word that drips from my mouth. You don't make me feel proud of myself."

"And Taylor does?"

"Yeah, but she's crazy."

"Agreed."

"I've been trying to get rid of her."

I glanced at him through the corner of my eye. A spacey expression set on his features. Perhaps I could get the truth from him under these circumstances.

"How many girlfriends do you currently have, Kevin?"

"Three. You, Taylor, and a friend in Phoenix."

"How many children do you have?"

"Just one."

I breathed heavily. "Are you engaged to Taylor?"

"I'm engaged to two women, actually." He rolled his eyes to a close.

Process of elimination—he was engaged to everyone but me. I had to know. "Why didn't you ever ask *me* to marry you?" The more the merrier, right?

"Because I do love you." His words came slower now. "Honestly, you're the only one I would seriously consider marrying."

"You're not making sense." I slapped his knee.

Startled, he snapped back, "What?"

"I want to know why you asked everyone to marry you except me?"

"I was going to one night. A long time ago. Before we even moved in together. I asked you to fly with me to New Orleans, but you said you couldn't leave work. That was the weekend I met Taylor. She dropped everything for me."

"So you hooked up with her."

"Yessss," he admitted. "But I never stopped loving you." He leaned against the headrest.

"You know what the saddest part is, Kevin? You actually believe your own lies."

No response.

"Did you hear me?"

Nothing. Once again, I'd been wasting my breath on him.

By the time we walked in the door of our apartment, it was almost three o'clock. Kevin's drugs had taken full effect. I helped him onto the couch, where he drifted off again with his injured arm slung across his chest.

I texted Lexa to see if she'd really meant good on her threat to meet with me any time I became available.

Preston and I still here.

Gr8. On my way.

Why did she always need someone else there when we met? Since we met last, plans for Inner-G had shaped up nicely. The numbers worked, the projections were promising. Our meeting today shouldn't be a ground-breaking experience.

As I swept up the glass in the kitchen, a sense of thankfulness in turn swept over me. Only a few hours earlier, I'd been trembling in this same area, hoping Taylor wouldn't kill Kevin right before my eyes. Praying she wouldn't get extra crazy and kill me, too. I'd even considered the fact that she might kill herself and leave Kevin and me to our guilt. "Thank You, Jesus, for protecting me."

For some odd reason, I wanted to call Jacob, but I knew better. No need in exposing him to my craziness, putting my sanity on trial.

I shelved the situation with Kevin the way I'd learned to push people, and pain, aside in order to function. A normal person would be seething, yelling, screaming, boo-hooing. Not me. I was raised by Margie Carolyn James. She taught me how to activate the little "disconnect" switch in my head that immediately released me from all emotional turmoil. Off to work.

Jacquelyn felt it her duty to fill me in on the latest office gossip while I waited for Lexa to get set up in the conference room. Two people in accounting were pregnant by a married man. One of our newly hired employees was fired for visiting questionable Web sites. "Getting crazier by the day, I tell you," she said, laughing.

"We'd better get to praying," I commented. Maybe, before all the drama with Kevin, I might have been slightly amused. Suddenly other people's misfortunes weren't so funny anymore.

Don't go there with her. Jacquelyn did an about-face. "You are so right." She changed tunes almost immediately. "Yesterday, my pastor preached about the power of prayer. He had everyone jumping out of their seats! We shouted for thirty minutes, I tell you!"

I gave her a flat-lipped nod. "And while you're at it, could you pray for me, too?"

"What's wrong?"

I wasn't foolish enough to share my business with Jacquelyn, but I did want her to know that some of us were no longer on the gossip mill. "Just pray God's will be done in my life."

"That's the best prayer ever."

"Amen."

Lo and behold, the foundation for Lexa's panic presented itself in the first minutes of our meeting. Lexa,

Preston, and I would meet with Inner-G's VPs Wednesday morning.

"Okaaaay. This is certainly useful information." *What is this—surprise Tori day?*

Preston asked, "I thought you knew?" He faced Lexa.

She fumbled through an explanation. "I . . . thought I sent you an e-mail."

"Nnnooo. You didn't. If you had, I would have probably come in a day or two last week."

Preston's eyes traversed between Lexa and me. One of us was lying and he knew it. "Each time I've texted or e-mailed Tori, she's replied within a day."

Yes! Tell her, Preston!

Lexa touched her phone's screen. "I don't understand what's happening with this thing."

"I do." He shut her mouth.

Me, too! She's not using it!

"Lexa, you need to get to the bottom of your communication problems or any *other* problem you might have with Tori." Preston stood. "I'll be in my office until at least six. Let me know if you need my help with anything. Inner-G is finally on the right track, but we're not out of the woods with their execs yet. We need to look sharp Wednesday."

Preston excused himself. Lexa followed suit. I sat there wondering what she expected me to do with all this paperwork but no partner.

Ten minutes later, Lexa returned with puffy eyes and a red nose.

I leapt from my seat and closed the conference room door. We couldn't afford to be seen as the emotionally unstable women behind the wheel of this reckless account. Preston might have our back to some degree, but there were always sharks like Brian lurking in the water. One whiff of blood and he'd strike to take both our spots.

"Lexa, calm down."

She leaned forward until her forehead thopped on the table. She thopped again and again.

I reached across her body and pulled her shoulders upright. "Lexa, this will all work out. It is not that serious."

"How can you say such a thing? This is everything— my life, my whole career!" she croaked.

"Your career is not *you*." Look who's talking.

"Yes, it is." She escaped my grip and settled her head on the table again. "I've given everything—I mean *every single part* of me—for this account. And now the whole thing's backfiring."

I didn't have the nerve to ask her to run that "every single part" by me again. Suffice it to say, her actions told the complete story.

"Lexa, I'm gonna tell you something that changed my life." This time, I swiveled her chair to face me. Mascara etched a river of sadness down her face. She struggled to maintain control of her bottom lip.

"Listen. The day of your funeral, what do you think your coworkers are going to do after the ceremony?"

Her droopy eyes questioned. "I don't know. Cry, I guess."

"No. They're going to go to lunch." I stated the facts just as Ms. Sanchez, the hospital social worker, had done for me. "Then they'll come back through the office, rummage through your desk for fresh stacks of Post-it Notes. The next week they'll welcome the new girl."

She sniffed, wiping her face. "But you guys are like my family. I got passed around when I was a kid—this is the first time I've ever really fit in. Are you going to lunch after my funeral, too?"

"I mean, I'll be sad, but, yeah . . . I will probably go to lunch with them. What I'm saying is, come in, do the best you can at work. But do *not* give this job every single part of you. We work for companies whose goal is to manipulate the general public into buying their products—good or bad. In the grand scheme of life, what we do is not that serious. Save some of you for Lexa."

A trancelike expression covered her face. "But I did some . . . really, *really* bad things to land this deal."

"Lexa, if it helps, we've all done really, really bad things for wrong reasons."

"Like what? I mean, how many people do you know who've slept with a ratty-looking hip-hop rapper's manager just to get a tentative appointment with his agent?"

Slow your roll, Lexa, I'm not a priest. "I don't personally know anyone who's done *that* . . . um . . . I just know you have to forgive yourself and move forward. And it helps to have someone who'll help you forget."

"Who helped you?"

The sound of her heart creaking open was almost audible, as though our time alone had been divinely ordered. "My Aunt Dottie—the one I'm helping in Bayford. She was my rock when I fell on the consequences of a bad decision. I leaned on her, she leans on Jesus."

"Oh, God, no. Not Jesus!" She buried her head in her arms on the table. "My grandfather is a Baptist minister. Are you trying to kill me with guilt?"

I threw her a lifeline. "Lexa, Jesus doesn't make people feel guilty about what they've done wrong. He's the answer, not the problem."

Honestly, I wanted to excuse myself and leave Lexa to her meltdown, but now that I'd brought Jesus, the epitome of compassion, into the picture, bailing on her didn't seem possible.

She endured another crying spell while I sat by help-lessly. *What would Aunt Dottie do right now?* Probably the most unprofessional thing in the book—touch her. I placed my hand on Lexa's back and traced big, gentle circles. "It's going to be all right, Lexa. No matter what you've done, you can get up and move forward. Jesus will help you."

Her sobbing subsided, finally. She whisked wetness from her face, sniffed up her snot. *Atta girl!*

"I'm sorry."

"No need to worry about getting things right with me, Lexa. I think you know Who's top priority."

"I didn't mean to spazz on you." Quickly, she re-assembled her businesslike persona, shuffling papers, avoiding eye contact. She unhooked her ponytail clamp, shook out her mane, and then fastened the holder again. "Can we just pretend this never happened?"

"If I were you, I wouldn't." *Snap!*

That wisdom came out of . . . somewhere deep inside me.

Chapter 27

Lexa and I worked until almost eight, bringing my long day to a whopping close. Every i dotted, every t crossed. Tuesday we'd review, Wednesday we'd hit 'em hard, make Inner-G's representatives forget all about our previous blunders.

I stopped for sushi—the dish I missed most while in Bayford. While at the counter, the cashier asked if this order was "for here or to go?" Kevin's image popped in my head.

"To go. And double the order, please."

The source of my kindness couldn't be explained. Phantom Tori wanted to finish Taylor's job. Who could blame either of us? Kevin was a cross-country player who'd used his job to live a triple life. If both of us snapped, it would make a really cool movie: one of his fiancées shot him, his live-in girlfriend delivered the fatal blow.

Was I actually his live-in girlfriend? Did he have a place in Phoenix and New Orleans, too? Suddenly our living arrangements made sense. He didn't want my name tied to any of his bills. Maybe the other women were snoopers. Maybe they had better sense than me.

He must have gotten pretty bold when I went to Bayford.

Kevin lay in the same spot where I'd left him five hours earlier. "Hey, ba—Tori."

I'd worked myself up so on the way home, I felt like throwing his container of sushi across the room, aiming directly for his arm. Instead, I tossed it on the coffee table.

"Thanks for everything."

"You're not welcome," I sassed, entering my bedroom and slamming the door shut behind me. My appetite for sushi vanished during the route home. *How could he do this to me? Why am I doing this to myself?*

I ran a hot bath and soaked until my toes and fingers shriveled up. I wondered if this was how wives reacted when they discovered husbands' affairs. Did they sleep in the same house the night of the discovery? I mean, wives had to be around the lowlife tricksters for at least a day or two before counseling could be arranged. Many of them had kids to protect and didn't want to alarm the whole family if they intended to salvage the relationship. Not so, in my case.

Shouldn't I be in a hotel right about now?

Kevin shuffled into our room, stripped down to his birthday suit and crawled beneath the covers. He used throw pillows to prop up his arm.

His big nasty behind all up in my bed after fooling around with Taylor. "Aren't you going to take a shower?"

"Can't."

"Then go back to the couch."

"Can't."

"You don't have a choice," I fussed from the tub.

"Come on, Tori," he whined. "My arm is killing me. I really need the bed. Don't worry, I just took more pain meds. You won't even know I'm here."

"I can't sleep in the same bed with you, Kevin."

"Please."

Here we go. Once again, weak, pushover Tori—the one who was always smiling and doing the right thing, the same one who even tolerated Kevin's presence—said, "He's in pain, Tori. Give him the bed."

Old Tori argued, "He ought to be in pain! He's a cheater, a liar, a bad dad! He's pitiful."

Then have pity on him, just as God has pity on you.

I wondered how much time should lapse before I obeyed the command. Couldn't I postpone being nice until the next day, or until the day I moved out? Besides, what did God have to do with all this anyway? He doesn't like liars, either. There.

"You are *not* sleeping in this bed tonight, Kevin. Take some more pills and make yourself a pallet on the floor." Guess I wasn't spiritual enough yet to whip my attitude around so quickly.

Kevin failed to rustle out of bed.

"Did you hear me?"

No movement.

I sat up in the tub and raged, "Kevin, I'm talking to you!"

"Huh?" in bewilderment.

"Get out! Get out of our bed!" The anger converged behind my eyes, compromising my composure. *Where's my disconnect switch?*

"Are you serious?"

"Yes. Get up, get your pillow, get out, or I'll move you myself."

The mattress springs squeaked. "This is ridiculous, Tori."

"No. You're ridiculous. You think you can cheat on me, have a baby with another woman, get shot, then come home and roll in the bed like nothing happened today? You're lucky I'm here, willing to look after you, making sure you don't bleed out in your sleep!"

Slowly, he stumbled out of the room. "It's not my fault I got shot."

"Yes, it is your fault. You should pick your secret fiancées better."

Score one last point for Phantom Tori.

Jacob texted me way too early Tuesday morning. After my comment about Kevin bleeding to death, I had to climb out of bed twice to make sure my prediction hadn't jinxed him. Seven twenty-five A.M. seemed more like five twenty-five.

How r things n H-town?

The only honest reply on my fingertips: U don't want 2 know.

Since I was up, I called Aunt Dottie's to catch DeAndre before his bus ran.

"Hey, kiddo. You ready for school today? Don't forget, baseball practice tonight. You got your glove?" I sounded like a card-carrying, minivan-driving soccer mom.

DeAndre didn't answer either of my questions. "When are you coming back?" Sadness tinged his voice.

"Maybe tomorrow. I'm not quite sure. Why? Is everything okay?"

"Can I come to Houston with you?"

"No. I don't have time to drive back to Bayford. You all right?"

"Can Pastor Jacob bring me to Houston?"

"DeAndre, what's wrong?"

I heard rustling, followed by Joenetta's voice. "Ain't nothin' wrong with him. He just don't wanna mind, that's all. Got mad 'cause I wouldn't take him to the library. I told him I ain't none of you. I can't be runnin' all over town catering to him, spoiling him rotten."

In what world does taking a child to the library constitute spoiling? "Is his book overdue?"

"I don't know. Too bad if it is. You gon' have to pay the fine 'cause I ain't goin' to no white folks library."

It occurred to me just then that Joenetta needed counseling. How else could she be so bitter before eight in the morning? I wondered what must have happened early in her life to propel her onto this gloomy path. For the first time, I realized I needed to pray for my *other* aunt rather than despise her.

"You're right. I'll handle the library issue when I get home," I agreed.

"You ain't got to tell me I'm right. I *know* I'm right," she pushed.

I held my tongue for a second. "Can I talk to DeAndre again?"

"He's already outside at the bus stop." Then she hollered, "Get off at your daddy's house again after school today, DeAndre!"

After my hearing returned, I asked, "Why's he going over to Ray-Ray's?"

"If you must know, I'm keepin' baby Shanisha. Ray-Ray and Fontella ain't got no money for day care this week. DeAndre's a big help," she reluctantly explained.

Despite my gut feelings about Ray-Ray and Fontella, I figured it might be good for DeAndre to spend time with his little sister. "Awww . . . How old is the baby?"

"Too young to be talked about on the phone long distance. You got somethin' else to say?"

"Have a good day, Joenetta."

She grunted, "Uh huh. Why you bein' so nice to me all of a sudden?"

Because you're pathetic. No. Couldn't say those words. "I'm a nice person."

"People aren't nice, not 'less they want something," she accused.

"People can be nice for no reason at all, just for the love of God inside."

"Hmph. You talkin' like Dottie now."

"Thank you."

"Bye."

I doubt this conversation affected Joenetta one way or another, but my attitude changed. No matter what she did or didn't do, *I* could choose to treat *her* well.

Yes! Ever have one of those moments when, suddenly, everything makes sense? Those verses Jacob and I discussed our first night at Starbucks—the night of the marvelous massage—First Corinthians thirteen. Love. Being forced to care for cheating-lying-Kevin, working with trifling-Lexa, and dealing with she-needs-Jesus-Joenetta taught me to preserve my own sanity through love. *Thank you, God, for revealing this inside me.*

Jacob would be so happy for me. I sent him another text: Will b home n time for service 2morrow. Dinner after?

He answered: u cookin?

Cooking? Me? Don't get me wrong, I knew how to boil water, but most of my creations were far too healthy for Jacob's palate. For Bayford's palate.

I had to warn him: u like lettuce wraps?

Willing 2 try.

Ok. See you.

He surprised me with Miss u.

Awww . . . miss u 2. LOL!

LOL?

I forgot he was a newbie. Means laughing out loud.

Gotcha. LOL! C u later. C, I'm trying to get this!

I fell back on my bed in laughter. Jacob's refreshing sense of humor set me up for a wonderful day.

Kevin's rumblings called. I dressed and joined him in the kitchen. He'd done a decent job of making one-armed scrambled eggs from the carton of whites we kept in stock.

"Morning," he said with his back to me.

"Same to you."

"Want some eggs?"

"Yeah."

I took a seat at the bar while he whipped up another serving for me. I would miss admiring Kevin's legs. His no-worries approach to life. His insistence on paying major bills, as ill-inspired as his motive might have been. In light of the love scriptures, there was much to love about Kevin. He would make a good husband, if he could stop cheating. Maybe if he didn't travel as much, he could maintain a substantial relationship.

With one good agile arm, he slid my eggs onto a plate. He opened the refrigerator and grabbed an apple. Two slices of whole wheat toast popped out of the toaster. He put one on his saucer, one on mine.

He served my food on the bar counter. "Here you go."

"Thanks."

"Least I could do."

"Yep."

He leaned back against the mini-island. "I know it's over between us, but I would like to remain friends."

His statement struck me oddly. Taking our relationship down a notch wouldn't affect much. "I don't think we've ever been more than friends."

He took a bite of toast and chewed. Tossed his head back and forth. "You're probably right."

"No offense, but I've never been super mad crazy about you. Not like"—*Jacob*—"the thought of you makes me smile inside."

He swallowed eggs. "Yeah. I know what you mean. We're roommates. With benefits."

"No more benefits," I declared.

He bowed in agreement. "I want you to know that I am sincerely, truly sorry."

"Did you take meds already?"

"No. I'm in complete, sober pain right now," he declared.

"As you should be."

"Touché."

We finished our breakfasts. I rinsed our dishes and placed them in the dishwasher.

"What's on your agenda today?" he asked.

"Going in to work."

He laughed. "I can't believe you're still here."

"That makes two of us."

"You're so . . . over everything that's happened. I mean, I know you. You should *so* be in a hotel or moving out right now."

"I *am* moving out. Give me a few weeks to handle the details."

He nodded. "Sure. Take all the time you need. I figured you would be leaving. But I'm saying—you're so calm. Except when you kicked me out of my own bed, but otherwise . . . you're acting like this was all *supposed* to happen."

"Shut up!" I touched my lips with my fingers. "It *was* supposed to happen. I prayed and asked God for clarity about our relationship. And He showed me exactly where we stood."

Kevin angled his head downward, doubting me. "So you prayed?"

"Yes!"

"And you believe God set this whole thing up with Taylor to answer your prayers?"

I shrugged. "You got a better explanation?"

He shrugged, too. "Whatever. All I know is, you've changed, Tori."

Smiling ear to ear, I gloated, "That's the best thing you've ever said to me."

Chapter 28

Kevin caught a red-eye flight to Salt Lake City early Wednesday morning. Despite his doctor's recommendations, Kevin thought it best to get back in the swing of things. He said he couldn't do the whole laying-around-the-house thing.

He walked out minus our routine good-bye kiss. Simply "See ya."

"Adios."

Our second honest exchange in years, probably.

Now for the big meeting with Inner-G reps. Lexa and I were pumped. In my heart, I felt as though I had been training my leader, but I knew Lexa's self-esteem needed the boost. She needed to at least look like the lead on the account. I had groomed her for every question they might ask. I even gave her a lesson on how to say "I don't know" without sounding incompetent.

When we wrapped up our review, Lexa had asked me if I'd ever considered a career in law. "You could prime witnesses for cross-examination."

Lexa was ready to rock, and I was more than happy to have her back.

I picked the most sophisticated suit in my closet. A black single-button pant suit tailored to professionally accentuate my every curve. My twists unrolled perfectly, spiking at all the right angles. Every aspect of my appearance screamed *Power!*

Green lights led the way to work. Always a good sign. "Thank You, Lord. This is going to be a great day."

As I took one of the closest parking spaces, courtesy of prompt arrival, my cell phone blared its ringing tune. I checked the display before answering. *Why is Aunt Dottie calling me?*

"Hello?"

"Tooor."

"Yes, it's me, Aunt Dottie," I said.

"Deeeon."

"DeAndre?"

"Yaaaahs."

"What's the matter with DeAndre?"

She babbled off a series of incomprehensible words. "I can't understand you, Aunt Dottie. Is anyone else there?"

"Jonay."

"Put her on the phone, please, Aunt Dottie."

Eternal seconds ticked before Joenetta took the phone. "Who's this?"

"This is Tori. What's going on?"

"DeAndre's got himself in trouble again with white folks."

"His bus hasn't even come yet—what kind of trouble?" I ranted.

"Worse than school. The law. Police found him riding his bike on the highway service road at three o'clock in the morning, clear over in Plainville. Now the folks at

Child Protective Services got him. Might keep him for good."

Fear clogged my throat. My voice trembled. "What? Why would they keep him? Why did he run away from Aunt Dottie's?"

"No. I'm trying to tell you what happened if you'd stop all this whining. Whoo!" She paused. "You ready to hear what happened?"

"Yes, please."

"He ran away from *Ray-Ray's*. Serves DeAndre right if they keep him for a little while," she spurted callously.

Lexa tapped on my car window, pointed at her watch, then toward the building. I acknowledged her hint with a go-away wave. She sped inside.

"You still there?" Joenetta yelled.

Barely able to breathe, I said, "Yes. Are you, or can someone go get him? Please."

"Naw. They ain't releasin' him yet." A baby's shrill cry filled the background. "I got to go. They might turn DeAndre loose to you if you can get to the county fast enough, I don't know. I said I gotta go. Bye."

Quickly, I scrolled my call log to Jacob's name.

"Top 'o the mornin' to ya."

"Joenetta says DeAndre ran away last night. The police caught him riding his bicycle and took him into custody. She says they won't release him to anyone." My voice broke with emotion.

In his consistent, easy tone, Jacob assured me he would dress and get to the Bayford County building as quickly as possible. "I'll call you when I know something. Don't worry, Tori. DeAndre is tough. He'll be all right."

Maybe he was tough at school when people ragged on his mother, but the DeAndre I'd come to care about was probably curled up in a little ball in the back corner of some room filled with malicious, foul-mouthed, pot-smoking delinquents.

I gathered my attaché and laptop, frazzled from head to toe. My phone in hand, I flew past the empty reception area and straight to the conference room.

"Here we go!" Lexa cheeped. Her eyes danced with confidence. "We make such a good team, Tori. I'm so sorry I ever doubted you."

Nerves churned in my stomach. "I'll be back."

My digestive system took the news of DeAndre's confinement as a cue to cleanse itself. Sitting there on the paper-lined toilet seat, I whispered to God in this secret place.

Father, I don't know what to pray, but You know what to do. Be with DeAndre. Intervene in this situation, O God. I . . . I can't believe this happened. But You already knew. So in Jesus' name I pray Your presence in this craziness. Amen.

Lexa must have sensed my distress upon return to the conference room. "Is there something I should know about?"

"My nephew. He ran away last night."

She inhaled sharply. "Is he all right?"

"Thanks for your concern. Yes, he's okay, but the police have him. Or maybe Child Protective Services has him, I don't know."

"Wow. Does he run away often?"

"Not that I know of. He's actually a pretty good kid," I boasted.

"Wait a minute." Lexa's brows furrowed. "Is this the one who peed in your trash can?"

"Yep. He's the one."

"That was unbelievably hilarious. Sounds like something my brother would have done when we were little."

"DeAndre had his reasons for peeing in the trash." Conscious of my own statement, I quickly recognized he must have had cause for running away, too.

I read Jacob's name and heard the phone simultaneously. "Hello?"

"Okay, here's the deal. They're keeping DeAndre on the grounds he wasn't properly supervised."

I protested, "But didn't he run away? You can't supervise someone who's run away!"

"Hold on, hold on." Jacob attempted to calm me. "They just explained the protocol. Any time an eight-year-old is found wandering around town in the middle of the night, a formal inquiry automatically ensues."

Put in those terms, the county's concerns made sense. "So what's next?"

"Child Protective Services will appear before a judge this afternoon and determine DeAndre's temporary custody arrangements pending a complete investigation," he explained. "If someone, preferably a family member, steps in to assume temporary guardianship, they may release him to that family member. Otherwise, they'll put him in foster care."

"What time?" I glanced at my watch.

Lexa slapped her hand on the table and shot me wide-open eyes. She mouthed "no" twice.

"One o'clock."

Mental calculations put me back in Bayford at twelve-thirty if I left immediately and traffic cooperated with me.

"I'm on my way."

Lexa amplified her nonverbal theatrics, standing and placing both hands on her head.

"I'll meet you at the courthouse," he volunteered. "You know where it is?"

"No."

"Call me when you hit the loop. I'll lead you in."

"Thank you, Jacob."

"No problem . . . hey."

"Yeah?"

"Pray," he suggested.

"I have."

He closed the matter. "Then it's already done."

My ear buzzed with Jacob's words while Lexa fumed in vain. "I can't believe this! You're *leaving*? *Now*?"

All I could do was imitate Jacob's calmness. "Lexa, you know this account backward and forward. You're perfectly capable of conducting this meeting without me. We've practiced, we've prepared. You are *so* ready for this."

"Preston will *not* be happy," she snarled.

"He *will* be if you shine. In fact, he'll be extremely impressed if you pull this off without me."

She sank back into her seat. "What is this—reverse psychology?"

I sat in the chair next to her. "Lexa, I'm not trying to trick you. I'm trying to make you see that you *are* capable, you *can* lead a successful major campaign, you *can* succeed without compromising yourself."

"But I *need* you," she squealed.

"Yes, you *did* need me to prepare you, and I've prepared you well. I mean, all I'd planned to do during the meeting was sit here and smile while you did all the talking."

She took in a deep breath. "What will happen to your cousin if you don't go?"

"He'll be put in state's custody."

Tears softened her flustered expression. "I wouldn't wish foster care on my worst enemy." She closed her eyes. "Go."

A brief hug sealed the deal. "Thank you for under-standing, Lexa. I meant every word I said about you pulling this off. You'll cover for me with Preston?"

She pushed me away. "Yes. Just go, go, go before I change my mind already."

She didn't have to tell me twice. I rushed out of the building, thanking God I'd been humble enough to teach Lexa how to shine. I thought I'd been helping her, but in reality, I'd helped myself.

I called Aunt Dottie to give her an update. In her own way, she told me to be careful and not worry. Maybe it's wrong to speed when God has made a way, but my right foot didn't get the memo. I made it back to Bayford in record time and called Jacob for final instructions.

At the courthouse, we touched and agreed in prayer. Jacob squeezed my trembling hands as he muttered in closing, "Amen."

As we walked into the building, Jacob said, "I saw DeAndre earlier. He's fine. He thinks he's on an adven-ture." Jacob unfurled a paper he'd been holding onto and explained, "Here's some paperwork you need to complete and give to the secretary before the hearing. I've already listed you as a concerned party."

My biggest fear assuaged, Jacob and I took a seat on the left side of the courtroom. Looked like something straight out of a scene from the Salem Witch Trials. Hard-wood floors, intimidating gargoyles in all four corners of the room, simple chairs for everyone except the judge, whose ample behind had obviously been sitting in big, comfortable lounge chairs most of his adult life. I had to cut him some slack, though. Maybe listening to people's arguments and troubles all day drained him of all energy. If his life was half as dramatic as my week, he needed to stay seated.

"Are we on the correct side?" I whispered to Jacob as two attorneys approached the bench to consult with the judge.

"Quiet in the courtroom!" the judge boomed.

Out of habit, I tweeted, "Sorry."

"I said quiet, or I'll have you both removed!"

Jacob grabbed my hand. The bailiff flashed me an apologetic grin. *Okay, so it's not me.* This judge *had* to be some kinda kin to Joenetta Lester. I checked out his nameplate. Judge Peter Kiplinger, JD.

"Lord, You are good and Your mercy endureth forever," someone's ring-tone blasted. The guilty party, an elderly redheaded gentleman two rows ahead, scurried to silence the phone before the line repeated.

Oh my gosh!

Judge Kiplinger slammed his gavel. "Bailiff, remove that man from the courtroom and issue a ticket for disrupting our proceedings."

Maybe DeAndre had been right after all about these Bayford County judges being bad. Jacob and I both double-checked our phones to make sure we wouldn't be the next victims. In the process, a text from Lexa caught my eye. We lost Inner-G. Heads will roll. You were wrong about me. I froze.

How could this be? After all we'd done, after I prayed to God? Nothing made sense, but I had to refocus.

I gave myself the same pep talk I'd given Lexa only hours before. *I am a big girl. I can do this. I'm a trained professional. I can market myself.*

Not helping, especially after Lexa's awful news.

When my own words didn't work, I tried the scriptures with greater success. *I can do all things through Christ, who strengthens me.*

When they called all concerned parties in our case

forward, I was still trembling—but only on the inside. The state's caseworker actually smiled as she passed me. I stood, not sure of exactly what I was supposed to do. The knee-level swinging doors hit the back of my legs as I cautiously entered Judge Kiplinger's playpen.

"You coming forward or what?" he asked.

I cleared my throat. "Yes. You want me to come up there?"

"Affirmative."

I can do all things through Christ, who strengthens me. I took another step toward the judge's stand, surprised my joints hadn't given out on me already. In a passing manner, I looked back at Jacob. He nodded slightly, confirming the scriptures.

"Your honor," the caseworker began, "this is simply a matter of formality. DeAndre Lester was found riding around town this morning on his bicycle. The state requests custody until we can determine whether or not he is being properly supervised."

He turned to me. "And who are you?"

"I'm Tori Henderson. DeAndre is my cousin. I'd like to request temporary custody."

"Oh." The caseworker smiled again, her curly blond wig mirroring her bubbly personality. "You must be the one he was trying to visit. When the police asked DeAndre where he was going, he said he was riding to Houston to be with Cousin Tori. Evidently, he's very fond of you."

Emotion flooded my body. *He was coming to see me?* I had to stay centered.

"Miss Henderson," the judge inquired, "what is your relation to DeAndre?"

"He's my cousin . . . by marriage."

"Whose marriage?"

"My mother married his uncle."

"So he's not your *first c*ousin?" Here we go with all this numerical stuff!

"No, your honor. But his aunt, *our* aunt, was caring for him until she had a stroke. I stepped in to help and I've been taking care of him for several weeks now."

Judge Kiplinger took a moment to review DeAndre's file. "His mother's incarcerated?"

"Yes," the caseworker and I said.

"But you live in Houston?" he questioned again.

"For now."

"For *now*? When do you plan on moving—and where to?"

"I'm not exactly sure, we're—*I'm* . . . in the process of making a decision . . . about moving."

Judge Kiplinger leaned back in his chair and crossed his arms. The caseworker bit her lip. I felt my face tingling under the judge's ogling eyes. He pressed a finger on his temple, raising a row of wrinkles that covered his fingertips.

"Who lives with you in Houston?"

Suddenly, I wished Jacob hadn't come along. "My friend."

"Your friend *who*?"

"Kevin Walker. But we just broke up. I won't be living with him much longer."

Judge Kiplinger raised his voice. "So you're living in Houston with your ex-boyfriend—for now—and you want me to grant you permission to drag little DeAndre hundreds of miles away to thrive in *your* unstable home?"

The caseworker focused on the floor, where my heart lay.

"Absolutely not," Judge Kiplinger lambasted. "I will not subject this child to a questionable living arrangement. DeAndre Lester is hereby awarded to the state pending further investigation by the Department of Child Protective Services."

That stupid gavel sealed DeAndre's doom, in my wretched opinion. "Next case."

Numb, I passed through the hinged doors wondering how my life could get any worse. Jacob met me at the aisle and put an arm around my shoulder, escorting me from the courtroom. I burst into tears on the courthouse steps.

"They wouldn't let me have him, Jacob. He's in foster care and it's my fault," I cried into his chest.

He wrapped his arms around me, kept me from melting right there on the concrete.

With snot dripping from my nose, I looked up into Jacob's eyes. "I'm sorry, Jacob, about the whole Kevin thing. I wanted to tell you, but—"

"Shhhh," he stopped me. "We can talk about that later."

I felt a slight tap on my shoulder. "I'm so sorry," the caseworker tried to comfort me. "We'll take good care of him. Here's my card." I read the name: Stella Gentry. "Call me if you have any questions. I'll do my best to keep communication open between you and DeAndre. You obviously love him very much."

"Yes. I do."

"Well, don't you worry, Miss Henderson. The foster families in Bayford County are *very* receptive to colored children."

Ain't that special?

Chapter 29

I worried myself sick that next week. Literally. Fever, chills, runny nose, no appetite. Despite Cassandra's whopping daily cash register balance, I was bummed about DeAndre, Jacob, and NetMarketing. In essence, my entire life had bottomed out. My nightly prayer centered not on my problems, but on DeAndre's well-being.

God, I don't know why You allowed him to be put in foster care. People say I'm not supposed to ask You questions, but since I'm already thinking it, You might as well know—I do wish I knew why You allowed this. Just like with Job.

Anyway, I trust You know what You are doing. Please protect him. Please work this whole thing out like Your Word says. Amen.

Instead of me reading scriptures to Aunt Dottie, she read to me nightly. If I followed along in my Bible, I could decipher her words. She emphasized encouraging passages—mostly in Jeremiah and Isaiah. Every day, her speech improved. This must be what DeAndre did for her—sat and listened to her talk.

Jacob dropped by once to check on me. Being subject

to his bright, cheerful aura made me feel even worse. Why was he being so nice to me after what I'd disclosed in court? The woman he deserved in his life certainly wasn't sharing an address with another man.

Aunt Dottie left us alone in the kitchen. My hair was as dry and brittle as my lips but I didn't even care. This was the *real* me Jacob claimed was dead. Yeah, he had the Bible on his side, but my phantom was stronger than most, I guessed.

"You don't have to keep playing this charade." I granted him a get-out-of-jail-free card.

"Who's playing?"

"Achoo!"

"Bless you," he conferred. He snatched a paper towel from the holder on the counter and rejoined me at the table. "Here."

"Jacob, stop with the kind come-as-you-are thing already. Don't you want to know who I was living with and why?" I grilled him.

"Yeah." He came clean finally. "But I figure you'll tell me when you're ready."

"I'm ready to get it over with."

He tightened the corners of his lips. "Go."

"Kevin's my ex-boyfriend. We lived together for eighteen months. In fact, I was living with him when I came here to Bayford."

Jacob's brows jumped.

"But he's never home. He's a traveling salesman. We hardly ever see each other."

Jacob solicited, "But you *were* living together?"

"Yes."

"And you never moved out?"

"No. But I plan to."

He posed another question. "What's the holdup?"

"I don't know. I mean, my life was cut and dry before I came back to Bayford. Then the store, and DeAndre, and . . . you. Everything changed."

"I told you things would be different once you started walking in the Word."

"I thought you meant for *better*, not for worse. Now DeAndre's in foster care, my job is in jeopardy, and you know *all* my personal business."

He laughed quietly to himself. "Yes, ma'am. I sure do."

"I'm sorry, Jacob." I laid my hand on top of his. "Being with you has shown me what it's like to be in a real relationship with someone who actually has my best interest at heart. The more I got to know you, the more I realized . . . what I had with Kevin wasn't real. He became less and less significant until there was nothing to tell, really."

"Is that the whole truth?"

I laced my fingers between his. "Yes. Kevin and I were finished a long time ago."

"Well, since we're putting all our cards on the table, there's something I need to tell you, too."

"Surprises are not welcome. What?"

"I already knew about Kevin."

"How?"

"How else?" he hinted.

"DeAndre."

"Yeah. You might not want to tell him too many of your secrets," Jacob warned. "He told me Kevin *lived* there, but he didn't *stay* there. Had me confused."

"Why didn't you just ask me?"

"It wasn't time. We haven't committed to anything formal, haven't made any declarations about this relationship—if that's what it is. I didn't want to pressure you," he rationalized. "I still don't."

"Don't what?"

"Don't want to pressure you."

Jacob probably didn't mean to sound like Kevin in his effort to prevent stress in our relationship, but I'd heard this all before. In my brain, no pressure meant no obligation. No accountability. And, by the same token, no passion.

"I like pressure, Jacob. Pressure makes me sharper. Gives me something to look forward to."

He smiled. "Me, too. So here's my first and probably my only pressurized question."

"Already?"

Stress lines formed on his forehead. "How soon can you move out of the apartment you're sharing with the old dude?"

"Depends on what happens with my job. I'm meeting with my boss soon."

His facial muscles relaxed. "All right, Schnookums."

"Uh, let's *not* do pet names."

"Aw, come on, Honey Bun."

I protested, all the while leaning in for our second kiss. My only regret was lack of lip gloss. I cut the kiss short, from sheer embarrassment. "Sorry about my lips."

"Yeah." He laughed. "You kinda nicked me there."

I whacked his unyielding shoulder. "Stop."

"Might need stitches."

"Anyway!"

Cassandra hauled me out of bed and up to the store as soon as I'd been fever-free for a day. "Look, girlie, we gotta keep it jumpin' and humpin'. Walmart's been open for a week already, and we're holding our own."

I pulled the sheets over my head. "Who let you in here?"

"None other than your favorite person on earth."

Now that Aunt Dottie could amble around the house with her scooter (she ordered a red one), she'd gotten into the habit of taking company again. We had guests galore, just like I remembered from my high school days.

"I'm sorry about DeAndre," Cassandra fussed, "but he's gonna be all right. Did you talk to the caseworker lady?"

"Yes." I spoke into the bedding. "Ms. Gentry says he's with a nice colored family with other colored children his age and adjusting very well. She says he's playing baseball, too."

"Okay, so she was wrong for the colored thing. But this is Bayford. Look on the bright side," Cassandra perked. "He might actually win a game or two."

I ignored Cassandra's optimism. "I'll bet she tells every family member this same story. What else can she say? She won't tell me DeAndre's crying his eyes out every night, that he wants to come home so he can be around other coloreds who actually love him."

Cassandra's feet halted their pacing. "DeAndre is in God's care. He always has been and he always will be. How do you think he made it to the sanctity of Aunt Dottie's house with a momma like Zoletha Simpson and a daddy like Ray-Ray Lester? God's protecting DeAndre for His purposes. Have a little faith."

I tucked the sheets under my chin and watched as Cassandra authorized herself to open my closet doors and select my clothing. She laid a pair of jeans and a baby-doll T-shirt on the end of my bed. "Now get up before I get Aunt Dottie to roll in here and pop you with her good arm. She might ziggle you with the other one, too. She's getting pretty strong, I see."

Cassandra opened the top drawer of my bureau, grabbed my black hat with silver rhinestones, and tossed it to me. "Here. Take this, too. We're going to Walmart after we close Dottie's tonight."

"Why?"

Her eyes became slits. "We need to scope out the competition. See what kind of specials they're advertising, see which products they've put on their end caps. Only best-selling items get prime placement in a store, you know? I've been doin' my homework, fo' rizzle."

"So why the hat?"

"Celebrity disguise. Can't have Dottie's customers thinking we're Walmart groupies," she whispered.

"I'm not wearing this hat."

She took a look at my do. "You might wanna rethink your position. Your hair is straight Shaka Zulu right now."

"So. You got a problem with Shaka Zulu?" I objected. "There's nothing wrong with my natural African naps."

"Girl, please. Shaka wouldn't claim you. He'd say 'she no in our tribe. Enemy afro texture. Seize her! Wool-loo-woolloo-woolloo!'"

Cassandra's clowning sparked a giggle deep inside me that ballooned into a full-blown guffaw. "You are crazy, for real!"

"Woolloo-woolloo-woolloo!" she shrieked again, repeatedly tapping my afro with a hanger.

Elbows covering my head, I surrendered. "Okay! I'm up! I'm up, Shaka!"

I noticed Aunt Dottie parked at my doorway, her body bouncing with laughter.

"Aunt Dottie, why did you open the door for Cassandra?"

She waved my question away.

Cassandra shouted, "'Cause she loves you, girl."

Aunt Dottie corroborated with a glint in her eyes, "Aaah luuuh you, Toor."

There it was, spoken from her own lips. Sometimes those three words make all the difference between a life falling apart or coming together.

"I love you, too, Aunt Dottie."

"Awwwie! Group hug!" Cassandra decreed. "Group hug!"

We got to the store just before Cassandra released the Dottie's Throwback text, which always brought in a rush of patrons.

Virgie and Elgin welcomed me back, as well as the entire town of Bayford, it seemed. "We've been praying for you, Tori"; "We know God will work everything out for you and DeAndre"; "Missed you."

The support from people who didn't know me personally lifted my spirits tremendously. Some of them probably knew me because of Aunt Dottie. Others maybe because of Jacob. Nonetheless, they cared because, in some way, we were connected.

Almost made me forget about my problems. Almost.

We closed the store with another successful count. Though Cassandra was supposed to go home hours ago, her dedication to the success of Dottie's knew no end.

Cassandra and I helped Elgin lock up, since Virgie had to work her other job that evening. "Elgin, we'll see you tomorrow," Cassandra discharged. "Don't break anything on the dance floor tonight."

"Can't make no promises," he clucked.

We made it to Walmart a little after eight. The parking lot was packed, which surprised me. I guess I figured since we were in such a small town, there wouldn't be so many shoppers. Wrong. Super-wrong.

"Dang!" Cassandra gawked. "Everybody and their *second* cousin is here! Shabooty!"

We drove around for a while hoping for a good spot. Nothing opened after creeping up and down three aisles.

"Looks like we're going to have to foot it, homie," Cassandra concluded. She gave in to a block on row H. After parking, she tapped my hat's bill. "Pull it lower."

"I will not," I griped.

"All right," she hissed, "if the paparazzi catches you in the enemy's territory, don't blame me."

"You are too serious about this," I warned her. "We are not spies."

"I know. For real, though, I need a new kitchen rug."

"Get out, Sandra."

We entered the store. Bright lights illuminated the warehouse motif. Polished concrete floors, exposed beams high overhead, humongous signs marking the various departments.

"We need signs in Dottie's," Cassandra noted on a mini-spiral she'd produced from nowhere.

"Everyone knows Dottie's layout," I reminded her.

"Doesn't matter. The signs aren't up to let you know where everything is—they're suggesting things you hadn't even thought about buying before you walked in the store," she explained. "Suggestive selling."

Shut my mouth.

"You go down the snack aisles. I'll check the meats and produce." She tore off a sheet of paper and handed me a pen.

"What am I looking for?"

"Go down the aisles and see which items are at eye

level and on the end caps. Write down their names and prices," she instructed. "And if you see anything that shocks you—layout, placement, pricing—make a note."

I had to give it to her. "Girl, you've really got your stuff together."

"You ain't said nothin' but a word, double-o-seven, nothin' but a word. One last thing."

"What?"

"Keep your head low. I've already seen three people I know."

"Gotcha."

Pumped by Cassandra's sense of adventure, I took off on assignment, taking notes as I perused the aisles: "Doritos—$2.99, powdered doughnuts—$2.39. Graham crackers on the bottom shelf? I definitely needed to notify Cassandra of these findings.

I was on my second page of notes when I heard the loudest, countriest, most welcomed scream. "Miss Tori!"

Like a mother who recognizes her child's voice among a sea of youth, I immediately turned toward the voice. "DeAndre?"

He squeezed through two people's shopping carts and hopped over a bag of fallen Tostitos to reach me. *DeAndre!*

He leapt into my embrace and wrapped his arms around my neck. I spun him around twice, savoring the distinct odor of little-boy-needing-a-bath. "Hey, you! I'm so glad to see you!" I kissed his cheek.

He wiped it off. "Miss Tori, you can't kiss me in front of other people."

"But I miss you," I laughed. In just a few weeks' time, he looked older already. "How are you? Who are you here with?"

"I'm fine. I'm shopping with Miss Retford. She's my

foster mother." He pointed down the aisle toward a plump brunette woman who was temporarily blocked by other carts in maneuvering her way toward us. Two other school-age boys tagged along.

"What are you doing here?" he asked.

"I'm working. What are you doing here?"

"You're always working, Cousin Tori."

I winked at him. "I'm sorry. I should have spent more time with you. So, how's your foster family? Are they treating you right? Are they hitting you? Has anyone touched you where they're not supposed to?"

"No, no bad stuff." His face shined. "Guess what!"

"What?"

"We get to play video games on Fridays and Saturdays."

"That's great, DeAndre!"

"But I'm not that good yet."

"Hey." I squinted my eyes. "Why'd you run away from your daddy's house?"

"'Cause they made me sleep in the closet."

It took every ounce of self-control in me to remain calm. I needed to get the full story out of him without going off or breaking down. "Why?"

"'Cause my baby sister was crying. So I was trying to wipe her tears, but I didn't see a towel. So I used the pillow to wipe her eyes. And my stepmom said I was trying to summo . . . suffum . . ."

"Suffocate the baby?" I finished his sentence.

"Yeah. That."

I stabbed his chest with my index finger. "DeAndre, you didn't do anything wrong. If they think you would suffocate a baby, they obviously don't know what a wonderful, nice young man you are."

"Right!"

We high-fived on it.

As Miss Retford neared us, I set DeAndre's feet back on the ground.

"Miss Retford, this is my cousin Tori. Tori, this is Miss Retford. And this is Paul and Jamie. We're brothers. Kinda."

"Gail," she deformalized the conversation, shaking my hand.

Paul and Jamie politely spoke for themselves. "Hello, Miss Tori." I noted Paul's curly locks and droopy eyes, traits also present in Gail's gene pool.

"Hello there. I hear you two are teaching DeAndre how to play video games, huh?"

"Only on weekends," Gail reiterated. "Homework and baseball on weekdays."

"Double-o-seven," Cassandra summoned behind me. "What are you—hey, DeAndre!"

"Hi, Miss Sandra."

I stepped aside, putting Gail in Cassandra's line of sight. And then God answered my prayer right before my very eyes.

"Hey, Gail! Haven't seen you in a while! How's my favorite uncle's wife?"

Gail and Cassandra hugged. "So you've got DeAndre, huh?"

"Yes," from Gail. "He's an absolute joy. Fits right in, no problems."

"Good," Cassandra cheered, then she turned to me. "Tori, Gail is married to my very favorite uncle on my father's side, Uncle Stoney. He spent a lot of time in the military, been all over the world. He and Gail have been keeping foster kids for—what? Five years?"

"Seven, actually," Gail piped with pride. "But we only

do short-term placements. It's too hard on Paul when we keep kids for a long time and then have to let them go."

I feel you, Paul.

Cassandra added, "Uncle Stoney's a truck driver, Gail's a full-time mom."

Keeping up with three boys DeAndre's age was probably a double-time job. Everybody ain't able. "Well, I'm glad to know DeAndre is with good people." Understatement of the day.

"Next to Aunt Dottie's, this is the best place he could be," Cassandra confirmed.

Remembrance of a verse kindled within me. "All things work together for the good of them who love the Lord." This time I even recalled the reference—Romans 8:28. My shoulders lightened, my heart lifted. Cassandra had been right—DeAndre was in God's care all along.

Gail extended, "If you'd like, we can contact Miss Gentry and arrange for visitation."

"That would be great. Thanks."

"No problem. She's pretty good about keeping kids in touch with their families."

"Ooh! Momma, can we get some Gushers?" Paul pleaded.

Gail pushed her basket forward. "No, no Gushers. Let's get off this aisle completely."

"Awww," he whined.

"Ladies, we've got to get home before too late."

I reached down for another hug from DeAndre. He grabbed me tightly. And just before we let go of each other, he murmured in my ear, "I love you, Cousin Tori."

"I love you, too, DeAndre. You be good."

"Okay. See you later." He took off to catch up with Gail and the boys. Before they left the snack aisle, he secretly waved good-bye to me.

Cassandra rested her shoulder against mine. "God truly worked that out, my sister."

I stood in amazement, almost breathless. "I know."

Cassandra puckered her lips for a moment, then testified, "You know I'm pretty cautious about white folks. But I can vouch for Gail. She's good people. My sister even takes her boys to play at Uncle Stoney's house sometimes, when she feels like driving the distance."

"How far are they from Bayford?"

"Well, they're another fifteen minutes west, so I guess altogether about forty minutes from Aunt Dottie's."

I marveled, "Are you related to every single person in Bayford County?"

She tittered. "Darn near. Let's just say my daddy got around, and so did his daddy. Tell you what, though. I ain't marryin' no crazy joker who can't keep his behind in the home zone." She turned an imaginary key. "Click! Click! Lock it down or . . ." She struggled for a rhyme.

"Your body won't be found . . . alive?" I tried.

Cassandra flared her nostrils. "Dog, girl, I ain't say nothin' 'bout killin' nobody."

"It rhymes—*down, found.*"

"Nuh uh." She snapped her fingers. "And you're dating my *second* cousin?"

"Who in this entire region of Texas *isn't* your cousin?"

She laughed. "I gotta keep my eye on you, Tori."

After a few more spying missions, we shopped for Cassandra's rug and got in line. The woman two carts ahead of us, Miss Macie Corbie, a daily Dottie's customer Cassandra and I both recognized, was in a heated argument with the cashier.

"I thought you said y'all beat the competition's coupons," Miss Corbie insisted.

"Ma'am, we do match our competitors' advertised prices in *print*."

Miss Corbie wagged her cell phone in the cashier's face. "Here's the coupon from Dottie's right here. Chicken noodle soup for a quarter a can! Can't you read!"

Cassandra and I turned to each other in shocked unison.

"Ma'am, this is a text message, not a coupon."

"Well, I don't want nothin' in this basket then! Nothing!" Miss Corbie announced to everyone within hearing distance, "False advertising in here! I'm shoppin' at Dottie's like I always have!" She left her basket and slowly shuffled away.

Cassandra and I high-fived. "Can't nobody do it like Dottie's," she chanted. "Can't nobody do it like Dottie's."

Chapter 30

I slept well after learning DeAndre was in good temporary hands, but I knew Judge Kiplinger wouldn't consider returning DeAndre to me and Aunt Dottie so long as I was technically living in sin with Kevin. I needed a new address, and this meeting with Preston weighed heavily on my residential status.

From my perspective, there were only two options. Door number one, Preston could fire me for unsatisfactory job performance. Forget all the good things I'd done before Inner-G and while Lexa headed the account. Current bottom lines weighed more than past accomplishments.

Door number two, Preston could save my neck but conclude that the telecommute trial had failed and kindly request/order me to hightail it back to the office, where he could micromanage me until I proved myself again.

In either case, I'd need to move back to Houston; to find another well-paying job (which could take forever, given the economy); or maintain the one I'd been graced to keep.

Neither scenario would satisfy Judge Kiplinger, whom

I gathered wasn't exactly gung ho about moving DeAndre out of Bayford County.

Preston, who was scheduled to attend a weeklong summit in Dayton, Ohio, said our meeting couldn't wait until he returned. "Could we possibly meet on a Sunday?"

"Sure," I replied. Sunday was just as good a day as any to get raked over the coals.

Cassandra wanted to go along for the ride, so with Kevin safely out of state, she and I set out for Houston after closing the following Saturday night.

She marveled at my apartment. "Oh my goody-woody! Love your floors! The architecture!"

"All Kevin's. I can't wait to move."

She visually searched the walls. "No pictures?"

"No," I admitted. "This was *his* place, remember?" I'd filled her in on all the Kevin drama while we drove.

"Right, right. Maybe you could stay in this complex, just move to another unit."

"Hmmm." I considered. "Might not be a bad idea. Except I'm sure I'd run into Kevin here every now and then."

"So?" she balked. "*He* should be ashamed to look *you* in the eyes, not the other way around."

Good point.

Cassandra and I spent a few hours packing up my belongings, marking and labeling boxes for storage. Kevin had promised to arrange for moving and storage when he got back in town so long as I organized my belongings.

After a late night, Cassandra and I got up early Sunday morning searching for a church. "I'll go online and find one," I offered.

"Not necessary. I do have one cousin in Houston. He said just look for a Williams Chicken and there'll be a Missionary Baptist or a CME church within a three-mile radius," she quoted.

"I'm not familiar with Williams Chicken locations."

She bucked her eyes at me.

"I don't eat much fried chicken."

"Could have fooled me."

My cell phone got us to a small, white frame church tucked behind—where else?—a Williams Chicken restaurant. Cassandra and I withstood curious stares and speculative smiles, but soon got into the service as the members realized we knew the words to the choir's hymns. We weren't heathens.

After church, we grabbed lunch at Panera. I dropped Cassandra off at the apartment and gave her a satellite TV lesson to keep her occupied while I ran off to meet with Preston.

I used my key—maybe for the last time—to enter the locked building. Preston, uncharacteristically flanked by piles of paperwork, was waiting for me in his office. Framed pictures of his family had been overtaken by spreadsheets, charts, and graphs.

"Hi, Tori. Sorry for the mess. I've got a ton of work to accomplish before I fly out tomorrow. Thanks for agreeing to meet with me today."

"No problem." I moved a stack of papers from the least cluttered chair, placed them on the floor next to my feet.

Preston's tranquil demeanor scared me. Was this the calm before the storm? *God, do whatever is best.*

"So, what gives?" I asked.

He tapped a few last computer keys, cleared an area on his desk, folded his hands, and finally faced me. "I don't have to tell you the meeting with Inner-G didn't go well for Lexa."

I sighed. "She texted me."

"They were not impressed with her. To be honest, neither was I. What *did* impress them, however, was the number of times she referred to you as the magic key holder. They'd ask a question, she'd say, 'Well, as soon as I hear back from my colleague, Tori, I'll be able to respond accurately, blah, blah, blah.'

"Long story short, they pulled the plug on us. And I let Lexa go."

I flinched at the news, wondering how Lexa would process this disappointment. Before this incident, I might have gloated in her demise. Not now.

"Late last week, Inner-G's head honcho called me. He said after he'd heard your name so many times during the botched meeting and saw Tori Henderson computer-stamped at the bottom of the only comprehensible data Lexa produced, he and his team decided they'd stay with NetMarketing if and only if they could work directly with the infamous Tori Henderson.

I took a deep, processing breath.

Preston continued, "If you take on this assignment, your old clients will be reassigned. I'd want you dedicated to Inner-G alone. You need to get out there, travel with them, immerse yourself in sports and hip-hop culture. Learn this market like the back of your hand. Eat, drink, and live Inner-G. Lots of long, hard, nose-to-the-grindstone hours."

Overwhelmed by his demanding spiel, I interrupted him. "Can I still work remotely?" Given my Bayford-inspired prioritizing skills, I might be able to pull this off. Well, everything except the travel.

"No." Preston killed the dream. "I need you here."

When my face hinted disappointment, Preston tried flattery. "I can't think of anyone who's more dedicated to NetMarketing than you. So, what do you say, Tori?"

A few months ago—before appendicitis, before DeAndre, Jacob, reconnecting with Aunt Dottie, God, and the good people of Bayford—I would have dived head-first into this opportunity, no questions asked. *Isn't this the recognition and position I've always wanted?*

My mouth went dry. "H-how soon must I make a decision?"

Muscles knotted in Preston's neck. "Tori, what's there to think about?"

"My life," I said under my breath.

He peered at me, bemused.

"I have to think . . . and pray about this."

"You *do* want to keep your job, don't you?" he threatened, clicking the top of his ink pen repeatedly.

"Yes, I do," I admitted. "But I've learned life isn't about me. I have other priorities, other people I care about to consider." *For once.*

He hurled his hands back onto the keyboard and started typing again, severing eye contact with me. He bit off the final words of our meeting. "Let me know by tomorrow morning."

"Okay."

I dismissed myself, wondering where this new and depreciated Preston Haverty had been hiding all these years. I'd seen him angry, of course, but never rude. Never disrespectful. Then again, we'd never had so much at stake.

Before I left the building, I made a conscious decision to forgive Phantom Preston. No way could I arrive at the best option under the influence of anger.

I veered off the path to the exit doors in order to use the ladies' room. The need to hear from God pressed heavily on my heart. What if Preston removed his offer from the table by morning? What if Judge Kiplinger's attitude never changed, no matter what my circumstances? Was it fair to move DeAndre to Houston so I could drown myself in work? What about Jacob?

As I pushed through the women's bathroom door, two little girls, younger than DeAndre, scampered into empty stalls, slamming the doors shut. *Odd.*

"Hello?" I called to them. "Are you girls okay?"

Just then, a woman nearing Aunt Dottie's age slipped into the restroom, softly closing the door behind her. Her wispy, cotton-spun hair retained her Sunday-morning roller set with great effort. The fancy curls contrasted with the mop and bucket she'd managed to glide into the restroom noiselessly.

"I'm sorry, ma'am. I hope they're not bothering you."

"Oh, no," I assured her, "I was only making sure they weren't alone."

The woman smiled relief. "These are my granddaughters. I have to bring them to work with me on Sundays."

"It's like that sometimes," I related.

She leaned in and whispered, "Please don't tell anyone."

"My lips are sealed."

"Come on out, girls. It's time to go."

Bows and bouncing twists emerged from the stalls. The girls shied toward their grandmother. The woman winked as she walked away. "You understand the importance of family, I see. God always rewards a tender heart."

Peace filled my chest so completely, I didn't need to wait until morning to give Preston my answer. I confidently strolled back to his office. With a hint of cheer in my voice, I caught his attention at the doorway. "Preston?"

"Yes." His brow arched and rounded, mimicking my optimism. He clapped twice. "I knew you'd make the right choice. Welcome back, Tori."

"No, no. I'm not coming back. I can't take the Inner-G account." I burst his bubble.

He gulped and chewed his bottom lip. "I hate to lose you, Tori. You're a smart lady, but the economy's in a slump. You sure about this?"

"Don't worry about me. I've got faith and family. I'll land on my feet. I'll be in touch." Turning my back to him, I ended the conversation.

"Tori, wait."

"Yes?" I stopped, looked in his direction again. *Oooh, those glasses.*

Preston shifted nervously in his chair, his jawline tightening. In that instant, I realized Preston wasn't concerned about me. His anxiety centered around NetMarketing. Losing Inner-G meant losing money and blowing the contract of a lifetime. Preston had more at stake than me, actually. I mean, really, what sense would it make to fire the one person who could save NetMarketing's reputation with its biggest client ever? He'd be next on *his* boss's chopping block.

"Let me rethink the remote alternative," he compromised. "If we hired a production assistant to travel with Inner-G and handle the minute details, this might work. Colleges are always looking to place eager interns. We might even get a tax break for giving someone else a chance to get their feet wet."

"Okay," I agreed, stunned at his unexpected rollover. "I'll wait to hear from you."

Cassandra and I laughed about Preston's change of heart half the long way home, then we praised God for His intervention.

"Girl, God's lining your entire, best life up for you," she teased. "Before long, Daddy'll have you spoiled rotten, thinking every good and perfect thing you pray for is supposed to happen."

"Well," I hesitated, "it *is* supposed to happen, right? I mean, why pray if you don't expect God to move?"

"That's what I'm talkin' 'bout!" She clapped. "Preach, girl! You talkin' like somebody who knows the Word now!"

Chapter 31

I could hardly wait to tell Jacob what happened with the NetMarketing situation. I called him immediately after I dropped Cassandra off at her paid-for home.

"Hey, how are you?"

"Good. How was the trip?"

His lowered tone concerned me. "You all right?"

"Yeah."

"You busy?"

"No," he sighed. "Not really."

My brows furrowed instinctively. "I'm no voice analysis major," I teased, "but you certainly don't sound like yourself."

He laughed softly. "Got a lot on my mind."

"Would a frappuccino help?"

"No. Not this time."

"Well, you know," I imitated him, "I'm not God, but I'm a pretty good sounding board."

Out of the blue, he perked up and asked, "You want to go bowling?"

"Sure. When?"

"Now."

"Now?"

"Yeah. Lanes don't close for another couple of hours."

Ten minutes later, Jacob was opening the passenger's door for me. We made it to Bowl-King on my testimony of God's hand moving at NetMarketing. "I think I'm going to be able to work from home, too. Isn't that great?"

"That's great, Tori," was the full extent of his excitement for me—for us.

"Jacob, are you listening to me?"

He parked the Camry. "No. I'm sorry."

We sat in silence for a moment, looking out the car windows, then at each other.

"What's wrong?"

He ran a finger across his lips. "My dad. He told me, after church today, the doctors say he's in the first phase of Alzheimer's. He wants me to start transitioning the church, preparing them for my leadership."

The second I heard Jacob speak those words, one of Aunt Dottie's favorite verses arrested my spirit. "What about Jeremiah twenty-nine and eleven?"

Jacob recited the scripture. "'For I know the plans I have for you, declares the Lord, plans to prosper you and not to harm you, plans to give you hope and a future.'"

I reiterated, "God has *good* plans for you *and* your father."

Jacob shook his head. "But Alzheimer's is Alzheimer's, you know? It's slow. Humiliating. Degenerating. I can't watch him decline and be there for my mom while taking over the church, too. I don't think I'm up to it, Tori. I really don't."

Jacob sounded like me when I first moved to Bayford. Overwhelmed with new responsibilities, unsure of how to accomplish the daunting tasks ahead. I still didn't know what was going to happen with the store or exactly how DeAndre would fare, but when I looked back over the past few months and saw God's faithfulness, I had no reason to doubt His ability to figure out the rest of my mess.

"Jacob, you'd be surprised how much pressure God can handle inside you. He's amazing. He just lines up circumstances and people in your favor. I can't even explain how He does it."

Jacob's eyes sought mine. "You truly believe His Words, don't you?"

"With all my heart."

Jacob smiled again. He grabbed my hand and kissed my palm. "Thanks for being here, and for being one of the people sent to help me through."

"Any time."

He tilted his head, jokingly, and asked, "You mean like *any* time any time, or like *some* of the time any time?"

"*Any* time."

"Like you're moving out of your apartment *any* time?"

"Like I've already arranged to put my stuff in storage *any* time," I informed him.

He pressed once more. "Okay, so is this like you're moving to Bayford *any* time?"

Fully aware of the commitment he was groping for, I replied, "Yes, I'm relocating to Bayford."

Jacob's smile faded. "What if your new client won't allow a remote office?"

"Then I won't work for them," I stated. "DeAndre's placement is only temporary. Aunt Dottie still has a long way to go in her recovery. And you."

"What about me?" he fished.

"*You.* And whatever God is doing to us. Another amazing surprise."

"I'm not surprised," he bragged, pinching his chin.

"Oh—you already knew Aunt Dottie would have a stroke and I'd come back to town and fall in love with you?"

Did I just say that?

Jacob covered my face with his, kissing me softly. Almost solemnly, as though we'd just made an everlasting agreement.

Yeah, I just said that.

Chapter 32

"All parties in the matter of DeAndre Lester, please step forward."

Jacob squeezed my hand. "Be strong."

I'd wanted to wear my power suit, but I didn't think Judge Kiplinger would take kindly to me projecting an authoritative stance in his courtroom. I couldn't come off like a city-slicker. By the same token, I needed to appear confident and capable of taking care of an eight-year-old boy, without a husband.

Ms. Gentry approached the bench along with another gentleman, Mr. Ybarra, whom I'd never met before but was expecting. He was a volunteer who'd been assigned to DeAndre's case by an organization named CASA (Court Appointed Special Advocate). As I understood things, this gentleman's job was to speak on behalf of DeAndre's best interest.

We all introduced ourselves as we stood before Judge Kiplinger, who took his time about reviewing the notes in DeAndre's case.

Man, you've had seven weeks to look at those notes! I literally bit my tongue to keep my attitude in check. The judge had already thrown out two people in the half hour we'd been waiting for our hearing.

"Ms. Gentry, please inform the court of your findings."

"Your honor," she began, "DeAndre was left in the care of his father, grandmother, and stepmother when he ran away. We find those caregivers unfit to care for him due to the disturbing family dynamics recorded in DeAndre's file. The state would prefer to place DeAndre in the care of other, suitable family members." She gestured toward me.

Thank you, Ms. Gentry!

She continued, "However, if that's not possible, we recommend he remain in state custody."

Judge Kiplinger asked, "How's he doing with his current foster family?"

"Oh, he's fine, your honor, but the family he's with now only accepts temporary placements. He'll have to be moved again next week."

"I see," from the judge. He eyed me for a second, then shifted his focus back to the papers. "Mr. Ybarra, what are your recommendations?"

"I agree with Ms. Gentry, your honor. DeAndre is doing well now, but it would be best for him to be placed with responsible family members. He's head-over-heels about his cousin Tori. She's the best fit for him."

Two votes for me!

Finally, Judge Kiplinger addressed me. "Miss Henderson, has your living situation been stabilized?"

"Yes, your honor. I'm living in Bayford now."

"And you have steady employment?"

I nodded eagerly and slapped my letter of employment verification from NetMarketing on the platform. "Yes. My job in Houston allows me to work from home."

He examined Preston's letter. "Says here you're traveling ten percent of the time."

My throat tightened. "It'd be more like once every couple of weeks, mostly just to Houston and back. They hired an assistant for me and everything, Judge Kiplinger."

"I don't give a rat's behind who they've hired. I want to know who'll watch DeAndre while you're trotting the globe in your fancy suits."

I hadn't figured that part out yet. "My aunt. Jacob." I pointed behind me.

Judge Kiplinger grilled me. "Who's he? Your new boyfriend?"

"Yes, but I'm not—"

"So you left one man, moved back to Bayford and now you're living with another one? Is this your idea of an ideal environment? Have you run a background check on him?"

"No, no, no." I could almost feel DeAndre slipping away. I took a deep breath and tried, unsuccessfully, to hold back the tears welling in my eyes. *Jesus.* I was sure my words sounded like jibber-jabber, but I had to get them all out before he slammed that gavel on me again. "Your honor, I don't live with my boyfriend. It'll be just me, DeAndre, and Aunt Dottie, and I don't know exactly how—"

"Did you say Aunt *Dottie*?" Judge Kiplinger's sparse eyebrows shot up.

"Yes."

He set both hands flat on the platform. "You mean Dottie Mae *Lester*?"

"Yes?"

He smiled—I didn't know his muscles knew the formation—and caroled, "Why didn't you mention Aunt Dottie before? She's a saint. Impeccable character. She brought food to my sister when she was in the final stages of breast cancer."

Wordless, I nodded.

"You say DeAndre will be staying with you and Aunt Dottie?"

"Yes, your honor."

"Well, if Aunt Dottie's got anything to do with raisin' DeAndre, he'll be perfectly fine. The court hereby places DeAndre Lester in the temporary custody of Miss Tori Henderson. We'll review this case in six months to determine permanent custody. Court's adjourned."

He slammed the gavel. "And tell Aunt Dottie Judge K says hello."

Outside the courtroom, I crumbled with joy in Jacob's arms. "We got him back!"

"We sure did, Tori. Praise God."

Epilogue

One Year Later

"Go!" I screamed from the stands.

"Runnnn, Dadre!" Aunt Dottie echoed as we watched DeAndre run from third base to score for the Yellow Jackets.

Jacob yelled, "Come on in, DeAndre!" from the dugout.

DeAndre tore across the field, sliding into home plate, ensuring every thread of his pants absorbed as much red dirt as possible. He repositioned his helmet, wiped his knees, and gave me a thumbs-up. I gave it right back to him.

Aunt Dottie giggled. "Heeee sompin else."

"He sure is," I agreed.

I wished Aunt Dottie and I weren't the only ones cheering DeAndre on. Most of the other kids had uncles, cousins, great-grandparents present. (There's not much to do in Bayford on a Saturday morning.) After the state deemed Joenetta and Ray-Ray unfit, they'd basically wiped their hands clean of DeAndre, which is what they'd wanted to do the whole time anyway. To date, Zoletha hadn't replied to my letter.

DeAndre deserved better, and I was determined to give him all the love and support he could possibly contain, so help me God.

I checked my watch. Two-thirty. Almost time for me to go to Dottie's and help Cassandra plan next month's throwbacks. Though Cassandra was more than capable of handling Dottie's herself and even more committed (as if possible) to the store's success now that Aunt Dottie had made Cassandra part owner, I didn't want Cassandra to fall into I'm-every-woman syndrome. More than anything, I kept an eye on Dottie's to make sure Cassandra didn't bring a cot and move into the back office.

"I gotta go, Aunt Dottie. Jacob will take you and DeAndre home after the game. We're all going to the movies tonight in Henrytown."

"Kaaay."

Exiting the stands, my mind shifted to things-to-do mode. Help Cassandra, update Inner-G's weekly reports, and visit with Jacob's mother, who was slowly working through Senior Pastor Carter's passing, a month earlier. In His infinite wisdom, God had taken Pastor Carter home to glory before Alzheimer's could reduce him to Jacob's greatest fear.

Even unto death, God is always watching over us. Always.

Thank You, Father.

Don't miss the newest novel in Vanessa Davis Griggs's
Blessed Trinity series

The Other Side of Divine

In stores August 2013

Prologue

And take the helmet of salvation, and the sword of the Spirit, which is the word of God.

—Ephesians 6:17

When I tell you how beautiful, you're not going to believe just how much so. In fact, beautiful doesn't even *begin* to describe or give it justice.

I'm sorry. Please forgive me. I'm getting ahead of myself here. I hate when someone starts in the middle of a conversation as though you've taken part in what was apparently going on in their heads before they began to speak and you have no *earthly* idea *what* they're jabbering on and on about.

To those who don't know me, my name is Esther Crowe. Those who know and love me best call me Esther, Aunt Esther, or Miss Crowe. A few folks even call me Zion from my days when I had a dance group called the Daughters of Zion many forgotten years ago. The miss part of Miss Crowe is actually a *miss* statement. There I go again: my attempt at a little humor and playing on words.

I love words. For anyone who may have missed it, I was playing on the word misstatement.

I was born Esther Morgan, no middle name. I married into the last name of Crowe. My husband died young (much too young), early into our marriage from complications of an illness called lupus to be exact. I don't like talking much about it. Suffice it to say: I never remarried; I never got around to finding anyone special enough to fill his space.

Then there was that terrible automobile accident that pretty near claimed my life here on earth. I was spared, although barely. For ten years, it was as if I didn't really exist. But then my nephew, Dr. Zachary Wayne Morgan, stepped into that Chicago nursing facility, bringing with him someone near and dear to my heart: my dear, sweet Gabrielle Mercedes Booker all the way from Birmingham, Alabama, and all grown up now.

Gabrielle dropped the last name of Booker and goes by Gabrielle Mercedes. That poor child has indeed lived a hard life. That wretched woman who was given charge over the almost four-year-old at that time was actually the cause of (eight years old when I first met her) me and Gabrielle becoming acquainted. I was out in the community on a summer jog and Aunt Cee-Cee was out there treating that sweet child like she thought her name was Cinderella (before the glass slippers). I laugh sometimes because Gabrielle has told me on more than one occasion that I was like her very own fairy godmother.

I suppose it's true what some folks say: What Satan meant for bad, God will use it for good.

I figured out a way to get that precious little girl some joy into her life while she endured being treated even worse than a redheaded step child. At least I'd like to believe I brought some good into that child's life. But Gabrielle could dance, oh my *goodness*, she could dance! The first time my eyes fell on her running around picking up after those four other children like she was their hired help, I saw the greatness in her. I often described her movements as like the seeds on the feathers of dandelions being carried in the wind: Graceful with a capital *G*. I saw the greatness in her future.

Gabrielle's aunt Cee-Cee (Cecelia Murphy) tried to say I believed Gabrielle was the child I never had. She even joked (or so she claimed after she didn't get the response she hoped for) that I could have Gabrielle outright, for the right price, of course. If I could have gotten Gabrielle without the insult of seemingly buying her, I would have taken that child in a heartbeat, in a *heartbeat*. After I learned how badly Aunt Cee-Cee had done Gabrielle after my automobile accident—taking the money I'd paid for Gabrielle to attend Juilliard, then putting her out on the streets with nowhere to go. . .

I don't even like thinking about that. Why couldn't I have been here? I wanted so much to see the look on her face when she received the information about Juilliard. But to think: That wretched woman took that money, stole it is what she did . . . Well, needless to say, Cecelia Murphy's day of reckoning is coming. And you can believe *that*.

I didn't think of Gabrielle as the child I never had. What folks have to understand is: None of us *truly* own anything or anybody here on earth. Everything belongs to God. Psalm 24:1 provides the title and the deed. "The earth is the Lord's and the fullness thereof; the world, and they that dwell therein." My father used to say, "If folks think they own it, then let them die and see just what they really own. You brought nothing into this world and for certain, you'll take nothing when you leave, not even these earth suits we call our body."

I miss my father. We were taught by our parents that if we saw someone in need, especially a child, we should try to do what we can to help. That's how things were back in my day. Yeah, I'm over sixty years old. Now and days, if you say something to a child, not only might the child cuss you out, but nine times out of ten, when the parents find out, one or both of them will hunt you down and cuss you out.

Yes, I meant cuss and not curse. Having also been a schoolteacher, I know the difference between the words. Cussing is a whole other word and a whole other level than cursing. High society folks, who make their subject and verb agree, curse. Folks who want to get you good and told cuss.

But back to what I was saying. I don't want to get off on that because that's a whole other story in itself. I was in this horrific automobile accident. Everybody, including me, believed my life as I'd known it was over. Then Gabrielle stepped into my room and danced me back on my journey to recovery. There was such an anointing in my room that day, oh my goodness! I felt the glory of the Lord sitting . . . the weight of His glory on me. There's nothing like the glory of God to lift you up.

Yes, God raised me right up off of that sick bed. I heard Him speak to me just as clear as you hear me speaking now. "There is more that I require of thee. Get up, Esther! There's too much still left for you to do."

So I girded myself up. I began putting on the whole armor of God. I held up my sword, I'm talking about the Word of God, and I was ready to get back on the battlefield.

If God has ever told you to do anything, please know that God equips those He calls. He raised me up off that deathbed, and in a little less than a year's time, my speech has become ninety-five percent clear again. My dance returned, no so much in my legs and feet as in my heart. There's something glorious to be said about dancing from the heart.

People come up and say, "Esther, how are you doing?" And I say, "I'm still kicking, just not as high."

After God got me back on my feet, He told me I had to go help Gabrielle one more time. That there was a huge battle coming, and I needed to be there to help. All I needed was a Word from the Lord. Over the objections of my family (mostly from my sister-in-law Leslie Morgan, Zachary's mother), I packed my bags and told Zachary what time to pick me up from the airport. These new flying rules are horrible. I feel like Rip Van Winkle· with everything that appears to have changed while I was out of it. What's all this taking off your shoes and folks with gloves patting all over you? I'm an old woman. What exactly do they think I'm going to do?

There I go again: another subject for another time.

In mid-November, 2010, I left Chicago and arrived in what had been, for a few years, my hometown. When you obey God, things fall into place even if to us it doesn't look like that's what it's doing. God knows what He's doing. *I* thought I was coming to Birmingham to help Gabrielle plan a wedding she and Zachary were taking much too long to do. There was also a little legal matter left undone between me and Mrs. Cecelia Murphy, better known to me now as "The defendant."

So after a beautiful Christmas with my nephew, Zachary, and his fiancée, Gabrielle, not to leave out the biggest surprise of all for me: little Jasmine Noble, who can dance just as great as her mother Gabrielle, who would have guessed that at the beginning of 2011, all Hell would break loose. No, I did not cuss here. When I say Hell, I mean Hell in every biblical sense of the word with the devil, his imps, and fire and brimstone. Well, all of Hell broke loose. It's definitely what you would call the *other* side of divine.

God knows in advance of spiritual warfare when prayer warriors are needed to be in place. God sent me to Birmingham for such a time as this and . . .

You know what? Instead of me telling you everything, why don't I just let you see for yourself.